ROMANTIC COMEDY

CURTIS SITTENFELD

doubleday

TRANSWORLD PUBLISHERS
Penguin Random House, One Embassy Gardens,
8 Viaduct Gardens, London SW11 7BW
www.penguin.co.uk

Transworld is part of the Penguin Random House group of companies
whose addresses can be found at global.penguinrandomhouse.com

First published in Great Britain in 2023 by Doubleday
an imprint of Transworld Publishers

A CIP catalogue record for this book
is available from the British Library.

ISBNs
9780857527493 (hb)
9780857527509 (tpb)

Printed and bound in Great Britain by Clays Ltd, Elcograf S.p.A.

The authorized representative in the EEA is Penguin Random House Ireland,
Morrison Chambers, 32 Nassau Street, Dublin D02 YH68.

Penguin Random House is committed to a sustainable future
for our business, our readers and our planet. This book is made
from Forest Stewardship Council® certified paper.

For beloved and funny C

PROLOGUE

February 2018

You should not, I've read many times, reach for your phone first thing in the morning—the news, social media, and emails all disrupt the natural stages of waking and create stress—which is how I'll preface the fact that when I reached for my phone first thing one morning and learned that Danny Horst and Annabel Lily were dating, I was furious.

I wasn't furious because I was in love with Danny Horst or, for that matter, with Annabel Lily. Nor was I furious because two more people in the world had found romantic bliss while I remained mostly single. And I wasn't furious that I hadn't heard the news directly from Danny, even though we shared an office. The reason I was furious was that Annabel Lily was a gorgeous, talented, world-famous movie star, and Danny was a schlub. He wasn't a bad guy, and he, too, was talented. But, for Christ's sake, he was a TV writer, a comedy writer—he was a male version of *me*. He was pasty skinned and sleep-deprived and sarcastic. And, perhaps because he was male or perhaps because he was a decade younger than I was, he was a lot less self-consciously people-pleasing and a lot more recklessly crass. At after-parties, he was undisguisedly high or tripping. He referred often, almost guilelessly, to both his social anxiety and his porn consumption. When he'd considered going on Rogaine, I had, at his request, used his phone to take pictures of the top of his head so that he could see exactly how much his hair was thinning there, and when he applied the medication the first time, I'd checked to make sure the foam was evenly rubbed in. And I was so familiar with the various genres of his burps that I could infer from them what he'd eaten recently.

Danny was like a little brother to me—I adored him, *and* he stank and got on my nerves. But his foul and annoying ways had, apparently, not precluded Annabel Lily's interest. She'd been the guest host of *The Night Owls* three weeks prior, coinciding with the release of her latest film, the fourth in an action franchise in which she played a corrupt FBI agent. She'd delivered the opening monologue while wearing a one-shouldered black satin cocktail dress with a thigh slit, highlighting her slender yet curvy body; her long red hair had been styled into old Hollywood waves. Annabel was beautiful and sweet and charming, and if she didn't have the best comic timing, she was completely game, which was just as important. In one sketch, she'd been called on to play a woodchuck, which entailed crawling around on all fours and wearing a furry suit and two enormous prosthetic front teeth. In fact, Danny had written this sketch, meaning it was plausible that they'd first been attracted to each other while rehearsing it.

The woodchuck part was endearing enough that I might have been able to forgive them both except that theirs was the third such pairing that had occurred at *TNO* in the last few years, and, as anyone knows who's ever written a joke—or heard a fairy tale, or read an article in the style section of a newspaper—there's a rule of three. In this case, it constituted the trend of a romance between a bona fide celebrity and a *TNO* staffer who'd met on the show. But, crucially, a bona fide *female* celebrity and a *male* staffer. The year before, at a wedding I'd attended, an icy blond Oscar-winning British actress named Imogen Wagner had married a cast member named Josh Beekman, best known for his recurring character Backne Guy.

And the year before that, the head writer, Elliot Markovitz (five-foot-eight, forty, and my Top-Sider-wearing boss), had married a multi-platinum-album-selling pop singer named Nicola Dornan (five-foot-ten, thirty, and a special envoy for the U.N.). And this, of course, was the essence of my fury: that such couples would never exist with the genders switched, that a gorgeous male celebrity would never fall in love with an ordinary, dorky, unkempt woman. Never. No matter how clever she was.

But I also knew, as I lay in bed glaring at the screen of my phone—Danny and Annabel's debut as a couple had occurred the night before, in the form of making out at the club where Annabel's twenty-fourth birthday party had been held—that I would write about my fury. Just as I always did, I'd turn my feelings into comedy, and that was how I'd cure myself.

CHAPTER 1

April 2018

WEEKLY SCHEDULE FOR
THE NIGHT OWLS

Monday 1 P.M. pitch meeting with guest host

Tuesday 5 P.M. start of all-night writing session

Wednesday 12 P.M. deadline for submitted sketches

Wednesday 3 P.M. table read of submitted sketches

Wednesday 9 P.M. preliminary show lineup posted internally

Wednesday night–Saturday morning rehearsals; scripts revised; sets built; special effects designed; hair, makeup, and costumes chosen and created; pre-tapes shot

Saturday 1 P.M. run-through of show

Saturday 8 P.M. dress rehearsal before a live audience

Saturday 11:30 P.M. live show before a new audience

Sunday 1:30 A.M. first after-party

Monday, 1:10 P.M.

For the meeting that marked the official start of that week's show, I planned to pitch two sketches. But I had three ideas—you could write and submit more but pitch only two—so I'd play by ear which ones I went with, depending on how the guest host reacted to the pitches preceding mine. About forty writers, cast members, and producers were crammed into the seventeenth-floor office of the show's creator and executive director, Nigel Petersen. Nigel's seventeenth-floor office—not to be confused with his office on the eighth floor, adjacent to the studio where the show was filmed—was both well-appointed and never intended as a meeting place for anywhere close to forty people. This meant that Nigel sat behind his desk, the host sat in a leather armchair, a few lucky staffers nabbed a place on the sole couch, and everyone else leaned against the wall or sat on the floor.

Nigel started by introducing the host, who, as happened about once per season, was also that week's musical guest. Noah Brewster had twice in the past been the musical guest, but this was his first time hosting. He was a cheesily handsome, extremely successful singer-songwriter who specialized in cloying pop music and was known for dating models in their early twenties. Though he looked like a surfer—piercing blue eyes, shaggy blond hair and stubble, a big toothy grin, and a jacked body—I'd learned by reading the host bio we were emailed each Monday morning that he'd grown up in a suburb of Washington, D.C. He was thirty-six, the same age I was, and had been famous ever since releasing the hit "Making Love in July" more than fifteen years before, when I was in college. "Making Love in July" was a paean to respectfully taking the virginity of a long-haired girl with "glowy skin," "a pouty mouth," and "raspberry nipples," and it was one of those songs that had for a year played so often on the radio that, in spite of finding it execrable, I accidentally knew all the words. In the time since then, Noah Brewster had won many awards and sold more than twenty million albums, a figure I also had learned from his host bio. It was not a coincidence that his tenth album was being released the following week; hosts, musical guests, and the combinations therein were usually either celebrating newfound fame or promoting imminent work.

After Nigel introduced him, Noah Brewster looked around the room and said, "Thanks for letting a musician crash the comedy party. Hosting *TNO* has been a lifelong dream, ever since I was a middle school misfit sneaking down to the basement to watch after my parents went to bed." He smiled his big smile at us, and I wondered if his teeth were real or veneers. After nine years at *TNO*, I was as accustomed as one could be to interacting with high-wattage celebrities, though it often was surprising to discover who was even better-looking in person (most of them), who was an asshole (not many, but definitely a few), who was shockingly vacuous (the lead from a popular police procedural stood out), and who you wished would stay on the show forever because they were so great in the sketches and also just so fun to hang out with in the middle of the night.

Nigel glanced to his left, where a writer was sitting at his feet, and said, "Benji, why don't you kick things off?"

Benji pitched a sketch about the former FBI director, James Comey, writing the memoir he'd just published, dictating Dear Diary–style girlish reminiscences. Then a cast member named Oliver said he was working on an idea with Rohit, another writer (it wouldn't become clear until the read-through of the sketches on Wednesday if this was true or an excuse on Oliver's part). Then a writer named Lianna pitched a sketch where Noah Brewster would play the token hot straight boy in a high school chorus, then a writer named Tony pitched a sketch where Noah Brewster would play a preppy white guy running for office and guest-preaching in a Black church. Henrietta, who was one of the two cast members I worked with the most, said she and Viv, who was the other cast member I worked with the most, wanted to do a sketch about Internet searches made by dogs. I went sixth.

"I think of this one as The Danny Horst Rule," I said. "Because it's inspired by my very own officemate, whose big news I trust we're all aware of." Everyone clapped or hooted. Over the weekend, after seven weeks of dating, Danny and Annabel Lily had gotten engaged, as revealed in a post on Annabel's Instagram account showing a close-up of a ring on her finger, her hand resting atop Danny's. Celebrity gossip websites immediately reported that the diamond was an emerald-cut halo with a pavé setting, and estimated that the ring had cost $110,000. Although I myself had been married briefly in my twenties, I had no idea what *emerald cut, halo,* or *pavé setting* meant—my ex-husband and I had both worn plain gold bands.

As the cheering died down, Danny, who was sitting on the floor two people to my left, said, "Thanks, everyone. And, yeah, pretty fucking psyched that I get to be Mr. Annabel Lily." There was another round of cheers, and Danny added, "If you're wondering, Sally did warn me that she'd be exploiting me to advance her career."

"I'm trying to convince Danny to write it *with* me," I said. "But we'll put a pin in that for now. Anyway, I want to write about the phenomenon where—sorry, Danny, I really do love you—but where men at *TNO* date above their station, but women never do."

There was widespread laughter, though laughter at the pitch meeting could mean you'd revealed your punchlines too early. For this reason, some people pitched only decoys, though I took the risk of sharing my real ideas in order to lay claim to them in case anyone else was considering something similar. And anyway, to a surprising degree, laughter was never the ultimate determinant of a sketch's fate; Nigel's whims were. Of the forty or so scripts that would be submitted for Wednesday's read-through, about twelve sketches would make it to the dress rehearsal Saturday and just eight to the live show. Sketches featuring the host had a better chance of surviving, but beyond that, it was impossible to guess what Nigel would decide. All of us in his office at that moment, cast members and writers alike, had had our hearts broken many times.

"Obviously, Danny should be in the sketch in some capacity," I added, "either as himself or as someone else. And, Noah, it could work really well if you're a guy who gets arrested for somehow breaking the rule, like you're on a date with either Henrietta or Viv made up to look less gorgeous than they are in real life." Though I was close to Henrietta and Viv, I wasn't just flattering them. They really were both gorgeous, which wasn't unusual for female comedians, *and* they were both so funny that their funniness often obscured their beauty, which also wasn't unusual for female comedians.

"Just so I understand—" Noah Brewster said, and the confusion on his face made me wonder if he'd turn out to be one of the ding-dongs. I'd never previously spoken to him. The first time he'd been the musical guest had been before I worked at the show, and the second time, I hadn't had any reason to interact with him. Occasionally, musical guests appeared in sketches, or you could watch them rehearse their songs on Thursday afternoons if you weren't otherwise occupied, but that didn't mean you'd meet. "In this sketch," he said, "I'd be breaking the law because I'm so much better looking than a woman I'm dating?"

There was some chuckling, and a writer named Jeremiah said, "The bail for your hair alone would be a billion dollars."

Noah's expression was agreeable as he looked at me and said, "No, I'm really asking."

"Well, yeah," I said. "Basically." I was seated with my back against the west wall of Nigel's office, about ten feet from Noah, and many of my co-workers were between us.

Noah's voice remained cheerfully diplomatic as he said, "I've always thought it works better when the host is making fun of himself—or herself—instead of mocking other people, so I'm inclined to pass on this one."

That self-deprecation was a winning strategy wasn't wrong. But declaring this early and this publicly that he didn't want to participate in any particular sketch was both unnecessary and irritating; Nigel always gave hosts veto power. In fact, I was irritated enough that I decided to pitch as my second idea the one I'd been on the fence about, which I'd been on the fence about because I wondered if it was insulting to Noah Brewster.

"Fair enough," I said in a tone intended to be just as diplomatic as his; I knew I had to tread carefully. "And if you really want to make fun of yourself, I have some good news. My next idea is that obviously you have tons and tons of fans, and one of the reasons they love you is for how romantic your music is. Since romance and cheesiness go hand in hand, I wonder about a sketch where you play a cheesemonger and the cheeses you're selling correspond to your songs. So you can show a customer some Brie and be like, 'This has a silky flavor with delicious raspberry hints, perfect for making love in July.' Or 'The saltwater flavor of this Gruyère is reminiscent of the breezes at Lighthouse Beach.'"

"This velvety taste goes down on me very smoothly," said Danny. As it happened, someone else riffing on your idea was higher praise than an outright compliment.

Noah wasn't visibly insulted, though he again seemed more puz-zled than amused. He said, "So it's like descriptions of wine but for cheese?"

"You can think on it," I said. My third idea, the one I'd submit for the read-through but wouldn't mention at this meeting because of the two-pitch limit, was for Noah to be a guest judge in a Blab-bermouth. Blabbermouth was a recurring sketch I wrote based on the singing competition show *American Lungs,* which aired on the same network as *TNO* but was shot in L.A. It featured three famous musician judges who coached the contestants, and the part I parodied—I'd borrowed this directly from real life—was not only that the two male judges spent a great deal of time telling the female judge she talked too much when giving feedback to contestants, but that the male judges spent far more time telling the female judge she talked too much than she spent talking. Most galling to me on the real show was that instead of refuting the accusation, the female judge would good-naturedly respond, "Y'all, I know! What can I say? I'm a blabbermouth."

"Thank you, Sally," Nigel said. Nodding toward the writer next to me, he said, "Patrick?"

As Patrick started with an idea about Trump melting down his gold toilet to make teeth fillings, I watched Noah Brewster's cheesily handsome surfer face watching Patrick, and I continued to watch Noah's face, off and on, for almost three hours because that was how long pitch meetings lasted. Before Nigel released us, he asked Noah, as he asked all hosts, if he had any sketch ideas of his own. By this point, I had come to the conclusion that Noah was not, in fact, a ding-dong. He smiled and laughed often but didn't seem to be trying too hard, as some hosts did, to prove that he was funny. And his requests for clarification had come to seem confident in a way that, in spite of my lingering annoyance about his response to my Danny Horst Rule pitch, I respected.

Once again looking around the room, Noah said, "Hearing all this has made me even more excited about the week ahead. A little terrified, but mostly excited. I'm psyched to roll with your ideas and

I don't have a big agenda. I'll admit there's an idea I've been noo-dling over, kind of trying to write it myself, and I'll have to decide before the table read if it should or shouldn't see the light of day, but, in terms of your sketches, I'm down for any of it."

You mean any of it other than pretending to date a woman less attractive than you, I thought. I was wondering if his aversion was somehow tied to having dated so many models in real life when I heard a long, low belch and immediately became aware of an un-pleasant odor, a noxious version of a breakfast burrito. I snapped my head in the direction of Danny, and he pursed his lips and wid-ened his eyes in a ridiculous way—as if to say, Oops!—and I scowled. Burping was part of life, yes, but could he not have held it in for the last thirty seconds of a three-hour meeting?

Patrick, who was the writer sitting between Danny and me, leaned toward me. He murmured, "That was you, right?"

MONDAY, 4:47 P.M.

I was responding to emails when Danny entered our office carrying a can of Red Bull. "Yo, Chuckles," he said as he sat backwards on his desk chair and rolled toward me. The room was narrow enough that the only way to fit a couch was for both of our desks to be against the same wall. Gesturing at my computer screen, he said, "How's the great American screenplay coming along?"

"I wish," I said. "I'm telling my agent I don't want to write a"—I held up my fingers in air quotes—" 'humorous animated short for an organic douche company.' "

"How much does it pay? Because maybe I want to write a hu-morous animated short for an organic douche company."

"Ten thousand, but also douching is bad, and I assume the or-ganic part is bullshit. Your vagina is a self-cleaning organ."

"Maybe *your* vagina is a self-cleaning organ. But yeah, ten grand is a nonstarter. I don't sell out for less than six figures." I suspected Danny earned close to what I did. He'd been hired as the youngest-ever host of News Desk, *TNO*'s satirical show-within-the-show, and he wrote and occasionally appeared in other sketches, meaning that, as a second-year cast member who wrote, he probably earned the same amount as a ninth-year writer who never appeared on-screen. This was currently $12,000 an episode, or $252,000 a year—not a huge amount for a TV job where you pulled several all-nighters a week, and obscene compared to, say, a fourth-grade teacher's salary. Even if Danny didn't yet earn more than I did from *TNO*, he'd recently begun appearing in movies, whereas I used my summers off for the considerably less lucrative activities of reading novels and traveling.

"Okay, I need your advice," Danny said. "Annabel is freaking out because she just found out our signs are incompatible. Belly's a Pisces and I'm a Sagittarius."

"Oh my God," I said. "I can't even believe you've lasted this long."

"I get that it's ridiculous to you, but she takes this shit very seriously."

"Did she not know when your birthday is until now?"

"She had a session with her astrologist yesterday, who told her even though our connection is authentic, our communication styles are inharmonious and I'm not the person to walk beside her on her healing journey."

I bit my lip, and Danny added, "It's okay, you can laugh. But I still fucking love her."

"What about *your* healing journey?"

Danny made an aw-shucks face. "I'm all healed, Chuckles."

My resentment about their relationship and the sketch I'd just pitched notwithstanding, I found Danny's unbridled love for Annabel sweet. Their sincerity and spontaneity and sheer optimism all seemed so misguided, so destined to fail, that how could anyone, including a cynic like me, not root for them? Getting engaged after seven weeks was only the latest in their dramatic and very public declarations of love. After a week together, they had traveled to Paris for a make-out session in front of the Eiffel Tower, and after two weeks they'd gotten matching tongue piercings, and all of this had been documented on social media then breathlessly described by celebrity journalists.

In general, Danny's emotional openness made me hopeful about either Gen Z, males, or maybe both. A year and a half prior, I had been less than thrilled when I learned that I was being moved from the office I shared with Viv to an office with Danny, who was then new to *TNO*. I hadn't yearned for this proximity to Danny, who'd found success as a stand-up comic with bits so steeped in irony that I couldn't always tell what the joke was, which then made me feel extremely old. Relatedly and even more unsettlingly, I wondered if the office change was intended to send a message to me. *TNO* and Nigel specifically were notorious for indirection, with people often literally not knowing they'd been hired or fired. Was putting me in a crappy office with a new twenty-four-year-old dude a way of nudging me toward the exit without telling me to leave? For the first few weeks of the 2016 season, Danny and I had barely spoken, as he worked a lot in the office of the dedicated News Desk writers, whose names were Roy and Hank, and quickly became the most visible new cast member. Then, five weeks into the season, it was election night—a Tuesday, so we were at the office, ostensibly writing, though no one was getting any work done. Around 11:30 P.M., just after Florida was called for Trump, following North Carolina and Ohio, with Wisconsin and Pennsylvania looking bad, Danny and I were walking toward our office at the same time from opposite directions, got within a couple feet of each other, made eye contact, both began sobbing, and threw ourselves into each other's arms. It was shortly after Trump's inauguration, as our democracy started to unravel, that Danny took to calling me Chuckles. This was short for *chuckle slut*, which was the term for women who slept with comedians, and Danny bestowed the nickname after I told him I'd never once slept with a comedian.

Almost eighteen months later, I said to him, "Maybe Annabel just needs a day or two to absorb what the astrologist said. Like, she was thrown by it, but she'll realize it's not that big a deal."

"I wish people could change signs," Danny said. "I'd totally convert to Scorpio for her."

"I think she'll come around," I said.

He nodded toward my computer screen. "It's very demeaning that you think my vagina needs cleaning. It shouldn't smell floral when I'm getting oral." He grinned. "I'll invoice you for the ten grand."

MONDAY, 7:32 P.M.

Mondays were the only days during a *TNO* workweek when I got home at a remotely normal hour, and I tried to use them to continue recovering from the previous week if there'd been a show—from October to May, shows typically aired three weeks in a row then we got two or three weeks off—and to brace myself for the week ahead. I'd walked the forty minutes from the *TNO* offices in Midtown to my apartment on the Upper West Side, picking up Thai takeout near my building. I ate pad see ew from the container while sitting at my kitchen counter and talking on speakerphone to my seventy-nine-year-old stepfather, Jerry. My mother had died three years prior, devastating both Jerry and me in ways we couldn't really express. Four months after the funeral, I'd convinced Jerry to get a beagle named Sugar, who brought him so much happiness that I considered her presence in his life to be my crowning achievement. Plus, she gave us something to chat about every Sunday or Monday instead of our feelings.

"She was a very good girl getting her nails cut today," Jerry said jovially, then dropped his voice to a whisper—presumably because Sugar was nearby and he didn't want to offend her—and said, "She really wasn't. It took two attendants to hold her because she was wiggling so much."

"Was she whimpering, too?"

"Like a baby," he said. Jerry and Sugar lived in Kansas City, in the house I'd grown up in. I tried to visit twice a year, though since my mother's death I hadn't been able to bring myself to go for

Thanksgiving or Christmas. I'd either stayed in New York or traveled far away, once to the Seychelles with Viv and once, with Viv and also that time with Henrietta, to Mexico City. Jerry spent the holidays with his sister.

"I saw on the Internet that your host this week is also the musical guest," Jerry said. "That sounds awfully tiring." My mother and I had debriefed about each show on Sunday afternoons, and in her absence, Jerry had, on Sunday afternoons, taken to emailing me two formally written paragraphs sharing his feedback. The kindness of this impulse almost made up for the fact that, apart from appreciating Sugar's antics, Jerry didn't have much of a sense of humor and wasn't familiar with almost any of the pop cultural phenomena or people that *TNO* satirized. Though he and my mother had been in the studio audience twice, he'd never have even watched it on TV if I didn't write for it.

"You've probably heard Noah Brewster's songs playing in the background in a restaurant or department store," I said. "And I'm sure it *is* really tiring to host and be the musical guest, but he gets to promote his new album."

"I meant to tell you," Jerry said. "I ran into Mrs. Macklin at Hy-Vee, and she said to give you her best. She said Amy just had another baby, which I believe is her third."

Who's Mrs. Macklin? I thought. *Who's Amy?* Then I remembered a high school classmate named Amy Macklin, a girl I'd worked with on the student newspaper. (I'd been the copy editor, not a reporter, because reporting would have required interacting with other humans in a way I couldn't then have managed.) I said, "Good for Amy." A third child inspired in me more gratitude for my own circumstances than envy for Amy's.

Jerry described a tapas restaurant he'd eaten at the previous Friday with his sister and her husband, which had featured a garbanzo-bean-and-spinach dish he thought I'd like (though I didn't perceive myself as having a special relationship with garbanzo beans, Jerry's belief that I did arose from the fact that when I was staying with him, I often bought hummus). Then we circled back to Sugar. A family with two daughters had moved in next door the month before, and Sugar had taken to sitting on Jerry's back deck, facing the other house, and barking, as if to summon the sisters. "I think she likes it when they tell her how adorable she is," Jerry said.

"Who wouldn't?" I said, and Jerry laughed.

"All right then," he said. "Be careful on the subway, honey." This was how he always ended our conversations.

After I'd hung up, I refrigerated the leftovers and took a shower. I still rented the seven-hundred-square-foot apartment I'd moved into almost ten years before, when I'd arrived in New York. The difference was that for the first two years, I'd had a roommate who slept in the real bedroom while I slept in a shoddily built loft above the living room, where the ceiling was four feet from the mattress. It was hard to say in retrospect if I hadn't had sex during those two years because I was me, because I was adjusting to my divorce, or because there simply wasn't space.

When I emerged from the shower, I put on the huge T-shirt I slept in, brushed my teeth, rubbed cheap lotion on my legs and expensive lotion on my face, then retrieved my phone from the pocket of the jeans I'd left on the bathroom floor and got into bed. Four texts were waiting, three of them from Viv.

The first: *I still look like a zombie*

The second: *You think I should skip dinner?*

The third was a close-up photo of her right eye, the white part of which had a red and blurry-edged dot slightly bigger than her pupil. In a sketch during the live show the previous Saturday, a cast member named Gregor had thrown, of all things, an oven mitt that had been intended to lightly hit Viv's chest but had somehow struck her eye. She'd noticed the blotch when removing her makeup after the show but it hadn't hurt and she'd attended the after-parties that lasted long into Sunday morning. When the blotch hadn't gone away by Monday, she'd seen *TNO*'s set nurse, who recommended Viv make an appointment with an ophthalmologist just to be safe.

I texted back, *Take a pic where I can see your whole face*

A few seconds later, another photo arrived of Viv's entire and very pretty face, in this moment unsmiling and preoccupied-looking, with both her eyebrows raised. Viv was Black and thirty-one, five years younger than I. I knew that both she and Henrietta, who was white and thirty-two, used preemptive antiaging measures like Botox and chemical peels. At the same time, Viv appeared in a recurring sketch where she played a famously well-preserved middle-aged TV host talking to her reflection in her dressing room mirror, uttering with pleasure the phrase "Black don't crack."

It really doesn't look that bad, I texted. *I'd decide about dinner based on how you feel*

Still doesn't hurt, Viv replied. *But*

She sent the female zombie emoji, green skinned and holding out curled fingers.

No you look fine, I wrote.

By which I mean great!

I think ok to go to dinner or ok to skip but you don't need to skip to spare anyone

On Monday nights around eleven o'clock, Nigel always took that week's host and a few cast members to dinner at a fancy restaurant. The only writer ever included was the head writer, which I actually didn't mind because even after nine years, I was more comfortable having fleeting rather than sustained encounters with Nigel. Many people in- and outside of *TNO* were obsessed with the man who'd created the show in 1981 and produced it ever since. Born Norman Piekarkski in Oklahoma City, Oklahoma, in 1947, Nigel Petersen was indisputably the comedy kingmaker of twentieth- and twenty-first-century America, and it was often said that your relationship with your father was revealed by the relationship you had, or thought you had, with Nigel. But I'd long believed that being quietly competent would serve me better than trying to curry favor with him directly. For my entire first year, I hadn't even been sure he knew my name, and then at the after-party following the season finale, he'd said in his surprisingly soft and understated voice, "The field trip sketch was very funny, Sally." These eight words were possibly the greatest compliment of my life, which might have revealed that I had daddy issues if I hadn't already been well aware I had daddy issues. The following year, we'd interacted more because I had many more sketches on air, but we spoke only when he was giving notes on them. Our annual superfluous exchange came after he'd complimented with similar brevity a sketch I'd set at a Kansas City barbecue restaurant, when I'd dared not just to mumble thank you but to follow up by saying, "I know you're from Oklahoma. Do you think of that as the Midwest or the South?"

Again in his soft and understated voice, he said, "According to the census, it's the South." That was that for the 2010–2011 season.

Did you make appointment with eye dr, I texted Viv.

Tomorrow at 11 AM, she texted back.

Oh great, I replied.

Go tonight!

Have fun!

She replied with a winking emoji, and I opened the other text that had arrived while I was in the shower. It was from Gene, the guy I'd been hooking up with off and on for the last eight months: *Hey Sally how's it going?*

It occurred to me to invite him over—it wasn't yet nine o'clock, I'd just washed my hair and the rest of myself—and then I thought I'd rather go to sleep early. I almost never saw Gene during show weeks; even when I knew by Wednesday that I'd have no sketches on the live show, I was expected to attend Thursday rewrites, which could go until nine or ten, and it was all just so mentally consuming that I found it easier to give myself over to *TNO*'s rhythms. It was perhaps the one workplace in America where people who had spouses and kids were not only in the minority but were looked at with vague pity, because how could anyone possibly manage that, too?

Also, though we had decent sex, I didn't like Gene that much. He was a financial analyst who'd early on mentioned that the University of Florida's business school, which he'd attended, was ranked among the top fifteen in the country. Though I'd never previously wondered about the University of Florida's business school ranking, of course this had prompted me to look it up and discover the claim was off by about ten. Far more alarmingly, he'd once used the word *snowflake* to disparage a co-worker who regularly took sick days because of migraines. While it was possible he meant the term apolitically, the meaning he apparently did intend wasn't much better. And I hadn't called him on it because I feared doing so would result in my needing to find another sexual outlet, meaning I'd have to resubscribe to a hookup app and meet enough strangers at enough bars to determine which one probably wouldn't kill me if we went back to my apartment.

If, on the plus side, Gene wasn't homicidal, he wasn't particularly cute, either. He was of medium height and build, with light brown hair, and there was something so generic about him that he could have played an extra in any *TNO* sketch set in an office. He was unobjectionable in the way that a person you sat next to on an airplane was usually unobjectionable; unlike with an airplane seatmate, though, most of what we did was get each other off. In the months this had been going on, he'd asked me exactly two questions. The first was if I'd ever tried butter coffee (no), and the second was if I'd ever been to Rockaway Beach (also no).

None of Gene's predecessors had been particularly inquisitive, but they'd asked enough that I'd given a fake job, which I never had to do with Gene. I'd told other guys I'd "dated" that I was a writer for the newsletter of a medical device company, which had been one of my jobs before *TNO*. Though I wasn't much of a liar generally, I feared the guys I hooked up with would be overly interested if I mentioned my real employer. In a best-case scenario, they'd merely want tickets to the live show, but in a worst-case scenario, they'd be aspiring improv performers. Or maybe the real worst-case scenario was that they'd know me in a way I didn't want to be known by them. Even I wasn't sure if my in-person self (a mild-mannered woman of average intelligence and attractiveness) or my scripts (willfully raging sketches about sexism and bodily functions) reflected my real self—or if I had a real self, or if anyone did. But I suspected that much of my writing emerged from this tension or lack of integration; I believed the perceptions undergirding my sketches arose from my being invisible or at least underestimated, including being mistaken for someone nicer than I was. Since childhood, I'd often felt like a spy or an anthropologist, and I was fine with others at *TNO* knowing who I really was only because they, too, were, at their core, spies and anthropologists and weirdos.

I'd had the arrangement I had with Gene with a series of guys, ending the previous one when I discovered an unsettling three months in that he was a married dad (I'd always imagined that being someone's mistress would feel compromising yet glamorous, but in this case it had mostly been marked by my unwittingly catching the guy's preschool-aged kids' colds). Though I sometimes joked with Viv and Henrietta about being a man-eating career woman, I felt confident that I wouldn't have found a deeper connection with Gene or his predecessors if only I'd given them more of a chance. If I'd gone out for a meal with them, or walked around Governors Island with them, if we'd been required to hang out clothed and sober, I'd have ended things immediately.

I was typing *Busy this week, what about meeting up next Tues or Wed?* but before I could send it, presumably when he could see the three dots of my impending reply, another text from Gene arrived, and it was a dick pic. He appeared to be at his Queens apartment, which I'd visited just once. Taken from his navel down, the picture showed him lying on gray sheets, wearing no shirt and navy-blue mesh athletic shorts that he'd pulled toward the inside of his right thigh so that his wrinkled balls tumbled out and his veiny erection sloped left and upward. Given the nature of our relationship, such a photo wasn't out of bounds, and far from the first he'd sent, but I'd never found a way to express that they had the opposite of what I assumed was their desired effect. In fact, the personal details peripherally revealed—the mesh shorts and gray sheets, the nightstand in the background on which I could discern a plastic container of watermelon-flavored antacids and a book about the leadership principles of billionaires—were oddly poignant but alienating. They reminded me of a truth I was usually unbothered by, which was that I knew what Gene's dick looked like, but I hardly knew him at all.

I deleted *Busy this week, what about meeting up next Tues or Wed?* and typed *Wow!!*

Right now, he replied. *Thinking of you*

Flattering! I replied.

Send me one? he wrote.

At dinner w/ friends, I typed back. Then I added, *Busy next few weeks unfortunately but hope you're well*

At some point soon after that, I fell asleep with my phone in my hand, the better to look at it first thing upon waking the next morning.

TUESDAY, 12:10 P.M.

TNO's offices and studio, along with many other offices and studios for our network, were located in an iconic building referred to as 66—it was sixty-six floors, and when the building had been completed in 1933, such a number had been more noteworthy. As I walked there just after noon, I knew I wouldn't set foot outside again for the next twenty-four hours.

The writers' hall on the seventeenth floor was, as I'd anticipated, ghostly in its emptiness, and I sat at my desk and inserted my earbuds. I always listened to classical music, usually Haydn or Schubert, while writing sketches about things like dog farts, tampons, and Title IX. I worked for two and a half hours without standing or removing my earbuds and in this way generated a rough draft of the Danny Horst Rule sketch (nine pages) and then a rough draft of the Blabbermouth one (ten pages). This early on, I was more focused on getting the structures into place than coming up with jokes.

One of the legends of *TNO* was that most of the show was written between the hours of 5 P.M. Tuesday and, because sketches were due by noon, 11:59 A.M. Wednesday. Another of the legends was that much of the creativity of *TNO*'s early years had been fueled by cocaine. While both of these rumors were in fact true, I personally had never done coke in my life and didn't do most of my own writing overnight. I stayed at the office overnight because it was when I worked with cast members on their ideas and because it was considered bad form not to, and I often did find myself feverishly revising at 11:55 A.M. on Wednesday. But I wrote first drafts much better and faster during the day, and I sometimes wondered if, the cult of the overnighter aside, most of my colleagues would have, too.

At some point in my first year, I'd realized that the all-night writing sessions were, in a different way from the sketches, largely performative. Occasionally, it really did take six hours to write a sketch, but far more often, people fucked around for five hours then wrote a sketch in forty minutes. At any point on the writers' hall, as Tuesday turned into Wednesday, you were as likely to see someone goofing off as typing. The *TNO* writing staff was still three-quarters male, and they'd be wrestling or making bets or peeing in trash cans. Some writers or cast members left before midnight to do a set at a comedy club; returned to wrestle, make bets, or pee in a trash can; *then* started writing. But these days, I knew of only one cast member who used hard drugs at work. Far more of my co-workers wore Fitbits, drank kale juice, and meditated in their off hours, or at least claimed to.

It was Nigel himself who was clearly a natural-born night owl, and though the schedule he'd set in the beginning seemed objectively crazy, it was after all this time justified by an if-it-ain't-broke logic. Many sketches that had found their way into the country's collective consciousness and spawned beloved characters and catchphrases had indeed been written at one or three or four-thirty in the morning. And really, if you were lucky, Tuesday was just the beginning. If one or more of your sketches made it past the table read, you might stay up late on any or all of the remaining nights until Saturday, rewriting, rehearsing, or directing a shoot for a pre-tape. Then you'd probably stay up all night Saturday, too, commiserating or celebrating at the after-parties, because your sketch had been cut at the last minute and you felt despondent or because your sketch had made it to air but bombed and you felt despondent or because your sketch had aired and killed and you felt exhilarated.

Prior to joining the show, I'd kept typical sleeping and waking hours, but *TNO* truly had rewired my biology, as if I were a third-shift factory worker except vastly better paid, or an ER doctor except not saving anyone's life. It now seemed normal to me that most people arrived at the office around 5 P.M. on Tuesday, and we placed our orders for dinner around 9 P.M. I spent the hours before and after dinner working with cast members, most often Viv and Henrietta, on sketches they were developing. Around one or two, I lay on the couch in my office, set a T-shirt over my eyes and earplugs in my ears, and, except when I was awakened by chaos in the hall, I nodded off for about five hours, which was downright decadent by *TNO* standards. I'd set my phone alarm to go off at six or seven then brush my teeth in the women's room. There was a shower in the private bathroom off Nigel's office that some of my co-workers used after he went home, but I wouldn't have had the nerve or the ambition and merely kept a toiletries bag in a desk drawer. After brushing my teeth, I'd have coffee and an energy bar and sit down again at my desk for revisions. At this point, plenty of people were still awake, never having slept at all, and usually emanating a half-dead exhaustion, though sometimes giving off a loopy camaraderie reminiscent of the kids who'd stayed up all night at an elementary school slumber party. I'd revise for a few hours, turn my sketches in at the last minute like everyone else, and go home for a few hours to poop in peace and shower before returning to work for the read-through at three.

On this particular afternoon, I still had a draft of the Cheesemonger to hammer out but decided to get coffee—real coffee that I'd buy from a place in the lobby of 66, not from the office kitchen—and while I was waiting in line, I texted Viv, *How was doctor apptmt?*

So, she replied immediately.

Interesting story

I didn't see my usual doc

I saw someone else
And he was
She added three fire emojis.

Then came a screenshot, clearly taken off the eye clinic's website, of a man who looked to be in his early forties, was smiling earnestly, was either light-skinned or biracial, and was wearing a white dress shirt, yellow tie, and white lab coat. Next to the photo were the words

Theodore P. Elman

Certification: American Board of Ophthalmology

Education: M.D., Perelman School of Medicine, University

of Pennsylvania

Specialty: Comprehensive Ophthalmology

Another text from Viv: *OK he looks kinda middle aged dorky here but trust me*
We had crazy chemistry
And he wrote his email on business card if I have Qs
But he can't ask me out right?
Because it would be illegal
I typed: *Wait how's your eye?*
Then: *I don't think illegal but maybe unprofessional?*
Want me to ask my college roommate who's a pediatrician?
From Viv: *I have a subconjunctival hemorrhage*
Which grossness aside isn't that serious
Should heal on its own 1-2 wks
From me: *Oh good*
Obviously you don't look gross if there was crazy chemistry
Was he wearing a wedding ring
From Viv: *No*
From me: *Did he know who you were*
From Viv: *Unclear*
If I think there was chemistry, was there chemistry?
From me: *Yes*

From Viv: *What if there was chemistry but only for me*
From me: *Pretty sure that's not how chemistry works*
When are you getting to office
From Viv: *4:30?*
Can you write some sketches that make me look hot and hilarious in case the love doctor watches this week
From me: *Hmm should I assign not hot woman in Danny Rule sketch to you or Henri*
From Viv: *Me me me me me*
From Viv: *All airtime is good airtime*

TUESDAY, 10:08 P.M.

Viv, Henrietta, and I had brought our food from the dinner order—on this night, Greek—into the office they now shared. I sat at Henrietta's computer, Viv sat on her own desk, and Henrietta sat on the floor. We were working on the idea about dogs' Internet searches, and first we debated whether the sketch should feature real dogs or Henrietta and Viv in dog costumes (because cast members were always, unfailingly, trying to get more air time, we quickly went with the latter). Then we discussed where it should take place (the computer cluster in a public library, but, even though all this mattered for was the establishing shot, we got stalled on whether that library should be New York's famous Main Branch building on Fifth Avenue, with the lion statues in front, a generic suburban library in Kansas City, or a generic suburban library in Jacksonville, Florida, which was where Viv was from). Then we *really* got stalled on the breeds of dogs. Out of loyalty to my stepfather and Sugar, I wanted at least one to be a beagle. Viv said that it would work best if one was really big and one was really little, and Henrietta said she was fine with any big dog except a German Shepherd because she'd been bitten by her neighbor's German Shepherd in third grade. After forty minutes we'd decided on a St. Bernard and a Chihuahua—I eventually conceded that Chihuahuas were funnier than beagles. We decided to go with the Florida location for the establishing shot because the lions in front of the New York Main Branch could preempt or diminish the appearance of the St. Bernard. Then we'd arrived at the fun part, which was the search terms.

With her mouth full of beef kebab, Viv said, "Am I adopted?"

With my mouth full of spanakopita, I said, "Am I a good girl?"

With her mouth full of falafel, Henrietta said, "Am I five or thirty-five?"

"Why is thunder scary?" I said.

"Discreet crotch-sniffing techniques," Henrietta said.

"Cheap mani-pedis in my area," Viv said. "Oh, and cheapest self-driving car."

"Best hamburgers near me," I said.

"What is halitosis," Henrietta said.

"Halitosis what to do," I said.

"Where do humans pee," Viv said.

"Taco Bell Chihuahua male or female," I said.

"Target bull terrier married," Viv said.

"Lassie plastic surgery," Henrietta said.

"Funny cat videos," I said.

"Corgis embarrassing themselves YouTube," Viv said.

"YouTube little dog scares away big dog," I said.

"Doghub two poodles and one corgi," Henrietta said.

"Waxing my tail," I said.

"Is my tail a normal size," Viv said.

"Refinancing my mortgage," Henrietta said, and, though all of us had been laughing intermittently, this was the one that made me laugh so hard I had to stop typing. I had been both in- and outside of this moment many times at *TNO*—laughing uproariously with my co-workers on a Tuesday night, and hearing writers and cast members in other offices laughing uproariously, without me, on a Tuesday night. After I'd recovered, I said, "How to tie a tie."

"What is bitcoin," Viv said.

We'd all started laughing again when a foam football sailed

through the open door, and someone—I quickly realized it was the writer Rohit—yelled, "Stop gloating, you succubi!"

TUESDAY, 11:29 P.M.

Rather shamelessly, I'd been planning to ask Danny to give me some dialogue for his part in my Danny Horst Rule sketch. When I entered our office, he was slouched on the couch, holding his phone in front of him, a female voice I recognized as Annabel's coming out of it.

Danny glanced up at me and said, "Hey, Chuckles," and, though I couldn't see the screen, Annabel said, "Hey, Sally."

"Hi, Annabel," I replied.

Apparently continuing where they'd just left off, Annabel said to Danny, "But if you want to compliment someone, you say they look hot. If you say how impressed you are by their body positivity, it means, 'That's great you're so confident even though you're fat.'"

"Baby, you're the hottest girl ever," Danny said. "You're reading too much into it." Judging from his cooing tone, I assumed the preceding day's concerns over their astrological mismatch had been resolved.

"The worst part," Annabel said, "is that being criticized makes me want a donut."

"You could eat a hundred donuts and be just as sexy as you are now."

As I sat at my desk, in exactly equivalent amounts, I did and didn't have the impulse to put in my earbuds. In the last seven weeks, Annabel had with her entourage in tow attended all the live shows except for the one when she'd been in Tokyo for the opening of the flagship store of a luxury clothing brand for which she was a spokesperson. During the shows, Annabel hung out not in our office but either in Danny's dressing room or, befitting her status, with Nigel. Nigel was both Buddha-like in demeanor *and* an intergenerational celebrity mega-schmoozer, as likely to walk through the studio, on any given day, accompanied by a septuagenarian rocker from one of the world's most famous bands as a rising teen starlet.

"I don't know why she has to be such a bitch," Annabel was saying. "I thought our feud was over after we presented together at the Globes."

Danny lowered his voice, which still meant, because he was sitting about four feet from me, that I could clearly hear every word he said. "You know how perfect you are?" he murmured. "You're so perfect that I'm getting hard just looking at you. I don't think I could stand up if I tried."

Did he realize I wasn't yet wearing earbuds or did he not care? I suspected the latter; every day, things were said at *TNO*, often on camera, that would have constituted sexual harassment in any other workplace except the current White House.

"Instead of eating a donut, I'm getting on the treadmill right now," Annabel said. "I'm going to turn the gradient up to 15 percent. Body-shame that, you bitch."

"What if instead I come over and fuck you really hard and tell you how beautiful you are?"

After a pause, in a much softer voice, Annabel said, "Yeah?"

"So beautiful," Danny said. "So, so, so beautiful."

"Should I send Mickey to get you?" This was her driver or bodyguard, or maybe both.

"It's faster if I take an Uber."

"I'll get in the shower now."

"Don't take a shower. Don't do anything. I'm hanging up now and I'm on my way. I'll call from the Uber. I love you so fucking much, baby."

"Hurry, baby."

He'd already stood and was halfway out the door when I said, "Please if you ever jerk off in here don't get it on the couch. That's all I ask of you."

Danny paused and glanced over one shoulder with his back to me, which offered the advantage to both of us of my not having to know if he actually had an erection. "I'd never jerk off in here." He smirked. "That's what my dressing room is for."

WEDNESDAY, 1:14 A.M.

I heard someone saying my name, but at first I was so deeply asleep that I incorporated the voice into my dream. I thought it was Bernard, the janitor, coming to empty my trash can, and, senselessly, I mumbled, "You can leave the mollusks." I felt a hand lightly pat my shoulder, and the person said, "Sally, I'm really sorry to bother you"—not a commonly uttered phrase at *TNO*—and I pulled the T-shirt off my eyes and the earplugs from my ears, sat straight up, and said, "What do you want?"

Hunched over the couch at such an angle that my sitting up had brought our faces within a few inches of each other was Noah Brewster.

"Sorry," he said again. Even in my disoriented state, I noted that he looked, in his cheesily handsome surfer way, uncomfortable. Though I was accustomed to being awakened by random people in an office in the middle of the night, perhaps he was not accustomed to waking people in this fashion.

"No, it's fine," I said. "What do you need?"

"Well, Bob O'Leary suggested—should I give you a minute? I can come back."

"Now is good." I wiped the back of one hand across my mouth in case I'd drooled in my sleep, which it felt like I had.

"Bob said you'd be the best person to help with the sketch I've been working on." Bob O'Leary was a longtime supervising producer at *TNO*, one of the many magicians who had been there since the beginning and made the show run, while remaining almost totally unknown to the public. Noah was no longer leaning toward me—he was standing straight up—and I noticed then that he was holding a few papers.

I pointed at them. "Is that the sketch?"

"Seriously, though, if you need a minute—"

"I'll read it now." I extended my arm, and when he passed me the script, I swung my feet off the couch. I gestured toward the couch's other end. "You can sit. This is the idea you mentioned at the pitch meeting?"

He nodded as he sat. "Should I tell you what it is or just let you read it?"

"Let me read it."

I grabbed a blue ballpoint pen and pulled a two-month-old issue of *The Atlantic* off the windowsill to use as a surface to write against, and began reading. I was dimly aware of Noah Brewster a few feet away from me, scrolling on his phone. It would have been a lie to claim I didn't feel some vestigial stress about keeping a huge celebrity waiting. I still often recalled an observation made by a writer named Elise with whom I'd overlapped for my first two years, which was that when we nonfamous people talked to famous people, we wanted the encounter to be finished as soon as possible so that we could go describe it to our nonfamous friends. But my stress was mostly offset by the knowledge that I was keeping Noah Brewster waiting for his benefit. The overriding goals of any episode of *TNO* were to entertain and to make the host look good; a genuinely funny or endearing host could reap the benefits in terms of public perception for years.

The sketch was seven pages, set in a dance studio, and featured a musician meeting with a choreographer in the presence of two record label executives, an agent, a manager, and a videographer. The choreographer was saying things like "When you do rainbow arms, the people sitting all the way in the back will feel your passion" and "A retrograde will bring closure to the song in your heart." In reply, the nameless musician was saying things like "But I'm a singer-songwriter. I'm not a member of Cirque du Soleil." In the ten minutes it took me to read, I marked the script in a few places, though more gently than I would have for a cast member or fellow writer's work. About two-thirds of the third page achieved nothing and could easily be cut, but instead of drawing a blue line through that section, I made a question mark in the margin next to it. On page four, when the choreographer asked the musician if he'd ever considered incorporating some kind of panther into his show, I laughed out loud.

After I'd finished, Noah Brewster and I made eye contact, and I said, "Is this based on personal experience?"

"It's been a while, but when I first started playing arenas, the record label had me work with a choreographer who had a lot of ridiculous suggestions. Her ideas made sense from a visual standpoint, in terms of the size of arenas, but they were really influenced by the boy band craze and completely off for me personally. Just all these very melodramatic hand gestures and pauses."

"Your script is actually in pretty good shape, although I think it can be tightened. Do you want me to give you feedback and you go work on it or we can revise it together now?"

"I'd love to get your help revising. Bob said you're a genius with structure."

"Ha," I said. "I'm pretty sure that's a euphemism for being more hardworking than funny. Can you email me the version I just read?" I stood, stepped toward the desks, and pulled over Danny's chair so it was next to mine.

As I took a seat in my chair, Noah sat in Danny's. He was tapping his phone, and he said, "What's your email?"

I gave him my address and asked, "How long have you been working on this?"

He smiled. "I'm tempted to pretend I started it earlier today, but at least a few weeks. Whenever it was that I got the confirmation I'd be hosting."

"There's no shame in preparation. Obviously, a lot of stuff here happens on the fly, but sometimes a sketch that ends up being a big hit is something the writer was pitching week in and week out for an entire season." After I hit the return key on my keyboard to bring the monitor to life, my open email account came into view. At the top of the inbox was an article my stepdad had forwarded with the headline as the subject: *Daily Garbanzo Beans, Other Legumes*

Lower Bad Cholesterol. Just under that was an email from Henrietta, related to a sketch she wanted us to write together and filled with links, that had as its subject line *Batshit evangelical mom influencers.* Though it felt weirdly intimate to expose my inbox to Noah, the wall behind the computer monitor made me even more self-conscious. I'd taped two photos there, the first of which was of me and Hillary Clinton in December 2015, taken in her *TNO* dressing room before she'd appeared in a sketch I'd written. The other was of my mother holding me as a baby in early 1982, my mother wearing a buttonless denim vest over a yellow blouse and me wearing a yellow onesie. Between the photos I'd taped a rumpled piece of printer paper with two columns. In the first column, handwritten by me, were the words *boner, balls, dick, cock, blow, golden shower, manhood, hand job, suck, prick, beat off.* In the other column were the words *pussy, tits, titties, eat out, nipples, finger, hairy vagina, vagina, vulva, pink, wet, queef, cervix, fist.* Next to *pink* were parentheses with three exclamation points inside them and next to *cervix* were parentheses with eight exclamation points. As Noah's email appeared in my inbox, and I downloaded and opened the file, he remarked on none of this.

I said, "Your attachment isn't going to give me an STI, is it?"

He laughed. "I hope not."

"Okay." On my desk, in the space between the monitor and the keyboard, were my almost-empty coffee cup from the afternoon and about two dozen hair elastics. I lifted an elastic and looped my hair into a bun. "You actually have all the ingredients you need, but they're not in quite the right order. And it's kind of subtle in places, but, because of the sketch's physicality, it can be more slapstick. Does that make sense?"

"It does."

"Also, I'm sure setting it in a dance studio is realistic, but it'll confuse the audience. It should be set in the stadium where the musician is performing. So you collapse space and time for the sake of clarity."

"Got it."

"Another thing for clarity, and this would kill a few birds with one stone, is we could start with a title card that gives the date and place. Wait, what if the musician is explicitly your younger self? And wardrobe can come up with some awesome early-two-thousands clothes? So the title card says *Madison Square Garden, May 2001,* or whenever your first album was really exploding—when was that?"

"The album was released in May 2001."

I'd already typed *Madison Square Garden,* and I glanced at him. "I'll email the document back to you afterward, and obviously you can change any wording that you don't like."

"Go for it. Please."

I added *May 2001.* "The other characters will address you by name, so the audience immediately knows it's you. But the next issue is there are too many characters. Do you think anyone serves a purpose here besides you and the choreographer?"

"Isn't it important for the record label execs to be there? To show that these are directives coming from above and the musician—well, me—can't just shrug them off?"

"True. Maybe we should even play that up." The current first line was from the choreographer, who said, "I want to give you some ideas to jazz up your dance moves onstage." Above it, I inserted an executive saying *Noah, we've summoned you here because we at your record label are getting feedback that your live shows lack excitement, and we think some cutting-edge choreography will really enhance the audience's experience.*

"It's ridiculously obvious," I said, "but, unless there's a payoff for withholding the premise, you might as well give it as fast as possible."

"What if the guy is like, 'According to some focus groups . . . '"

"Oh, that's even better," I said. "How about 'According to focus groups held with one hundred twelve-to-fifteen-year-old girls residing in four mid-Atlantic states . . . '"

He laughed, and I retyped the sentence.

We both were quiet, and after a few seconds, I said, " 'We're con-

cerned that the girls sitting up in the nosebleed section aren't sufficiently receiving your soulful emotions.'"

"'And this could affect your long-term sales,'" Noah added, and
I typed both parts.

"'So the world-famous choreographer'—we need to give her a
silly name—'is here to offer her expertise.' Hmm. Lulu von Floppy
Bosoms?"

Again, he laughed in that light way. "Sure."

"Just FYI, some stuff that reads on the page as only mildly funny
is automatically ten times better when the cast is acting it out. Okay,
now we can cut everyone other than the record label guys, you, and
Lulu. The celebrity entourage clutters up the sketch because they
aren't really what it's about. So we give everyone else's dialogue to
the execs, but you pick who plays the parts, and their names go in
the script, not the characters' names. Who do you want to be Lulu
and who do you want to be the executives?"

"Shouldn't I ask people if they're interested before assigning
them a role? I don't want to be presumptuous."

I laughed. "You're the host. Any cast member will be happy to be
in your sketch."

"What do you think? For one of the execs, Josh always cracks me
up."

"Yeah, he'd be good." I typed Josh's name before the first record
executive's dialogue. "And maybe Hakeem is the other? And for the
choreographer—" Either Henrietta or Viv would do an excellent job
and each was likely to appear in multiple other sketches. Naming a
chronically underused cast member, I said, "What about Grace?"

"Sure."

"Then from here on out, really the only change I'd make is to put
Lulu's choreography suggestions in order of ridiculousness from
least to most. It's more satisfying if they escalate, so it starts with
waving your hands around a lot and ends with the panther idea."

"There's one thing I didn't put in there because it didn't come
from a choreographer but from kind of like, I guess he was an image

consultant. He recommended I perform shirtless and in leather pants."

"Oh, that's perfect. But let's make the pants into shorts. Shorts are even better. Or what if you're the one who suggests this, and it's the pivot at the end? So up 'til now, it seems like you're so resistant to these silly ideas, but you're just resistant to *their* silly ideas. And you're wearing tear-away clothes that you pull off, and you say something like 'I'm confident that audience engagement will be enhanced by my beautifully sculpted body.'"

Noah shook his head good-naturedly, and his blond surfer hair shifted a little. "I'm starting to feel like I just dug my own grave. And I'm still with the same label I signed with in 1999. That's the irony here, as I vilify them in public."

"If it reassures you, there's no guarantee any sketch will get picked for the live show." When our eyes met, I said, "But I bet this one will."

"I guess I'm a winner either way," he said. "Or a loser?"

I scrolled through the document, making the changes we'd discussed. When we got to the third page, I said, "This chunk can go because it doesn't establish anything new. It's kind of filler."

I could tell he was reading the lines onscreen, then he said, "No, you're right."

At the end, I inserted the stage directions for him to rip off his clothes then I glanced at him once more. "Want to read it through out loud? You can do the you part, and I'll be the execs and the choreographer."

We both laughed a few times as we read. When Noah said, "Because my beautifully sculpted body will enhance audience engagement," I realized it unintentionally echoed the earlier line about cutting-edge choreography enhancing his live performances. I cut the second *enhance* and replaced it with *increase*. In general, word repetition worked only when it seemed intentional.

"We need a title," I said. "But just as a placeholder, so don't overthink it. Something like Choreographer."

"Done," he said. "Choreographer." He pointed down at the elastics on my desk. "Is it when you pull your hair back that your magical editing powers kick in?"

I laughed. "I've heard of novelists who are very precious about their writing rituals, like they have to light a candle or drink herbal tea first, but *TNO* beats that out of you."

"Well, I feel like I just took a master class in comedy writing. I seriously can't thank you enough."

"Again, it still has to make it past the table read and rehearsals, but I actually think it's really fun."

"The way you keep saying *actually*," he said. "It's like you're surprised."

"Sorry. It's just that very few hosts write sketches, and even if they do, a writer probably drafted it. And honestly, for a musician host, it's almost unheard of."

"Do you know I write my own songs?"

"But don't you think songs and sketches are different animals?"

"Well, structure is really important in both, right? And rhythm? And what you withhold versus what you reveal up front?"

"True."

"What kind of music do you like?"

"What kind do *I* like?" The question caught me by surprise.

"If you're making dinner at home or you're on the subway, what are you listening to?"

"I guess a range. If we're talking about genres, mostly folk or pop."

"Which specific artists?"

"I don't have particularly cool taste if that's what you're asking. Have you met the writer Jeremiah? He always knows about bands before they blow up."

"I'm just curious. I swear this isn't a trick question."

"When I was in third grade, I had a cassette of The Supremes' *Greatest Hits* that I played so much the tape started unspooling out the bottom. And then, because of how upset I was, my mom took me on an emergency trip to the mall that same day to replace it."

He smiled. "And since then?"

"Mostly female singer-songwriters. My mom liked Linda Ron-stadt, Patti LaBelle, Joan Armatrading, so we listened to them a lot. Dolly Parton, of course. And Sade. And then my taste sort of segued into more countryish like Lucinda Williams and Emmylou Harris. And then, you know, Mary Chapin Carpenter, Dar Williams, or more recently Brandi Carlile. Oh, and Janelle Monáe." I glanced over and said, "My favorite singers of all time are the Indigo Girls."

"Yeah, they're incredible," he said.

I looked at him—we still were side by side, perhaps six inches apart—and said, "Are you serious?"

"Why wouldn't I be?"

"A lot of people—meaning male writers here—would use the Indigo Girls as a punchline. Or have used them as a punchline, to make a joke about something that's very female or that's lesbianish or that's earnestly political. And I fucking hate it. Partly because it's sexist, but even more because it's not funny. It's lazy. The Indigo Girls are super talented and have been doing what they do for a long time, on their terms, regardless of cultural trends, and now that we're a budding autocracy, it's a little harder to mock the people who have always stood up for the rights of the disenfranchised. Plus, they just have such beautiful, complementary voices." I paused. "That's why you came to my office, right? You were hoping for a rant about the Indigo Girls."

"I love rants about the Indigo Girls. Have you seen them live?"

"Yes, a bunch of times. Have you?"

"I performed with them at a fundraiser in L.A. years ago. And Amy does backup vocals on my song 'East Matunuck.' I'm trying to think if they've ever been on *TNO*."

Of course he had played with them, of course he was on a first-name basis with them. But how had I not known Amy Ray was on one of *his* songs? "Funny you should ask," I said. "They haven't been the musical guests, but there was once a spoof of them where the cast members playing them were dudes. This was before my time."

"How long have you worked here?"

"It's my ninth season. Another fun fact is that *TNO* and I are actually the same age. I was born the month of the premiere, in October 1981."

"That seems auspicious, right?" Noah said. "I was born in September '81, so you and I are the same age. If you've been here nine years, I take it you like it?"

I had to admit that, for all his cheesiness, he had impeccable social skills. Most hosts were charismatic and many were polite; some were curious about the history of the show; but almost none would ask a writer multiple questions about herself. It didn't seem rude to me that hosts registered writers the same way the outside world did, which was far lower in the hierarchy than cast members. A lot of writers aspired to be cast members, and some had auditioned for the cast at the same time they'd auditioned for the writing staff, but I felt liberated by not wanting more. It wasn't by accident that I had never appeared on camera.

"For sure, this is my dream job," I said. "Even with the baked-in sexism, even when I've barely slept. I just can't imagine a job where I laugh more, or the people are more talented and hard-working. And to get paid to make fun of stuff that deserves to be made fun of and have this huge platform—what more could a misanthrope from Missouri wish for?"

He laughed. "Are you a misanthrope from Missouri?"

"Yes and yes."

"I feel that way about my music—like, This counts as a job? Sometimes I get scared that someone is going to tell me the jig is up. I fooled everyone for a couple decades, but now they've realized I'm a fraud."

"What's the fraudulent part? That you don't really know how to play guitar?"

He laughed.

"That could be a sketch, actually," I said. "With you just sort of wiggling your fingers on the strings."

"Actually," he repeated. "See? You do say it a lot. But no, the fraudulence is being rewarded for something I'd gladly do for free. You'd have to be super, super entitled to experience that and never second-guess yourself or at least be amazed by your luck."

"The thing I worry about is overstaying my welcome," I said. "There's supposedly a *TNO* curse where if you stay too long, you get stale here *and* you miss the boat on the next stage of your career. It only applies to writers and cast members, though. A lot of the producers and wardrobe and makeup people have been around forever."

"What's the boat you'd miss by not leaving? Like, what's your next act?"

"I'm going to write non-condescending, ragingly feminist screenplays for romantic comedies."

He glanced at me. "What makes a romantic comedy non-condescending and ragingly feminist? Besides an Indigo Girls soundtrack."

"Mostly the quality of the writing. And related to that, the character development. When one of those movies doesn't work, it's usually because it's horribly written and/or the script hasn't done the work of convincing you the couple is attracted to each other, so then you don't care if obstacles get in their way and keep them apart. Another of my pet peeves is that the female characters used to all be sort of cutesy, like having flour on their nose after they baked cookies and not knowing it. And now they're all a mess, like waking up really hungover and getting fired. I want to create characters who aren't flawless but also aren't ridiculous or incompetent at life." After a second, I added, "Wow, was that two rants in a row? I swear I'm actually not a total asshole."

"You actually don't seem like a total asshole."

"I think I'll leave at the end of next season, thirteen months from now." Oddly, I hadn't told this to anyone else yet, including Viv, Henrietta, or my agent. "And then I will have been here exactly ten years. But who knows if I'll really be able to cut the cord?"

"I'm glad you're here now, tonight." Noah pointed at my computer screen. "To save me from myself." After a pause, he said, "I have to ask—" and he leaned forward and tapped the piece of paper with the two lists of words.

"The first column is words the network censor has allowed in sketches," I said. "The second column is words the network censor said were offensive and had to be changed. It's almost like there's a double standard for terms related to men's sexuality and terms related to women's, huh?"

"That's crazy. Even *pink*? And *wet*?"

Hearing Noah say *pink* and *wet* together—I felt an unprecedented sympathy for the censor, who, as it happened, was currently a woman in her fifties named Janice. Aloud, I said, "It's all contextual, of course. Obviously, you can have somebody say 'That's a nice pink sweater.' The problem with the standards rules is that they aren't even rules. It's just at the discretion of one person."

"Do you think getting censored has ever forced you to find a workaround that's better than what you originally had?"

"For sure," I said. "But I still don't like the hypocrisy."

After a companionable silence, he said, "If I never sang 'Making Love in July' again, I'd be okay with that. I wrote it when I was eighteen, and I'm grateful, if it's possible to feel grateful to a song, because it opened so many doors for me. But the chord repetitions are simplistic and, yeah, it *is* kind of cheesy. The reason I still perform it isn't for my own enjoyment." We made eye contact, and he said, "Obviously, we live in a world where fans have ways to be very vocal when they think they've been shortchanged."

So *this* was behind all his questions about my favorite musicians—he felt defensive about the Cheesemonger idea I'd pitched. His declaration that sketches worked better when the host was making fun of himself notwithstanding, perhaps he was as vain and touchy as anyone else.

"I haven't written the Cheesemonger sketch yet," I said. "My instinct is that it could be fun, but you're under no obligation to do it if you think it's dumb or insulting or you just don't want to."

"I have to see how it turns out, right?"

I tried to think of a gracious way to convey that if it was likely he'd push to cut the sketch, I'd prefer not to spend any of the next ten hours writing it.

"Random question," he said, "but are there any male singer-songwriters you like?"

"Oh, sure. Jason Isbell. Neil Young. And you, of course."

"Of course. Which would you say are your three favorites of my songs?" In this moment, surprisingly enough, he didn't sound vain. If I hadn't known better, hadn't known that charming people was part of his job description and that he dated twenty-two-year-old models, I might even have thought he was flirting.

"It's hard to choose," I said. "Something I really admire is the level of quality you've operated at for so long."

"Nice try. Just three."

"Okay, well—" I held up my right fist then extended my thumb. "One, 'Making Love in July.' Then, hmm—" Frantically, I searched in my mind. He was ubiquitous enough that even though I didn't like his music, I surely knew at least three of his song titles, but it was difficult to summon them on command. Then a title came from nowhere, and, releasing my index finger, I exclaimed, " 'Best Laid Plans!' " What had he said was the name of his song with Amy Ray on backup? Or had I already revealed my ignorance? I then recalled a collaboration he'd done with the mononymic pop singer Fran-çoise. "Oh, and 'Sepia.' " I wasn't sure if "Sepia" counted more as Noah's song or Françoise's, but I did sort of like it. Plus, I was now triumphantly holding up three fingers.

"It's an amazing coincidence," he said, "given what a fan you are, because those are my three most popular songs. In fact, those are probably the songs that someone who's never really listened to my music would be familiar with. Wouldn't it be wild if you wrote an entire sketch about how cheesy my music is, but you'd barely ever listened to it?"

"If by wild you mean egregiously irresponsible, then yes," I said. "But since I'm the president of the Manhattan chapter of your fan club, that suggestion is deeply wounding."

He was grinning and shaking his head, and I was grinning, too, and I said, "You know how I said I'm not a big asshole? Maybe I am a big asshole."

"Impossible."

"When the fan club meets, it's in a church basement and we hang a life-sized poster of you on the wall and gaze at it."

"Oh, really?" he said, and he then did something very confusing. He turned toward me, cupped my chin with his hand, and looked intently into my eyes. "Like this?" he said. "Is this what you do?"

Was the gesture brotherly? Or flirtatious? Or just strange?

It seemed he was wondering the same because he quickly dropped his hand and said, "Sorry. I feel like it's weird I just did that."

Because of how surprised I was, I overcompensated. In a merry voice, I said, "Around here, you have to try *much* harder to be weird. If you peed in a pickle jar and left it on my desk, that would be a start. Anyway, seriously, you'll meet with Nigel and Elliot and the producers after the table read, and I'm sure they'll let you have the final say on the Cheesemonger sketch."

"No, I trust the process," he said. "I've always been under the impression that when—" But I didn't learn what he'd always been under the impression about because this was the moment we were interrupted. Autumn DiCanio, who was head of *TNO*'s talent department, appeared in the doorway, along with one of her assistants. Most of Autumn's assistants were pretty, long-haired blondes just out of college—this also described Autumn herself, except she was forty—and because I had trouble telling the assistants apart, I wasn't sure of this one's name.

"Noah!" Autumn said warmly. "We've been looking everywhere for you! How're you doing?"

It occurred to me for the first time that it *was* rather odd this revision had just happened in my office, that Noah had found his way to me solo. Hosts were regularly in the office during the wee hours, especially as the week went on, but they were almost always chaperoned by Autumn or a member of her staff, or writers visited the host in his or her eighth-floor dressing room, supplicant-style.

"I'm good," Noah said. "Sally's been helping me with my sketch."

"Fantastic," Autumn said. "Sally's one of our very best. We have a car downstairs to take you to the hotel whenever you're ready, unless you guys are still working?" For my first few years at *TNO*, I'd instinctively disliked and distrusted Autumn because of her upbeat, briskly corporate energy. However, I'd realized over time that she was highly organized and competent in a way that was hard not to respect. And she had great taste. In addition to booking and then babysitting the hosts and musical guests, she scouted for new cast members, whom Nigel rejected or hired. As with Bob O'Leary, the public didn't know Autumn existed, but she'd discovered many of comedy's household names.

Noah turned and looked at me—I was farther inside the office, farther from Autumn—and he said, "I guess we're wrapping up?"

"I'll email the revision back to you."

"Sally, just email it to me and cc Madison, and we'll take care of the rest," Autumn said, and I could tell that she was trying to protect Noah from sharing his email address with a writer; she didn't know he already had. She added, "Noah, we'll make sure your sketch is in the pile for the table read. That'll be at three, and the car will come for you at 11 A.M. for the photo shoot and promo videos, so hopefully you get to have a relaxing morning."

Noah had turned back in Autumn's direction but once again looked at me. "Do you need a ride home?"

Was he joking? I said, "Oh, I stay here on Tuesdays," and Autumn laughed and said, "I'll bet Sally's night is just beginning."

Noah stood then and said, "Thanks again. I really appreciate it."

"I'm here to help," I said, and I suddenly felt cringingly awkward. I had no idea if the awkwardness had originated with me, or with the arrival of Autumn and the assistant, whose name I was now 87 percent certain was Madison, or with the fact that Noah had recently grabbed my face. Both Autumn and maybe-Madison wore very tight black jeans, angular black shirts, and pointy black boots. I was abruptly conscious that I was wearing gray sweatpants, a black sweatshirt, light green running socks, and no shoes. Noah was somewhere in the middle of their style and my slovenliness, in jeans, sneakers, and a long-sleeved brown T-shirt with a refrigerator on it.

Before the three of them left, Noah waved from the doorway. "See you at the table read," he said.

WEDNESDAY, 4:43 A.M.

When Danny returned, he looked exhausted but gave off a happy energy. Before I could ask, he said, "All's well in Bellyville."

"Glad to hear it." Since my editing session with Noah, I'd spent two and a half hours working on the Cheesemonger sketch. After he'd left, I'd felt churned up, presumably from his celebrity aura, and I hadn't tried to go back to sleep. I currently had four pages of the sketch, which weren't very good, and the overstimulation that had gripped me at 2 A.M. was long gone. I reached for the pages of the Danny Horst Rule sketch sitting on my desk and held them out to Danny. "Will you help me with your dialogue?"

"Man, Sally, have some self-respect."

"I'm trying to turn in three separate sketches," I said.

"That's on you. Do you think it would be weird if Belly and I break a glass at our wedding? She suggested it."

"Do you want to?"

He shrugged. Though he rarely mentioned it, a widely known part of Danny's origin story was that he'd grown up in an Orthodox Jewish enclave in New Jersey. As the oldest boy of seven siblings, he'd attended a yeshiva through high school and had been expected to become a rabbi like his dad. But he'd secretly watched comedians on cable from the age of twelve on, and he'd left his community after his first year at a rabbinical college, when he moved into a homeless shelter for young adults that, by coincidence, was about a mile from the *TNO* studio. Seven years later, Danny was still estranged from all of his family except a brother, which he joked was a reasonable price to pay for getting to eat fried shrimp. And he was far from the only person at *TNO* who'd endured misfortune; tragedy, of course, often begat comedy.

Danny had taken the pages from me, and he read them so quickly that if I didn't know him, I'd have thought he was skimming. "This is brutal," he said. "In an awesome way." He took a pen off his desk and began filling in the spaces I'd left blank. When he'd finished, he said, "It's definitely better if I'm the second cop who comes in, not the first."

"Because it increases the tension of when will you appear?"

He nodded.

"I wonder if Noah would be willing to be the first cop instead of the guy on the date," I said. "But he was so negative about the sketch in the pitch meeting that I don't even want to ask."

"Yeah, that was a real slap-down from him in Nigel's office."

I thought of telling Danny about my recent encounter with Noah, but how would I tell it? I wasn't sure. Instead, I said, "Thanks for noticing."

Danny smirked as he handed back the pages. He said, "Chuckles, everyone noticed."

WEDNESDAY, 2:57 P.M.

In the interlude between turning in my sketches and the table read, I took a cab home, fell asleep for an hour, woke, showered, and walked to the Seventy-ninth Street subway station. As I stood on the platform waiting, I read the texts that had come in during my nap, which included two from my college roommate, Denise, the pediatrician, who lived in Austin. Responding to my question about if Viv's ophthalmologist could ask her out, Denise had written:

Doctor should not ask her out. But I don't know specific laws or rules. I know it is different with psychologist/psychiatrist where it might be unethical.

Then: *Is this for a sketch or real life?*

Real life, I typed back. *Can my friend ask the dr out?*

From Henrietta, to both Viv and me, there was a photo of a bag of coffee-flavored potato chips, along with a text: *Did we know these exist?*

When I reached the seventeenth floor of 66, Henrietta and Viv were sitting on the couch of my office, and Danny was at his desk. Viv tilted the potato chip bag in my direction, and I took one, which looked like a regular potato chip topped with a dusting of cinnamon. I bit off a tiny amount as Danny said, "It's not the worst thing ever."

I swallowed. "Or is it?"

Danny reached out and took a few more, stuffed them in his mouth, and said while chewing, "They're wrong but weirdly compelling."

Henrietta said, "Like Log Cabin Republicans."

"Or that monkey in Japan who was caught trying to fuck a deer," Viv added.

As we all walked down the hall to the conference room, I said to Viv, "My college roommate said Dr. Eyeballs isn't supposed to ask you out, but I asked if you can ask him. I'm waiting to hear."

Viv grimaced. "Yeah, I don't really do that."

"What's it like to be so beautiful you never have to make the first move?"

She laughed. "Advantageous yet burdensome. Also, in my case, complicated by America's ongoing misogynoir."

The conference room was full as we entered, with most seats taken around the pushed-together tables in the center, as well as around the perimeter of the room. There were even more staff members at read-throughs than at pitch meetings, including from hair and makeup, wardrobe, set design, and the music department. Spread over the tables were scripts of the sketches and, because we'd be there for three hours, bottled waters and scattered platters of sandwiches, salad, cut-up fruit, chips (presumably not coffee-flavored), and cookies. Whether you considered this meal breakfast, lunch, or dinner depended on how late you'd been up the night before.

Danny, Viv, and Henrietta all took seats at the table that had been saved for them. I took a second-perimeter seat, my back to the windows that overlooked muffled honking traffic and muffled frolicking tourists seventeen stories below. Noah Brewster was in the middle of the tables' south side, to the left of Nigel, who always narrated the stage directions in all the sketches. The worse the sketch was being received, the faster he read.

It happened that I was about twenty feet from Noah but directly in front of him, and when we made eye contact, he smiled and I felt a wild surge inside me, though I wasn't sure if it was panic, excitement, or something else. He was painfully handsome, yes, but I had already known that. I reflexively looked away, as if we were strangers who'd accidentally locked eyes on the subway. Then I realized that looking away had been rude and odd, because we *weren't* subway strangers. We were, if only for this week, colleagues, and part of my job was to make him comfortable. I quickly looked back, saw that his smile had been replaced with a more quizzical expression, and forced a smile of my own. When I did, he raised a hand and waved. Then a cast member named Bailey, *TNO*'s first nonbinary performer, leaned in from Noah's left and said something, and Noah turned toward them and replied, and they both laughed.

Elliot, the head writer, called the meeting to order by sticking two fingers in each corner of his mouth and whistling, and we got down to it. Cast members who'd turned in sketches always gave themselves the leading role, which they'd read, whereas writers assigned roles to various cast members, and these assignments sometimes stuck and sometimes didn't. If Nigel decided a cast member, especially a favored one, had a "light week," he might unilaterally make reassignments as a sketch advanced.

We started with a sketch about the porn actress alleging that Trump had paid her to keep quiet about their affair, then there was a sketch where Noah was performing the national anthem before an NFL game as a duet with a famous diva played by Henrietta, and they were competing over the high notes. The first sketch to make me really laugh was the one now titled Blue-Eyed Soul, by Tony, in which Noah was the white politician preaching to a Black congregation.

Even after nine years, I found table reads fascinating because they represented the intersection of multiple creative and psychological forces. In a room filled with the people who mattered in my life, but with no outside audience, I was always desperate with curiosity to find out how my sketches would be received and what the other sketches were like; I was often shocked by the brilliance of some sketches and the crumminess of others; and it was unsettlingly easy to infer social dynamics by the laughter and warmth, or lack of, with which a sketch was received. More than once, it had been at a table read that I'd first suspected two people were romantically involved, or that someone was going to be let go at the end of the season.

An hour and five minutes in, we got to The Danny Horst Rule. After what I'd thought of as my best line, there was only half-hearted laughter, while, to my chagrin, the loudest laugh lines were the ones Danny had written for himself. Still, I could feel that the sketch's catchily self-referential premise meant it was likely to make it to the next stage.

Formal feedback didn't happen during a table read—whether your sketch ended up in the lineup for the show *was* the feedback. But before we went on to the following sketch, the writer Jeremiah, who was sitting behind Nigel, said, "What I really respect is Sally's fearlessness in the face of offending half the staff here."

From my chair against the window, I said, "I'll take that as confirmation that it strikes a chord."

A writer named Jenna said, "And they lived heteronormatively ever after," and Bailey leaned back from the table to fist-bump Jenna.

By coincidence, my Blabbermouth sketch came right after The Danny Horst Rule, and Blabbermouth also got respectable if not inordinate laughs. Writers often sought out the cast members, including the host, who'd be reading their sketches to make suggestions about what tone to use. Though I hadn't sought out Noah—I'd arrived at the read-through just before it started, and also, for some reason, I would have felt weird instructing him—he did a good job. The conceit was that the male judges of the singing competition were speaking over him, too, in addition to speaking over the female judge, and he and the female judge began doing other things, like filing their nails, playing checkers, and pulling out yoga mats and sitting in the lotus pose. The alchemy happened that I'd described to Noah the previous night, when a sketch went from words on a page to a much funnier live enactment.

After Blabbermouth, though, there was a string of duds, including one by a first-year writer named Douglas whom Henrietta, Viv, and I referred to behind his back as Catchphrase because his primary goal at *TNO* seemed to be to send a catchphrase into the zeitgeist. This week, the catchphrase that Catchphrase was trying to coin was "Ridin' toward ya, ridin' from ya"—the sketch featured Catchphrase himself on a unicycle—and I felt a flare-up of loathing. How and why had Catchphrase been hired? How and why was he so confident? In his second week, I'd suggested during rewrites for someone else's sketch that a woman get on all fours to force a fart out before her date arrived. Referring to a viral sketch from seven years earlier, Catchphrase had said in a casual yet knowing tone, "That's too derivative of My Girlfriend Never Farts." I'd replied, "Hmm, I wonder if that's because I'm the person who wrote My Girlfriend Never Farts." Appearing not at all chastened, Catchphrase said, "Ah, so you're a self-cannibalizer."

Noah's sketch—Choreographer—was after Ridin'. It got laughs right away, when Nigel read the *Madison Square Garden, May 2001* title card, and though the laughter dwindled rather than building as the sketch continued, it still seemed funny enough to make the cut on its own merit and not just because it had been written by the host. At the conclusion of the sketch, Noah made eye contact with me and nodded once. I nodded back.

The Cheesemonger was the very last sketch of the table read, by which point there was a palpable restlessness in the air. People were constantly getting up to use the bathroom or stretch their legs; even the midpoint break had been ninety minutes before. The earlier in the table read your sketch came up, the likelier it was, regardless of quality, to be well received. For this reason, and because I hadn't been feeling all that inspired when I wrote the Cheesemonger, my expectations were low.

I was wrong, though; the sketch was met with lots of laughter. And most of it could be attributed to Noah. In the stage directions, I'd called for him to sing the lines that introduced the cheeses— "This is a Swissss," or "Here we have a delectable Camembert"— and he really went for it, in an operatic way. I'd given the roles of the three customers, who approached the cheese stand one after the other, to Henrietta, Viv, and Bailey, and they all had great chemistry with Noah. Or perhaps it was just that everyone was relieved to have reached the end of the meeting.

As we all finally stood and people threw away their paper plates and chatted, I pulled my phone from my jeans pocket. Sometimes, of course, I had the impulse to check my phone during meetings, before remembering that there was an infinitesimal chance that any message from outside could matter to me as much as what was happening in this room.

I'd heard back from my college roommate Denise: *Your friend can definitely try to ask out the doctor but most doctors would be like, "Oh thank you. You are too sweet." And then move on with the visit. Basically not even acknowledging the asking.*

I screenshotted the text, sent it to Viv—who was standing fifteen feet away, talking to Nigel and Autumn—and added, *Obviously my roommate doesn't know the friend here is you and the law of gravity doesn't apply*

WEDNESDAY, 9:13 P.M.

After the table read, Nigel, Elliot, Bob O'Leary, and another producer named Rick Klemm would go to Nigel's seventeenth-floor office and close the door. An hour or two later, you'd find out if your sketch had been picked for the Saturday show—or more accurately, if it hadn't yet been eliminated—when an intern appeared in the conference room and posted a copy of the list of sketches from the read-through with the picks highlighted, then unceremoniously left additional highlighted lists on the table. Meanwhile, in Nigel's office, brightly colored index cards featuring sketch titles were pinned on a corkboard in order of their tentative appearance. All this information could have been sent out via email, sparing the mingling of people receiving good and bad news, but this was another *TNO* tradition that Nigel apparently had no desire to change. Typically, a handful of people were waiting in the conference room to see the list, and those who weren't waiting quickly filtered in as word spread that picks were out.

The interval between when the table read ended and the lineup got revealed was always kind of tense and weird—some people deliberately left the building, including a bunch of the male writers and cast members who played basketball—but I stuck around. It wasn't that long to wait, and I wanted to know as soon as possible whether I'd be working frantically, exhilaratingly, between this moment and Saturday night, or if I'd have nothing much to do besides attend Thursday rewrites. More often than not, one of my sketches made it past the table read, and I was particularly optimistic for this week, but it still was far from a given.

In Viv and Henrietta's shared office, Viv had us assess her eye injury, which was fading from a red dot to a yellow one, from various distances. She was trying to determine the exact number of inches away from which it was visible.

"It's really not obvious," I said. "I'd have forgotten about it by now if you didn't keep reminding me."

"You're not watching me in high-def."

The next way we killed time was that Henrietta and I tried to convince Viv that emailing the eye doctor and offering him a ticket to the show wouldn't violate her policy of not making the first move. Or that, if it did, perhaps that was fine, too?

Viv was lying on the floor stretching, bending and turning her left leg sideways and pressing her right elbow against her knee, and Henrietta and I were both slumped on the couch. Looking at Henrietta, Viv said, "You better not use this." She was referring to Henrietta's recurring Are Straight People Okay segment on News Desk, in which Henrietta offered faux earnest updates about the ridiculousness and outright toxicity of prominent heterosexual couples. Supposedly for material, Henrietta, whose wife was an art history professor named Lisa, followed celebrity gossip more avidly than anyone else I knew. The irony of Henrietta being a celebrity herself, albeit an extremely private one who, also ironically, wasn't on social media, was lost on none of us. Though I tended to be solidly conversant in such gossip, Henrietta always heard every morsel first. It had been in a text from her, accompanied by a link, that I'd originally learned Danny and Annabel were dating.

"How about this?" I said and read aloud the email I'd been composing on my phone. "'Dr. Elman, it was nice to meet you yesterday, and I'm feeling good today. As a thank-you, I'm wondering if I can give you a ticket to *The Night Owls,* where I'm a cast member. Let me know if you're interested and we can figure out a date. Either way, thanks again for your help. Viv.'"

"'Let me know if you're interested in removing all my clothes and boning me, and we can figure out a date,'" Henrietta said. "But, Viv, do you even have his email?"

"He gave it to me in case I had follow-up questions about my eye."

"Right." Henrietta made air quotes. "'About your eye.'"

"No offense, Sally, but that email is boring and not at all funny," Viv said.

"Granted, but it's open-ended and doesn't hit the medical stuff too hard. I purposely didn't include the word *eye,* but it does have the words *feeling good, interested,* and *date* to subliminally lure him in."

"Seriously?" Viv said.

"No," I said. "Well, maybe. I think it gives you both the cover you need at this point. Are you asking him out or expressing appreciation for treatment? Who can say? And you seem modest for not assuming he knows you're on *TNO,* right? Even though I bet he does."

Viv wrinkled her nose. "Calling him Dr. Elman is so formal."

"Do you know what he goes by? Ted? Teddy?"

"I may or may not have done some reconnaissance and found an alumni update he sent to the Penn class of '88. He's fifty-two, and he goes by Theo."

"Holy shit, he's fifty-two? Not holy shit like that's so old—I mean, it's kind of old—but holy shit like I'd have guessed ten years younger."

"Have I taught you guys nothing?" Viv looked both amused and impatient. "Black don't crack."

"Sorry," I said. "But still."

"Have you ever dated someone that much older than you?" Henrietta asked.

"Like five years ago, this Italian guy hit on me when I was flying back from Paris, and we went on a few dates." She grinned. "You think Dr. Theo had one of those starter marriages like you, Sally?"

I said, "If he did, his would have been back in the early nineties. When you were, what, in kindergarten? But I actually like the sound of him. Professionally successful but not in the entertainment industry, so he won't be threatened by your career. Most doctors—" And then all three of our phones exploded with texts from other cast members and writers telling us the sketches had been picked.

It also would have been easy, of course, for someone to send around a photo of the picks, but no one ever did. We stood and hurried to the conference room, and, as we rounded the corner, a cast member named Duncan said to me, "Not bad, Milz." Danny was standing in front of the posted list, and he raised his eyebrows and said, "You got a hat trick, Chuckles." He held up a hand for a high five, and I slapped it.

Included on the list, in addition to The Danny Horst Rule, the Cheesemonger, and Blabbermouth, were Noah's Choreography sketch; a digital short written by Tony and Lianna that juxtaposed shots of a dismayed Black grandpa who'd be played by Jay watching social media videos of white women showing the ways they "improved" various recipes, like by adding raisins to mac and cheese or marshmallows to fried okra; the James Comey sketch; Sister & Father, a recurring sketch where Henrietta played a nun in love with a priest played by Hakeem, which this week featured Noah as the Pope; a sketch by a writer named Tess about talking medications in a bathroom cabinet; a Three Tenors sketch by Joseph; and Catchphrase's terrible Ridin' Toward Ya sketch. Neither the dogs' Google searches sketch I'd co-written with Viv and Henrietta nor my favorite sketch from the table read, the one by Tony about the white politician at the Black church, had made the cut. And the likelihood was that two or three more would be eliminated. There were no guarantees at *TNO,* but still: I'd never in nine years had three sketches in the same episode.

One of the writers, Patrick, said warmly, "Is it sexual harassment to say that I hate you right now?"

I and the other writers whose sketches had been picked wandered into a room next to Nigel's office to speak to the heads of all the departments who would make our words three-dimensional: wardrobe and hair and makeup and production design and special effects. The sets would be built at a warehouse in Brooklyn then transported back to 66, ideally on Friday, to be painted. While talking to a set designer named Buddy, I said, "Yeah, a mix of triangular hunks of cheese and wheels but both are way bigger than life-sized," and then I said to a woman in wardrobe named Christa, "For Blabbermouth, I'm picturing Noah in something like animal print leggings and a jean jacket so I guess a hair metal vibe?"

The rest of the week would be challenging and exhausting and consuming and magnificent, and I thought, as I met with Bob O'Leary to confirm which cast members were in each of my sketches so he could coordinate the whole crazy chessboard of *TNO,* that what I'd told Noah the night before, what I'd thought a thousand times, was true: Without question, I had the best job in the world.

Thursday, 1:08 A.M.

I was walking toward the elevators to leave when I heard someone say, "Hey, Sally." When I turned, Elliot—the head writer, who was married to the multi-platinum-album-selling singer named Nicola—was leaning out of his office.

I paused.

He said, "Nice lineup on the corkboard."

Because he'd been part of the meeting where the first round of sketches had been selected, I said, "If you're offering me the opportunity to thank you, I'll hold off 'til the live show." I didn't point out that I'd never know if he'd argued for or against any of mine.

"I'll be shocked if at least one doesn't make it to air," Elliot said, which didn't seem particularly encouraging. He added, "I just wanted to say—not to touch the third rail—I hope—" He paused, and I was reminded that, although he had over time remade himself into a well-groomed, successful cultural arbiter married to a pop star, he was still, fundamentally, an awkward writer.

And though I myself was no stranger to awkwardness, I wasn't going to help him out. "You hope—?" I repeated.

"That someday you'll be able to let bygones be bygones."

If I'd had any acting skills, I'd have said, "Meaning what?" But of course I knew what he was alluding to; even though he was wrong, I knew. Elliot had started at *TNO* the year before I had and was legendary for landing what became a wildly popular sketch on his first episode ever. By the time I joined, he seemed like a beloved veteran. In contrast, my first year had been bumpy and confusing, I'd often been too intimidated to even speak, only two of my sketches had made it on air in the whole season, and I hadn't known if I would be invited back. The week in August after my contract had been renewed, a few months before the next season started in October, I'd run into Elliot at the Strand, next to a table of novels in translation, and we'd ended up getting coffee and having a surprisingly frank conversation. I had confided all the insecurities I'd been wracked with—my total lack of experience in stand-up or improv, the fact that I hadn't attended Harvard—and he'd matter-of-factly said that was all normal, almost everyone felt insecure, even people who had lots of experience with stand-up or improv and people who had gone to Harvard, and his trajectory was more anomalous than mine. *TNO* liked raw talent, he said. Nigel preferred hiring people for their first TV job because then the show could mold them. Elliot pointed out that I didn't always submit a sketch for the table read and asked if I was writing them and not submitting or not even writing them. The former, I said. He said that I should never be the one to preemptively reject my ideas; I should force other people to. In fact, I should submit a minimum of two sketches each week, even if I didn't think they were in perfect shape. There were so many variables affecting a sketch's outcome—the host, the national moment, Nigel's mood—plus an idea could always be drastically improved in rewrites. Also, Elliot said, I should seek out cast members who'd started around my year, who were as green and hungry as I was, and we should pool our talents and climb the ranks together. Our time might not be now, but if we persisted, it would come. The only way to learn, he said, was by doing it. He didn't put it in these terms, and I'm not even sure if he knew this was what he was saying, but his message was: Act like a guy. It was a message that turned out to be invaluable.

At that time, he was years away from being named head writer—we were part of a writing staff of twelve—and we became close friends. We didn't write together, but for my second season on the show, we were editors of each other's work, brainstorming ahead of time and punching up early drafts, and our compatibility had the unfortunate effect of making me think we were in love. I hadn't dated anyone since my divorce, which had become official a few months after I'd arrived at *TNO*. Unlike in the dynamic with my ex-husband, Elliot and I shared a shorthand, a general sensibility, and the same incredibly weird schedule. After holding in my feelings for seven months, I half-drunkenly confessed my love to him at the after-party following the season finale of my second year, he rebuffed me, I cried to a writer named Stephanie while she ate a plate of grilled sesame shrimp and scallions, and I never again was close to Elliot. For the subsequent seven years, while frequently attending the same meetings and passing each other in the studio, we'd spoken only when necessary.

But I neither longed for nor resented him, as I'd always sensed he believed. Though I'd been hurt and humiliated by his rejection, it had, I soon realized, freed me and offered clarity. I would never again risk poisoning *TNO* for myself by falling for or trying to date anyone there. And this decision made me see that there was a different way I wrote when, even subconsciously, I was seeking male approval, male *sexual* approval: a more coy way, more reserved, more nervous about being perceived as angry or vulgar. It was the syntactical equivalent of dressing up as a sexy zombie for Halloween. From my third season on, I'd embraced my anger and vulgarity. I'd been a gross zombie.

I began writing about ostensibly female topics—camel toe and wage inequity, polycystic ovary syndrome and Jane Austen, Do-si-dos and Trefoils and mammograms and shapewear and *Dirty Dancing* and the so-called likeability of female politicians. By October of that year, I'd written my first viral sketch, Nancy Drew and the Disappearing Access to Abortion, in which Henrietta played the amateur detective. By December, I'd written my second, My Girlfriend Never Farts, which was a digital short that interspersed men at a bachelor party remarking on how their girlfriends and wives always smelled great and were hairless interspersed with shots of the women grunting and sweating as they moved a couch up a staircase, writhing on the toilet with explosive diarrhea, and giving instructions to an aesthetician who was waxing their buttholes. I didn't try to be disgusting for the sake of being disgusting, but I didn't try not to be disgusting.

A few years after not reciprocating my feelings, Elliot appeared to develop an almost identical friendship with another new female writer except that I had the impression they *were* hooking up, but it didn't last. The same season that Elliot became head writer, Nicola Dornan was a musical guest on the show, they began dating, and a year after that, they got married. This development did seem to vindicate his apparent belief that he shouldn't have settled for me. Quite a few people from *TNO* had been invited to the wedding, and I hadn't been one of them.

All of which was to say, as we stood in the hallway outside his office, below a framed photo of a legendary *TNO* alum from the first season dressed as the Easter bunny—many such photos adorned the halls—I knew that Elliot was saying he hoped someday I could get over him.

I tried to sound persuasively non-defensive as I said, "Really and truly, Elliot, the Danny Horst Rule sketch isn't about you. It's not revenge for you marrying Nicola."

The expression on his face was sympathetic and disbelieving, which made me realize I'd have vastly preferred unsympathetic and believing. Somberly, he said, "You have good qualities, Sally. You're not out of the game unless you think you are."

I was filled with such loathing for him that it almost retroactively tainted the wise yet not entirely dissimilar work advice he'd given me years before. I was trying to come up with a reply that would seem polite while actually functioning as a retort—*Fuck you* was neither adequately clever nor subtle—when he added, "You know, you should try to get Annabel to do a cameo for the sketch."

Simultaneously, I thought that he was right; that this was a suggestion he'd have considered corny before he became head writer but now a celebrity cameo would increase the afterlife of a sketch online and gain him points with Nigel; and that I respected his ability to collaborate with me professionally even as he condescended to me personally.

"That's not a bad idea," I said.

THURSDAY, 1:51 A.M.

After climbing into bed, I lay on my back, propped up against the headboard by two pillows, and tapped the icon for the music app on my phone. As soon as I typed *No* in the search bar, the letters auto-filled to *Noah Brewster*. The first song that came up was "Making Love in July," which had, apparently, on this app alone, been streamed 475 million times. The number didn't make me like the song, but as someone who felt proud when a million people viewed one of my sketches on YouTube, I found it hard not to be impressed. I listened to a few of Noah's other most popular songs that I didn't recognize by name—one was called "Sober & Thirsty" and another was called "Topanga Sunshine"—then typed *Noah Brewster deep cuts*. A two-hour-and-forty-eight-minute playlist featuring thirty-nine songs came up, made by another subscriber to the streaming service whose username was BestBrewstyFanBarcelona. The playlist had zero likes, and the user had eight followers. I hit the play arrow, set my phone on the nightstand, and closed my eyes as a song called "All Regrets" started, a first person narrative about the promise and excitement of a new relationship, the heartbreak when it collapsed, and the sorrow not about losing the woman but about being wrong once again in his romantic optimism. Both the lyrics and melody were straightforward, and though I wasn't knowledgeable about what was going on with his guitar, the other instruments, or the backup vocals, the song was pleasurable to listen to at the same time that it was devastatingly sad.

Was Noah Brewster himself sad? With that hair and those big white teeth? I searched to see what year the song had been released—2013—then typed *who Noah Brewster dating 2013*. My precise question wasn't answered, but an avalanche of related articles offered themselves up, including a slideshow headlined "All the Famous Women We've Seen Noah Brewster With," and an essay headlined "Kissing and Telling with Noah Brewster," which was one fan's account of having sex with him in his hotel room after a show he'd played in Sacramento in 2009. The accompanying photo showed a pretty woman with lots of dark curly hair, wearing leggings and a zippered jacket; she was, or had in 2009 been, a nutritionist who'd attended his concert with a friend. She reported that Noah had been a considerate lover, that the Celtic tattoo on his back resonated with her because she'd spent her junior year of college in Ireland, and that her attempts to reach out to him following their night together had not been successful even though they'd had an "amazing connection." I then read a 2016 interview with Noah in *Rolling Stone,* which included several facts I had somehow already known, through either his *TNO* bio or pop cultural osmosis: that he had attended an elite all-boys' prep school in Washington, D.C., and was the son of a lawyer father and a mother who worked in education, who'd both initially been concerned about his decision not to attend college; that in his early twenties, after becoming famous, he'd had a period of heavy alcohol and drug use culminating in an accident in Miami when all the members of his band scaled a rising drawbridge and the drummer fell off and died, after which Noah became sober and gave a million dollars to the drummer's girlfriend for their child's college fund; that Noah had from 2010 to 2012 dated a model named Maribel Johnson, who was a decade his junior, was from a small town in Wisconsin, and had appeared during that time on the cover of *Sports Illustrated*'s swimsuit issue; that his most recent girlfriend had been Louisiana Williams, a jewelry designer to the stars, though the viability of her profession was difficult for me to assess because she was also the heiress to, of all things, a pest control fortune; that he was deeply interested in architecture and had sought out meetings with leading architects who were "impressed" by his knowledge; and that he was involved in several charities, including one that funded residential rehab for people in the music industry who might not otherwise be able to afford it. Unstated in the article was that he clearly had an excellent publicist, or probably more than one. Having interacted with him, I believed he was genuinely nice, but the leading architects' supposed pleasure at being sought out by a dilettante made me snicker.

By this point, I was on BestBrewstyFanBarcelona's sixth selection, "The Bishop's Garden." It was about a high school boy—the lyrics pointed to but didn't confirm its being Noah—whose classmates hooked up with girls from the neighboring school in a walled garden between the two campuses, and how the boy never participated in this ritual even though he wanted to. If the song was auto-biographical, I thought, then surely the nutritionist in Sacramento and the various models had righted this past injustice. But again, the song was melancholy and evocative—it made me think of the guys *I* hadn't hooked up with in high school—and it was not remotely cheesy. In fact, it was the kind of folky, poppy music I liked. If only I'd done this modicum of homework twenty-four hours earlier, I thought, I could have effortlessly answered his question about which of his songs were my three favorites. Though already, the memory of sitting side by side with him at my computer, revising his sketch in the middle of the night, felt like a dream the way life at *TNO* often felt like a dream: so vivid and goofy in the moment, so ephemeral once it ended.

I didn't know when I fell asleep, but when I awakened two hours later, the light was on and the playlist was still going. I reached out to turn off both and went back to sleep. When my alarm sounded at 9 A.M.—my first rehearsal, for The Danny Horst Rule, was at 11—I immediately began scrolling through my phone.

THURSDAY, 1:06 P.M.

I had stopped by the makeup lab to approve the purple eyelashes Henrietta would wear in the Blabbermouth sketch, along with a slinky sequined purple dress still being worked on by wardrobe. Henrietta herself was elsewhere, and the person showing the eyelashes to me was Francesca Martin, who'd led the makeup department for more than two decades. As I confirmed that the lashes looked good, the cast member Oliver, who'd be playing James Comey, came in to be fitted for his prosthetic nose, which would be made just for him out of silicone.

I was heading toward the elevators—I was about to join rewrites in the writers' room—when I got a text from Henrietta to both Viv and me: *Did Dannabel break up?*

Wait what, I replied.

Viv replied, *Oh shit,* accompanied by the broken-heart emoji.

Henrietta responded with a screenshot of an Instagram post Annabel had shared an hour before, a black-and-white photo of a topless female torso, one long-nailed, manicured hand set atop both breasts in a way that propped them up while concealing the nipples. Superimposed over the photo at a diagonal, a single sentence appeared in quasi-cursive font:

"Some of us think holding on makes us strong, but sometimes it is letting go."

—Hermann Hesse

I'd just pressed the elevator call button when another text from Henrietta arrived: *Also Herman Hesse?!*

I texted back, *Maybe she's into 20th c German novelists?*

Tho quote sounds fake

Like "Follow your dreams"—George Washington

Does this really make you think they broke up?

From Viv: *"We can do hard things"—Genghis Khan*

From Henrietta: *Google Dannabel breakup*

The internet thinks so

Bc she's not wearing engagement ring

I'd missed the first hour of rewrites because of rehearsal for The Danny Horst Rule, and since I was already late, I thought, *Why not be even later?* The actual desk that Danny sat behind during News Desk was stored, without pomp, in a random hall by the elevators, and I perched on the desk to investigate. The Internet was indeed abuzz: "Fans Asking if Cryptic Post Means Annabel-Danny Split" read one headline, of which there were many variations. How much of an asshole was I for wondering first how this development would affect my sketch and second how it would affect Danny? At the rehearsal, he'd seemed normal.

I was skimming an article on a particularly trashy website when Viv appeared beside me and said, "Hard at work?" Then she murmured, "I heard back from Dr. Theo."

"Good or bad?"

"You tell me." She passed me her phone, which was open to an email. As I began reading, I heard the tuning of a guitar through an amplifier in the studio.

Dear Viv,

This is a very kind offer! I have enjoyed TNO over the years, and I was aware that you were a cast member, although at your appointment I wanted to keep the focus on your eye :). In order for me to accept a social invitation from a patient, the patient would need to switch to a different practice (i.e., a different doctor at this clinic). Given that you are already a patient of Dr. Trumbull, a switch should not be onerous, but I want to be clear that I cannot continue to treat you medically if I attend the show.

Many thanks,
Theo

"What's bad about this?" I asked. "He's being responsible."

"It's so half-hearted. *Many thanks* is one degree away from *Best regards.*"

"He's saying he can't fall in love with you while he's still your doctor. Tell him you'll go back to seeing Dr. Trumbull, and the lovefest can start."

"Excuse me, Viv," said Trey, a production assistant in a headset. "Evelyn needs you in wardrobe for your Danny Horst Rule fitting."

Viv looked at me. "This is the one where it's my talent and not the outfit that has to make me look cute in front of Mr. Many Thanks?"

"I actually told Francesca *not* to give you a unibrow, so you're welcome," I said. "But it's Dr. Many Thanks." As Viv walked toward the wardrobe department, I called, "That's a good email!"

From the studio, I heard someone, probably a roadie, say, "One, two, mic check, one, two," and it was then that I realized that the guitar tuning I'd heard before was for Noah Brewster's song rehearsal. Thursday afternoon was the time that musical guests, who of course usually weren't also hosts, showed up to rehearse. These casual, free quasi concerts were a huge perk of working at *TNO,* and the bigger the act, the more people "just happened" to be passing through the studio, including employees of other shows at the network. Several times, I'd stopped to watch a musician I was minimally familiar with and walked away forty minutes later a fan.

I turned around and reentered the studio proper, walking toward the main stage, which was known as Home Base. The floor in front of Home Base was currently a mess of disorganized audience chairs; multiple cameras, including the iconic crane that for every episode swooped in for the guest host's entrance; and random set walls. Crew members were wandering around, while about twenty people were actively watching Noah, including Autumn, two of her assistants, and a cast member named Lynette. I sat on a chair about fifteen feet from the stage's lip. Noah, who stood with a guitar hanging from a strap over his left shoulder—he wore clothes similar to the ones he'd had on the previous day, a gray T-shirt, dark jeans, and black suede sneakers—was talking to the drummer and the sound engineers. A bass guitarist stood on one side of him and a rhythm guitar player on the other, and toward the rear of the stage were a keyboard player and two backup singers.

"All right," Noah said. "We're going to try 'Ambiguous' now."

"You texted me late," he sang into the standing mic. "Like it hadn't been years . . ."

I'd never heard the song, which I assumed was on his forthcoming album. It was somehow both energetic and mournful. Noah closed his eyes as he sang—"This is always your way / Like it isn't too late"—and his blond hair flopped around as he did something that wasn't exactly dancing, but was a kind of rhythmic bouncing that nudged me into the vicinity of embarrassment. Which was ridiculous! Noah didn't need me to feel embarrassed on his behalf; this was what he did, and had done thousands of times before stadiums full of people. After he opened his eyes, he occasionally glanced down as his fingers changed chords, sometimes stepping away from the mic as he did. Other times he was looking out into the studio, and because I was so close to the stage, we soon made eye contact. A jolt went through me similar to the jolt at the table read. But how had Noah Brewster earned the right to unsettle me?

As he continued singing, we continued making intermittent eye contact that turned into sustained eye contact. Was he mocking me? Proving something about my musical ignorance or his talent? Or was he, like, *serenading* me? In the most literal sense, he was definitely serenading me—he was standing on a stage with a guitar, and I was a few feet away, and he was singing—but what did it mean? Perhaps, as was often the case with human interactions, it meant nothing. Yet instead of the jolt induced by our first eye contact dissipating, some feedback loop was occurring in me, a thrumming awareness of my own physical body.

The song lasted probably three and a half minutes and ended with a multi-guitar flourish, his bandmates clustered around and synched up with him, and I felt both transcendently alive and immobilized. It was only when I heard other people clapping, though there weren't enough of them in the space to achieve a critical mass, that I realized I ought to clap, too.

Noah grinned, and I thought that surely I was experiencing the ache of being around incredibly beautiful people. I'd believed that I'd become immune, but it seemed I was having a breakthrough infection.

Noah was looking at me as he said into the mic, "Thanks, everyone. This next one is called 'Inbox Zero.'"

My phone vibrated in my pocket, and when I pulled it out, I saw that I had three texts from the supervising writer, Kirk, who was Elliot's deputy.

Sally can you come to writers room, said the first.

Then, *About to discuss Cheesemonger*

Then, *Where are you*

Needing to leave Noah's rehearsal was both a relief and a disappointment. For his next song, I didn't want him to keep singing to me. And also, I didn't want him to stop singing to me.

THURSDAY, 1:40 P.M.

For rewrites, any writer who wasn't at a rehearsal, along with a few producers, met at the big table in the writers' room, all of us with multiple freshly sharpened pencils and our own printed copies of the sketches. Weirdly, given that News Desk and the host monologue were probably the public's two favorite parts of *TNO*, they were handled separately and written last, the monologue primarily by Elliot and News Desk by Danny, Hank, and Roy.

When I entered the room, they were working on Sister & Father, then the Cheesemonger was up. It didn't get changed much, though we had a heated discussion about whether *provolone* was a funnier word than *Gouda* before we moved on to The Danny Horst Rule.

As with the table read, sketches were read aloud at rewrites, and some of the writers who aspired to be cast members did so theatrically, but I read more perfunctorily; Elliot had assigned me to Viv's role. I'd written the sketch so that it started with a couple on a date, played by Viv and Gregor, the most conventionally handsome cast member and the one who'd accidentally thrown the oven mitt at her eye. They were finishing their meal at an Italian restaurant and saying what a good time they were having when a cop, played by Josh Beekman—that is, another *TNO* cast member married to a star, in his case the Oscar-winning Imogen—approached their table and said, "Both of you are under arrest for violating the Danny Horst Rule. A man is allowed to date a woman way hotter than he is, but a woman isn't allowed to date a man way hotter." As Viv and Gregor protested, Josh handcuffed them, and the other diners at the restaurant expressed either dismay or approval. When Gregor tried to escape, Josh said "Code eight" into his two-way radio, then Danny appeared, also in a police officer's uniform, and said, "I got your call for backup. Oh, wow, this isn't a misdemeanor. It's a felony."

When we'd reached the end of the sketch, Elliot said, "The more times Josh explains the rule, the less sense it makes."

"Yeah, Elliot, I'm sure you have *no* idea what the rule is about," said Benji, and I was grateful he'd been the one to point it out.

"I get it that I'm Joe Schmoe who's married to Nicola," Elliot said. "Elephant in the room acknowledged. But in terms of the logic here, isn't there a counterargument that it's commendable when a successful man ends up with an even more successful woman? He could lead a life where people kowtow to him, yet in this relationship, he'll always be the second fiddle."

Tony said, "Group therapy alert," which someone almost always said at some point during Thursday rewrites.

"Seriously, though," Elliot said. "When a gorgeous woman dates some old, gross dude who's rich, everyone accepts that it's transactional. By that logic, shouldn't a gorgeous woman dating an ordinary guy be a sign that it's not transactional?"

"But the sketch is about *powerful* gorgeous women dating quote-unquote ordinary guys," I said. "The women aren't ingenues."

Elliot shook his head. "If you put too fine a point on the rule, you call attention to its incoherence."

Less because I agreed than because I knew that, behind closed doors, Elliot could encourage Nigel to cut the sketch, I said, "I'm fine tightening Josh's dialogue. The second and fifth lines can go with no problem."

"Where Annabel says, 'Come on, honey,' to Danny," said a writer named Alan, "is that the real Annabel? If so, we should do more with her."

He was right. But because I hadn't yet asked Annabel if she was willing to do a cameo, I'd inserted just one line for her as a placeholder. "Hopefully, it's the real Annabel," I said and wondered again if the breakup rumors were true. I still hadn't seen Danny since our morning rehearsal. "But TBD."

"Assuming it's her," Benji said, "what if she goes off on the rule?"

"But not in a way that breaks down the logic," added Lianna.

"Wait," said Patrick. "What if some famous feminist like Gloria Steinem comes into the restaurant and kind of chides Viv for being outraged, and Annabel is the feminist? She's like, yes, it's absurd that someone like Danny is marrying someone like Annabel, but who cares about that shit compared to the earnings gap and reproductive rights?"

"I've got it," I said. "Annabel should be the ghost of Susan B. Anthony."

"In a suffragist white dress and a sash and a gray bun," Patrick said. "And those little glasses." Patrick was about five years younger than I was, a slim, quiet, bearded Harvard graduate who'd once told me that he'd been so nervous before he'd interviewed with Nigel that he'd sincerely pondered purchasing a package of adult diapers. In this moment, I loved him deeply.

"Isn't Susan B. Anthony canceled because she was a racist beyotch?" said a writer named Fletcher.

"We can acknowledge that," I said. "By someone saying, 'Shut up, Susan, you've been canceled.'"

"This you?" said Tony.

"If Annabel is Susan B. Anthony, then Josh or Danny should hit on her at the end," Elliot said. "Like"—he switched to a wheedling New Yorker impersonation—"'Yo, Susan, you're a feminist icon, I make 60K a year and I'm only twelve years away from my pension, whaddaya say we make some magic together?'"

In spite of myself, I laughed. I really, honestly didn't have feelings for Elliot, but there was something about him that did, if I thought about it enough, make me sad. I experienced a disorientation around the ways our sensibilities did and didn't overlap, and had led us to draw opposite conclusions. He hadn't wanted to be romantically involved with a person with whom he shared a sense of humor, whereas I hadn't been able to imagine anything better. Or maybe he'd just thought I wasn't pretty. Either way, his aversion had made me question my view of the world, my own beliefs about what attracted two people, to such an extreme degree that I'd given up on romantic partnership completely.

In the writers' room, Elliot seemed to consider the Danny Horst Rule rewrites finished then, because he said, "Sally, can you make those changes and email it to Sheila, Kirk, and me? Next up, let's do Three Tenors."

THURSDAY, 6:18 P.M.

During a break in rewrites, I returned to my office to revise and found Danny facetiming with Annabel in what seemed to be a normal way. As usual, he lay on the couch holding his phone in front of him, and he nodded at me and said, "Hey, Chuckles." Glancing back at the screen, he said, "Belly, I don't think it has to be the same."

"Let's ask Sally," Annabel said. "Turn me around."

I revolved my desk chair as Danny held his phone screen toward me. Annabel's red hair was in a bun, and she wore a white velour sweatshirt and appeared to be sitting on the floor of a walk-in closet with shelves of very orderly, brightly colored stiletto heels just behind her. Her face furrowed as she said, "Isn't there supposed to be the same number of bridesmaids and groomsmen? Or, not to be homophobic, whoever's getting married—the bride and the bride? But just for balance?"

I looked above the screen at Danny, who was visible only to me and whose expression was surprisingly earnest. "That's a custom more than a rule," I said. "A couple can do whatever they want."

"But if Danny just has Hank, Roy, and Tony standing next to him and I have nine girls next to me, plus I'll probably include Farren"—was I supposed to know who Farren was? Had she even said Farren or had she said Darren or maybe Farrah?—"then what? That's lopsided!"

"How about if some of your bridesmaids stand on Danny's side?"

Before Annabel could respond, Danny turned the screen back toward himself and said, "Now that's using your noggin, Chuckles. Belly, I gotta be in wardrobe in a sec. You gonna be there in like an hour?"

"My eyebrow person is coming at 6:30, then I'm free again."

"Okay, love you, my moon."

"Love you more, my sun."

As soon as he'd hung up, I said, "Maybe you guys should elope."

"Yeah, that's not Belly's style." He stood up from the couch and stretched his arms above his head, revealing his pale, hairy navel.

"Do you think she'd be in my sketch about you and the dating rule?"

"Ask her," he said, and though I could see that he was tapping his phone, I didn't realize until I heard ringing followed by Annabel saying, "Yeah?" that he had called her back. "Sally has a question for you," he said and again turned the phone toward me.

I vastly preferred communicating via text or email to making phone calls, and even when I was calling someone I knew well, I often thought through what I'd say beforehand. Given the delicacy of this particular request and Annabel's fickle personality and high status, I might have gone as far as jotting down a few words—wasn't this one of the advantages of writing dialogue for a living? Caught off guard, I blurted out, "Hi again. Sorry to bother you. I'm working on a sketch about how at *TNO* it's happened a few times that huge stars like you fall in love with male cast members or writers, and I was wondering—"

"Don't sugarcoat it," Danny interrupted, sounding amused. "It's about how gorgeous girls go for dudes who are unworthy of them. You're so chickenshit, Chuckles."

"Not unworthy," I said. "Just like, maybe there's a perceived discrepancy in professional standing."

In a prim voice, Danny repeated, "Maybe there's a perceived discrepancy in professional standing." Still holding the screen toward me, he leaned his head around the side of it, stuck out his tongue, and wiggled it either seductively or mockingly. "Sally wants to know if you'll be in a sketch about how I'm disgusting and you're a smoke show."

"Baby, you're not disgusting," Annabel said.

"That's not what it's about," I said. "You know Elliot and Nicola? And Imogen and Josh? The sketch is, kind of, uh, celebrating that trend. And I'm sure you're super busy, but I think it would be really funny and the audience would love it if you were up for a cameo."

"Baby, turn the phone around," Annabel said, and when Danny did, she said, "Baby, do you want me to do it?"

"I don't care."

"Would I have to wear prosthetics? Because the glue for that woodchuck nose gave me a rash for literally two weeks."

"You don't have to wear prosthetics. You can just, like, share your Annabel splendor with the world."

Danny had turned the phone back toward me, and from behind it, he shook his head, presumably at my obsequiousness.

"Can I think about it?" Annabel said. "And I need to talk to Veronica."

As with not knowing who Farren was, I also didn't know who Veronica was, but I imagined an agent or manager. "Of course," I said. "And we can connect your team with Autumn DiCanio and her team if you have any special requests. You could skip rehearsals tomorrow, but, ideally, you'd get here by Saturday midafternoon. I'm sure you remember the schedule."

"Oh, shit, my eyebrow guy is here," she said.

"Thanks so much for considering this," I said as Danny ended the call.

"'Sharing your Annabel splendor,'" he repeated. "Chuckles, you're a world-class kiss-ass."

I shrugged. "Isn't the reason you're marrying her that you think she's splendid?"

FRIDAY, 11:03 A.M.

From the minute I entered the studio to rehearse the Cheesemonger sketch, which was about to happen on Stage 4, I was gripped by an agitation that may have been predictable, that was certainly misplaced, and that I hadn't experienced for many years: I was completely preoccupied with Noah Brewster. When I saw him from behind as I walked toward the stage—he again wore a light T-shirt and black jeans—I felt a stomach-churning, pulse-quickening swooniness that I was so unaccustomed to I almost didn't recognize it. But I did recognize it, just barely. It was the kind of attraction I'd felt in middle and high school, a full-body, brain-dominating excited terror.

Naturally, I pretended that nothing irregular was happening. I nodded curtly at Noah when he turned in my direction, and then in a businesslike tone, I said, "Hi, everyone. Hope you're all feeling cheesy-tastic." In addition to Noah, there were four cast members— the customers were played by Henrietta, Viv, Bailey, and, as an addition during rewrites, Wes—and three times that many crew members. Autumn DiCanio and her assistant Madison had also shown up.

As with other sketches, there was a rudimentary set in place, a gesture at what would exist by the following night. I as the writer was also the producer (one of the distinct privileges of *TNO*), while the sketch director was a guy named Rick, and the production manager was Bob O'Leary. Bob led the blocking, figuring out who went where in what order and communicating with the control room about camera angles. Though the cast had copies of the script, crew members also stood next to the cameras, holding cue cards.

I thought I'd calm down as we got going, but my roiling agitation continued. Why had this happened? How had I developed a consuming, imbalance-inducing crush on Noah fucking fake-surfer Making-Love-in-July Brewster? In my defense, I didn't think the revision session in my office had single-handedly done it, nor had his musical rehearsal the day before. But the combination of the two had tricked my brain into thinking there was some particular energy between us; it had tricked me into being *hopeful*. And maybe, because I liked irony and plot twists as much as the next writer, the hope was weirdly exacerbated by working on the Danny Horst Rule sketch, which focused on the very impossibility of a romantic connection between someone like Noah and someone like me. I often lived parts of my sketches before or after writing them. Many were autobiographical, not in a way that was intended as catharsis but because that was the material available to me, and sometimes, the ones I hadn't lifted from my past turned out to be lifted from my future. For a few years, I'd written sketches about a couples therapist who was a twelve-year-old girl, played by Viv, and though my ex-husband and I hadn't seen a therapist, the sketches were a kind of holding place for my occasional uneasiness about whether we should have. And I'd once written a sketch about a woman who hid her job from her hookups before I began hiding my job from my hookups. The difference was that the woman wasn't a TV comedy writer but a spy.

The cast read through the script twice, and after they'd gone over their lines a second time, I hoped I sounded like a competent adult and not a crush-addled middle schooler as I said, "Great job, everyone. This is really awesome and fun. Noah, you're occasionally veering into an Italian accent, and I don't think you need it—singing really passionately and earnestly is enough. I see your vibe as less European, and more the kind of dude who unironically talks about love languages."

"I *am* the kind of dude who unironically talks about love languages," Noah said, and everyone laughed.

"Bailey, you can show more skepticism toward Noah," I said. "While Viv, you're fully into his schtick."

"Aye, aye, captain," Viv said, and Bailey said, "Like hostile skepticism? Or like I just don't get him?"

"Hmm." I turned to Rick and Bob.

"I vote for the latter," Bob said.

"I agree," I said. "More like middle-aged baffled."

"This might be random," Noah said, "but what if I sing a duet with one of them at the end? If one of the customers is as, you know, cheesy as me."

"Oh, I love that," I said. "Henrietta, let's have you do it."

"Ab-so-luuuuutely," Henrietta trilled. Almost all *TNO* cast members could sing respectably, and some, including Henrietta, had truly beautiful voices, though she rarely used hers in a beautiful way.

I turned back to Noah. "But do you mean a real song of yours or would I write one?"

Noah looked amused. "If you want to write a song by tomorrow night, I can't wait to hear it."

"Yeah, let's go with an existing song. Are you okay with it being 'Making Love in July'?"

He grinned. "Sally, I'd expect nothing else."

Noah grinning, Noah using my name, Noah's ability to be warm and normal, while my insides churned—it was all somewhat devastating. Did he remember that, the previous afternoon, he'd serenaded me? Was I supposed to never mention that he'd serenaded me? Had he *not* serenaded me?

I said to the group, "We'll get the updated scripts to you ASAP. Otherwise, thanks again, everyone."

I was standing just offstage at this point, and Noah stepped down and approached me. In the same friendly tone from before, he said, "Did you hear Elliot's idea for my Choreography sketch? I guess I have no one to blame but myself."

"Wait, what's the idea?"

"You know how the choreographer suggests putting a panther in my show? Elliot's asking Nigel to spring for a real panther."

"Oh, wow. Are you comfortable with that?"

"God, no." Noah's forehead wrinkled. "Would you be?"

"You'll for sure hear from animal rights activists. Which I understand—I sometimes get stressed out on the animal's behalf, but the truth is that my greatest moment here involved a reindeer."

"What sketch was that?"

I shook my head. "Nothing I wrote. In my third season, in the episode right before Christmas, Diana Ross was the musical guest, and at the very end, she sang 'Joy to the World,' and fake snow fell from the rafters. The cast was standing behind her singing along, and Nigel came out with a reindeer that had antlers and everything. I knew it was corny, but I almost couldn't contain my happiness."

"Were you onstage?"

"Oh, God, no. Never. I was on the studio floor."

"I somehow missed that episode, but it sounds awesome. And I'm not even a person who wore out her *Supremes' Greatest Hits* tape in grade school."

I laughed—although we'd discussed it less than three days ago, I certainly wouldn't have expected him to remember that detail from my life—and he added, "My greatest show was in Glasgow, during a crazy summer storm. For the entire last hour, there was a torrential downpour, and everyone and everything got soaked. Me, my band, the instruments, the stage, the audience. I ruined my guitar, and it was so completely worth it."

"I guess the common denominator for epic live performances is a weather event involving precipitation," I said, and he grinned again.

"And it doesn't even have to be natural," he said. "It can be manmade. Have you really never appeared onstage here?"

"Yes," I said. "I really never have. I prefer lurking in the shadows like a goblin." He made a concerned expression, and I said, "I don't mean goblin in a bad way. It's a point of pride."

His expression shifted to something warmer as he said, "*Goblin* definitely isn't the word I'd have picked for you."

Surely, if I were a person adept at banter in real life, I'd have batted my eyelashes and said, "What word *would* you pick?" But I was adept at banter only on the page, and I said, "Anyway, about the panther, if you're into the idea, great, and if you're not, just say so to Elliot."

"Where's the fun in that?"

And then Autumn materialized at his elbow and said, "Noah, it's time for your tux fitting."

Looking at me, Noah said, "Aren't I fancy? See you at the Blabbermouth rehearsal." Before I could reply, he'd been whisked away.

I pulled out my phone and texted Viv, *Where'd u go*

She responded with a photo of herself sitting in the armchair in her dressing room, making a festive expression and holding aloft a can of Diet Coke the way a person might hold up a champagne flute. Within a minute, I was knocking on her dressing room door.

"Bad news," I said as I entered. "I realized Noah Brewster is hot."

She laughed. "Welcome to 2001."

"Why didn't anyone tell me?"

"That an aging white boy heartthrob walks among us? Sally, there are certain insights a woman has to have on her own."

"Do you think he's a cocky jerk?"

"Probably."

"But based on working with him so far?"

"At the dinner on Monday, he was pretty down-to-earth. He told a story about spraining his ankle while doing parkour with his agent."

I wanted to convey that it seemed as if there was some sort of attraction between Noah and me, but it felt embarrassing because Viv occupied a different plane than I did and there were options available to her that were unavailable to me. And didn't this discrepancy mean that if I described what it had been like when Noah was in my office, or when I'd watched him sing, or just now after the rehearsal where Viv had been present, that I'd need to make a joke of it? And was I really ready to make a joke of it, if only to purge myself of my agitation, or would some small part of me be hoping that Viv would confirm that an attraction between Noah and me was possible? Not that we were about to violate the Danny Horst Rule and start dating but that there could be a moment of fleeting flirtation. Except that if there could, wouldn't Viv have picked up on it at the rehearsal?

Aloud, I said, "Did you respond to Dr. Theo?"

Viv wrinkled her nose. "The whole thing with how I need to see a different doctor—now it's just another thing on my to-do list."

"Didn't Dr. Theo say your eye will probably heal on its own?"

She nodded.

"And you're already the patient of a different doctor there, right?"

She nodded again.

"Then you don't have to make another appointment now. You don't have to do anything. All you do is email Dr. Theo and say great, in the future you'll go back to the other doctor, and you look forward to seeing him here on Saturday."

There were three hundred seats in the studio, and for each show, writers got two tickets to give away, cast members got six, and the host and musical guest got a few dozen. The remaining tickets not claimed by Nigel's famous friends were distributed to the public through either a lottery or a standby system of avid fans, mostly college students or tourists, willing to wait on the sidewalk for more than twenty-four hours.

"You'd invite him to the after-party, right?" I said.

"Let's not get ahead of ourselves."

"By the way," I said, "I'm trying to get Annabel to be in my Danny Horst Rule sketch. They didn't break up."

Viv made a face—she was one of the people who considered celebrity cameos to be pandering. "Yeah, Henrietta told me Annabel posted something on Insta saying people need to chill."

"I didn't see that, but Danny was talking to her in our office. Do you think Annabel intentionally fans the flames, or she's just sort of experiencing her emotions and they get overinterpreted?"

"I wouldn't be surprised if she's hired a reality TV writer to script her life."

"Are you serious? That makes me terrified for Danny."

"Maybe he's the writer."

"I'm pretty sure their relationship is real to him."

"Oh come on—as if there's a clear distinction between real and fake for any of us. Aren't we all performing the role of ourselves?" I was standing a couple feet from her armchair, and she extended her right foot and lightly tapped the tip of her athletic slide against my sneaker. She said, "Even you, you behind-the-scenes pseudo-purist."

FRIDAY, 2:28 P.M.

And then, because *TNO* was like a summer camp where you ran into everyone all the time, over and over, I saw Noah again at the rehearsal for Blabbermouth, which was on Stage 2; less than three hours had passed since I'd seen him at the Cheesemonger rehearsal. Again, a dozen crew members had gathered around the stage, plus Autumn and a different assistant (I thought this one's name was not Madison but Addison, and then I thought that surely I had to be making that up). Blabbermouth had a bigger cast than the Cheesemonger: Noah playing himself as a guest judge; Henrietta, who played the supposedly talkative female judge; cast members named Jay and Dillon, who played the male judges; and four other cast members playing auditioning contestants, most of whom sang only a line or two before the judges began dissecting their performances.

The metallic silver judges' table was in place, though many other props were missing. A recurring joke of the sketch was mock versions of the show's sponsored beverages—oversized wax cups with logos that last time had been for "PepsiCo Ostrich Ovaries Hibiscus Iced Tea," and this time were going to be "Manic Armageddon Masculine Caffeine with Extra Caffeine."

Sometimes my relief and excitement at a sketch making it past the table read was followed at rehearsal by overwhelming doubt about its quality—*this* was what I was hoping to send out into the world?—that then was followed, as the days passed and the script, set, and costumes came together, by renewed confidence. But as Blabbermouth got under way, there was a lot of promising intra-sketch giggling, and at one point, I noticed even Bob O'Leary laughing.

Then Elliot arrived, and the giggling stopped. He often attended rehearsals, and his presence often decreased the amount people laughed. Whether you thought this was because everyone wanted to play it cool to impress him or because he was a buzzkill probably depended on your view of Elliot.

As we wrapped up, after the director, whose name was Abraham, and I had both given our notes, Elliot said, "It's ending with a whimper instead of a bang. Either we need to punch up Jay and Dillon's lines or make Noah and Henrietta do something more dramatic."

"Well—" I said. The sketch ended with Noah and Henrietta doing yoga, and the idea that immediately occurred to me was simultaneously obvious, reliable, and, because of Noah's presence, slightly embarrassing to articulate. But because approximately 30 percent of me had developed a crush on Noah while 120 percent of me was a comedy writer, I said it anyway. "Why don't we have one of them fart? Or both of them, and that's the one time Jay and Dillon actually listen?"

Dillon said, "Or I turn to Jay and am like, 'Wait, did you hear something?' And he's like, 'Nope, I don't think so.'"

"Alternatively," Elliot said, "while, Sally, I hate to deny you that old chestnut, you know when kids play the game Airplane? What if that's what they're doing, with Noah on the ground holding Henrietta up on his legs. Is that doable, Noah and Henri?"

One of the ways it was obvious that Noah was a good sport was that he didn't hesitate before lying flat on his back on the not especially clean stage floor, his golden hair draped over *TNO* dust and debris. He lifted his legs and arms, and Henrietta leaned over him so his heels lined up with her hipbones, their hands clasped. As he bent his knees, he said to her, "Want me to take off my shoes?"

"Nah," she replied—Henrietta was also a very good sport—and then she leaned in even farther and suddenly was aloft on his feet. Watching them, I felt a strange and not immediately identifiable feeling, though I knew it wasn't good.

"Can we get some airplane sound effects?" Abraham said. "Or they just make them with their mouths?"

"Vroom, vroom," Henrietta said. "Or no, that's cars."

"Let's try it both ways," I said to Abraham.

We went through the sketch again, start to finish, and when we got to the airplane part a second time, I understood. I was *jealous*. Not because Henrietta was famous and I wasn't, or because she was objectively prettier than I was. I was jealous because she got to tussle in this silly way with Noah, to hold hands with him. I was jealous of the physical contact and the proximity. I thought then of Gene and his dick pic. Apparently, I was due for a session with him after all, to stave off exactly this type of inconvenient yearning.

After Bob, the camera guys, and the control room had decided which camera would cut to Noah and Henrietta on the floor, rehearsal was finished, and I thanked everyone. "Hey, Sally," Noah called and waved me over from the stage, where Elliot had joined him. "Breaking news on the wildlife front. Turns out Nigel suggested a snake instead of a panther."

I glanced at Elliot. "Like Britney Spears at the VMAs way back when?"

"I know she's not the Indigo Girls or Diana Ross," Noah said, "but don't you think a Britney homage would be pretty cool?"

I blinked, trying to determine how much he was joking. Could it be that Noah was one of those rare guys who didn't essentially dislike or mock women, and who also didn't ignore our existence, and who also didn't see us primarily as objects of lust? That he was weirdly, disarmingly fine with us?

"On the one hand, yes," I said. "On the other hand, a snake is even more terrifying than a panther."

Looking between us, Noah said, "How do animal rights activists feel about snakes?"

"Who cares?" Elliot said.

"I think people are less protective of reptiles than mammals," I said.

"All things being equal, I'd rather not offend anyone," Noah said.

At the same time, I said, "*TNO* wouldn't be *TNO* if no one was offended," and Elliot said, "Good luck with that."

As Bob approached Elliot with a scheduling question, Noah said to me, "I have something else to run by you. The future of comedy hangs in the balance over this. You ready?"

"I hope so."

"This is also for Choreographer. When I rip off my clothes to reveal my leather shorts and vest, someone in the makeup department asked if I want my tattoos covered with concealer. I said no because I'm playing myself, right? But then I started overthinking it and I was like, but I'm playing myself back in the year 2000, when I didn't have any tattoos yet. So is the answer yes or no?" Before I could respond, he said, "I know this is trivial, but I got worried about breaking some comedy rule that I don't even know exists."

"If there's a rule, I don't know it, either," I said. "But what kind of tattoos are we talking about? Do you have a gigantic dragon across your chest or something?"

He smiled. "Not yet, although the night is young. No, I have three and they're all run-of-the-mill."

Oh, yes, I thought. *The Celtic symbol I read about in "Kissing and Telling with Noah Brewster."* Aloud, I said, "Where are they?" We were standing about three feet apart, with Bob and Elliot still nearby, and I probably sounded less relaxed than I intended to as I said, "Do you want to just show me?"

"This one, for starters." Noah held out his left arm, pushing up the long sleeve of his T-shirt, and on the inside of his forearm, I saw an image of music notes on a staff. "Not cheesy at all, right?" he said.

"Is that from one of your songs?"

He shook his head. "It's 'Blackbird.' Kind of a touchstone song for me."

"I don't think anyone gets points deducted for 'Blackbird.' And I bet that would be pretty subtle on camera." The tattoo was a few inches in size, but the truly salient fact about his forearm was that it was perfect. Both the skin and the barely visible hair on the other side of his arm were golden, and it was muscular but not too muscular, not steroidally muscular. I could accept that my lot in life was never to get to touch an arm like that, but it was torturous to be so close to him.

"Then there's this one," he said, and he was turning away from me and pulling up his jeans on the right side, from the ankle. There was a crow on the back of his calf, and it was much bigger and blockier than the musical notes.

"Less subtle," I said. "But likely off camera."

"The last one is on my shoulder blade." He glanced back at me. "Is that okay to show you? I don't want to be the guy who finds pretextual reasons to start taking off his clothes. I promise that I really do want to know what you think about this."

Again feigning relaxation, I said, "Wardrobe changes during the show are so rushed that they happen in plain sight. So not only have I seen every cast member in every state of undress, but the audiences have seen them, too."

"In that case," he said, and he crossed his arms and pulled his T-shirt up in the back, not over his head, but so that it was resting on his shoulders. There was indeed a Celtic knot of interlocking black lines and circles, and this tattoo was the biggest of all. Were my co-workers aware of this display? I didn't dare look around and break the spell. By this point, there was even less than a foot between us, and the skin on Noah's back was also painfully, gloriously golden, and also there was something oddly domestic about the moment, as if we were boyfriend and girlfriend, standing in the bathroom in the apartment we shared, and he'd asked me to look at a red mark on his back because he wondered if it was a tick bite, and also I wondered for the first time if this *was* pretextual. If he'd be wearing a vest, presumably it would cover his back.

Yet because it seemed like a once-in-a-lifetime opportunity, while still standing behind him, I reached out and pressed a fingertip against the tattoo. "You mean this?" I said.

Of course he meant this.

"Yeah," he said.

Never had I wanted so badly to just smash myself against another person, to tear off another person's clothes. And wasn't he complicit, hadn't he gotten about 13 percent of the way to naked? Or was I delusional and was he accustomed, as cast members were, to having his body exposed and handled? My fingertip was still touching his tattoo. I swallowed, unbending my other fingers, and pressed the rest of them to his perfect skin. Calmly, I said, "I wouldn't worry about this one, either." As I pulled my hand away, I added, "Although I do like the word *pretextual*. I might have to start using it."

He yanked down his shirt and when he turned around so we were facing each other, he said, "Help yourself. My dad's a lawyer, and I learned it from him. I hope you didn't just lose all respect for me because of the basicness of my tattoos. I got them within a couple years of each other, quite a while ago."

"I think I know something that will reassure you." I was wearing an unzipped fleece jacket, which I shrugged off, then I lifted the right short sleeve of my T-shirt and angled my arm toward him, elbow out.

Peering at my bicep, he said, "Is that a . . . mouse?"

"In fourth grade, my class had a hamster named Barnaby who I loved so much that I told my mom I wanted a tattoo of him. She said if I promised to wait until I was twenty-one, if I still wanted it, she'd get one with me. Obviously, by the time I was twenty-one, the *only* reason I still wanted a hamster tattoo was to hold my mom to her end of the bargain."

Just as I had, he reached out his fingers—they, too, were perfect, long and slim and straight—and when they brushed against my skin, I thought that if I could live inside this moment forever, I would. But he withdrew them quickly. He said, "I take it that's why it says *Mom*."

"Hers said *Sally*, but the amazing part is that we didn't coordinate it. We did it separately, in different rooms, to surprise each other. And when we realized what we'd done—" I paused. This had been fifteen years before, at a place in downtown Kansas City, and afterward we'd gotten enchiladas for lunch. Because my mother hadn't been an ostentatious or performative person, it had taken me a long time, until college really, to realize how smart and funny she was, and how generously compassionate. Whenever I described embarrassing things I'd done, she'd say, "Oh, I can imagine doing that," or "I think most everyone feels that way."

To Noah, I said, "When we realized that she'd gotten her hamster to say *Sally* and I'd gotten mine to say *Mom,* I started laughing and she started crying. And she wasn't one of those moms who cry all the time. But now, I understand why she did."

Noah's expression had turned serious as he said, "Your mom—is she—?"

I knew what he was asking. "She passed away in 2015."

"I'm sorry."

"Thank you." I pulled my fleece jacket back over my shoulders. "Whenever it was that you got your tattoos, I don't think you need to cover them up. It's not like people fact-check sketches. And there'll be enough going on that you might as well simplify where you can."

FRIDAY, 4:39 P.M.

The car was, apparently, parked in front of the main entrance to 66 on West 50th Street—in other words, not in a parking space, meaning God only knew what strings Annabel's publicists had pulled to avoid its being towed immediately. After summoning Danny down from the seventeenth floor, Annabel, who'd been sitting on the hood, leapt off it in order to passionately kiss him, as the paparazzi, of whom there were more than a dozen, clicked away with their cameras and shouted questions about the price of the car and the date of the wedding. The car itself was a silver Mercedes-AMG G 65, a collection of letters and numbers that meant nothing to me, though Henrietta reported that the Internet said that it had cost $220,000. I happened to know, though I wasn't sure if either Annabel or the general public did, that Danny didn't have a driver's license.

I'd witnessed none of the spectacle firsthand because I'd been in rehearsal for Blabbermouth, trying to behave normally around Noah. But when I ran into Danny back in our office, he was the one who showed me the pictures from Annabel's Instagram account, which featured them with their lips locked in the foreground and the car in the background. These photos had been taken not by a paparazzo but by a photographer on Annabel's payroll present at almost all of her public events. Across the first photo was the sentence *I heart my bb,* and Danny's response in the comments below was *love u my moon girl.*

I said, "The weird part is I heard you and Annabel had broken up yesterday." Danny and I were sitting side by side on the couch, and though he'd denied having just burped, the air was filled with the smell of a half-digested Reuben.

"No, we did break up." His tone was equanimous. "But only for half an hour."

"Have you broken up other times?"

"A bunch."

"Has it been stressful?"

"I wouldn't choose it."

"Is Annabel always the one who initiates the breakups?"

"Yeah, but she's also the one who reaches out to get back together. She gets jealous, which is crazy because it's not like I could ever do better than her. Once I told her when she wore her hair all pushed to the side, she looked like Bethany Brick, and she freaked out."

"Who's Bethany Brick?"

"That was her question, too. Tell me you don't watch porn without telling me you don't watch porn."

"I find it narratively unsatisfying," I said.

"Yeah, I think you might be missing the point. Anyway, another time I told her I don't really get jealous, and it was like she got jealous about me not getting jealous. All I meant was that I know she's out of my league. I've already exceeded my wildest dreams." We both were quiet, and he said, "This must all sound so stupid."

"No, no," I said quickly. "The sketch about The Danny Horst Rule—that's me being pissed about the double standards of heterosexuality. It's not a comment on your specific relationship with Annabel."

"But all me and Belly's ups and downs—they probably seem real juvenile to you."

"Have I ever told you I was married in my early twenties?"

"Seriously? Damn, Chuckles!"

"I didn't think this at the time, but both the marriage and the divorce were bloodless. My ex-husband and I were the opposite of you and Annabel. We were very calm and restrained, and look where that got us—I haven't spoken to him for almost ten years. And it's not like I've figured out much since then. I have no idea what makes any couple stay together or break up, so who am I to judge?"

"What other secrets from your past have you never mentioned? Did you shoot a man in Reno just to watch him die?"

"I think you have to trust your own instincts," I said.

"I've been meaning to ask if you'll be my groomswoman. That's a groomsman with a vagina."

"What, to even out the numbers with Annabel's bridesmaids?"

"Partly, but I also really want you there."

I turned my head toward him and smiled. "Then sure. I'm honored."

We were quiet again, and it was an agreeable quiet, before I said, "I need a ride to Poughkeepsie, but I can't remember—do you have a car?"

Danny laughed. "Fuck you, Chuckles," he said warmly.

FRIDAY, 5:07 P.M.

"I did exactly what you said," Viv said. "I emailed him like, 'I'm officially not your patient, your name will be on the VIP list, see you tomorrow.'" We were in her dressing room, before she went for the fitting for her Sister Colleen nun's costume.

"Did you hear back?" I asked.

"He made a joke about how he'll need to take a nap on Saturday afternoon to stay up so late, which—" She curled her upper lip and flared her nostrils. "You know how I said he looks middle-aged and dorky in that website picture but he was really hot in person? Maybe he looks middle-aged and dorky because he *is* middle-aged and dorky. He also said he'd be here with bells on."

"I actually think that's sweet," I said. "Open your heart."

Viv rolled her eyes. "Says the woman who's basically dating a disembodied penis."

FRIDAY, 8:07 P.M.

"Sally, wake up," a female voice said. "Can you hear me? Wake up because I have an amazing piece of gossip!" While waiting for my sketches' sets to arrive at the studio from the warehouse, I'd lain down for a cat nap in my office, and when I opened my eyes, Henrietta was kneeling beside me. In a tone of true glee, she said, "Noah Brewster wears a wig!"

I was on my back, and I propped myself up on my elbows. "Wait, what?"

"His beautiful blond locks are fake! I have to say that the quality is impressive. Do you think he's been wearing a wig since he first got famous or his hair started thinning as he got older?"

I sat up, reached for my water bottle on the windowsill, took a sip, and said, "How do you know?"

"Terrance was just figuring out my hair for the Cheesemonger, and Gloria pulled him over for this hushed discussion, but I pieced it together. It sounds like Noah didn't say anything about it to Gloria, and it's an issue because in at least two sketches, he's supposed to wear a wig. So he'll be wearing his wig, then a wig cap, then a second wig." She clapped her hands. "It'll be a wig sandwich!"

"What does his real hair look like?"

Henrietta sat back on her heels and shrugged. "I assume sparse."

Was it weird that this knowledge made me feel protective of Noah? It made him seem vain and insecure in ways that were understandable rather than laughable. "I actually wouldn't mention it to anyone else," I said. "It could be distracting."

"Really?" What she said next made me recall telling Noah that I wasn't an asshole and then telling him that I was. "Because I was sure you'd get a kick out of it."

SATURDAY, 1:55 P.M.

At first, I assumed that Annabel was merely late. The run-through was both the first time anyone at *TNO* experienced the week's show as a coherent whole, albeit without makeup or some final costumes and special effects, and also the last rehearsal before the dress rehearsal. Dress would occur at 8 P.M. in front of an audience who would then be switched out for a different audience for the 11:30 P.M. live show.

As the cold open started on Home Base, with Oliver playing Comey, I hurried from the cue cards room, where I'd been checking changes, to Stage 1, where the Cheesemonger was fourth in the lineup. In the hall, I passed Danny in his police officer costume and said, "Hey, is Annabel in your dressing room?"

"Her team was gonna check in with Autumn when they got here."

As I entered the studio, I looked around and didn't see Autumn; it was likely she was in the narrow space behind Home Base with Noah, waiting with him before he went on for his monologue. I started to text her, realized I didn't have her number, and opened an email. I typed Autumn's address and one sentence in the subject line—*I need Annabel on Stage 3 for 5 slot*—and hit Send. Then I asked a production assistant to find out where Annabel was, and he briskly walked away. The cold open segued into the house band playing the sax-heavy theme song over what would at dress and live be the announcer, whose name was Rusty, reciting the opening credits. But Rusty didn't appear until dress, and it was the assistant director Penelope exclaiming, "And your host, Noah Brewster. Ladies and gentlemen, Noah Brewster!" Noah walked out the door onto the stage in a tuxedo and fist-pumped in time to the house band's introductory crescendo, and I tried not to notice, yet again, how outrageously handsome he was. Then I thought, *Wait, really, that's a wig?*

As he began his monologue by saying, "I'm completely thrilled to be hosting *TNO* tonight," I scrutinized his hairline and the blond layers that framed his face, the chunks tucked behind his ears. Truly, I'd never have known. I wondered if Henrietta could have misunderstood, but it seemed unlikely. And then Elliot appeared onstage, and I thought, *Elliot? What the hell?* Like me, Elliot wasn't on camera from one year to the next; in his bones, he, too, was a writer as opposed to a performer. But it turned out the premise of the monologue was that *TNO*'s head writer thought Noah was there to be the musical guest and not the host, and Noah was trying to explain that he was both. I wasn't sure why Nigel wasn't the one filling Elliot's role. Had Noah and Elliot developed some friendship in the last week that needed to be conspicuously celebrated?

After Noah's monologue, a rough cut of the white women's recipes digital short aired on the many monitors hanging throughout the studio, then it was time for the Cheesemonger sketch on Stage 1, which would be followed directly by the Danny Horst Rule sketch on Stage 3. As the Cheesemonger started, I stood just off set, holding my script open against my left forearm and gripping a pencil in my right hand. I used my left hand to quickly check my email and see if Autumn had responded; she hadn't.

The run-through was more relaxed than the dress rehearsal in the sense that there were pauses and do-overs—some sketches happened twice in a row—and I could still make changes based on my own judgment. For the dress rehearsal, each writer watched their sketch *with* Nigel in a little space set up for him under the balcony seats, a kind of cave in which he sat in a director's chair drinking rosé, his eyes trained on the feed on a monitor so that he saw the sketches as viewers at home would. Also present, watching with Nigel, would be one or two of his assistants, a couple senior producers, Autumn, and sometimes one of Nigel's very closest celebrity friends (his less close celebrity friends were invited to watch the live show from his studio office). This meant that these were the people who overheard Nigel give feedback to the writer, which meant the septuagenarian rocker from one of the world's most famous bands had once been privy to Nigel matter-of-factly saying to me, "When Viv tells Henrietta to treat her yeast infection with a garlic clove, I take it Viv means inserting it vaginally, but the current language is unclear." Before dress, I always applied the deodorant I kept in my desk toiletries bag because I never sweated more than when watching one of my own sketches with Nigel.

At the run-through for the Cheesemonger, as in the previous rehearsal, Noah threw himself into the role, and a green screen behind him made the image on the monitors show rats festively running around in the shop. But even as his duet with Henrietta landed perfectly, I kept turning around and scanning the studio for Annabel. The sketch finished, and Bob O'Leary, who'd been watching from a few feet away, said to me, "Any notes or are we good to go?"

I looked at the cast members and said, "Wes and Viv, can you stand closer to Bailey? You're all too far apart. Otherwise, do it exactly like that at dress and air." I glanced back at Bob. "But Annabel Lily is supposed to be in the next sketch, and I'm not even sure she's here yet."

Bob said into his headset, "Can anyone tell me if Annabel Lily is in the studio? Looking for Annabel Lily for The Danny Horst Rule on Stage 3." His voice was audible via speakers throughout the studio, including, I knew, in the dressing rooms.

Noah was literally being led away by the hand by a member of the wardrobe department named Peggy who always escorted the host during performances. He wordlessly held out his free right hand for a fist bump, and I brought mine up to his. Given how overwrought I was about him, I might have expected sparks to fly at the point of contact; they did not, and then he was gone, off to wherever Peggy was taking him next.

As Bob and I walked toward Stage 3, I could tell when he got a response on his headset, though I couldn't hear it. He turned to me and said, "Annabel's not here. How about if Lynette or Bianca stands in for her?"

What a flake, I thought, and said, "Bianca." Bianca was a first-year cast member in her early twenties, meaning Annabel's age or even younger.

Bob said into his headset, "Sally says Bianca. You know where she is?" After a pause, he said, "Great, send her out."

And then The Danny Horst Rule started: Gregor and Viv on their date at the restaurant, smiling and laughing, Josh in his cop uniform appearing to arrest them. My preoccupation with Annabel's absence made it hard to evaluate how it was going, especially when Danny entered. About thirty seconds later, Bianca walked on wearing Crocs, jeans, and a black crop top and announced that she was Susan B. Anthony, reading the cue cards so smoothly that I doubted an outsider would know she'd been informed of her participation in this role in the last five minutes. When the sketch ended, I said, "Thanks so much for pinch-hitting, Bianca." I made quick eye contact with Danny. "That was solid overall," I continued, "although, Josh, you came in a little late. Don't wait for Viv and Gregor to get through their lines. Just charge in and interrupt them."

"Got it," Josh said.

"You want to see it again?" Bob asked me.

Was it my imagination or was a weird energy coming off Danny? "I think we're good," I said.

As everyone dispersed, Bianca approached me. "I just want to tell you," she said, "this sketch is a really important statement. It's funny, but it's also, like, what the fuck? Because the rule is a real thing here. I'm glad you're calling it out, and I'm glad that now I get to be part of it."

"Oh—" I paused. "Thank you. But I'm sorry, the plan is still for Annabel to be in the sketch for dress and air. I think she's just running late."

Almost as quickly as Bianca's face fell, she composed it again. "Yeah, of course," she said. "No, that makes sense."

"I really appreciate you filling in, and I'd love to work with you on something else soon—"

"Yeah, yeah," Bianca said quickly. "Yeah, same." She darted away.

As the next sketch started—it was on Home Base and was the one where Viv was a nun and Hakeem was a priest—I checked my email again and saw that Autumn had replied. Her email read: *Annabel is not here*.

You don't say, I thought. I walked to the bathroom—my next sketch, Blabbermouth, wasn't until the eleven slot—and I felt the awkwardness of the misunderstanding with Bianca clinging to me as I peed and washed my hands. I'd never been a cast member, but it had once been my first year at *TNO*, and I remembered how it had seemed as if whether or not I got a break was determined not by anything I did but by what other, more senior people allowed.

When I reentered the studio, Noah was performing his first song, which was the one that he either had or hadn't been serenading me with. Because of the lighting, I knew he couldn't see beyond the first couple rows of chairs, now arranged into orderly lines. I stood behind the floor seats with my arms folded, and as I listened to him sing and watched him play guitar, I felt the respect I often felt at *TNO* for people who not only knew how to do things I couldn't but who were so good at those things that they made them look easy.

After Noah's first song, I stayed where I was standing for News Desk, with Danny deadpan in his coat and tie. As he walked onto the set to take his seat behind the desk, the pale pink joggers he wore on the bottom half of his body instead of suit pants were visible. I wondered what Annabel's excuse was—perhaps her aromatherapy massage had run over, or maybe she was having a plasma facial. Not unusually, Danny barely cracked a smile as he delivered his lines.

Then came Noah's Choreography sketch, which was fun and silly, and which concluded with Noah tearing away his shirt and pants to reveal the black leather shorts and midriff-exposing leather vest, meaning that what was really being revealed were his six-pack abs and toned arms and legs; his forearm tattoo was barely noticeable. As if the sight of his golden body wasn't sufficiently stimulating, during what would be a camera cutaway, a prop guy placed a long green snake around Noah's neck and shoulders. It took me a few seconds to realize the snake was rubber. Noah gripped both ends of it and wiggled his hips in a faux sensual way that I didn't find as ridiculous as I knew I was supposed to, or maybe it was because he wasn't afraid of being ridiculous that he was so attractive.

Then it was time for Blabbermouth, and though Noah and Henrietta were high-spirited as their silliness culminated in the airplane bit, I felt a deep, uneasy knowledge that the sketch wasn't quite good enough; it wasn't making a point that earlier iterations of Blabbermouth hadn't made better. I also knew that I wasn't going to start wildly revising this close to dress and air. Some writers kept making changes for as long as they could, but I believed a point arrived when potential gains in quality came at the expense of the cast's familiarity and comfort with the script.

After Blabbermouth was Catchphrase's horrible sketch, during which I had the unpleasant experience of realizing Catchphrase could simultaneously unicycle *and* juggle, which impressed me in spite of myself; then Noah's second musical act, the song called "Inbox Zero"; then the Bathroom Cabinet sketch, which seemed to me to be about 75 percent of where it needed to be writing-wise; then the Three Tenors. Then Noah reappeared on Home Base and said, "Thank you for coming to this rehearsal that was perfectly smooth in all ways." Over the speakers, I heard the assistant director Penelope say, "And that's a wrap on the run-through, folks."

Bob, Nigel, Autumn, Penelope, and Elliot converged on the floor in front of Home Base, and Noah hopped offstage and began speaking with them. I tried to discreetly approach Autumn from the back, touching her elbow. When she turned, I murmured, "Annabel is still coming for dress and air, right?"

Autumn frowned and shook her head. The other people in the conversation all had gone quiet and were looking at me.

I said, "I'm just trying to figure out what's going on with Annabel Lily."

"Annabel's not coming today," Autumn said. "Period."

"Why not?" I asked.

"Because something came up for her."

"I can reach out to her," Noah said.

"Or Danny can," I said, just as Bob said, "Noah, you'll have your hands quite full between now and air."

"It's no big deal," Noah said. "I kind of know her."

In a much warmer voice than the one she used to address me, Autumn said, "That's above and beyond of you to offer, but guess what? It's time for you to meet your snake." She glanced among the others and said, "The handler recommends that Noah and the snake have one-on-one time to get used to each other."

My eyes met Noah's, and I said, "Wait, you *are* using a real one?"

He grinned. "I've been reassured it's non-venomous."

Elliot patted Noah on the back and said, "It's gonna be awesome, man."

Bob said, "In the last thirty-seven years, we've only lost, what, Nigel? Three hosts? Four?"

Dryly, Nigel said, "No more than that." Then he looked at me and said, "A strong show for you tonight, Sally."

SATURDAY, 6:01 P.M.

I was back in the cue cards room when my phone buzzed with a text from Henrietta: *OMG Annabel and Danny have broken up for real?!?!!! Is Danny okay?*

"Oh, shit," I said aloud and turned to the nearest cue card guy. "I'll be right back."

I hurried to Danny's dressing room and knocked on the door several times. There was no answer, but, when I turned the knob, I saw Danny lying facedown on his brown corduroy love seat. The room was about six by eight feet, a windowless box with a Formica counter under the mirrored wall, and Danny had done little to personalize the space other than installing the love seat. His legs hung off it, and he still had on his blazer from News Desk.

"Danny, it's me," I said.

When he turned his head, his face was red and tear streaked. "I guess you heard," he said.

After I'd perched on the edge of the love seat—he was taking up so much of it that my right thigh was squeezed against his left hip—I could smell him. But it was a scent that was recognizable and human and not disgusting; the recognition of it felt familial.

"I'm really sorry," I said. "Although do you think it's *over* over? Given your history—"

"Remember on election night, when it was like, the worst *could* happen? And then all of a sudden, it was like, Oh my fucking God, it's happening. And then it had happened." He sniffed. "Her publicist called my publicist, and Belly already put out a statement, which I'm sure the publicist wrote because it's phony bullshit wording." He grinned darkly. "Then she blocked me on all her socials."

It seemed, among other things, either stunningly insensitive or deliberately cruel to behave this way hours before Danny was scheduled to perform live on national TV. And it would have been a lie to say that I didn't once again wonder about the fate of my Danny Horst Rule sketch, but this time it wasn't the main thing I was thinking about. The main thing I was thinking was that Danny had dodged a bullet.

"Did something specific happen?" I asked.

He rolled onto his side, his back against the corduroy cushions. "I was at her apartment this morning, right? We're chilling in the kitchen, we're making smoothies, and she has this super powerful, top-of-the-line blender. We're talking about how it has a ten-year warranty, and I start making dumb jokes like, by the time the warranty expires, all cars will be self-driving, all meat will be grown in labs, and we'll probably be divorced but we won't even care because we'll both be banging robots."

He was quiet, and I said, "Is there more?"

"For real, I was barely even awake. I was just talking shit. But she flipped out."

"Did she understand you were kidding?"

"She said I've never been serious about her because I'm incapable of being serious." He shrugged. "I come back here thinking, Okay, that sucked, but we've been through it before. She'll show up here and we'll have make-up sex"—it was not, I told myself, the moment to ponder which emissions this couch had absorbed—"and instead she went scorched earth."

"I know this is easy for me to say, but what if you ignore social media, get some sleep after the show, and go see her in person tomorrow?"

"She's a little crazy," he said. "But when she's not being crazy, she's the sweetest, most caring person I've ever known. She has this huge bed with a million pillows and a big down comforter like in the fanciest hotel, and we just lay on it, looking into each other's eyes. I didn't know people did that gazing shit outside of movies until I met her."

"That sounds nice," I said.

Neither of us spoke for a few seconds, and Danny's stomach grumbled.

"When did you last eat?" I asked.

"Good question."

"Let's have a page go get you a sandwich. What about something plain, like turkey and cheese? You should have some protein." But when I stood, he held out an arm to stop me.

"You know when you're really vibing with another person?" he said. "Like for once the loneliness lifts, and you fully get each other—do you think that's all bullshit?"

I took a deep breath and said, "I don't think it's bullshit. I think it's rare, but real."

SATURDAY, 6:27 P.M.

I told the two assistants at desks in front of Nigel's office that I urgently needed to see him, and one stood, entered his office, then reemerged and motioned for me to come in. Inside, standing around the corkboard, were Elliot, Bob O'Leary, and two other producers.

Nigel himself was behind his desk drinking from a tall, clear glass, and when he set it down, he said, "Sally, never underestimate the value of water."

"We need to cut The Danny Horst Rule," I blurted out. Because I hadn't done this before, I wasn't sure if the pronoun should have been *we* as in *we need to* or *you* as in *you need to*. "Danny and Annabel just had a big public breakup, and she's putting stuff on social media, and it's very messy."

In a calm tone, Bob said, "Annabel is hardly essential in the sketch. Bianca was fine."

"We need to cut it for Danny's sake," I said. "He's really upset."

"Danny's a pro," Elliot said. "He'll be okay. Plus, don't they break up a lot?"

"It seems different this time."

"Might the sketch be cathartic?" Nigel asked.

Looking among their faces was disorienting; trying to get them to *cut* one of my sketches, after nine years of doing the opposite, was disorienting. Perhaps I was wrong and they were right? Both for Danny's well-being and so that I could have a hat trick, I wanted them to be.

"It wouldn't be cathartic," I said. "It would be kicking him when he's down."

"Should we keep it in dress and see how it goes?" Bob asked.

"Or see if they've gotten back together in an hour," Elliot said.

"We need to put Danny out of his misery now," I said.

"Either way, he's still on News Desk," Elliot said.

"That's not *about* him," I said.

"You're certain of this?" Nigel said.

Naturally, in this moment, I wasn't. "Yes," I said. "I'm certain."

Nigel turned to Bob and said, "Let's put Medicine Cabinet back in."

Elliot and I made eye contact and—not judgmentally but more musingly—he said, "If I didn't know better, I'd think you'd lost your edge."

SATURDAY, 6:35 P.M.

Both the host's dressing room and the musical guest's dressing room were on the same corridor, and their doors had been closed on my way to Nigel's office. As I returned to the studio, the host's was open and filled with people. I heard someone say, "Hey, Sally!" and Noah appeared, gesturing for me to come in. Behind him, standing or sitting on the surprisingly crappy furniture in the surprisingly unfancy space, were Autumn, Madison *and* Addison, one white man with a well-tended goatee, one Black man with a well-tended goatee, a spiky-haired woman in overalls, a blond-haired woman who looked like a suburban mom, and a white guy in a suit and tie. I assumed the ones that weren't Autumn, Madison, and Addison were his agent, manager, and other members of his business team.

Noah was wearing a tuxedo and also a layer of makeup, and—perhaps because I was used to seeing both men and women in foundation, bronzer, and blush—I thought he looked radiantly handsome. If he really did wear a wig, it was exceptional.

"Hey," I said. "How did bonding with the snake go?"

"We're like this now." He held up crossed fingers. "Honestly, it wasn't bad. I thought it would be cold because of cold-blooded, but it was warm. Or I should say her, not it. Her name is Eleanor."

"For real?"

He nodded. "I wanted to tell you—I texted Annabel, and it sounds like she and Danny broke up."

"They did," I said. "And the sketch was cut."

"Oh, I'm sorry."

"It happens. I mean, thanks for trying. How are you feeling?"

He made a self-mockingly anxious expression. "Maybe not one hundred percent calm?"

"I think you're going to be great and have a great show," I said. "Truly." It was common for hosts to be palpably nervous as the live show approached—and some were so nervous all along that they were vomiting and shaking for the entire week—but I personally had never offered reassurance to any of them. I had, however, once randomly found myself in a hall hugging the panicking male backup dancer of a female rapper, a bald, extraordinarily muscular man wearing a tight tank top and short denim shorts. To Noah, I added, "This week's show is actually in much better shape than a lot of them are at this point."

"Yeah?" Noah said. Then, simultaneously, we both said, "Actually?" and smiled. It felt in this moment like we knew each other much better than we did, and I thought that Noah clearly was a good guy, in addition to being radiantly handsome, and also that it would be an enormous relief when the live show was finished and we were no longer having dozens of ostensibly casual encounters. If *TNO* was like summer camp, at least his session would last only a week. I gestured with my thumb and said, "I should go tell Danny my bitchy little sketch about his love life is cut."

"Before you go—" Noah leaned into the room and set his palm on the shoulder of the blond woman, who wore a maroon dress with brown flowers on it and was eating a hundred-calorie bag of cashews. There was a bowl of such bags on a table, along with bananas, apples, grass-fed beef jerky, a crudité platter, tiny brownies, and water bottles. The woman turned toward him, and Noah said, "Sally, this is my sister, Vicky, and Vicky, this is Sally, who's a writer here."

Warmly, Vicky said, "You're one of the people making Noah's dreams come true."

"Well, not personally," I said, which immediately seemed weird on my part. "Nice to meet you," I added as we shook hands.

"Likewise."

"Do you live here in—" I began, but before I could finish, Autumn was upon us in her Autumn-ish way, saying, "Sally, I'm going to steal both Noah and Vicky and show them where Vicky will stand when she introduces Noah's first song."

"Oh, fun." I took a step backwards and waved vaguely. "Break a leg!" I said, then I scurried away.

SATURDAY, 11:08 P.M.

Working at *TNO* was often hectic, but the most hectic time was between the end of the dress rehearsal and the start of the live show. The three-hundred-plus audience members needed to be escorted out, and another three hundred–plus needed to be brought in. All the writers and all the producers and all the cast crammed into Nigel's office—this time, his office overlooking the studio—so he could reveal which two or three sketches he was cutting for time, and how he thought the sequence of the remaining ones needed to be rearranged, and which last-minute adjustments he wanted made to the scripts, sets, and costumes. If at times his attention to detail seemed ludicrous—he'd decree that a potted plant in a sketch should be moved from the right side of a desk to the left—the counterargument was that he was Nigel Petersen, and the rest of us were not.

Dress had gone well, with the audience laughing a lot, but it hadn't gone so well that it made me fear for the live show; sometimes you went into live knowing you couldn't top dress, and this wasn't one of those nights. There'd been a true dud—Sister & Father, the one that featured Viv as the nun—where the audience was quiet from start to finish, but it had been right before Noah's first musical performance, which to some extent served as a palate cleanser and prevented the dud from ruining the rest of the show. It was understood that, although all of us always preferred to kill, the fact that sketches *could* bomb, that the audience wouldn't reward us just for showing up, gave killing its value and meaning.

In keeping with Nigel's frequent inscrutability, he wasn't cutting Sister & Father; instead, he wanted it rewritten so that rather than Noah as the Pope coming in two-thirds of the way through, the sketch started with Noah, and Noah's headgear changed from a miter to a skullcap. Both Blabbermouth and the Cheesemonger survived dress, though Nigel wanted twenty seconds cut from Blabbermouth, which raised the question for me of whether to eliminate the recent addition when Henrietta flew airplane-style on Noah's feet or to thin out the chatter between the male judges. I went with the latter, while wondering if doing so would undermine the entire sketch. And Catchphrase's Unicycle sketch had been moved to the last slot. Later sketches tended to be wild cards—clearly, including them wasn't Nigel's priority, because they might need to be cut for time *during* the show—but they sometimes became unexpected classics.

After the meeting, I raced to the cue cards room and ran into the writer Benji, who said, "That's a bummer Nigel cut The Danny Horst Rule. I thought it was solid."

Even if I'd wanted to, there wasn't time to clarify; we both needed to check new cue cards. I simply said, "I know." There were ten minutes left to air, and I could hear the house band playing on Home Base, and the chatter of the audience members eagerly waiting for the show. Usually, Danny took the stage for a couple minutes before air to warm up the audience, but I heard Bailey, who also had gotten their start as a stand-up, doing it instead. Then Bailey left the stage and the cast member Jay bounded out, with Bianca, Lynette, and Grace taking their places behind him. Though I couldn't see Home Base, I knew because this was how it always happened that Jay was wearing a three-piece, seventies-style pale blue suit, and the women were wearing matching short silver halter top dresses with tall white boots. They all belted out "We Are Family," and the audience went nuts.

As I walked toward the spot under the balcony where I usually watched the live show, a no-man's-land quite separate from Nigel's cave, and without rosé, I passed Viv, who was about to play Comey's book editor in the cold open. In the seconds before a cast member went on, when they were surrounded by a makeup artist, a hair stylist, and someone from wardrobe all making last adjustments, the clusters always reminded me of when the mice and birds in the original Cinderella movie dressed her for the ball. I didn't want to get in the way, or to call out Dr. Theo's name, so when Viv's eyes met mine, I merely held up my right hand, first with the thumb up, then with the thumb down, and raised my eyebrows. She nodded and held up her own thumb. I wasn't sure whether I'd been asking if Dr. Theo was there or if they'd spoken, but, either way, the confirmation seemed promising. "Awesome," I said, and kept walking to take my place next to two other writers, Patrick and Jenna. Unless things went awry during the show—if another sketch went way over and I was told by a producer I needed to make more cuts—this was where I'd stay. Even on nights when none of my sketches were in the lineup, it was thrilling to be in the studio seeing the cast members perform and knowing the sketches were appearing on television screens all over the country. Like Noah and millions of other people, I too had once been a kid who lived far from New York and watched *TNO* and was electrified.

And then it was 11:28, 11:29—one of Nigel's pearls of wisdom that people outside *TNO* borrowed was "The show doesn't go on because it's ready. The show goes on because it's 11:30"—and I could hear Penelope saying, "Thirty seconds to air, people, thirty seconds to air. Keep moving, everyone." The cold open started, and Oliver was smarmily self-righteous as Comey, and Viv was impatient as his editor and Lynette came onstage as a world-weary Hillary Clinton and then there was the moment at the sketch's conclusion when they broke the fourth wall, leaned their heads in, looked at the camera, and shouted in unison, welcoming viewers to the show just as *TNO* cast members had been doing since 1981. Hearing the famous line never failed to release something in me, some ecstasy that was like lifting the tab on a soda can, or maybe like having an orgasm, or maybe like knowing I'd have an orgasm in the near future—some excitement and anticipation and nervousness and delight. The essential thing I'd failed to understand about *TNO* before working there was that, even though there were flubbed lines and late camera cuts and sketches that bombed, the live part wasn't the show's weakness; it was its strength. And really, so was the way all the preparation had to be crammed into a week. These were the things that made us inventive and wildly ambitious, that gave the show its unpredictability and intensity and magic. Though, oddly, even after thirty-seven years, plenty of viewers still didn't realize the show *was* live.

By this point, I'd been around Noah enough that I could tell he was nervous during the monologue, but in an endearing way—that he was both happy and jittery. When Elliot came out for their faux-misunderstanding, Elliot's comparative stiffness—and frankly, his comparatively mediocre looks—amplified Noah's charms. And then Noah was saying, "Our musical guest is, well, also me, and we've got a great show tonight, so stick around and we'll be right back," and it was all spinning forward, with Peggy whisking Noah offstage (another of my all-time favorite moments had been the night when a petite starlet in extremely high heels finished her monologue and Peggy simply hoisted the starlet into a piggyback to get her from Home Base to her first sketch). I often thought that *TNO* was like a sped-up version of life itself, and that whether something proceeded magnificently or disastrously, time always kept rushing by and the next moment was happening. During commercial breaks, or as other sketches unfolded, the swarms of techs in all black were calmly moving set walls and unrolling rugs and carrying sofas and desks, and before each sketch started, Penelope was saying over the speakers, "Ten seconds," and then, "Three, two," and then we were live again. After Noah's monologue, the commercial break, and Tony and Lianna's digital short, the Cheesemonger killed (of course the sketch I'd cared about the least killed, and the one I'd cared about the most had been cut, even if I'd been the one to cut it); then there was the Medicine Cabinet sketch that had replaced The Danny Horst Rule, which was both clever and a little soft still, not as sharp as it would have been if it had been revised more; then the overhauled Sister & Father, which made the audience roar as soon as Noah appeared in his white cassock and skullcap and in which Viv as the nun innocently spouted filthy double entendres that prompted me to scan the backs of the heads of the audience in the floor seats for Dr. Theo; then Noah's first musical act was being introduced by his sister, Vicky, and it was "Ambiguous," the song I'd watched him rehearse. This time around, it made me unexpectedly sad and then made me think maybe I should end things with Gene and try, after all this time, for a real boyfriend. Not anyone from *TNO*, certainly, and not Noah Brewster because he was Noah Brewster. But *someone,* someone whose eyes I'd want to gaze into and who'd want to gaze into mine while we lay on a huge bed with a million pillows. Then it was News Desk, in which whatever mood Danny was in was indistinguishable from his usual deadpan delivery and which, apart from Danny's current-events jokes, featured Bailey in a cooking segment for Minnesota hot dishes—Bailey was, in real life, from Duluth—and as they dumped a massive pitcher of cream of mushroom soup into a clear glass pan of tater tots, I could already tell this was going to be a recurring bit. Then there was Noah's Choreography sketch, and I saw the snake handler waiting just off set; I'd expected the snake to be green like the rubber prop, but her scales had a pattern of reddish-orange diamonds over paler orange, and the audience cheered after the handler placed her around Noah's shoulders then moved away, and my heart thudded, and then that sketch was finished, too, and I'd once again seen Noah's muscular abdomen and so had many other Americans. Then there was Blabbermouth, and though it got laughs, just as I'd been able to tell that Bailey's hot dish segment was the beginning of something, I could feel that Blabbermouth had run its course. Then Peggy was pulling Noah from Stage 3 to Stage 2 for his second song, the Cinderella mice and birds were outfitting him in a retro mint-green-and-black bowling shirt and touching up his makeup, Jay was introducing this time, and Noah was singing "Inbox Zero," and then, after a commercial break, it was already time for goodnights, when Noah stood on Home Base, joined by the cast members and his band, and said thank you and everyone hugged each other. Catchphrase's Unicycle sketch had been cut, but so had Joseph's Three Tenors sketch. Danny didn't appear for goodnights, and the house band was still playing the ending music and the audience was still cheering as I left the studio and walked down the hall toward his dressing room.

A producer and a wardrobe assistant both congratulated me on my sketches, and I thanked them perfunctorily. I knocked on Danny's door and opened it without waiting for a response. He was sitting in front of the mirror removing makeup with a wipe.

"How are you doing?" I asked.

"How do you think?"

"If you don't want to go to the after-party, we could go get pizza or whatever."

In the mirror, we made eye contact, and he smiled grimly. "No offense, but you're giving such intense vibes right now of 'Honey, I know you didn't get invited to prom, but wouldn't it be way more fun to stay in and bake cookies with Dad and me?'"

"I do have a delicious recipe for snickerdoodles," I said, and he didn't laugh.

He said, "I'm gonna go home, smoke some weed, and try to sleep."

"Will you text me tomorrow and let me know how you are?" We had never previously communicated on our day off.

"Okay, Mom," he said.

Before I left his dressing room, I patted him on the shoulder.

Cast members, unlike writers, were each provided with a car and driver to get to the after-parties—more specifically, with a gigantic black Cadillac Escalade SUV—and I'd arranged to ride along with Henrietta and her wife, Lisa. Before I met them in Henrietta's dressing room, which was just a few doors from Danny's, I needed to stop by the seventeenth floor, drop off my scripts, and get the black nylon fanny pack I used as a purse. When I entered the office, an enormous bouquet of flowers sat in the center of my desk, dark and light pink roses and frosted-looking greenery. As I lifted the large square vase from the open cardboard box, I thought that if this was Noah's way of thanking me for helping him with his sketch (four days, and also a lifetime, before), it was both excessive and extraordinarily gracious.

But when I pulled the note from the clear plastic fork in the bouquet's center and unfolded it, it read:

Sally, please forgive me. xoxo Annabel

SUNDAY, 1:51 A.M.

That week's official after-party, before the after-after party or any parties after that, was at a huge fancy old-school French restaurant. It featured a slightly trendy bar on the lower level—not a bar that a twenty-three-year-old who lived in Bushwick would consider trendy, but one that, say, a thirty-six-year-old who lived on the Upper West Side might. Every official after-party was a weird blend of quasi-mandatory work event, necessary emotional release, celebrity scene, and 1:30 A.M. dinner.

Almost immediately after arriving, Henrietta, Lisa, and I went through the buffet—Henrietta had once told me this was the one meal of the week when she ate in a completely unrestrained way—then we sat in a big round booth already occupied by Viv; Dr. Theo; Bailey; Bailey's partner, Sterling; Oliver; Oliver's manager, whose name I didn't know; Oliver's ex-girlfriend Bettina; and Oliver's cousin, whose name I also didn't know. Even as the cast members and I debriefed about the show—who'd messed up their lines, who'd broken character, which sketches had been received more or less enthusiastically than we'd expected—I wondered what Dr. Theo made of being at this place, at this hour, surrounded by people a minimum of a decade and a half younger than he was. In person, he was as handsome as the online photo I'd seen or maybe more so: medium height, slim, with closely cut salt-and-pepper hair and warm brown eyes. He seemed simultaneously calm and hard to read. Viv was on his left, and I was on his right, and as the debriefing continued, I said, "I hope the inside baseball isn't boring you to death."

"Not at all," he said. "It's fun to see behind the curtain."

"You're an ophthalmologist, right?" I said.

"I am."

"What's that like?"

He laughed. "It's good."

I laughed, too. "I guess you already know this, but people's eyes are important to them."

"I do know that," he said. "And it's true."

"Although I always forget to do that thing where you're supposed to look twenty feet away from your computer screen for twenty seconds every twenty minutes. Are you from New York?"

He shook his head. "I've lived here since right after med school, but I grew up in St. Louis."

"Wait, really? I'm from Kansas City."

We turned to look at each other—we both were holding forks over our plates—and he said, "Well, hey."

"Do you get back home much? I just go a couple times a year."

"I go for the holidays. My parents and sisters are still there, and my nieces and nephews. As a matter of fact, my oldest niece is now at NYU, but the rest of my family is there."

"Viv went to NYU," I said. "As you probably know."

From Dr. Theo's other side, Viv said, "Viv went where?"

"Viv went to NYU," I said. "Where, if I'm not mistaken, she was an econ major and the star of the student improv group."

To Dr. Theo, Viv said, "Sally moonlights as my publicist. I don't know if she mentioned that."

"It's not a job," I said. "It's a calling." But even as we joked around, my gaze was drawn across the expanse of the restaurant's dining room to where Noah sat in a booth exactly like ours with Nigel, Elliot, Autumn, Noah's sister, one of the guitarists who'd performed with him, and both of the goateed guys I'd seen in his dressing room. They all were speaking animatedly, and I thought how relieved Noah must feel that the show had gone well. I wondered if I'd end up saying goodbye to him. I could approach him, of course, but did I really have anything to say?

For the next hour, I continuously monitored Noah's location and activity, neither of which changed much, except for when he rose from the booth as Franklin Freeman, who was the house band's director, was passing by. Noah heartily clapped Franklin on the back, then they embraced and talked for a few minutes. Would I ever see Noah again? The most plausible time would be if he returned to host in two or three or seven years, if I still was working at *TNO*, which I didn't think I would be.

"Sally," Viv was saying, then, "*Sally?*" I turned. "Want a ride to Blosca?" This was the dive bar on the Lower East Side where the night's first after-after party was being held. The bar was down a narrow staircase to a basement level, and the party would be much smaller, more like forty people instead of the hundred milling around this one, and the main attractions were a pool table and cheap drinks (somewhat astonishingly, we all, even the cast members who'd been driven there in Escalades, had to pay for our own drinks at the first after-party). My first year at *TNO*, I'd been too intimidated to attend the after-after-party, then from my second to my sixth or seventh years, I'd attended all of them, though I ended the night there instead of going on to strip clubs rumored to be the sites of after-after-after parties. A few times, I'd found myself at a diner around 7 or 8 A.M., but that was the extent of my adventurousness. And in the past couple years, I often skipped the after-after-party altogether because I was more enticed by my own bed.

But Viv was already wearing her jacket, looking at me expectantly, still waiting to hear if I wanted a ride.

"Sure," I said.

SUNDAY, 3:09 A.M.

At Blosca, I went straight to the bar for a drink, turned around, and almost collided with Noah Brewster.

"Hey!" He smiled broadly.

"Hey!" I said back. "Congratulations! You were great." Though I wasn't drunk, I'd just taken a large, reassuring sip of vodka tonic, following two drinks at the earlier party.

Noah leaned over the bar and asked for a club soda—presumably, he was completely sober—and I heard the bartender say, "Love your music, man," and Noah said, "Thanks, man," and then he turned back to me and said, "I wasn't sure if you'd be here." Even in the dim lighting, his eyes were bright blue, and his blond surfer hair was, well, convincingly hairlike. Sometimes at after-parties, the hosts would still be wearing their TV makeup, but it looked like he'd wiped his off.

"I wasn't sure if *you'd* be here," I said and held out my arms. "But here we both are." Not that he'd know it, but this was as theatrical, and as tipsy, as I got. "Are you exhausted or still running on adrenaline?"

"I don't know how you guys do it week in and week out."

"But being the host and the musical guest is the craziest of all possible worlds. I could never do either, let alone both. And you really were awesome. Choreographer was fantastic."

"Well, you were right about the Cheesemonger."

"No, you get credit," I said. "It's all in the delivery." Tipsiness notwithstanding, I already was aware of monopolizing a celebrity's time when I was no longer professionally useful.

This was when Noah said, "Now will you admit you've never really listened to my music?"

I genuinely laughed. "If I hadn't, how would I have written the sketch? Also, I'm a human being in the world. Do you think there's any man, woman, or child who hasn't heard 'Making Love in July' while lying in the chair at the dentist's office?"

"Yeah, exactly. I mean that you haven't listened beyond the bare minimum. You haven't listened on purpose." He still seemed to be good-naturedly teasing as opposed to needily grasping for a compliment.

"Also not true," I said. "I love 'The Bishop's Garden' and 'All Regrets.'"

He squinted a little, scrutinizing me.

"Here's what I'll admit," I said. "There are two categories of pop songs I'm not crazy about, and because 'Making Love in July,' through no fault of its own, is in one of the categories, it biased me against you early on. I mean almost twenty years ago. But I've realized that I underestimated the range of your"—I paused—"your oeuvre." I paused again. "What kind of asshole do you think uses the word *oeuvre* in a bar at three in the morning?"

"Just guessing but maybe an asshole who went to Harvard?"

"No, no," I said. "I'm not one of *TNO*'s Harvard assholes."

"Where'd you go?"

"Duke," I said.

This time, his smile was more sarcastic. "As in the world-famous university in North Carolina? Do you mean that Duke?"

"I get that having gone to Duke might not sound that different from having gone to Harvard, but, trust me, the writers who went to Harvard think it is. Also didn't you go to some fancy prep school in Washington, D.C.? Because I went to a gigantic, crappy public high school in suburban Kansas City."

"But I never went to college at all, so that negates my fancy prep school degree. I was supposed to go to Kenyon, but instead I started busking at Metro stations. When do I get to find out the two categories of songs you hate?"

"Well, my disclaimer is that music isn't my area of expertise."

"Noted."

"One category is the kind of song where it's about a long relationship or marriage, and the lyrics are like 'Sometimes it was so bad that we almost didn't make it, but we've survived.' I think those songs are unintentionally funny because they're supposedly a celebration of the endurance of love or whatever, but the lyrics sound more like 'Being married to you is hell, but let's congratulate ourselves for gutting it out.'"

"Hmm," he said. "I guess I've never thought about that."

"There's a ton of them," I said. "'We both were attracted to other people, you drove me crazy, I wanted to kill you. But, baby, after all these years, you're still the one.' That actually might be a good sketch. Even though you poisoned my cat, even though you puked on my needlepoint pillow. Have you ever been to a wedding reception where they make all the married couples stand up and then the DJ says, 'Sit down if you've been married less than ten years, less than twenty years, less than thirty years?' And the last ones standing are some ninety-year-old couple who's been married since 1950?"

"Did you meet my backup singer Jimmy? I've only seen that at his wedding. I think it's not a WASP thing."

"I think you're right. But there could be a freeze-frame on each couple as they're applauded, and they do a confessional. So all the other guests are like, 'This is so touching,' and the ninety-year-old woman is thinking to herself, 'For seven decades, the sound of his chewing has made me want to strangle him.'"

"That would be funny," Noah said. "Actually."

Our eyes met, and I said, "Thanks, actually."

"The thing is," he said, "I'm pretty sure I've never written that kind of song, partly because I've never been married."

"Oh, sorry. 'Making Love in July' is the other kind of song I was referring to. It's in the second category. That kind is always a man singing to a woman and it's like, 'Baby, you don't know how beautiful you are. You're so perfect, I never thought I'd find this, am I in heaven?'"

Noah looked both amused and uncertain. "What's wrong with 'Baby, you're so perfect, I never thought I'd find this, am I in heaven?'" At an almost subliminal level, I found it gratifying that I'd tricked Noah Brewster into saying to me, while we stood a foot apart, "Baby, you're so perfect, I never thought I'd find this, am I in heaven?"

I said, "I don't like the You-don't-know-how-beautiful-you-are part. It makes it seem like the love is predicated either on a lack of awareness on the woman's part or else on her being insecure. And the woman in the songs is often both a child and a sexy enchantress. So the lyrics might as well be 'I'm attracted to you because you conform to the standards agreed upon to be desirable at this moment in human history, but you don't even know it and your cluelessness is what makes me feel like a real man.'"

"That's probably a little wordy," he said. "But point taken. Would you say it's similar to when the main character in a romantic comedy has flour on her nose after she made cookies and she doesn't know it? Because I've heard that's very annoying, too."

Although I was impressed that he remembered this part of the conversation we'd had in my office, I didn't know if he was agreeing or teasing me. I shrugged. "Didn't I warn you about my rants?"

"And didn't I tell you I love rants?" he said. "But I think you're conflating the second kind of song with something that's in a third category. Yeah, there are You-don't-know-how-beautiful-you-are songs, but I don't see those as automatically the same as the songs that are like, 'I can't believe you exist and I can't believe we found each other.' When one of those is done well, doesn't it capture the most transcendent experience two people can have?" When I didn't immediately reply, he said, "Don't tell me you think falling in love is bullshit."

"Well—" I thought of the oddly similar question Danny had asked just a few hours earlier. "I don't want it to be."

"I don't get why you'd write scripts for romantic comedies if you think romance is cheesy nonsense."

"That's just it, though," I said. "I don't write from a point of clarity. I write out of confusion."

"Then how about this—can you define cheese for me? Because I still haven't figured out, after two decades, where the line is between cheese and emotional extravagance that's acceptable. What makes a song or a movie or a moment in real life land on one side or the other? This is part of why the Cheesemonger sketch hit a nerve for me."

I was quiet for a few seconds and finally said, "That's a good question. But the line is subjective, right? Kind of like the Supreme Court definition of obscenity being 'I know it when I see it.'"

"What's a song you think is legitimately, non-cheesily romantic?"

"At the risk of being predictable, there's an Indigo Girls song called 'Dairy Queen.'"

"But isn't that about a relationship that doesn't work out?"

"Romance doesn't require a happy ending." Though I didn't convey it, I was surprised that he knew the song. Fans liked it, but it was no "Closer to Fine."

"Right," Noah said. "But you have to admit it's easier not to be cheesy when you're writing about lost love. Are your romantic comedies going to end sadly and that's their twist?"

I laughed. "I don't know how they end because I haven't finished writing one yet."

He was looking at me with intense curiosity, which wasn't a way I was often looked at. Then he said, "Have *you* ever been in love?"

"Well—" I paused. "I've actually been married." He glanced down at my left hand, the hand in which I held my drink, so I switched the glass to the other hand and wiggled my bare left fingers. "And divorced," I added. "I'm a brassy divorcée. I had a starter marriage in my early twenties, right after college."

"Does that explain why you're not a fan of songs about people who stayed married through all the ups and downs?" He took a sip of his club soda. "Or am I being facile?"

"Well, I definitely don't think divorces are inherently tragic. I saw my own as a personal failure, but it also was a huge relief. I'd never have had this career if I'd stayed married."

"In the beginning, when you and your husband were first together, did you feel like, 'Am I in heaven'?"

I laughed. "No." He laughed, too, a surprised-seeming laugh, and I said, "I think I've sort of been in love. Just not with my husband."

Noah was still regarding me with an expression that was both amused and strangely rapt, as if he found me riveting. This was the problem with celebrities, that they could deploy their charisma at will, and you basked in its glow, and then they shifted it away from you and the world reverted to being cold. "How does sort of in love work?" he asked.

Elliot had been at the after-party at the big French restaurant—he was far too ambitious to skip it—but he wasn't at the after-after-party; he'd stopped attending them when he got married. "It's pathetic," I said, "but there was someone at *TNO* who I thought was my soulmate. We never dated. We were just friends, but I thought we were comedy soulmates and life soulmates. The pathetic part is that he didn't feel that way about me."

"I can't tell," Noah said. "Are you saying 'soulmates' ironically?"

"Embarrassingly enough, I'm saying it unironically."

"And are you still into him?"

"Oh, God, no," I said. "This was years ago." There was a brief pause—over the bar's other conversations and the background music, which at that moment was a seventies rock classic, I heard the clacking sound of a new pool game—and I said, "Judging by your songs, I imagine you've been in love hundreds of times."

He shook his head. "Hardly."

"Do *you* still pine for people from your past?"

"I almost wish I did. I've never been in a relationship I thought could last forever, and when I look back, they seem even more doomed in retrospect. I wonder if I was deluding myself that the other person and I had anything in common. I guess if I start talking about attachment theory right now, I'll sound like I've been in a little too much therapy." He held up his glass. "But it definitely helps with staying sober."

"If it sounds like I haven't been in enough therapy, it's because I've chosen Midwestern repression instead."

He laughed.

I said, "Plus the time-honored method of channeling my neuroses into my writing."

"Another legitimate path, though not mutually exclusive from therapy."

"I think I know what attachment theory is from reading articles. It's replicating the dynamics of the family you grew up in?"

He nodded and set his drink on the bar. "I remember turning thirty and I'd just won this big award in the music industry—"

"Oh, come on," I said. "Don't be modest."

He grinned. "The Grammy for Album of the Year. Thank you for offering me that opportunity."

"If I won a Grammy for Album of the Year, I'd carry it with me at all times, including now. It's a little statue of a record player, right?"

"Except that you *have* won Emmys, so that doesn't really check out. Unless they're in there?" He nodded down toward my fanny pack.

Had he googled me? I didn't have much of an Internet presence—though I'd created social media accounts in order to follow other people, I'd literally never posted anything—but this was one of the few facts that would pop up if someone did a search. I patted my fanny pack. "If there was room for them, I would. As you were saying—you'd turned thirty, you'd won a Grammy, and . . . ?"

"Just that I thought I was on the cusp of figuring it all out. I'd had my early success, then I'd had a sophomore-slump album, then I'd redeemed myself critically—I mean, this feels like a misguided way of looking at it now, but it was what I believed at the time. I also thought I was on the cusp of getting married and having kids. For my thirtieth birthday, I'd gone to Costa Rica to surf with some friends. One night I happened to watch the sunset by myself from a balcony in the villa where we were staying, and I was really confident that there was some code I'd cracked. But six years have passed since then, I'm still not married, and I feel a lot more confused about everything—the state of the world, the direction of my life, how much I should use my so-called platform. Comparable to the cheesy versus not cheesy line, where's the divide when you're a celebrity who wants to be involved but you know plenty of people would just say, 'Shut up and play your guitar'?"

"When you thought you were on the cusp of getting married," I said, "was it to someone in particular?"

He shook his head and smiled. "You think that could have been part of the problem?"

"For what it's worth, when I was in high school—at my big crappy public school—a math teacher once said at assembly that the point of life is to find the thing you're good at and enjoy doing, and to do it for other people. Can you imagine having the audacity to declare what the point of life is? But I never forgot it, and I'm not so sure he was wrong."

"I've heard worse."

"It might sound silly, but I think of—" I paused. Even after two and a half drinks, this felt like a lot to reveal to a person I barely knew. But I kept going. I said, "I think of *TNO* as the love of my life." Unaccountably, my eyes filled with tears. And then I realized it wasn't because I thought what I was saying was sad. It was because it was true, and not sad at all.

"Oh, yeah," Noah said immediately. "I feel that way about my music."

"We're so lucky," I said. "Don't you think? Most people don't have that. I know, everywhere other than New York, if you have a good job and a spouse and kids and a house and a car, those are the markers of maturity and stability and completeness. And you eat your dinner at seven P.M. and go to bed at ten, and go for vigorous jogs on the weekend. If you're into that, great. But there are lots of other ways to put a life together."

"Do you know that Thoreau line 'The mass of men lead lives of quiet desperation'?"

"Not only do I know it," I said, "but in high school, I had a poster with famous quotes on it, and that was one of them!" I'd spoken with such excitement that I had spit a very tiny amount of saliva onto his right cheek. He did not wipe it away; he beamed back at me, and though I couldn't prove it and certainly wasn't going to ask, I suspected not that he didn't know I'd spit on him but that he didn't want me to be embarrassed or truly didn't care, that he didn't find me at all disgusting. Even after six days, his easygoing warmth was so unexpected, and so endearing. "Just to be clear," I said, "I do lead a life of quiet desperation. I wouldn't want to be friends with anyone who doesn't, or anyone who isn't filled with ambivalence, because I assume they'd be incredibly shallow. But I'm sure I'd be ten times more quietly desperate if I were living in the suburbs with a two-car garage."

"Do you know you don't want any of that? The marriage or kids?"

It occurred to me to say, "With you or someone else?" but what if he thought I was serious? Instead, I said, "I don't know for certain, but I'm not sitting around waiting for either one. And I bet not settling down when you were thirty has made you a better musician. And continuing to feel confusion has, too, probably. I just can't see how anyone who thinks they have everything sorted out and have come out on top could write very good songs. Or, for that matter, very good comedy sketches or very good screenplays."

"Maybe *you* should be a therapist." He lifted his glass from the bar, took a sip, swallowed, and said, "By the way, I don't believe in the Danny Horst Rule. I thought your sketch was funny and I'm sorry it got cut, but the rule itself—personally, I've definitely dated— you know—"

I didn't try to conceal my amusement. "Women less attractive than you?" I suggested.

"That's not what I was going to say. But non-celebrities."

"You've dated them in a serious way?"

"Of course. It's not like the only relationships I've been in are the ones that have been reported in gossip columns. But you're damned if you do and damned if you don't. If you go out with another celebrity, it's like Danny and Annabel, where you're under this distorting microscope. You have the advantage of understanding each other's worlds firsthand, but the disadvantage of both having really complicated schedules. Whereas if you date someone who isn't another celebrity, you feel like you're always asking them to accommodate you. Plus, it's easy for them to feel insecure. You're looking at me with a very mocking expression right now. I realize these are privileged problems."

"I think you think I'm looking at you with a mocking expression because I'm a writer for *TNO*."

"I guess that might be an occupational hazard." And then something happened that later was hard for me to explain to myself, hard to understand. As when he'd cupped my chin in my office, it might have been nothing. His expression became both very tender and very amused, as if there were an excellent inside joke between us, and he tilted his head to the right and looked at me with a focused kind of sweetness and warmth. Then he again set his glass on the bar and leaned forward incrementally, and I thought, *Oh my God, is he going to* kiss *me? Because Noah Brewster cannot kiss me here, in front of my co-workers, in a setting that isn't really private be-*

cause nowhere is private in the age of cellphones, in a world in which he is him and I am me. And because if he kisses me, what will happen next?

Also incrementally, I took a step back. "All your insights about love and romance," I said. "Did you get them from dating twenty-two-year-old models?"

He squinted with what appeared to be genuine confusion. "What's that supposed to mean?"

My heart was beating more quickly, and not in a swoony way. In a pre-combat way, like in rewrites when I steeled myself to argue with Elliot. I said, "I didn't realize models were so educational."

Noah's expression was no longer confused. It was stony, and a few seconds elapsed before he said, "I thought we were just having a real conversation. Why would you say that to me?"

"*Haven't* you dated a lot of models? Is that not factually correct?" He scowled—it was definitely the handsomest scowl I'd ever seen, and it was also, to an extent that I was only starting to absorb, horrifically regret-inducing—and I added, "I didn't mean to offend you."

"Right," he said.

"Sorry, but I did warn you that I'm an asshole."

"Wow. That's just—" He shook his head. "That's the lamest excuse I've ever heard."

We looked at and away from each other with a new awkwardness, a not-fun awkwardness, while the hum of the room, which had previously been almost unnoticeable, seemed to swell. On the one hand, I desperately wished I could rewind the conversation ninety seconds and un-say those things about models. On the other hand, feeling attracted to this man, experiencing his attention—it had been stressful and confusing, not just in the bar but for the last several days, and now it seemed like that stress and confusion had run their course. I could get back to my regular non-hopeful, non-tormenting life.

"If you don't want to accept my apology," I heard myself say, "then I guess that's that. It was nice to meet you or whatever." I lifted my drink toward him in some sort of farewell salute.

He seemed deeply frustrated and maybe even angry as he said, " 'I didn't mean to offend you' and 'I told you I'm an asshole'—neither of those is an apology. I just wish—" Then he paused. Again, he shook his head. "You know what? Never mind. I guess I should be grateful that you warned me who you are before things went any further." He tucked his hair that I knew was a wig behind his ears in a way that was oddly decisive. "So, yeah. Take care, Sally."

And then he turned and walked away.

THE FOLLOWING DAYS

I'll describe what happened next not chronologically, because even now the chronology is hazy to me, but in order of my awareness of the events. The first thing I was aware of was that Noah did not leave the bar immediately, but chatted briefly with a cluster of cast members, then left ten minutes later. I sought out Viv, who was talking to Dr. Theo in such a soft, intimate way that if I hadn't been so worked up, I'd have left them alone. As I stood about fifteen feet from Noah, I watched him out of the corner of my eye, wondering if I should approach him and try to make things right; if I were drunker or more impulsive, I'd probably have attempted it, but it seemed unlikely that I'd succeed. Also, I didn't want to overestimate the importance to him of our skirmish. Might he barely remember it by the following morning? I felt devastated and relieved when he walked away from Josh and Hakeem and Lynette, toward the exit sign at the bottom of the staircase, paused to pull out his phone and type something on it, then disappeared up the steps to the ground floor. But of course I'd already felt devastated—I'd felt that way as soon as I ruined our conversation. It was the dramatic shift in tone, the fact that I *could* ruin it, that allowed me to admit to myself that the dynamic between us, not just at the after-after-party but for the last six days, had had enough heft and energy to be something; it had not been nothing. If he hadn't been famous, I'd definitely have thought he was hitting on me. Though whether we really had been about to kiss a few minutes prior—now I'd never know if I'd been shockingly correct or laughably wrong.

The second thing that happened was that the Cheesemonger sketch went viral. By Sunday night at 8 P.M. it had more than five hundred thousand views on YouTube, by Monday it had more than a million, and by Friday it had more than three million.

The third thing that happened was that a week and a half later, Noah's tenth album was released, and when he returned to New York to promote it on both morning and late-night talk shows, he was asked repeatedly about the Cheesemonger, discussed it warmly, and never mentioned me. Even worse, he and Annabel Lily were photographed hanging out together on two separate occasions. One afternoon, they went window-shopping in SoHo, and the next day, they had dinner at a sushi restaurant in the East Village. That night, he was seen leaving her apartment around 11 P.M. It was Henrietta who alerted me, texting after the first round of photos showed up online, *What are they thinking????* And then, as if I didn't understand, *Poor Danny!!!*

I masochistically continued to google Noah for a few weeks, and there wasn't any more documentation of him with Annabel. Though the photos had been accompanied by disavowals from unnamed sources, meaning their publicists ("Noah and Annabel are just old friends"), another diner at the Japanese restaurant had noted their "flirty vibe" ("They were really enjoying each other"), and the episodes seemed patently staged. I mean, window-shopping—did anyone do that in real life? And for fuck's sake, just get takeout sushi! But I couldn't have said if album promotion was the point and cruelty was the byproduct or if exploring a sincere attraction was the point and album promotion was the byproduct.

The fourth thing that happened was that Viv and Dr. Theo became a real couple, a long-term couple, though, as she told me later, they didn't have sex that first night. They did go home together, and they did sleep in the same bed, but they actually slept, after what Viv jokingly but ecstatically described as heavy petting.

It was with Viv and Dr. Theo that I'd left the after-after-party not long after Noah's departure. We all climbed into the second row of the Escalade, with Viv in the middle, and as I fastened my seat belt, I leaned forward and said to Dr. Theo, "How are you holding up?"

"Not sure I've been awake at this time since I was a resident, but I'm hanging in there."

Viv said, "Should we pop into Bellevue and you can deliver a baby for old times' sake?"

"I'll take a rain check on that."

The driver pulled into the street, and less than a minute had passed when I heard a rhythmic breathing, a quieter sound than snoring, and when I leaned forward again, I saw that Dr. Theo had fallen asleep. Viv and I made eye contact, and she smiled.

"I like him," I half whispered and half mouthed.

"I do, too," she whispered back.

"You know the Danny Horst Rule?" I said quietly. "Do you believe it?"

"No," she said immediately.

"Really?"

"For sure our culture is obsessed with how women look, and we've all been infected. But at the individual level, people are way freakier than we acknowledge. Attraction has to do with so many things besides appearance." After a pause—we were headed up FDR Drive, nearly empty at this hour, riding alongside the dark swath of the East River, beyond which the lights of Brooklyn were visible—Viv said, "Would you rather marry Danny or Annabel?"

"Definitely Danny," I said.

"Right? Because hot eventually gets boring, but funny never does."

"With you, the person won't have to choose," I said. "They'll get funny and hot."

"I know." Viv pointed to her left, where Dr. Theo slept, and, in the same lowered tone we'd been speaking in, said, "Lucky dude."

I hesitated before saying, "On Tuesday night, I helped Noah Brewster with his sketch. He randomly showed up in my office, and it was just the two of us for about an hour, before Autumn came and found him again. After that, all this week, I kept feeling like there was chemistry between us. Then I'd think, it's impossible. There's no way."

"Of course it's possible," Viv said. We were passing the landing of the East Twentieth Street ferry when she said, "You're like *Roman Holiday*."

"What do you mean?"

"Noah sneaking away from his handlers. He's Audrey Hepburn and you're Gregory Peck."

"Ha," I said. "That didn't occur to me." After a few seconds, I added, "But if there was chemistry, I fucked it up tonight. At Blosca, we were having a weirdly soul-baring conversation, and I panicked and said something mean about him dating twenty-two-year-old models."

"Why'd you do that?"

"I have no idea," I said, and I began to cry.

Viv didn't reply. Instead, she took my left hand in her right one and held it, and the driver kept heading up FDR Drive, past the buildings on one side and the river on the other, at this quiet hour, on this spring night, on the island of Manhattan. On Viv's other side, Dr. Theo continued to breathe deeply.

CHAPTER 2

July 2020

from: Noah Brewster <NoahRBrewster@gmail.com>
to: Sally Milz <Smilz@TNOshow.com>
date: Jul 20, 2020, 11:42 PM
subject: Actually

Is this still you?

from: Sally Milz <Smilz@TNOshow.com>
to: Noah Brewster <NoahRBrewster@gmail.com>
date: Jul 21, 2020, 8:04 AM
subject: Actually

Yes, this is still me.

(Okay, my inner English major is experiencing a lot of turmoil right now. I want you to know that I know that, grammatically, Sentence 1 should be "This is still I," but I also don't want you to think I'm uptight. Have I successfully split the difference? Relatedly: As a kid, I thought turmoil was a kind of oil, like an alternative to canola.)

Hope you're hanging in there during this, um, deadly global shitshow.

from: Noah Brewster <NoahRBrewster@gmail.com>
to: Sally Milz <Smilz@TNOshow.com>
date: Jul 21, 2020, 1:36 PM
subject: Actually

Until I was in fifth grade, I thought noodles were made out of cheese. In my defense, noodles made out of cheese might be kinda good.

As for grammar, I'll accept both me and I. It's capitalizing Sentence that's confusing. Then again anyone who isn't an ignoramus would defer to the expertise of the person who graduated from a fancy college even if the college wasn't Harvard. Wait . . . is ignoramus an offensive term?

Are you in N.Y.? Not that you asked, but I'm in L.A.

from: Sally Milz <Smilz@TNOshow.com>
to: Noah Brewster <NoahRBrewster@gmail.com>
date: Jul 21, 2020, 7:04 PM
subject: Actually

I just googled ignoramus and I still don't know. But you remember plenty of people believe TNO's mission is to offend,
right? After the first episode of this year, before we all realized
we'd have a whole new set of problems to worry about, a high-
up person at the DNC tweeted about how a sketch I'd just
written was the apotheosis of twentysomethings' political apa-
thy. As someone turning 39 in October, I took the twentysome-
thing part as a compliment. But twentysomethings are the
least apathetic people I know! They're the ones who use metal
straws. They were going to BLM protests before everyone
was going to BLM protests. (Have you gone to any BLM protests this summer?) Anyway, you shouldn't look to me as an
arbiter of what's appropriate.

And I'm actually in (steel yourself for glamour ahead) Kansas
City, Missouri. In my childhood bedroom. Living with my
81-year-old stepdad and his beagle Sugar. The glamour never
stops! I'm sheepish about being one of those people who fled
New York, but after everything shut down, I started to feel like

I was losing my mind (like kind of for real, not as a hyperbolic expression). How's LA?

Noodles made out of cheese would be fantastic. You could fry them and dip them in marinara sauce and—oh shit, I think I just invented mozzarella sticks! Btw do random strangers ever write to you after guessing your surprisingly obvious email address?

from: Noah Brewster <NoahRBrewster@gmail.com>
to: Sally Milz <Smilz@TNOshow.com>
date: Jul 22, 2020, 10:36 PM
subject: Actually

I turn 39 even sooner than you, on 9/5. I'm not sure how some-one celebrates a birthday during a "deadly global shitshow" but maybe by using a metal straw and eating noodles made of cheese in the same meal? So many possibilities!

OK, speaking of the pandemic . . . in all seriousness, this brings me to why I first emailed you. Did you wonder? If you did, it was nice of you to act like it wasn't weird and out of the blue.

So . . . I had Covid in February. First, I will insert a disclaimer about how I shouldn't complain because of how privileged I am . . . then I will say it was fucking awful. For almost 3 weeks, I couldn't catch my breath, had the worst cough of my life, was exhausted, sore all over, constant headache. In addition to feeling like hell, I was terrified that I might never be able to sing again, or at least not like before. I'm lucky that this didn't prove to be the case, but for someone like me, anything that messes with voice and breath is very scary. As I type this all out, it occurs to me maybe you've also had it and are saying to yourself, what a baby! I hope you haven't had it.

But being sick gave me time to think about . . . to be honest . . . a lot of things. One was my week at TNO in 2018, specifically working with you, and how things took a kinda bad turn between us at the end. I regret that, and I want to officially say I'm sorry. I think you're cool and smart and I could have imagined us hanging out after that week and then . . . well, obviously that didn't happen. But maybe it should have, you know?

To answer your questions:

- I did attend a BLM protest. I went back and forth beforehand because I didn't want to do it in a performative way, but I decided it was more important to just go and let the chips fall in terms of potentially having my motives questioned . . . it wouldn't be the first or last time. I told the people that handle my socials not to post about it, although I think some pics did end up online. Did you attend any?

- Yes, a few times a year I get emails from random strangers that say either I'm your biggest fan ever, can I have $500 for my surgery, or your music sucks. I once heard from a guy who wanted his money back for my latest album and he went into a lot of detail about why. He made some fair points, so I emailed back Fine, dude, tell me your username on Venmo and I'll reimburse you the ten bucks. I never heard from him again.

I admit that my email address is unimaginative, but don't I get partial credit for sticking my middle initial in there? Does anyone ever tell you that your email address kinda reads as "smiles" . . . which I assume is exactly what you'd have picked if left to your own devices. Speaking of email, I think this is the longest one I've written since the early 2000s!

from: Sally Milz <Smilz@TNOshow.com>
to: Noah Brewster <NoahRBrewster@gmail.com>
date: Jul 23, 2020, 11:27 AM
subject: Actually

First of all, I'm sorry you were so sick. That sounds terrible. Are you completely better now or do you have those lingering symptoms? Did you have someone to take care of you? Were you in LA then? I haven't had Covid, or if I did, I didn't know it, which is extra lucky because right after TNO production shut down, a bunch of people got it, including Henrietta, Henrietta's wife Lisa (who is now eight months pregnant), and Viv (who by coincidence is also now eight months pregnant). For some reason, Viv's husband, who's a doctor, didn't get it. Viv, Lisa, and Henrietta all seem fine now, though I know they're worried about the potential effects of Covid in utero. Viv is also understandably anxious about her delivery. I confess that I didn't know until she told me that it's true even across class lines that Black women and their babies are much likelier to die in childbirth because of racism/bad healthcare.

Regarding BLM protests, I also went to one—you might know they were intense here, and some were very close to my stepdad's house—but it's safe to say nobody cared enough about my presence to post pics of me online. On the one hand, I find it so weird and awkward that white people and white-led companies woke up one day and decided to admit that racism exists. On the other hand, I guess better (400 years) late than never? Viv told me that after George Floyd was killed, she was getting check-ins from random white acquaintances being like, How are you? No, really, how?? and she was like, well, I'm exhausted from growing a human in my uterus, but I don't think that's what you mean. (Sidenote: Of course I newly worry that I'm one of the random white ladies presuming greater closeness with Viv than she feels, but I'm sure as hell not going to ask her for reassurance now. I've been wondering about a sketch along the lines of "Your handwringing will not protect you." Like about the phenomenon of white women believing that the mere act of expressing our discomfort or guilt gets us off the hook. Who knows what being at TNO this coming season will look like—there's a rumor we'll have daily tests—but last week I signed the contract to go back for my twelfth [!!] year.)

As for the end of your week at TNO, although I appreciate your apology, you were right about everything. (It's possible I've never before written those words to anyone so please enjoy them.) I've also thought a lot about that week, and I've also felt bad about it. The reality is that you don't owe me an apology, and I do owe you one. When you called me out, it was justified. What I said to you in that bar was rude. I'm truly sorry.

Is writing (and I imagine receiving) your longest email since the early 2000s a bad or good thing? In honor of the early 2000s, are you also fretting about the Y2K computer glitch and wearing one of those yellow Livestrong jerseys? I am, of course, wearing my yellow jersey right now. The breezy nylon keeps me cool in the humid Missouri summer.

from: Noah Brewster <NoahRBrewster@gmail.com>
to: Sally Milz <Smilz@TNOshow.com>
date: Jul 23, 2020, 3:50 PM
subject: Actually

What an honor to receive the inaugural Sally Milz "I think you were right about everything" declaration!! Would it be weird if I had the words tattooed on my arm? (Have you gotten any more ink since we compared notes on that front? I haven't, but remembering your hamster still cracks me up.)

It's fucking great to be writing and receiving long emails! Don't get me wrong, it's very intimidating to write to a TNO writer, but it's also so fun that even though I'm probably making all kinds of punctuation mistakes, I'm wondering if the thing I've been missing all these years is a pen pal. In all seriousness, this is the quietest my life has been in two decades and it's really nice to connect with another person. I sometimes used to wish I could hit pause for six months or a year and now it's like the universe called my bluff. No, I am not self-centered enough to think I caused a global pandemic, but still . . . be careful what you wish for.

To answer your question, I was in the middle of an 18 city tour in Feb, came back to L.A., and have been here since. I think it's a familiar story at this point, but we did a show in San Antonio that felt pretty normal, the next night was Houston and there was a strange energy in the air, two nights later was New Orleans and by the time I went onstage I knew we were postponing the rest of the tour. Though even that night we did the meet and greet and all the usual stuff . . . so I probably shouldn't have been surprised when I got sick a week later.

I am a bit sheepish, to use your word, about this, but I have a housekeeper/chef and a caretaker who live with me in their own section of the house, above the garage, and are married to each other. Then I have a P.A. who does not live with me. They all looked out for me when I was sick in a way I will be forever grateful for. None of them got sick . . . Margit (the housekeeper) left food outside my bedroom door and we didn't interact much, but it was reassuring to have people checking that I was alive.

I hope this isn't too weird of a question, but what's a "day in the life" for you now? Are you living with anyone besides your stepdad and his dog? Congrats on signing on for another TNO season! I remember you telling me in 2018 that you thought you'd leave in a year or two, but it sounds like you changed your mind. Did you consider staying in Kansas City?

So . . . I'm scared to broach this subject but since it seems like we are being honest . . . the thing I know I should apologize for is hanging out with Annabel L. that week after the show. I'm not sure if I owe you or Danny Horst an apology, but it wasn't cool on my part. There was nothing going on between Annabel and me, but I know it may have looked like there was and . . . well . . . I wish I could go back and change that impression.

(I'm sweating bullets here because one, this topic! And two, I first wrote "Annabel and I" but the 47 grammar websites I just checked suggested the other way. But I'm still not sure.)

I bet you look awesome in your yellow jersey. I've heard those never go out of style.

from: Sally Milz <Smilz@TNOshow.com>
to: Noah Brewster <NoahRBrewster@gmail.com>
date: Jul 23, 2020, 7:40 PM
subject: Actually

It's weirdly gratifying that I've infected you with my grammar anxiety. Sorry? Congratulations?

It actually (actually actually actually) could be a funny sketch to have various people explaining why they think they personally caused the pandemic. You're not the first person I've heard express this sentiment. The mom in the family who lives next door to my stepdad told me her 11-year-old daughter was worried she had caused it by telling the mom she traveled too much for work, and Henrietta's father-in-law told her he felt like he caused it because he was dreading a retirement party being held for him at the end of March. I mean, clearly, the combination of the 11-year-old, Henrietta's father-in-law, and you DID cause it, and you owe the entire world an apology. It had nothing to do with a bat at a market in Wuhan.

One of the weird things about working for TNO is that it's such a feast or famine schedule—either a ninety-hour week or I don't even go to the office for weeks or for the entire summer.

Before things shut down, I would have said that I'm excellent at keeping myself busy outside the show, but maybe the pandemic has called all of our bluffs.

I would NEVER stay permanently in Kansas City. I realize that might sound snobby and that smart, interesting people live everywhere and all that shit but still—never. Even when there's not a pandemic, restaurants are cleared out by 7:45 at night, the sidewalks all are empty, and sure, there ARE smart, interesting people here but not in the proportions there are in NY. That said, knowing that I'm staying with Jerry and Sugar temporarily makes it pleasant, if slow-paced. Jerry is very nice, very proper, and considers things like email and oat milk to be cutting edge. Sugar is not at all proper, especially when requesting belly rubs. This is by far the most time Jerry and I have spent alone together, and 75% of what we discuss is Sugar. I was 10 when my mom married Jerry (my biological dad, who was a pretty troubled guy, died when I was 8— a story for another time). When Jerry moved in with us, I'd been sleeping in my mom's bed since my dad's death, and the way she got me to return to my bedroom was by giving me my own TV. Which was how I began sneak-watching TNO as a fifth grader. So maybe I owe my career to Jerry?

This is A Day in the Life of Pandemic Sally (in exchange for my subjecting you to this, you are obligated to subject me to a Day in the Life of Pandemic Noah):

7: Wake up before it gets to be 99 degrees, take Sugar for a long walk, be shocked by how light it is, how many other humans are up and at 'em this early

8: Back home, shower, coffee, sit down at the wicker desk of my adolescence, open laptop to work on screenplay, accidentally spend the next 4 hours reading articles about when a vaccine will exist and what a gain of function mutation is

12: Lunch with Jerry, who gets up at 10 (when I'm not here he wakes up at 6 to walk Sugar and goes back to bed) then reads The Kansas City Star cover to cover for two hours while drinking a single cup of coffee and savoring a single bowl of Raisin Bran. Literally, he puts his breakfast bowl in the dishwasher and pulls out his lunch plate from the cupboard. For lunch we have baloney sandwiches on white bread with mayonnaise and lettuce. Fun fact: I've been a pescatarian for seven years. But is baloney REALLY meat?

12:30-4:45: Pretend to write screenplay, read more articles about anosmia and cytokine storms

5: Online "Chair Yoga for Seniors" with Jerry in the living room. The instructor is a foxy sixty-year-old named Marie, and Jerry would never in a million years discuss this with me, but I think he has a tiny crush on her. Not to brag, but as a non-senior (a junior?), I eschew the chair in Chair Yoga.

5:30: Jerry fixes a Manhattan for himself and a grapefruit seltzer water on the rocks for me, grills a pork steak for himself and a veggie burger for me, and we eat on the back deck if it's not too hot. In that case, we usually end up talking to the family next door (the daughters are 9 and 11, and the 11-year-old is the one who caused the pandemic by telling her mom she traveled too much for work). They ask us lots of questions like "If you could eat only one food for the rest of your life, what would it be?" and "If Sugar spoke human, what do you think she'd say?"

6:30: Another long walk for Sugar. For this one, I usually talk to Viv, Henrietta, or both. Viv is in the city—her husband is still seeing patients, which understandably makes her worry—but Henrietta and her wife have rented a place upstate.

7-9: I'm Jerry's tour guide through the Golden Age of Television. I try to find shows he wouldn't know about that might expand his horizons but won't horrify him. Yes: dramas set in the English countryside, wholesome reality show competitions, sit-coms about people who aren't white or straight. No: dating reality shows, fast-paced and extremely ironic millennial or Gen Z shows. When he doesn't like something, he says, "There's a lot going on, isn't there?" When he does like it, he says it was "very interesting" or "very amusing."

9:15: Jerry retires to his room, I can hear him puttering, I go to my room, two roads diverge and I try to take the one less traveled by putting away my laptop and phone and pulling out a book. I succeed about a third of the time.

Midnight: Lights out, peaceful slumber. Just kidding, lights out then logistical, corporeal, and spiritual panic.

Lather, rinse, repeat!

Have you ever been to Missouri? Also have you ever had a pen pal or am I, um, your first?

(Re: Annabel etc., I appreciate your honesty. I don't think there's much point in having a pandemic pen pal if you're not going to be honest. I actually just typed a whole other paragraph here about Annabel and life and my existential confusion, but I've decided to spare us both and deleted it. It's water under the bridge. If this makes you feel better, Danny is now happily dating Nigel's daughter Lucy, who recently graduated from Brown, works in publishing, and is predictably gorgeous yet oddly down-to-earth. I'm rooting for them as a couple and also rooting for Nigel to officially become Danny's quasi-Jewish quasi-dad.)

from: Noah Brewster <NoahRBrewster@gmail.com>
to: Sally Milz <Smilz@TNOshow.com>
date: Jul 24, 2020, 1:49 AM
subject: Actually

Of course I've been to Missouri! I've played a few times at Sprint Center in K.C., the Chaifetz in St. Louis, and years ago at the Blue Note in Columbia, MO, which is a cool smaller space (I believe a former movie theater). I can't say I've spent tons of time exploring Kansas City, but I did visit the museum with the huge badminton birdie sculptures on the lawn. On tour, if there is time apart from sound check and media stuff, I try to do one local thing, even if it's just a meal. But I also try not to be unhealthy, and eating the local specialty while not eating unhealthily can be at odds.

Sort of on this topic . . . I know this is a loaded question coming from me, but what would you say is your relationship with drinking and alcohol? You mentioned having "grapefruit seltzer water on the rocks" when your stepdad has a cocktail, although I am under the impression you sometimes drink. In case this doesn't go without saying, I realize drinking but not to excess is a normal part of life for lots of people . . . those enviably well-adjusted people!

Your stepdad sounds like a great guy and I bet he's really glad you're there. I look forward to hearing more about your biological dad or your mom if you ever want to share it. Unfortunately, I do not have a very good relationship with my parents. We don't fight, but we aren't close. Under normal circumstances, I see them about once a year, and I talk to them on the phone every few months. I have tried to make peace with who they are (I remember you and I discussed that I have benefited a lot from therapy, and certainly in this area). They still live in Arlington, Virginia, and they're both retired, but my dad was a tax lawyer and my mom worked in admissions at a K-8 private school. They are WASPs in every sense (read: snobs), and they've always seen my career as distasteful because of being so public. Plus, they think the music industry and L.A. are filled with unsavory people. Even before the pandemic, they led a very insular life of playing tennis at their country club, drinks and dinners with a small group of friends, and spending the summers in Maine. Obviously, I don't have anything to complain about, and there are clear advantages I have had in terms of my education even if I squandered the chance to attend college, and in terms of the financial safety net under me. But most of all there's the advantage of believing there would be a place in the world for my music. Because I was a shy, freaky goth weirdo as a teen, it took me years to cop to the entitlement or even arrogance inherent in thinking you have the right to pursue and share your art. It turns out a disproportionate number of people in the music industry grew up privileged, and many of them will go to great lengths to make you think otherwise. For sure, there are also a lot of musicians who overcame obstacles, including no money, and those people are usually more talented and much more enjoyable to hang out with.

I hope this isn't all too much information. I found your description of your stepdad so interesting that I thought I would try to give a comparable description. One thing I am very lucky about is that I really do consider my sister Vicky to be one of my best friends. She was there when I hosted TNO, and you two met briefly. Our parents disapprove of her in a different way from how they disapprove of me (she's a social worker who helps kids in foster care find "forever families," which to me makes her a hero while to my parents she is prioritizing other people's kids over her own—my nephew Jonah is six and my nephew Billy is four—plus she is divorced, which they also are ridiculously judgmental about). Vicky and I coordinate our annual visit to our parents so we can buffer each other.

Should I ask what your screenplay is about or does a genius not reveal the details of her work in progress? I assume it's a romantic comedy and that it features an Indigo Girls song at the climactic moment, but are you willing to say what happens in it beyond that? I am glad to now know that the secret to becoming an award-winning TNO writer is getting your own TV in 5th grade! I guess one of the reasons I had to go into music is that I didn't have my own TV until adulthood.

As for a day in the life . . . yours is a lot more interesting between dogs, chair yoga, and witty neighbors, but here goes:

9AM: wake up

10AM: at the risk of seeming like a cliché again, my trainer Bobby comes M/W/F. We do all our workouts outside and stay six feet apart. We stopped for a while in March-April, but for me personally working out is such an important way of maintaining an even keel with regard to sobriety and everything else.

1PM: lunch, then I catch up on emails or work stuff, which has slowed a lot. In the last few months, I have done some online fundraisers, including that notoriously glitchy one in late April.

4PM: either go for a hike to fight cabin fever or occasionally some friends come over. There are a few guys who I am messing around in a side project band with. One of the guys (two of the seven "guys" are women) is Erik Ventresca from Frontal Plumage, we've talked about working together for years, but for now we just jam in a totally low pressure way. Although I have a studio at my house, for obvious reasons, I carry everything outside, including amps. We've done this five or six times, and it's been a salvation. I'd meet up every day if they could, but the rest of them have families . . . including kids doing online school.

8PM: as mentioned, Margit cooks most of my meals but I have been cooking more than I did in the past. Now that I know you're a pescatarian, maybe some day I will make my pan-seared salmon for you. Do you like to cook?

About Annabel . . . yes, absolutely on water under the bridge. But I am intrigued by your missing paragraph of existential confusion. I love existential confusion! That missing paragraph reminds me of the missing Watergate tapes. (I'm trying to impress you with historic political references because that seems like something a TNO writer would be into. Is it working?)

You're my first pen pal! Am I, um, your first?

from: Sally Milz <Smilz@TNOshow.com>
to: Noah Brewster <NoahRBrewster@gmail.com>
date: Jul 24, 2020, 10:22 AM
subject: Actually

Okay, I have A LOT of questions! Were you really a shy freaky goth teen or is that what you tell people out of modesty? Do you work out for three hours a day?! What kind of music does your side project band play? But above all, how can your parents not be so proud and impressed that you are a super-talented and successful musician beloved by millions of people around the world? That's batshit crazy! In his heart of hearts, my stepdad doesn't even find TNO funny (it's in the "There's a lot going on, isn't there?" category for him), and he'll still tell anyone who'll listen that I'm a writer there. The best part is that he refers to it as The Night *Owl,* singular, instead of The Night Owls.

Maybe this is the moment to confess that since 2018, I've listened to your music a lot. Like, even before you emailed me a few days ago. It might be a tiny bit true that when you hosted TNO, I wasn't as familiar with your non-greatest hits as I could have been, but I've now gone back so far and so deep that I might even know the songs you forgot writing. (Have you forgotten writing certain songs? I've forgotten writing certain sketches, although if someone mentioned them, I'd remember. It's not unlike a high school classmate that you don't see for 22 years then spot in the cereal aisle of Hy-Vee after you've moved home during a pandemic and you recognize Vinny Kaplan immediately, but since you're both wearing masks you just slink away and you're pretty sure Vinny didn't notice you but maybe he was pretending exactly like you were.) Anyway, at the risk of sounding like a cringey fangirl, it turns out you're a great musician! Who knew?! Besides everyone??

I'm not sure whether a genius reveals the details of her screenplay, but I do reveal the details of mine (to a select few). It's about a single Supreme Court Justice who falls in love with a lawyer who regularly argues cases in front of her. Or maybe it's about a single advertising exec who oversees a cat food brand and falls in love with the single advertising exec who oversees the dog food brand. Or maybe the other single advertising exec oversees the rival cat food brand? Or, well, welcome into my brain. Several times, I've written about ten pages (probably not a coincidence that that's the average length of a TNO sketch) before I start questioning not just the premise of the screenplay but all the life choices I've ever made up to now, abandoning that idea, and starting over. Btw the other secret to becoming a TNO writer, besides getting your own TV in fifth grade, is being obsessed with Mad Libs. Did you like Mad Libs? In fourth grade, my friends and I were doing them on the bus ride back from a field trip to a nature center and, to this day, nothing has ever made me laugh more than the sentence "I was so happy that I couldn't wipe the smile off my penis."

I'm embarrassed that you remember when I said I'd be leaving TNO sooner rather than later. The truth is that it's probably time for me to go, but with all the other uncertainty now, I was too chicken. Plus, selling screenplays is a far less reliable paycheck than writing for a weekly show. I'm not that eager to work in a typical writers' room—the freedom and craziness and instant gratification of TNO may have spoiled me for life—although maybe I should try it before I decide. Now that there are Zoom writers' rooms, I could theoretically remain in Kansas City while joining one in NY or LA, which sounds like the worst of both worlds?

The full story of my departure from the city is that I lasted about two weeks after things shut down. My apartment (on the Upper West Side) is pretty small and dark, and ambulances were racing past at all hours. I wasn't interacting with anyone and I wasn't eating that much because I didn't want to go out and buy food, but I also felt uncomfortable asking some delivery guy to bring it to me. (I wasn't NOT eating, but I was eating weird shit I found in my cupboard like protein bars two years past their Best By date. And no, I don't like to cook.) One evening after a day of not leaving the apartment, I was washing my hands in the kitchen before eating a can of soup from when Obama was in office, I knocked a knuckle on my right hand against the faucet spout, and my knuckle came away smeared with some kind of black grime or mold. I bent over and looked up at the underside of the spout, and it was caked in this grime. I then went and looked at the faucet in the bathroom and it was the same. And I have a cleaning person who comes every few weeks. But I'd been drinking the water, using it to brush my teeth, etc. and I just felt so grossed out and like I'd been holding my sanity together so tenuously and feeling so worried about germs and the virus and what it was or wasn't on the surface of, and I almost couldn't withstand simultaneously confronting Covid and my disgusting faucets. (Do you remember speculating a few emails ago about if I'd think you were a baby for feeling terrible when you had Covid? Well, babies who live in glass playpens, etc., etc.) I got on a car rental website right then and I left at 5 a.m. the next morning, and I arrived at Jerry's house a few minutes before midnight

Kansas City time. Because I was terrified of making him sick, I then slept in the semi-finished basement for two weeks, and I wondered if leaving New York had actually improved anything, but after almost four months of chair yoga and conversations about a beagle, I'm sure it IS better. Although I don't want to stay in KC forever, Jerry has such good manners that he acts like I'm doing him a favor by being here. When really my only contributions are 1) the grocery shopping and 2) cutting Sugar's nails because the groomer he normally takes her to has shut down.

Btw it's an awesome flex that when I ask if you've ever been to Missouri, you can casually be like, Oh sure when I played in that stadium that holds 18,000 people. You might be appalled to hear I have never been to a show at Sprint Center (which was recently renamed T-Mobile Center), though if this is a good excuse, it wasn't built until after I'd graduated from college. Do you LIKE performing in stadiums? Is it stressful? Fun?

I really am sorry that your parents aren't supportive of what you do, and I imagine that that would be hard and very hurtful. I'm glad you're close to your sister—I remember meeting her and thinking she seemed nice. Regarding my parents, my dad was a pathologist (aka the people who look at biopsies, etc.), and also a depressive person who self-medicated (literally) through the inadvisable and illegal method of writing himself prescriptions for morphine. He and my mom, who worked in merchandising for Hallmark (yes, the maker of greeting cards and cheesy Christmas movies, though only the greeting card division is headquartered in KC) separated when I was a toddler. I have no memories of us all living together, though I do remember that when my dad came to get me for Saturday lunches, he almost always wore khaki pants and navy blue polo shirts, with a gray sweatshirt over them if it was winter. We usually got hamburgers. Even though from an early age I found hamburgers to be a disgusting bumpy circle of meat, I intuitively understood that I shouldn't express my disgust to him because it would be rude. That is, I understood I should be polite as you would with a family friend, as opposed to more blunt, as most kids would be with a parent.

When I was in second grade, on November 3, 1989, my mom picked me up early from school and took me to a park where we had never been and told me my dad had died from taking too much medicine. I assume the location was a strategic decision so that she didn't ruin a more familiar place, including our house. She told me that we'd never know if he'd taken too much medicine by mistake or on purpose but that really there wasn't much of a difference because even if he'd taken too much on purpose, it had been because he'd believed more medicine would make him feel better. I actually think this was a profound lesson about how with incomplete information, we choose our narrative. I also think my mom believed he did it on purpose, because before I left for college, she told me that no matter how bad I ever felt, the one thing I shouldn't do was kill myself. She said that ideas that seem right in the moment can seem wrong later, and that a lot of things are reversible but killing yourself isn't. She said this matter-of-factly, not unlike the way she used to say that you don't brush your teeth because it's interesting, you brush your teeth because you need to brush your teeth (as a kid, I complained that brushing my teeth was "boring").

I suspect that my dad's demons are part of what drew my mother to Jerry's stability and reliability. But from the time I was young, there was this category of things my mother would refer to as Mommy-Sally secrets, like eating leftover cake for breakfast, or both of us taking a sick day and having a picnic just because the weather was beautiful, or, even though she didn't curse in front of Jerry, if just she and I were in the car and she thought another driver was being unsafe, she'd say in a quiet but crisp voice, "What a fucking asshole." She conveyed to me without ever saying it outright that we all have public and private selves, which also was a very important lesson. Oddly, this ties into why I've been thinking I should leave TNO. With every passing year, I can feel how the writers coming up behind me are increasingly different from me. This, to be honest, is anxiety-inducing but also refreshing and appropriate and cycle-of-lifey—like, maybe it's time for me to make way for other people. And one of the ways that the writers in their twenties are different is that they DON'T seem to think we all have public and private selves. They're fine just having public selves and openly discussing their mental health issues and their medical issues and their sex habits and their family trauma. I find it really nice to be able to talk to you about all this stuff (or, so far, some of it), but I wouldn't talk about it with most people. Would you?

Regarding my relationship with alcohol, in normal life, I have a drink or two at the TNO after-party, and I don't drink much otherwise—maybe a glass of wine if I'm meeting Viv for dinner, but after she got pregnant, when she didn't order one, I didn't either. The one time besides the TNO party when I always have a drink is on a first date, to calm my nerves. So I guess the truth is that I do use it as a crutch, just not very often (oops, did I just reveal I don't go on first dates very often? By choice!). But it seems very understandable that you wonder about other people's drinking habits.

You actually are not my first pen pal. You're probably my best one, though, or at least this little diversion we have going is very enjoyable. Do you think it's beautiful when two people are each other's firsts, or do you think that inevitably creates awkwardness and it's better when one is more experienced and can guide the other?

from: Noah Brewster <NoahRBrewster@gmail.com>
to: Sally Milz <Smilz@TNOshow.com>
date: Jul 24, 2020, 3:01 PM
subject: Actually

I'm "probably" your best pen pal? In "this little diversion we have going"? You're breaking my heart here! Only kidding, but who are all these other pen pals that I probably compare favorably to? Are they current or past? Do I need to find them and challenge them to a duel?

In all seriousness, I am honored you've been enjoying my music. I might also sound like a cringey fangirl when I tell you that I think I have watched all your sketches. And this also happened in the past, right after I hosted TNO. I'm assuming you know it's hard to figure out which sketches you wrote because it doesn't say in the show credits so I had to venture into some deep dark superfan caverns. Now, just for the record, this does not mean I buy into the idea you refer to where I am a celebrity recognized far and wide and you are an unknown. You for sure have fans, even if you aren't recognized in the grocery store (except by Vinny Kaplan, who I am sure noticed you, knew you were pretending not to see him, and felt devastated). But I know you are a star in the comedy world. Also, plenty of people don't know or care who I am, and frequently when a stranger comes up to me in a restaurant (in normal times), I think they are about to say "I love your music" and what they say is "You look so familiar . . . are you my dentist?" But my point is that your sketches are really funny. Although it's hard to choose, the ones that made me laugh the most are the one about how women supposedly don't fart, the one about the ICE agents celebrating Thanksgiving, and the 1950s ads for housewives. I respect that you are not afraid to be dark or to acknowledge the awkwardness of life instead of glossing over it like we are all trained to do. Impressive to think your entire career is built on Mad Libs!

Thank you for the kind things you wrote about my parents. It took me a while to get here, but I try not to take their judgment personally. I'm grateful that I've had a much wider range of experiences and met many more people than they have. Also, it's not quite fair of me to claim they're completely unsupportive. Years ago . . . and warning, big namedrop ahead . . . I was part of presenting Mick Jagger with an award before joining the band onstage to play You Can't Always Get What You Want, and I invited my parents because my dad had been a huge Stones fan. Although they couldn't attend, I could tell he was impressed. Unlike my mom, my dad has some kindness inside him that he has trouble expressing (he doesn't talk very much overall) whereas my mom shamelessly takes digs at people, including people she gave birth to. I am really sorry about your biological father, but I'm glad to hear you had such a wonderful relationship with your mom. It seems like you have inherited a lot of her warmth and humor, and I bet she really loved having you as a daughter.

Do I like performing in stadiums and is it stressful? These are great questions. As you know from TNO, there is nothing else like the magic of a crowd feeling a collective and ephemeral joy, and in those moments, when I am onstage looking out at so many faces, I feel like a vessel in a way that's an incredible privilege. For sure, touring can get repetitive . . . the hotels and transportation but also the performing. Yet I know that for anyone in the audience, it might be a big night out for them, the tickets were not cheap, maybe they hired a babysitter and paid for parking. So my job is to bring as much energy in Omaha as at the Hollywood Bowl.

At this point, I don't usually feel stressed by shows. There are pros and cons to having "hit it big" early, and one that might be both is that by now, even as I recognize how much my career is a product of luck, it's the only life I know professionally speaking. Looking back, I was in serious danger of flaming out almost as soon as I got started. After my first and second albums came out back to back, I was drinking a lot, acting like a jackass in my early 20s, and generally letting success go to my head. In October 2003, there was a horrible accident in Miami where my drummer, whose name was Christopher and who was the sweetest guy, fell off a drawbridge over Biscayne Bay. This was a huge wake-up call, and following Christopher's funeral, I entered rehab for two months. I still think about him every day and wish I had stopped all of us from climbing the bridge. I considered quitting performing altogether. I wasn't sure if fans or the media would blame me for Christopher's death, and while this didn't happen, I have always felt very conscious of being given a second chance.

About your question of if I work out three hours a day . . . I do not work out from 10AM-1PM, as I may have implied. I work out from more like 10AM-11:15AM. But since we are being honest, it's questionable how healthy my relationship with exercise and food is. I am proud to say I have not relapsed with alcohol (and thank you for answering my question about drinking so straightforwardly), but I am pretty compulsive about exercising. This is not a humblebrag because I don't think it's good to be compulsive about anything. I was scrawny growing up and could eat whatever I wanted until I was about 30. At that point, as soon as I put on some weight, I stopped eating sugar and wheat. When I got Covid, I lost too much weight so I decided to start having bread again last spring and now, even though I've cut out grains again, I weigh 13lbs more than I did when I hosted TNO. Do you remember that sketch when I was wearing a very silly leather vest and shorts? I knew in advance I might be asked to wear something revealing for the show plus I'd be on TV and having my picture taken while promoting my album so I did a cleanse the week before. In the past, I have fasted in advance of photo shoots, but now that I have some distance on all of that, I think it's a habit I want to be finished with. I'm sure this will result in me looking less fit, and people will make snarky comments, but maybe I can learn to be at peace with it.

OK . . . I am seriously considering deleting that last paragraph because I am scared of how vain you will think I sound . . . but I also am curious what your reaction is. And no, I absolutely do not talk about this stuff with most people.

I know what you mean about getting older and having a different sensibility than the people coming up behind you. I feel aware of that when it comes to social media, which seems pointless to me and which I don't deal with myself but it is such a part of the machinery now. Another weird thing for me that's been true since the beginning is that, although my recent album sales are respectable, it's close to impossible that I will ever again reach the sales of my first album (even accounting for all the shifts in how music is sold during the last 20 years . . . which is, as you might say, a story for another time). Earlier in my career, this made me worry that I was failing the people at my label, but over time, it has helped me recognize that the one thing I can control is my music . . . not sales, not market trends, not critical reaction. I just can try to put my best work out there.

I swear to you I was a freaky goth, and for proof here's a picture of me from age 14. Please enjoy my way too long bangs, horrible-fitting jeans, and black nail polish. I was terrified of girls, worshipped The Velvet Underground and The Cure, and hated having to wear a coat and tie to my all-boys' school almost as much as I hated the mandatory sports.

I suppose the style of my side project band is . . . rockabilly? It's less poppy than my solo work, as I'm sure you will be sad to hear. I often wonder when I will play again before a crowd. I miss it like crazy and also, thinking of people pressed up against each other, sweating, singing at the top of their lungs . . . it's so hard to imagine that ever feeling normal.

I bet every version of your screenplay is great. I can't wait until I'm in a theater watching a movie you wrote.

from: Sally Milz <Smilz@TNOshow.com>
to: Noah Brewster <NoahRBrewster@gmail.com>
date: Jul 24, 2020, 7:22 PM
subject: Actually

You're definitely my best pen pal! Without question! I was just trying to play it cool.

There have been 3 others:

Pen pal 1 (4th-6th grade / 1992-1994)—Freja Mikaelsson who lived in Gothenburg, Sweden. My mom's college roommate married a Swedish man, and the moms cooked up this idea that their daughters, who were the same age, should write to each other. I have a hunch the main reason was for Freja to practice her English while the only Swedish I ever learned was "How are you?" and "I am fine, thank you." For a while, Freja and I corresponded a lot—mostly stuff like "My favorite color is yellow" and "I do not have any pets but would like a rabbit"— but it eventually petered out. Some of her letters might still be in a box in Jerry's basement, but the basement is, shall we say, not optimally organized.

Pen pal 2 (freshman year of college / fall 2000)—Martin Biersch. I went to high school with Martin (not to be confused with Vinny Kaplan of the Hy-Vee cereal aisle) and one night the August after we graduated, a bunch of people were hanging out at the pool at my friend Erin's house. I guess you could say Martin and I had a moment, and though we'd barely spoken in four years of high school, we started emailing each other after I went to Duke and he went to the U of Missouri, aka Mizzou (not sure if he ever went to see any shows at the Blue Note but I've heard it's a cool space, possibly a former movie theater). Martin and I emailed each other every few days from late Aug/early Sept to Thanksgiving break. Our emails weren't explicitly romantic but they weren't explicitly not romantic either (such things can be murky, right?). And then we both were back in KC for Thanksgiving break and there was this particular bar that people from my high school used to go to the night before Thanksgiving because they served you without an ID. When Martin and I saw each other there, it was probably the most awkward interaction of my entire life. Like, I could barely speak. And same for him. Looking back, I think the awkwardness was because whatever the dynamic was between us was unclear—neither of us knew if it was more friendly or flirty—and also, and I don't mean to be glib on this topic, I'm pretty sure we were both totally sober (I definitely was). We interacted for about six minutes, most in total silence (I think I talk an average amount now, but I was extremely quiet through college, and Martin was a quiet guy, too) and then I said I had to go to the bathroom and we haven't spoken or emailed since. Do you think he's still waiting for me to come back from the bathroom?

Pen pal 3 (my 3rd year at TNO / 2011)—You and I kind of discussed this at the after-after party, but by this time, I'd just turned 30, divorced, and had cycled through a mindfuck of a non-relationship with another TNO writer. Years after most people our age, I tried online dating for the first time. And I made a total rookie mistake by matching with a guy whose name I don't remember and exchanging emails with him probably three times a day for three weeks before meeting. And then we met and had NO chemistry. It wasn't awkward in the excruciating Martin way. It was more like when you sit down next to someone on a plane flight and mutually have not one iota of interest in each other. Obviously, endlessly emailing someone before meeting is a waste of time, but I do still wonder whether a person's writing self is their realest self, their fakest self, or just a different self than their in-the-world self? Or maybe emailing with someone a lot before meeting is ill-advised not because the other person is real or fake but because there inevitably will be a discrepancy between your idea of them and the reality. Have you ever tried online dating? For that matter, do you fly on commercial planes? If not, they're this thing where many people who don't know each other but are traveling to the same city board the same aircraft at the same time, like a bus in the sky.

Anyway, this is how all my pen pals measure up:

Freja: A- (Anything lower seems mean, right? Since she was a child at the time)

Martin: B- (It was kind of interesting to get a window into someone else's first semester at college, especially because I wasn't very happy freshman year, but his writing style was pedestrian)

Guy Whose Name I Can't Remember from Dating Website That No Longer Exists: B (I also can't remember any of our specific emails, but it has to count for something that I was motivated to respond)

You: A+ (Clearly!!) Also you were an adorable 14-year-old

It's very sweet and a little mortifying that you've watched my sketches. I'm tempted to give disclaimers about how topical comedy doesn't hold up well, but instead I am going to just say thank you. I'm sorry about the death of Christopher, which I did know about. The accident and his death both sound sad and terrible. I'm glad you decided after that to continue being a musician and I know a lot of other people are too.

And, in a different way, I also am glad you didn't delete the paragraph about eating and exercise. On the one hand, I think I know something about appearance pressures because I'm a woman who lives in America in the 21st century (maybe that could just be because I'm a woman, full stop), and because, working with people whose job is to be on camera, I've seen their insecurities and the criticism they get, even though they're really attractive. On the other hand, I actually can't imagine having my appearance publicly dissected by strangers, and it seems unfair that that matters so much when your looks are wholly unrelated to your ability to write songs and play guitar. For what it's worth, I remember you at TNO as terrifyingly fit, and it's very possible you look better having gained 13 pounds. In any case, in the last few days, my own sense of you as a Leather Shorts Wearer has been superseded by my sense of you as a digital consciousness that I'm communicating with (very enjoyably!). When I see your name in my inbox, I wonder what you'll say about your childhood or your life right now more than I think about what you looked like in leather shorts. Not that you DIDN'T look good in leather shorts. You looked as good in leather shorts as a person can . . . I mean, okay, eek, I fear this is reaching Martin Biersch at Thanksgiving 2000 levels of awkwardness.

One more sidenote: Apropos of my declaration above about thinking that I understand appearance pressure because I'm a woman, yet another of the reasons I suspect it's almost time for me to move on from TNO is that, while so much of my worldview has been shaped by beliefs about men and women and sexism and feminism, most younger writers at the show accept as a given that gender is a social construct. And to my surprise, the more I read on this subject, the more I agree. In 2012, when I got a sketch on air about elementary school girls playing four square at recess, it felt subversive and notable. I guess it's a sign of progress that now it's just accepted as fact at TNO that the world is wildly sexist (thanks, 2016 election?) and that "female" topics are as worthy as "male" ones. On a good day, this makes me think my work is done, and on a bad day, it makes me think I'm about to be put out to pasture.

Before I go, what is your favorite color? Do you have any pets?

from: Noah Brewster <NoahRBrewster@gmail.com>
to: Sally Milz <Smilz@TNOshow.com>
date: Jul 24, 2020, 10:40 PM
subject: Actually

This is all fascinating . . . but raises a lot more questions than it answers. For starters:

-I assume you only have the letters Freja wrote you and not the ones you wrote her? Which is such a bummer because I bet the letters that 4th grade Sally wrote were pretty spectacular. Maybe even national treasure level.

-What does "having a moment" with Martin mean? Is that a euphemism that everyone except me knows? It seems like the Martin anecdote is missing a few key details.

- I appreciate the reassurance about being the best pen pal ever but admit I am still feeling a little insecure that you are so much more experienced than I am. (I guess that's not a question.)

-Yeah, such things are sometimes murky. (I guess that's not a question, either.)

-Your marriage and divorce . . . is there a pdf somewhere I can download to get a comprehensive overview of when/where/why?

-Same question as above but about the TNO mindfucker.

About online dating . . . a few years ago I tried an app that is supposed to be "discreet" . . . not like for people doing shady things but for respecting users' privacy. I went on a couple dates through this, none memorable. I'm not convinced online dating is for me. Even with the supposed emphasis on privacy, when I was texting with women, I needed to keep in mind that any of them could talk to or even be a reporter for a shitty gossip website. I'm sure that being so wary didn't increase my likelihood of making a connection. For the record, I don't worry at all that you will sell me out.

About how I fly . . . it's usually in a space shuttle that takes off with rocket boosters. My time is so precious that this allows me to get where I'm going as efficiently as possible without having to interact with the riffraff. Yes, of course I sometimes fly commercial! Admittedly, it's first class and if the airport has a private terminal, that's where I wait. On tour, sometimes we charter a plane and sometimes it's a bus, and even with the fancier buses, there are very unglamorous parts . . . traffic, band members getting sick, band members washing their hair with the non-potable water, and on and on. And yet on those buses I have for sure had some of my happiest times.

My favorite color is yellow. I do not have any pets but would like a rabbit.

from: Noah Brewster <NoahRBrewster@gmail.com>
to: Sally Milz <Smilz@TNOshow.com>
date: Jul 25, 2020, 9:03 AM
subject: Actually

Sally,

Since sending that last email I have realized that asking if I can download a pdf about your marriage and divorce probably sounded disrespectful and I'm very sorry. I was trying to be funny, but I crossed a line. I want you to know that I realize (from watching my sister and some friends) that getting divorced is a very challenging life experience, and I shouldn't have been flippant about it. As I've said before, these emails right now are really a lifeline for me. I hope I have not done anything to jeopardize our communication.

Best,
Noah

from: Sally Milz <Smilz@TNOshow.com>
to: Noah Brewster <NoahRBrewster@gmail.com>
date: Jul 25, 2020, 9:32 AM
subject: Actually

I wish you could see how hard I'm laughing right now. You also get an A+ in squirming apologies. I especially appreciate how you included a salutation (I wasn't sure before this if you knew my name) and a signature (because before this I wasn't sure what your name was). But the "Best" is a really nice touch, like you were reaching out to ask if my marketing firm is currently hiring.

First of all, didn't I tell you back in 2018 that anyone who works at TNO is hard to offend? The reason I didn't reply yet wasn't that I was offended. It was just that it's taking me a long time to figure out how to summarize my marriage and the mindfuck. I'm still working on them! Maybe the emails should be divided into two parts, like Czechoslovakia in 1992.

Second, there are a lot of things about all marriages, including mine, that deserve flippancy and disrespect. Unfortunately, my marriage itself was kind of boring and not that funny, but it's safe to say that I am not someone who thinks marriage as an institution is sacrosanct. In fact, I aspire to find anything in life sacrosanct.

Seriously, your remorse here is very endearing, in addition to being hilarious. Please consider saying a few more things that you think are inappropriate and then apologizing for them.

In the meantime, as I write up my marriage/mindfuck opus, I have to congratulate you on your perceptiveness in realizing I left some details out of the Martin story. "Having a moment" with Martin means that (steel yourself?! Again?) I lost my virginity to him IN Erin's pool (!) while other people were sitting in the lounge chairs approximately ten feet away (!!). I guess out of deference to the other people, Martin and I didn't kiss while semi-publicly boning.

In other words, no, you don't need to worry about my selling you out because, although there's a smaller audience for my secrets, we're in a mutually assured destruction situation. Not that I'd sell you out anyway.

from: Noah Brewster <NoahRBrewster@gmail.com>
to: Sally Milz <Smilz@TNOshow.com>
date: Jul 25, 2020, 10:18 AM
subject: Actually

Phew!!!

I have to admit I got kinda spooked by that part about how you never emailed Martin again after the Thanksgiving awkwardness. I don't want you to ever stop emailing me!

I guess my main question about Martin is, was it a good experience for you? I have a bombshell to drop, something that no one in my whole life knows about me except my sister. See? I really do trust you! The bombshell is that my first album came out before I'd ever had sex. Everyone interpreted Making Love in July (a song I know you have great fondness for) as autobiographical, but I'd never "made love" in real life before its release and didn't until four months later. If you're trying to do the math, I was nineteen when the song came out and twenty by the time I lost my virginity. The song was a fantasy of sex, not a memory. When I wrote it, I'd kissed a couple girls, but that was it. My all-boys' high school was affiliated with a girls' school more or less on the same campus, and junior and senior year, we could take classes at their school and vice versa, so I can't even use the single-sex school thing as an excuse. I just had no game. Also my black nail polish phase, while brief, may have made girls think I was gay. (Speaking of, gender is absolutely a social construct . . . didn't David Bowie and Prince teach us that? At the same time, I'm sure there's always a place for your thoughts on men and women and sexism and feminism.)

A part of my virgin story that for some reason I think you might appreciate is that there are two separate actresses, Angela Shinske and Kathryn Woo, who the media often says Making Love in July is about, and Angela goes along with these claims, even though she and I only ever went on two dates, and by then it was 2004. Kathryn and I dated for longer, and she was my date to the 2002 Grammys, but I'd written the song well before then.

So . . . is your marketing firm currently hiring?

from: Sally Milz <Smilz@TNOshow.com>
to: Noah Brewster <NoahRBrewster@gmail.com>
date: Jul 25, 2020, 10:59 AM
subject: Actually

Wait, who DID you lose your virginity to? (Yes, I am ending a sentence with a preposition, but that's how urgently I need to know.) Did you tell the other person she'd deflowered you? I've always assumed that the Great Pool Boning of August 2000 was Martin's first time, too, and I wouldn't say it was magical, but it wasn't a negative experience, which I think counts as a win?

I hope you are not disappointed to learn that I don't find it shocking or embarrassing that you didn't have sex until you were twenty. I beat you by, what, just a year or two?

Regarding our emailing versus my emailing with Martin, this situation feels pretty different. Because you and I are adults? And because he and I had hardly spoken outside the pool (or in the pool, for that matter) whereas you and I have before this correspondence had many deep conversations about cheese, panthers, and snakes. Hmm, maybe these aren't such persuasive points after all. But I suspect unless either of us has changed dramatically in the last two years, we have a sense of what it's like to talk to each other in the same room.

Although, since we have arrived at this somewhat weird juncture . . . I don't know . . . do you have a handle on what we're doing here? Can you tell I'm borrowing your ellipses right now? To . . . convey . . . my . . . laidback . . . chill . . . personality . . .

from: Noah Brewster <NoahRBrewster@gmail.com>
to: Sally Milz <Smilz@TNOshow.com>
date: Jul 25, 2020, 11:26 AM
subject: Actually

Nope, I can't say that I have a handle on what we're doing. But it's fun, huh?

I lost my virginity to . . . I am white knuckling it here . . . a model named Brittain Smith. Brittain and I met at the premiere of a movie I had a song in and dated for just a few months. I much later seriously dated one other model, whose name is Maribel Johnson. For the record, those are the only two models I've ever dated, period. Not that I feel the need to justify it . . . in fact, it seems very sexist that anyone would automatically assume a relationship with a model is shallow. But the bigger reason I reacted badly when you said that thing in the bar about 22-year-old models is that when someone brings it up as a way of accusing me of being a playboy, it's not only insulting but just plain wrong.

Send the marriage/mindfuck pdf!

from: Sally Milz <Smilz@TNOshow.com>
to: Noah Brewster <NoahRBrewster@gmail.com>
date: Jul 25, 2020, 5:12 PM
subject: Actually

This might seem off-topic, but in my experience, there are two kinds of TNO hosts. With the good kind, the mood preparing for a show is fun. Everyone is aware of the host's higher status, and accordingly deferential, but we're all trying to achieve the same goal. With bad hosts, the person's status is the defining element of being in a room with them, because that's clearly the lens through which they view life—they're textbook narcissists. In that case, no matter how rude or unreasonable the host is, the TNO staff contorts itself to make sure they're happy with every situation while also getting the show on air by Saturday at 11:30. That kind of host isn't invited back. Even so, after their week, I feel dirty for having exerted a lot of energy to make them look good.

To be clear, you are 1000% not a noxious narcissist. But I can't help starting to wonder why I'm trying so hard to entertain you (and to compliment you! and to assuage you!). Because you're a celebrity? Who's bored during the pandemic? And I'm lucky to get attention from you? Until a vaccine exists and you can go back to surfing in Costa Rica and singing to a stadium of 18,000 people?

from: Noah Brewster <NoahRBrewster@gmail.com>
to: Sally Milz <Smilz@TNOshow.com>
date: Jul 25, 2020, 8:58 PM
subject: Actually

Sally, I'm really sorry if I've offended you. I'm confused because it feels like things just went off the rails, but I don't know
why. When I said I never want you to stop emailing me, did
that make you think I'm taking you for granted? I intended to
express the opposite. It is such a true joy to be in touch with
you and I was trying to tell you how grateful I am and how awesome I think you are. I'm not disputing that I may have done
something wrong here, but I'm not sure what it was.

If someone were to ask me, "Are you a celebrity?" my answer
would be "Yes, I'm a celebrity." If the question was "Does
America have a fucked up love-hate relationship with celebrities?" my answer to that is "Definitely, yes." Fame is kinda
something I chose . . . albeit without fully understanding what
I was choosing . . . and kinda something that chose me. It has
huge advantages and some disadvantages, but at this point
it's just a fact of my life. When you point out that I'm a celebrity,
you're not revealing something I'm trying to conceal. And it
isn't a part of my identity that can be separated from the other

parts. It's not something I have the option of leaving at home on some days, like an umbrella.

All of that said, I'm a person to exactly the same degree you're a person. I'm not a mannequin who stands on a stage and plays the guitar. Maybe my feelings, hopes, and worries aren't identical to yours, but I hope I don't need to convince you that I have feelings, hopes, and worries. The biggest bummer about your last email is the implication that I'm using you. I thought our emailing was mutual . . . mutually fun . . . and in the last few days when I have told you how into it I am, I was trying to compliment you, not make you feel like you are obligated to amuse me. Aren't we all just looking for someone to talk about everything with? Someone worth the effort of telling our stories and opinions to, whose stories and opinions we actually want to hear?

from: Sally Milz <Smilz@TNOshow.com>
to: Noah Brewster <NoahRBrewster@gmail.com>
date: Jul 25, 2020, 10:15 PM
subject: Actually

1) You HAVE been in therapy, haven't you? That's an ass-hole's way of saying I appreciate your very calm response to my half-crazy (75% crazy?) email that I have felt remorseful about ever since hitting Send. (Send is capitalized for a differ-ent reason from why Sentence 1 was capitalized in the first email I sent you—but maybe those will also be stories for an-other day?)

2) This is a weird question but do you remember when you were rehearsing the song Ambiguous at TNO and I sat near the stage and listened? And if you do remember, would you say you were serenading me?

from: Noah Brewster <NoahRBrewster@gmail.com>
to: Sally Milz <Smilz@TNOshow.com>
date: Jul 25, 2020, 10:21 PM
subject: Actually

I remember that perfectly. And I'm happy to answer your question but what do you mean by serenading?

from: Sally Milz <Smilz@TNOshow.com>
to: Noah Brewster <NoahRBrewster@gmail.com>
date: Jul 25, 2020, 10:24 PM
subject: Actually

Were you trying to seduce me?

from: Noah Brewster <NoahRBrewster@gmail.com>
to: Sally Milz <Smilz@TNOshow.com>
date: Jul 25, 2020, 10:33 PM
subject: Actually

I'm nervous right now because it seems like there's a right and wrong answer to your question, and I'm not sure which is which. So I'm just going to be honest because I've heard there's no point in having a pandemic pen pal if you're not honest.

I would say I was definitely trying to impress you and I was not trying to seduce you.

from: Noah Brewster <NoahRBrewster@gmail.com>
to: Sally Milz <Smilz@TNOshow.com>
date: Jul 25, 2020, 10:58 PM
subject: Actually

Where'd you go?

from: Noah Brewster <NoahRBrewster@gmail.com>
to: Sally Milz <Smilz@TNOshow.com>
date: Jul 25, 2020, 11:19 PM
subject: Actually

Wrong answer, huh?

from: Sally Milz <Smilz@TNOshow.com>
to: Noah Brewster <NoahRBrewster@gmail.com>
date: Jul 26, 2020, 12:25 AM
subject: Actually

Okay, here's the story of my marriage: As a middle class white girl, I can't claim I was out of place at Duke from a socioeconomic standpoint (this is how all juicy and romantic stories begin, right?), but I was a bad fit for the fraternity-sorority/country club vibe of the campus. I almost never went to parties and barely had friends until I joined the staff of the student newspaper my sophomore year. First I was one of the copy editors, and eventually I was the copy chief. This meant I stayed late, read practically every article that was filed, and was fairly invisible in a way that suited me. (Nigel says that TNO isn't a place for perfectionists or lone wolves, and because I'm naturally both, working there has taught me to fight those tendencies.)

Anyway, the sports editor of the newspaper my senior year was a guy named Mike. He'd also worked his way up, so we'd interacted tons of times (while I copyedited his articles about, say, men's tennis) without really getting to know each other. At a staff happy hour on Halloween, a columnist named Derrick got falling down drunk, and Mike and I ended up walking him back to his dorm room and putting him to bed. It was only maybe eight o'clock on a Friday, and campus was filled with people in all kinds of crazy costumes planning all kinds of wild nights, but both Mike and I were worried that Derrick was going to throw up, choke on it, and die, so we parked ourselves in his room, with the lights low, to keep an eye on him. We sat on the floor and talked for a few hours, until we decided it was safe to leave. I honestly don't think we'd have gotten together if not for babysitting Derrick (though I think this is true for plenty of relationships, that they're random at least as often as they're inevitable), but we quickly became a serious couple (in every sense). Mike was applying to law schools then, and he ended up deciding on Chapel Hill, which is just 20 minutes from Duke. He was (is? Because he's still alive, if not still part of my life) from Charlotte, NC, and it was already understood that when he finished law school, he'd go back there.

In the spring of our senior year, we decided to get married. Neither of us was being pressured by our parents—his parents actually were religious, but not in a way where they'd have been upset if we lived together without getting married. My mom said that she had concerns because people can change a lot in their twenties and Mike and I might evolve out of wanting to be a couple, but that she also thought I had the right to make my own decisions. We got married at the Durham County Courthouse the Friday after our graduation, in front of Mike's parents and brother, my mom and Jerry, and two of our friends from the newspaper. That Monday, I started my job as a writer at an in-house newsletter for a gigantic medical device company (AdlerWilliams).

When I look back, I simultaneously think it's fine that Mike and I got married, no animals were injured, etc., AND it seems like we did it for terrible reasons—at best, in order to cross off what we perceived as the biggest item on the to-do list of adulthood, at worst, because we were scared of life after college. Or maybe those are the same thing, or maybe I just mean I was scared. In theory, I wanted to move to New York or LA and write for TV, but I didn't know anyone in the industry and I was too chicken to go to one of those cities alone. I suppose I wanted to absolve myself of responsibility for my own happiness—I could blame Mike for trapping me in NC.

Every July, while working at AdlerWilliams, as a secret annual rite that no one besides Mike knew about, I submitted a sketch packet to TNO. The first time I ever did this, the head writer, who was then Ollie Toubey, called me eight weeks later and said something like "We can't make you an offer right now, but you're talented and we encourage you to apply again." It was a three-minute conversation that was the most exciting thing that had ever happened to me. I kept applying and being rejected for the next few years (and not hearing directly from anyone again), during which time Mike graduated from law school, we moved to Charlotte, and I got a new job as a writer at a magazine for a high-end credit card (Luxuries Monthly? Perhaps you subscribe? Against your will?). And then in late September 2009, on a Monday, I got a call from Ollie saying, "Can you come to the TNO office tomorrow to interview?" And I said, "Oh, wow, this is amazing, but I live in North Carolina." And Ollie said, "Cool, can you come to the TNO office tomorrow to interview?" I spent $880 on the ticket, which was the most I'd ever spent on anything. And I made a reservation at the Holiday Inn Express at the Newark airport, but I went straight from getting off the plane to the 66 building, so I was dragging my suitcase. I interviewed with Ollie and his deputy, Ursula, and they were the smartest and funniest people I'd ever met, then they told me to wait outside Nigel's office to meet him. I waited for seven hours, which as you might know is unremarkable—Henrietta had to wait outside his office for three days (the day I was there, he was taking a helicopter in from the Hamptons). I finally met him at ten o'clock at night, we had a very anodyne exchange that felt like it was over before it began, and I spent most of it describing working for Luxuries and for AdlerWilliams's newsletter (which was called Heartbeats). I assumed that he couldn't have found me more boring. I left his office after about eight minutes and sat in the hall again, and Ollie and Ursula went into his office for an even shorter time than I'd been in there then came back out, led me to Ollie's office, and said, "Can you start tomorrow?" Even now, I don't have the words to express how shocked and thrilled and overwhelmed and disbelieving I was. It was like swimming in the ocean and feeling something shift under you and the next thing you know, a gigantic magical sea creature that you never knew existed is rising out of the water with you on its back.

After this, outside 66, my suitcase and I got in a cab to the Holiday Inn Express, and I was shaking with excitement as I called Mike and told him the news. In this very subdued voice, he says, "It's too bad you can't do it," and I'm like, "Why can't I do it?" and he says, "Because we live in Charlotte."

Me: Why can't we move?
Mike: Because I'm licensed to be a lawyer here.
Me: Then why can't I commute?
Mike: Because what's the point of being married if we don't live in the same place?
(Long silence.)
Me: If you aren't willing to move to New York, why didn't you ever say that while I was submitting packets to TNO for the last five years?
Mike (matter-of-factly): Because I never thought they'd hire you.

I could say a lot of other things about this, but the salient ones are that 1) Mike did have a sense of humor and actively liked comedy. We went to see stand-up together, and we watched TNO and comedy specials. 2) He read my submission packets every year.

Although I realized somewhat belatedly that he didn't think I was funny or talented, Mike wasn't a jerk. He was a very calm, responsible, quiet person who believed he'd married another calm, responsible, quiet person. And, as my cab entered the Lincoln Tunnel, I thought to myself, Thank god we don't have kids because that will make our divorce much less messy. Sidenote: He still lives in North Carolina, is married, and is now a father of two.

My narrative instincts tell me I should take a breather here, that we should have some kind of palate-cleansing epistolary sorbet, or at least I should give you the chance to respond, but my wish for resolution propels me forward, to Part 2: The Mindfucker, which at least is far more succinct than Part 1: The Husband.

As you and I have already partially covered, in my second year at TNO, I developed a raging crush on a fellow writer (spoiler: It was your buddy Elliot). I half convinced myself he had a raging crush on me, in part because he wasn't espe-cially hot. That is, to my eye, he wasn't out of my league. At the season finale after-party, I told him (in a way that deserves a solid 9 out of 10 on the Martin Biersch Awkwardness Scale) that I was in love with him and he said, "Sally, you've confused the romance of comedy with the romance of romance."

I'm still not sure if this was a brilliant or supremely douchey thing to say. Maybe both? Certainly he was within his rights in not reciprocating my interest, and I soon concluded that if we'd dated and broken up, it could have ruined TNO for me, and if we'd gotten together and married and had kids, that could have ruined TNO for me in a different way. I decided I'd never again try to date anyone at TNO, which admittedly might have been a bit of a tree falling in the forest situation.

This is all a (very very) long way of saying that after being married to a guy who didn't like what made me me, and then being friends with a guy who adored me but didn't want to make out with me, I don't trust my own instincts. Both those situations scrambled my brain, and I know it's a small sample size, but I decided to be done with that shit. And now our emails are scrambling me again.

from: Noah Brewster <NoahRBrewster@gmail.com>
to: Sally Milz <Smilz@TNOshow.com>
date: Jul 26, 2020, 12:41 AM
subject: Actually

This might sound corny, but thank you for telling me all of that.
I'm glad I know it.

There are tons of things I want to respond to, but the one that
feels the most urgent now is why are our emails scrambling
your brain?

from: Sally Milz <Smilz@TNOshow.com>
to: Noah Brewster <NoahRBrewster@gmail.com>
date: Jul 26, 2020, 12:43 AM
subject: Actually

At the risk of destroying my favorite hobby of quarantine, because I'm in danger of confusing the romance of emailing with
the romance of romance.

from: Noah Brewster <NoahRBrewster@gmail.com>
to: Sally Milz <Smilz@TNOshow.com>
date: Jul 26, 2020, 12:44 AM
subject: Actually

Why wouldn't this be the romance of romance?

from: Sally Milz <Smilz@TNOshow.com>
to: Noah Brewster <NoahRBrewster@gmail.com>
date: Jul 26, 2020, 12:45 AM
subject: Actually

Because of the Danny Horst Rule?

from: Noah Brewster <NoahRBrewster@gmail.com>
to: Sally Milz <Smilz@TNOshow.com>
date: Jul 26, 2020, 12:46 AM
subject: Actually

Didn't I tell you in 2018 I don't believe in that?

from: Sally Milz <Smilz@TNOshow.com>
to: Noah Brewster <NoahRBrewster@gmail.com>
date: Jul 26, 2020, 12:49 AM
subject: Actually

I actually don't think I'm particularly insecure about my appearance. For both our sakes, I'll refrain from inventorying my face and body and just say that while of course I have some criticisms of myself, I feel lucky to be healthy, and never more so than now.

I'm also pretty sure it would disrupt the space-time continuum for a world-famous singer who looks like you to get involved with a TV writer who looks like me.

from: Noah Brewster <NoahRBrewster@gmail.com>
to: Sally Milz <Smilz@TNOshow.com>
date: Jul 26, 2020, 12:51 AM
subject: Actually

Sometimes, and this is one of your charms, it's hard for me to tell how much you're kidding. But I'm really attracted to you, and I have been since that pitch meeting in Nigel's office.

from: Sally Milz <Smilz@TNOshow.com>
to: Noah Brewster <NoahRBrewster@gmail.com>
date: Jul 26, 2020, 12:52 AM
subject: Actually

Sometimes it's also hard for me to tell how much I'm kidding.
But you didn't look so bad at that pitch meeting, either.

from: Noah Brewster <NoahRBrewster@gmail.com>
to: Sally Milz <Smilz@TNOshow.com>
date: Jul 26, 2020, 12:52 AM
subject: Actually

I realize this also might disrupt the space-time continuum but
can I just call you right now?

CHAPTER 3

August 2020

At the Hampton Inn in Albuquerque, New Mexico, halfway between Kansas City and L.A., I checked in while needing to pee so badly I couldn't stand up straight. I was the only person in the lobby other than the man behind the desk. He and I both wore cloth masks—mine featured strawberries, his was plain blue—and I said, "How full are you tonight?" and he said, "Not."

In the room, as I finished washing my hands, my phone vibrated in the side pocket of my leggings, and after I dried my hands (were the towels clean? Was anything?), I pulled it out.

LMK when you're at hotel, Noah had texted.

Then: *Have I mentioned I'm super excited you're coming here?*

Then: *I'm super excited you're coming here!!*

I looked at myself in the mirror above the sink and tried to figure out what expression a woman driving 1,600 miles to visit Noah Brewster would make. It would be sultry, right? Which was a problem because with effort, I could do friendly, and I could always do smirky, but I wasn't sure I was physically capable of sultry.

A week had passed since Noah and I had first spoken on the phone; twelve days had passed since I'd received his first email; and thirteen hours, counting stops to refuel, had passed since I'd pulled out of Jerry's driveway. I'd borrowed Jerry's sister's Hyundai, loaded up with a suitcase, a backpack, a purse, and an open cardboard box containing a water bottle, a twelve-count case of protein bars, four apples, three separate containers of 33.8 fluid ounces of hand sanitizer, and a bunch of masks inside a gallon Ziploc bag. Once I'd decided I was driving rather than flying, I'd calculated that I could make it in two very unpleasantly long days or three moderately unpleasant ones. Because I hoped (but was not sure) that I was on my way to have sex with Noah and because I wanted to have sex with Noah as soon as possible, I'd opted for two.

Presumably, after accepting Noah's invitation to visit, I ought to have been wonderstruck by the human capacity for connection even during the darkest times. And I was! But also I was preoccupied with how and when to address the disheveled and hairy state into which I'd descended during the pandemic. During our first phone conversation, he'd said that maybe the next day, we could facetime, and the minute we'd hung up, even though it was after three in the morning, I'd zealously tweezed my eyebrows and bleached the hair above my upper lip with the same possibly toxic cream I'd been using since middle school. But the following night, he'd called again rather than facetiming, meaning that I'd been denied the opportunity to pretend I was spontaneous and denuded and spontaneously denuded.

When we'd agreed that I was really, actually going to drive to California, I'd immediately begun strategizing about how I could arrive at his house (at Noah's house! The house of Noah Brewster!) after two thirteen-hour days on the road looking and smelling as unbeastly as possible. I planned to touch up my eyebrows and shave my legs, armpits, and bikini line in the morning, at the hotel in Albuquerque. And while of course I'd shower before leaving New Mexico, I'd devoted extensive thought to whether, upon reaching Los Angeles, I ought to find a place to shower again before getting to Noah—a truck stop? A hotel room? A friend's empty apartment?

But I'd decided not to introduce another logistical or social variable; I was telling no one I knew who lived there that I was visiting. Instead, before reaching Noah's house, I would stop at a gas station, which was just about all that was open in California at this point in the shutdown, to brush my teeth and perhaps apply a fresh coat of deodorant over my flop sweat.

All of which was to say that the sketches I'd written over the years about the absurdity and arbitrariness of beauty standards for women had arisen not from my clear-eyed renunciation of them but from my resentment at their hold on me. But more pronounced than my anxiety about whether Noah would think I was cute enough to smooch—even now, when it was plausible that he was so lonely that all he required was a warm body and a pulse—was my fear that it didn't matter *how* I looked because I'd misunderstood and this was not in fact a really, really inconvenient booty call.

I hadn't yet responded to Noah's texts from a minute before when another came through: *When we talk tonight there's something we should discuss*

Oh shit, I thought, and immediately my brain began supplying possibilities: *I'm celibate. I'm gay. I have Covid again. I've invited you here to ghostwrite my jokes for an upcoming Zoom appearance on a late-night talk show.*

And then one last text that wasn't exactly reassuring: *It's nothing bad*

On the night that I had emailed Noah my number, he'd called a minute later. Perhaps this efficiency shouldn't have provided enough time for me to get nervous, but my heart was thudding and I wondered as I said "Hi" if that one tiny syllable would reveal that my voice was shaking.

"Hey, Sally." Noah sounded relaxed and confident, like a man who stood on stages singing to adoring crowds, a man widely agreed upon by the American public to be exceptionally handsome. "Are you in your childhood bedroom right now? With all the Indigo Girls posters?"

"Sadly, I never had any," I said. "That would have been much cooler than the poster I did have with the Thoreau quote about lives of quiet desperation. Oh, and I also had an Audrey Hepburn poster to signify that I was classy and feminine." Because this wasn't the conversation I'd been expecting—I didn't know what I had been expecting, but not this—I could feel myself become marginally less nervous. "What posters did you have?"

"Just to be boringly predictable, mostly musicians. Jimi Hendrix, The Velvet Underground, the cover of Nirvana's *Nevermind* album. You are very classy and feminine, by the way."

"Is *Nevermind* the one with the pool and the baby penis?"

"I think it's supposed to be a condemnation of capitalism because the baby is reaching for a dollar bill, but maybe same difference."

"There really isn't much of my old stuff here anymore," I said. "There's the wicker furniture, but no graduation caps or stuffed animals or earring trees. No identifying markers of my teenage self."

"Oh, man," he said. "White wicker?"

"The bed frame, the bedside table, and the desk are all wicker, and there's a wicker armchair, which is where I'm sitting. I assume you're also sitting in a white wicker armchair?"

"Of course," he said. "Always."

This time, I laughed.

"I'm in my study," he said. "Does that make me sound intellectual?"

"Are you smoking a pipe and wearing a monocle?"

"And a velvet jacket," he said. "Truthfully, the main thing I study in my study is the TV screen. My bedroom is where I read."

"Reading and watching TV are both noble activities," I said. "That's important to remember."

"Especially watching TV on Saturday nights at eleven-thirty, right?"

"Do you not have a TV in your bedroom?"

He laughed. "No, I have one there, too. And one in the sitting room off the kitchen."

After I'd received Noah's second email—the one that mentioned he was in L.A. and that, like his first email, did not make it seem as if he was reaching out for a business-related reason—I'd googled *Noah Brewster Los Angeles house*. Of course I had; I wasn't brain-dead. As per the Internet: located in Topanga Canyon, purchased in 2014 for nine million dollars and *then* renovated down to the studs, a six-bedroom / eight-bathroom Spanish hacienda on ten acres with a pool, pool house, and freestanding recording studio built in 2016. A men's magazine had run photos of him taken in the studio as well as next to and in the pool—one shot showed him standing in the shallow end wearing a drenched white T-shirt that clung gratifyingly to the muscles in his arms and abdomen—while a shelter magazine had an online spread of the interior of the house accompanied by a long conversation between him and a British architect.

After I'd googled *Noah Brewster Los Angeles house,* the Internet suggested that I also google *Noah Brewster net worth,* and who was I to decline? The answer, which may have been accurate or completely wrong, was ninety-five million dollars.

On the phone, there was a brief silence, then Noah said, "So I think you should come visit me. And I think we should hang out and keep talking about all the things we've been talking about over email. What do you think of that?"

"Okay."

"Wait, do you think I'm kidding?"

"*Are* you kidding?"

"No."

"I wasn't kidding, either. And as luck would have it, my schedule is pretty open now."

He laughed. "So is mine. So how about, I don't know, tomorrow? The next day? You'll probably make fun of me for this, but one option is for my P.A. to arrange a plane to bring you."

"That sounds very *Fifty Shades of Grey.*"

"Yeah, somehow I haven't gotten around to reading that. But if we charter a flight, you skip the terminal and security, which I assume are the germ hotspots."

"I got the *Fifty Shades* books for some quick research for a sketch, and the next thing I knew I'd consumed fifteen hundred pages about Ben Wa balls and riding crops." I hesitated. I didn't know how much it cost to charter a flight, but it seemed like a destabilizing way to start things with Noah. I said, "A private plane sounds a little, uh, intense. But visiting you sounds great."

"You don't have to decide about the plane now. If you end up flying commercial, just promise me you'll wear a KN95."

"Do you know what people like me call flying commercial?" I said. "We call it flying."

"Yeah, I guess I asked for that."

This conversation had started after midnight, and we were then on the phone for two and a half hours more, discussing how the kids of one of his side project band members were sewing masks for residents of nursing homes; and how while walking Sugar that evening I'd passed a slim white woman in a T-shirt that said *Good Vibes Only,* and how that seemed like a thing a slim white woman shouldn't be wearing at this particular cultural moment; and how I was reading a novel set in Communist Romania; and how he was reading a book of nonfiction about the future of artificial intelligence but the truth was that he read it only at night and rarely got through more than a few pages before falling asleep; and how the previous week, he had started writing a new song for the first time since he'd had Covid and it hadn't gone incredibly well but also hadn't been a disaster; and about how in the Indigo Girls' "Dairy Queen," there was a lyric I'd never been clear on because it kind of sounded like "to hold you" but it also kind of sounded like "to haunt you" and if you looked it up online it said *hold,* but I wanted it to be *haunt;* and about the Dairy Queen chain and how he'd never been to one, and I said that was because he'd never lived in the Midwest; and about how I'd never been to In-N-Out Burger, and he said that was because I'd never lived in California. By then, it was almost three-thirty my time and I felt like the teenager I'd never been, drugged on lust and conversation. Just before we hung up, I said, "Usually I hate talking on the phone, but I don't hate talking on the phone to you."

"I'll try not to let that go to my head." He sounded very happy, and I felt a squeezing around my heart. Wasn't this all too good to be true? For the last week, whenever I hadn't actively been writing an email to or reading an email from Noah, as I'd scrambled eggs or dragged the trash and recycling bins to the curb, I'd often pulled my phone from my pocket and reread both the messages he'd sent me and the ones I'd sent him, especially if I was waiting for a response; more than once I read all the emails, in order, in their entirety. I also had continuously composed future emails in my head and assessed almost any experience I was having—not, admittedly, that I was having many—through the filter of whether they'd be worth describing to Noah. And now we'd spoken and it hadn't ruined everything!

He added, "Can I call you again tomorrow night?"

"You definitely can," I said.

"Can I email you seven times before I call you tomorrow night?"

"I'm hoping you will."

This was when he said, "I almost suggested facetiming now instead of calling. What are your feelings about facetime?"

"It depends on the face in question." After a pause, I said, "In your case, I'm pro."

He laughed. "What a relief." Then he said, "Good night, Sally. This was very fun."

"I agree," I said. "Good night, Noah."

But he didn't email the next day; instead, at noon my time, he texted, *Hope it's OK I just ordered these for you,* followed by a screenshot of a pink pillow that said *Good Vibes Please* in white cursive, followed by another screenshot of an orange pillow that said *Good Vibes Welcome* with an image of a sun below the words, followed by another text that said *It was hard to decide so I got both.*

I texted back, *That's an incredible coincidence because I just ordered this for you,* and sent a screenshot of a distressed wooden sign that said *In this house, we keep it real, we give hugs, and we dance badly.*

He texted back, *Truly amazing because for your kitchen I just ordered,* followed by a screenshot of a different distressed wooden sign that said *'Bout to Stir Up Some Shit* and featured an image of a whisk. And then we texted for three hours and then we talked again that night from 10 P.M. to 2 A.M. central. At 9:50 P.M. I had applied foundation and mascara and lip gloss, then I had wiped the lip gloss off, then I had reapplied it. At ten, the notification of a facetime call had appeared on my phone, but before I could see him, it had disappeared, and a regular call had come through.

Four hours later, at the end of that conversation, he said, "I just wanted to mention that I, well—I shaved my head. I don't have long hair anymore."

I thought of Henrietta kneeling beside me in my *TNO* office, waking me up as I lay on the couch to tell me about Noah's wig. Twenty-seven months had passed since then, which didn't seem like enough to account for how irretrievable that moment now felt.

I tried to sound casual as I said, "Cool."

"I didn't want you to be shocked if we facetime tomorrow."

"I'd like to think I'm harder to shock than that."

"Just since some people say my hair is, you know—" He paused, and when he continued, he seemed embarrassed for the first time that I could recall. "Like my trademark."

Again, I tried to sound light but sincere, and not at all mocking, as I said, "Aren't your songwriting and guitar playing your trademark?"

The next night, especially for the first minute or two, it was shocking and thrilling to see Noah on the screen of my phone. He looked both a little different and still joltingly, unreasonably handsome. His head was indeed shaved, with a few millimeters of stubble that was darker than the blond locks of yore but matched the stubble on his cheeks. He looked paler or more tired than in online images, which of course I'd inspected many times in the last week, meaning he looked like he wasn't wearing makeup and hadn't otherwise been professionally styled, and it was a pure and reflexive joy to gaze at this version of him: this private, real person. His piercing blue eyes were alert, and his expression was amused, and he was wearing an olive-green T-shirt and sitting in a low white armchair, and simultaneously, I wished I could dive into the screen and throw my arms around him, *and* I was self-conscious at the knowledge that he could see me, and I kept glancing at my tiny, grainy reflection in the lower right-hand corner of the screen. "This is so weird!" I blurted out.

He smiled. "In what way?"

"Do you not think so?" Quickly, I added, "Not because of your haircut. Your haircut looks great. I guess in the last two nights, I just got used to your disembodied voice."

"Is a disembodied voice better or worse than a digital consciousness?"

"Well," I said, "they're not dissimilar."

Then we discussed the book he was slowly reading about AI, and about how old we'd been when we'd acquired our first cellphones, and within fifteen minutes, I was much calmer. The next night it took only a few minutes to get over the shock of Noah's attractiveness, and the night after that I wondered if we were in the vicinity of phone sex—I'd already reversed the camera to show him my bedroom, he'd asked several rather silly questions about what kind of sheets I had and the positioning of my pillows—but I couldn't have facetime phone sex with Noah Brewster, or at least I couldn't sober, and I'd never drunk anything other than water while talking to him because it seemed unnecessary and maybe even inconsiderate. So instead, after we'd mutually pondered whether thread count made any real difference, I said, "What if I drive out to visit you instead of flying?"

"Seriously? Isn't that a million miles?"

"It's sixteen hundred."

"I don't want to do anything to discourage you, but wouldn't that be unnecessarily hellish?"

"I think it might be good for me. I could commune with my thoughts while the landscape poetically whips past."

"Is driving alone safe? Sorry if that's sexist, but—"

"Now you can send me a formal apology and sign it *Best*." Then I added, "It's not sexist. I think it would be safe enough."

"You'd have to text me a lot about where you are. I'm worried that my Sally radar might get spotty in some of those western states."

I could feel—and, in miniature, see—myself smiling goofily. Maybe I was a sucker, or maybe he had a little too much practice, but he was so disarmingly sweet. "How about if I attach a transmitting antenna to the top of my car?" I said. "Or to the top of my head?"

"That's a great plan, and then I can even track when you pop into a convenience store in, like, rural Utah."

"Don't judge me when I buy Doritos."

"Doritos are the best. So when can you leave?"

I had thought in our first phone conversation that some clarification would occur, some explicit acknowledgment that our contact was romantic, or presumed to be until proven otherwise. It hadn't. The dynamic between us was flirty and not explicit in any sense. And couldn't I have raised the subject as easily as he could? Except that didn't I have more to lose? Instead, we both kept chatting warmly. *Why wouldn't this be the romance of romance?* and *I'm really attracted to you, and I have been since that pitch meeting in Nigel's office*—if I was looking for confirmation, those lines from his emails were my strongest evidence. And those were lines I liked very much, lines I had reread many times even after memorizing them. But also: *I would say I was definitely trying to impress you and I was not trying to seduce you.*

"So that I know how to pack," I said, "how long do you envision me staying?"

"As long as you want," he said.

And then, instead of actually resolving the question, I said, "Are you the kind of Airbnb host who leaves out their framed family photos and their half-empty yogurt in the refrigerator or do you make it immaculate before your guests arrive?"

He laughed. "For you, I'll make it immaculate because I want you to give me five stars."

The next morning, I texted, *What if I leave KC morning of Aug 1 and get to you evening of Aug 2?*

You leaving KC morning of Aug 1 and getting to me evening of Aug 2 is a fantastic idea, he texted back.

On July 31, a FedEx package arrived at Jerry's house: the twelve-count case of protein bars, an eleven-by-sixteen-inch spiral-bound road atlas, and a gray T-shirt that said *California* in a yellow 1980s font. In the accompanying note, he'd written, *Sally, I can't wait to see you! Your pen pal, Noah.* I had never seen his handwriting, and even that seemed touching, and filled me with yearning: the way the *S* in *Sally* connected from its base to the *a*, the unadorned capital *I*, the straight unlooped line jutting down from the *y* in *you*. But was *pen pal* intended to be read as an inside joke or a reference to our platonic status?

That night, we ended our conversation at midnight, meaning early, and I set the alarm on my phone for 6:15 A.M. Though I'd told Jerry he didn't need to get up in the morning, he did; in his white-and-blue seersucker bathrobe, he carried my box of protein bars and masks outside and set it on the passenger side in the front seat, then he embraced me and said, "Some states let you drive eighty, but I think a bit slower is safer." Sugar frolicked at our feet, and I crouched to pet her. I had explained to Jerry that I was going to visit a friend in L.A. for a week or two, and his sister, my aunt Donna, whom I'd been grocery shopping for when I shopped for Jerry and me, had offered her car; she'd said since she and my uncle Richard hardly went anywhere these days, they didn't need two.

It was strange to leave Jerry's house; it was strange not to know how long I'd be in California; it was strange, even after five years, to live in the world without my mother; it was strange to be a person during a global pandemic. I started the engine and backed out of the driveway, waved goodbye to Jerry and Sugar from the street, and turned up the volume on the folky women satellite radio station, and a Mary Chapin Carpenter song I knew all the words to filled the car. I was both excited and melancholy as I drove south on State Line Road, through the early morning summer light, and my melancholy lifted some as I reached the Shawnee Mission Parkway and by the time I passed through Olathe, Kansas, half an hour later, it was almost completely gone, or at least eclipsed by giddiness and nervousness and sheer horniness. The highway in front of me was long and mostly flat, and I realized that I had been this excited and terrified only one other time in my life; it had been when I interviewed at *TNO*.

The Albuquerque Hampton Inn was four stories flanked by a mostly empty parking lot of bleak concrete, with the Sandia Mountains visible in the east. Sitting on the bed in my room, I ate dinner at 8:15 mountain time: two protein bars, a banana, and an orange I'd purchased earlier in the day at a gas station in the northwest corner of the Texas Panhandle. The drive had gone well enough, the highway taking me across the increasingly barren state of Kansas, then a brief dip through Oklahoma, an only slightly longer jaunt in Texas, and the final hours in New Mexico: the road straight and endless; the open expanses of land on either side a mix of bleached grass, sand, and scrub; the sky big and reassuringly blue. Though I'd planned while driving to either have profound thoughts about nature and humanity or else determine the structure of "Supremely," which was the working title of my barely existent screenplay about the Supreme Court justice, I'd mostly spaced out for long stretches. These stretches were abruptly punctuated with the impulse to grip the steering wheel when I found myself passing a truck or, far more pleasantly, by being intermittently startled at the knowledge that I might be having sex with Noah in about twenty-four hours. Mightn't I? As promised, I texted him each time I stopped, and he always texted back immediately.

Because Jerry was not a texter, I emailed to tell him I'd made it to Albuquerque. Then I put on a mask, left my room, hurried through the lobby—I passed a lone family carrying camping gear—and stood beneath the porte cochere inserting my earbuds. The sun had set, but the western sky was still faintly orange. When I called Noah, he said, "How was your dinner?"

"Thanks to your care package, delicious, and now I'm walking around the parking lot to get some air. How are you?"

"I'm trying to look at my house through your eyes to see if there's anything I should hide. Also, Margit is about to order groceries. You drink grapefruit seltzer water and put oat milk in your coffee, right?"

"As long as you don't have a Confederate flag, we're good. And yes."

"Even though Jerry thinks oat milk is weird."

"Yes. Even though Jerry thinks it's weird." Hearing Noah say Jerry's name, Noah knowing who Jerry was, still was both odd and sweet.

"One other thing along these lines, the thing I mentioned that we should discuss—do you remember that I don't keep alcohol in my house? Are you okay with that?"

"Of course," I said.

"Please don't say it's okay just to be polite. I'm being honest that not having wine or whatever in the house is my preference, but I'm sure we can figure something out if that feels too extreme to you. When I have friends over, they bring stuff and take it when they go, so it's not like I've banned it on the premises."

I was quiet for a few seconds before saying, "I'm honestly okay with it. If it was all the same to you, then sure, I'd have a drink when I get there, just because—well—not to sound dorky, but I'm a little nervous. But not having a drink isn't a big sacrifice." I thought, not for the first time, that plainly expressing your feelings about fraught topics was significantly harder than writing banter between imaginary characters.

"Will you tell me if that changes?" Noah said.

"The amount I'd want a drink is less than the amount I want it to be a non-issue for you," I said. "But yes, I will."

"Thank you, Sally, seriously. And last housekeeping item: My house is a little hard to find, up a bunch of winding roads, and I wonder if I should meet you in the parking lot of this shopping center and lead you back."

"Oh, I can find my way. Thanks, though." I felt the most anxious about the first seconds and moments in each other's presence. Though I'd told him in an email that I thought our interactions at *TNO* meant we already knew what it was like to be in the same room, I'd conveyed that sentiment when being in the same room again had still been hypothetical. Now that I was halfway to L.A., I was less sure. And wasn't meeting in a parking lot likelier to only increase the awkwardness?

"Let me know if you reconsider. Once you've gotten onto the 101, it'll be about twenty minutes to Topanga Canyon Boulevard, and things are more twisty-turny the farther south you get. When you really start to think you're in the wrong place, it means you're almost to my house."

"That doesn't sound ominous at all."

He laughed. "There's a stone wall along the property, then there's a gate in front of the driveway. Just pull up to the intercom, and after the gate opens, you go up the hill and I'll be waiting for you in front of the house."

Was this the moment to mention that I'd googled his house and the terra-cotta tiles in the front hall were lovely? Perhaps not.

"One other thing, in the interest of full disclosure," he said. "If you change your mind about meeting at that shopping center, there's a chance of paparazzi in the parking lot. They like to lurk outside the fancy grocery store. I'm assuming you're kind of used to that with your *TNO* friends, but I wouldn't want you to be caught off guard."

"Okay." A jitteriness swelled in my stomach, distinct from the swoony anticipation of seeing him; this jitteriness was sour.

"It seems like they're there less during the pandemic, but you never know."

I was passing the back of the Hampton Inn at this point; the curtains were closed in most rooms. In front of me, the mountains had turned black. According to my phone, it was seventy-eight degrees— already cooler than when I'd checked in and dry in a way that contrasted favorably to my last full day in Kansas City, when the temperature had reached a moist ninety-six degrees. Before I could stop myself, I said, "Would it be easier if I stay at a hotel?"

Slowly, after a silence, Noah said, "Easier in what way?"

"Logistically? I don't know."

"Would you be more comfortable in a hotel?"

Why had I introduced this possibility? What was wrong with me? It was almost like getting through the alcohol discussion unscathed had set me up for subsequent failure, like I was incapable of not somehow botching things. "I think it would be, uh—less fun?" I said. "But I also don't want to impose."

"I think it would be much less fun if you stay in a hotel," he said. "And just so you know, I have plenty of bedrooms so however you want to handle that—like, not to assume anything."

Surely there was some perfect, clever way to respond, some line that would make the conversation upbeat again instead of clumsy, that would charmingly convey that I appreciated his chivalry but very much hoped he wanted to share a bed. And if I'd had a day or two to come up with that line, or if I'd been writing it in a sketch for someone else, like Viv or Henrietta, I was pretty sure I could have figured out what it was. But as myself, in real time, I was tonguetied. After a few seconds, I said, "Yeah, that's fine."

Again, there was a second or two of silence, but his voice was warm when he said, "You know how you said you're a little nervous? I'm a lot nervous."

"Yeah, right."

"How could I not be? *TNO*'s star writer is coming to visit me."

"Are you more or less nervous than when you last performed at MSG?"

"Way more," he said, and we both laughed. It was a belated realization to have, but it occurred to me that perhaps this was how grown-up conversations worked—not that your communication didn't falter, but that you both made good-faith attempts to rectify things after it had.

In the morning, I woke at five, before the alarm on my phone went off, and even with my scrupulous showering and additional depilation, I was back on the highway by six. The sun rose behind me as I drove, casting a pink light on the land and vegetation on either side of the road. Because it was eight in New York, and because the highway was almost unsettlingly empty, I called Viv.

"Has the booty train left the station?" she asked.

"It's barreling toward L.A. at seventy-five miles an hour, and I think I might have a panic attack."

"Right now?"

"No, I'll probably wait until I get to California. How was the massage lesson?"

"We both kept it in our pants," Viv said. "Sorry to disappoint you."

Viv had hired a doula to attend her delivery, a silver-haired sixty-something woman named Gloria, and the previous night Gloria had provided a perineal massage tutorial over Zoom. In advance, Viv and I had speculated about whether Gloria planned to show her perineum to Viv or expected Viv to show hers.

"Did she use an anatomically correct mannequin?" I asked.

"She used a piece of paper and a pen. But speaking of perineal exploration, when do you get to Noah's?"

"Late afternoon or early evening."

"And why are you going to have a panic attack?"

"Real life is just awkward," I said. "What if he finds me boring?"

"What if you find him boring? By the way, I'm boiling eggs, and you're coming along with me now from the bedroom to the kitchen. You know what these eggs are?"

"Free-range organic?"

"They're my second breakfast."

"Congratulations."

I could hear a sort of shifting and rustling in the background, then Viv said, "Theo thinks you put the eggs in before you bring the water to a boil, but they're so much better when you boil the water *then* put in the eggs."

"I only make scrambled eggs, so I'm Switzerland here."

"Have you heard Bianca is getting fired? I got a text from Tony last night."

"Oh, that sucks," I said. "Patrick told me Elliot told him the retreat definitely isn't happening this year." This was an annual *TNO* getaway at a resort in the Catskills prior to the first show week, and it was meant to foster professional unity while invariably resulting in even more cliquish behavior than happened in the studio.

"I can't say I'm surprised," Viv said. "So is the thing you're worried about pooping at Noah's house?"

"Did I already tell you that?"

"Sally, I've known you for a long time."

The rule I'd imposed on myself after Noah and I had started emailing, but even before he'd announced how much he trusted me, was *No forwarding and no screenshots*. I could summarize to Viv and Henrietta what was happening, and certainly I could editorialize about my many, many feelings, but I couldn't show them anything, nor could I share any truly personal details that Noah revealed to me about himself.

I said, "What if because I've written sketches about diarrhea and BO, he assumes I'm comfortable with diarrhea and BO?"

"I don't think he's that much of a psychological simpleton."

"But we've never discussed that stuff."

"Really? While writing long, romantic emails about your yearnings and your inner souls, that didn't come up? I'm shocked. Okay, here's what you do. When you're on the toilet, as soon as the doodie comes out, like the second it hits the water, you flush. You might have to flush a few times, but that way, it doesn't stick to the bowl as much and you stink up the bathroom less."

"Is that true?"

"It's probably moot because he must live in a mansion with a million bathrooms. I'm giving you tips from when I'd go home with guys who lived in studios, but you'll be pooping half a mile away from Noah."

"Pooping under the same roof as a guy you like is a state of mind." Then I said, "What if I get there and he's like, 'I so value our robust platonic friendship'?"

"Then you platonically shake his hand, tell him good luck, rent a sweet little place on the beach, and get on Tinder." A timer beeped, and she added, "But since he unambiguously told you he's attracted to you, I'd be surprised."

"Are those your eggs?"

"Those are my eggs. Take deep breaths and keep me posted."

It was outside of Flagstaff, Arizona, five hours into the drive, that I realized how I should have replied when Noah had said "Not to assume anything" about sharing a bed. In a jaunty tone, I should have said, "Assume away!"

The gas station in Canoga Park, California, was, according to the directions on my phone, 10.3 miles and twenty-four minutes from Noah's house. It was a little after five Pacific time, a dry and sunny seventy-four degrees, and the stretch where I'd stopped didn't look so different from strip malls in Kansas City except for the palm trees lining the road. After I'd filled the tank, as I walked toward the entrance of the convenience store, my heart pounded and my entire body shook. Although I'd believed myself to be nervous when I'd spoken to Noah by phone the first time, and also when we'd first facetimed, those episodes seemed, in retrospect, quaintly mild. For Christ's sake, Noah was 10.3 miles away!

Outside the doors of the convenience store, I put on my mask. Inside, I found the bathroom, peed voluminously and washed my hands vigorously, then set my toiletry kit on the (germy? or recently cleaned?) counter by the sink. I removed my mask, brushed my teeth approximately three times more thoroughly than I normally did, rinsed my mouth with mouthwash from a travel-sized bottle I'd bought at a drugstore in Kansas City two days before, applied lip balm, and put my mask back on. Holding my travel-sized deodorant, my hand shook so intensely that I almost missed my armpit on the first try. I reminded myself of someone, and then I realized it was Sugar during a thunderstorm.

I had decided ahead of time that I'd change every article of clothing, even my underwear and bra, or especially my underwear and bra. I did so inside a stall, standing on top of my sneakers while trying to avoid setting my socked feet against the bare floor. After I was wearing my favorite and most flattering black T-shirt and cropped jeans, as my last act of transformation, I bent to peel off my socks and stepped into black sandals. My feet weren't horrifically sweaty, nor were they daisy fresh. I'd cleanse them with disinfectant wipes in the car, I decided, and wished that being aware of my own ridiculousness could somehow decrease my ridiculousness.

There was nothing left to do except go see Noah. I regarded myself once more in the gas station mirror and thought, as I hadn't for years, of what my mother had said after I'd repeated Elliot's line about confusing the romance of comedy with the romance of romance. First she'd said, "What a pretentious turd." Then she'd said, "I promise that someday you'll find the love you deserve, but it might not be when or how you're expecting it."

As I left the bathroom and passed the refrigerators of soda and iced tea and bottled water behind their clear glass doors, I squinted in uncertainty—could it be?—and then, under my mask, I couldn't help laughing. It wasn't that loud, but it was unmistakable: Through the store's sound system, a Muzak version of "Making Love in July" was playing.

It was true that as I entered Topanga Canyon, I quickly felt as if I were in the middle of nowhere, in a way that was beautiful and might, under other circumstances, have been calming. The winding two-lane road appeared far more rural than a place less than an hour from downtown L.A. had any right to. It led me past the craggy Santa Monica mountains on one side and steeply sloping descents on the other, past thickets of chaparral and sandstone outcroppings and the occasional house built into the tree-filled hillsides. Turning south, I caught my first glimpse of the hazy turquoise of the Pacific Ocean. It disappeared and reappeared as the road curved.

After fifteen minutes, I made a sharp right. I was by this point not sure my heart could beat any faster without it qualifying as a medical event. There was then the stone wall, the gate, and the driveway behind it, which rose up a hill of scrub and trees in such a way that it hid the house. I was so nervous that when I braked and tried to ease up to the intercom at the gate, I missed by about five feet. I backed out and tried again. Extending my left arm out the window, I pressed a silver button, and Noah's voice—as opposed to the voice of some manservant—said, "Hi there, Sally. Gate's opening now." Atop stone columns flanking the gate, I noticed video cameras, and I felt the same uneasiness I had when Noah had mentioned paparazzi in the grocery store parking lot. The gate opened, and I drove onto the property.

I'd ascended perhaps 150 feet when the land leveled off and the house appeared, the same sprawling stucco hacienda I'd seen online. The real-life fact of it reminded me of encountering one of the famous Monet paintings of water lilies at the Met after studying it in an art history class. Indeed—it did exist. I was still a hundred feet from the house, and a male figure was approaching the car in jeans and a teal T-shirt and a black mask, and my heart was an exploding firecracker. Even with a mask on, even from this distance, Noah was shockingly handsome.

I braked again when we were ten feet apart—Noah fucking fake-surfer Making-Love-in-July Brewster and me, Sally Milz—and my window was still open from speaking into the intercom, and my decidedly inglorious first words were "Should I be wearing a mask?"

From behind his mask, he said, "Should I not be wearing one?" Above his mask, his eyes crinkled in a way I was pretty sure meant he was smiling, and he said, "Welcome to California."

"Should I park here or pull up by the garage?" I asked.

"You should park here because you've been in that car for way, way too long." He pulled his mask down to his chin. "And I should take this off because starting now, we're in a pod together." He unhooked the straps from his ears and stuffed the mask into a back pocket, and the reveal of his face—well, it wasn't as if I needed confirmation that he was very attractive, but if I did, his blue eyes were intense, and his lips were slightly puffy and framed by laugh lines, and his thick eyebrows and stubble were light brown. And, though this was hard to fathom, there was some openness in his expression and bearing that made him seem palpably, disorientingly pleased that I'd arrived.

I turned off the engine, made brief and panicked eye contact with myself in the rearview mirror, and got out, and Noah was right there, zero feet away, and our bodies were smashed together and our arms were wrapped around each other. Because he was a few inches taller, my face was pressed to his partially stubbly neck, and the feel and smell of his skin and his stubble and his whole clothed body against mine was the nicest feeling I had ever felt. It all was both comforting and exciting in a combination I hadn't previously known existed, and we stayed like that for a long time.

And then, finally, because I was me and compelled to break the moment even as I wondered if we were about to begin kissing passionately, I pulled away and looked up at him and said, "Your directions were excellent."

"Do you need a bathroom or some water or anything?"

"I'm okay because I stopped before I got to Topanga." I appreciated not only his considerateness but also the unromanticness of acknowledging pee. I extended one leg. "I changed into my fancy shoes."

"Those are great fancy shoes." He tilted his head toward the house. "How about if I show you around? Just leave your stuff in the car for now."

"I have something for you." The driver's side door was still open, and I was careful not to retrieve his gift by bending from the waist and sticking my butt up at him, but by sitting down again in the seat and leaning over to grab the gray paper bag. When I'd reemerged, I handed it to him. I felt conscious of an ongoing, full-body shakiness.

"How exciting," he said.

"You might want to keep your expectations in check."

He grinned. "Oh, it's far too late for that." He reached into the bag and, one by one, extracted and opened each individually paper-wrapped key chain I'd purchased along the way. After the first, he said, "I've always longed for a key chain in the shape of New Mexico." As he opened the second, he added, "And I've also always longed for a Texas cowboy hat key chain. Oh, and an Arizona cactus." The remaining ones were a retro Kansas license plate with stalks of wheat and an Oklahoma state bird; I had, of course, thought of Nigel while purchasing it.

I said, "There's nothing for Missouri because I was over the Kansas border about five minutes after leaving the house."

"The funny thing is I never wanted a Missouri key chain," he said. "I have a new regard for Missouri. Don't get me wrong. But their key chains just aren't my style." He'd unwrapped them all by this point, and he said, "Thank you. I love them."

"I wanted to get you something I was confident you didn't already have."

He set his palm on my bare forearm, and I thought of the line from "Making Love in July" that went, "Did you feel it, too / my hand brushed against you." I thought of first hearing the song almost twenty years before, the summer between my freshman and sophomore years of college, and thinking it was silly and not having the faintest inkling of who Noah Brewster would eventually become to me. Also, when were we going to start kissing passionately? He said, "They're perfect."

Inside the house, we found ourselves in a high-ceilinged entry hall with white stucco walls and, as in the pictures I'd seen online, a floor of terra-cotta brick tiles interspersed with blue-and-white ceramic tiles. An interior arched doorway that opened onto a large living room confirmed that the aesthetic was Casually Fancy South-western and The Color White. As he led me through the living room, the dining room, and the study, almost all the rugs and couches and chairs were white—the furniture's fabric was often linen, with a couple cowhide ottomans thrown in—and almost all the tables looked expensively rough-hewn. Standing in the doorway of the study, I pointed at the desk and said, "Is that where you sat when you were emailing me? Where the magic happens?"

He laughed. "Some of the time."

There was a kind of instrument room, not to be confused with the freestanding recording studio, that was mostly empty except for a grand piano and bench, four guitars on stands against a wall, and a large (white) armless chair in one corner. The kitchen was also large and open, with a massive wooden island and a stainless steel refrigerator and a stainless steel range and an entire wall of floor-to-ceiling windows that revealed a long rectangular pool set in a patio of terra-cotta tiles. We stepped onto the patio, where Adirondack chairs circled a firepit. Beyond the pool, the land fell away into a valley then rose again into mountains, above which the pale blue sky was clear and expansive.

"Where are we right now in relation to the ocean?" I asked.

He jabbed his thumb over one shoulder. "It's that way."

"Nice view," I said. "And it smells even better than the inside of my car."

He laughed. "It's the eucalyptus."

"Do you actually swim, or is the pool more decorative? It's kind of Zen."

"Interesting you should ask. Much like with cooking, I've gone swimming more in the last few months than in the previous few years. I started out doing laps for exercise but now, just for fun, I float around on inflatables that I used to put out for parties but never used on my own."

"Where are your butler and chambermaid right now? Are they watching us on closed-circuit TV?"

He laughed. "I hope not. No, Glenn and Margit go see their grandkids on the weekends, and they usually stay overnight. Their daughter lives in Torrance."

"Do their grandkids come here? Have you met them?"

"They don't usually come here, but I have met them. It's a boy and girl who are close in age to my nephews."

I swept one hand horizontally, taking it all in, and said, "Well, you have a very nice backyard."

"The truth is that Topanga isn't the ideal place to be in terms of wildfires, but otherwise it's pretty great. And things have been okay this summer." Our eyes met, and he said, "Should I have mentioned the wildfire thing before you drove halfway across the country?"

"Wildfires sound terrifying, but I'm not sure that would have stopped me."

We reentered the kitchen, which segued into an entire second, or maybe third, sitting room, with a white couch and two white chairs facing a flat-screen television. I gestured toward it. "Is that where you watch *TNO*?"

"Every Saturday without exception." As we returned to the front of the house, he said, "I bought the place in 2014 but didn't move in until 2016 because of renovations. I guess the renovating would have been a pain if I'd been in a hurry, but since I'm really interested in architecture, I found the whole process fun."

I couldn't bring myself to inquire more—this interest still seemed affected in a way he generally wasn't—but I managed not to make some snotty joke about it, so wasn't that a wash, or even a minor victory?

We entered a corridor off which were three bedrooms, all of them so large and airy that I assumed the first was his, and experienced a silent titillation at the sight of the bed, until he said, "This is the room my sister prefers when she's here." I then assumed the second was his—like the first, it had a king-sized bed with a big white coverlet and a few Western-seeming leather throw pillows—and I then assumed the third was his. But in the third, he said, "I thought I'd give this one to you. I think it's the best because it's on the end, but if you really want privacy, we can set you up in the pool house." He was looking at me with an attentive and searching expression, and I wondered if we'd come to opposite conclusions after discussing the bedroom thing on the phone—if he'd thought I'd been sincerely requesting space instead of just trying to give him an out. And, seriously, *when* would we kiss? What if we waited too long and missed the window of opportunity, and I ended up not only coming up with jokes for his appearance on a late-night talk show but accidentally ghostwriting his entire memoir?

Or what if instead of waiting for him to kiss me, I kissed him first? If he rebuffed me, the bad news would be that I'd need to jump in my car and drive back to Kansas City immediately, but the good news would be that it would be such a vividly humiliating experience that surely I'd derive personal and professional inspiration from it for years to come.

But once again, I did nothing. I simply said, "Oh, I don't need to sleep in the pool house."

We crossed again through the entry hall, and then we were definitely in the master suite: twice as large as the guest bedrooms, with its own sitting area—it seemed so predictable as to almost not be worth noting that the bedroom was bigger than my entire apartment in New York—and the adjacent bathroom featured double sinks in a quartz countertop and an enormous quartz shower and a huge, oval, freestanding bathtub. As in the guest rooms, this bed was tidily made with a white coverlet, but, on the bureau and bedside tables, there were personal objects—an iPad and a legal notepad and a heavy-looking cylindrical silver clock with a lit-up face of shifting light- and dark-brown geometrical shapes. There really wasn't much clutter, though; either he was a tidy person or Margit or Glenn cleaned up after him, or both.

It occurred to me to point at the bed and say, "Is *that* where the magic happens?" But I managed to suppress this unhelpful impulse as well and instead said, "I feel like something is missing in here."

We were standing with our backs to the bathroom door, just inside the bedroom, and he glanced at me with an alert expression.

"An Indigo Girls poster," I said.

He laughed. "I guess people buy posters online now, right? I used to go to a music store at the mall and page through those giant plastic racks."

"Same," I said. "And then get an Orange Julius."

I felt conscious of having come to the end of the tour, conscious of being in his bedroom, conscious of the intimacy of our conversation. Even as I was exquisitely aware of his nearness, I also was thinking in an abstract way about how I had been one kind of person up until my divorce, a resigned and constrained person. Then I had been another kind of person for the last decade, a cynical and compartmentalized person. Was there any reason I couldn't now become a third kind of person, made more confident by experience and braver by the current reminder of how fragile and tenuous all our lives had been all along? And still Noah's head was turned to look at me, and my head was turned to look at him.

He smiled at me in a way I had never before been smiled at, a smile of such tenderness and openness and warmth. "Hi," he said.

"Hi," I replied.

We still were making eye contact as I brushed the back of my right hand against the back of his left one, and then our fingers intertwined a little. This, his complicity, bolstered me, and I stepped around so that I was facing him. The shift made it easier to properly hold hands, not just on the one side but, almost without my realizing it, on the other side, too. "So," I said, and I really did feel like I might disrupt the space-time continuum with the hugeness of what seemed to be about to happen. I had never initiated a first kiss with someone I cared about, and I had never initiated a first kiss while sober.

"So," he said, still smiling.

I took one more step toward him—again, the closeness of him, the mammalian smell of him, made me swoony—and then I stood on my tiptoes and leaned in and pressed my mouth against his.

There was, of course, a part of my mind narrating the action, declaring, *It's happening! Holy shit, it's happening!* But as we kept kissing, as we alternated between pursing our lips and pulling back and smiling and setting our hands on each other's shoulders and backs, as his tongue slipped forward and touched mine, my inner narrator receded, or went somewhere else. And then there was just the sheer physical pleasure and excitement of my mouth touching his mouth and the skin on my hands and arms and face and neck touching the skin on his hands and arms and face and neck and the rest of my clothed body pressed to the rest of his clothed body. It felt like a relief, like something I'd been waiting for since *TNO* and much of the world had shut down in March, and also like something I'd been waiting for since he'd shown me his tattoos in 2018, and also like something I'd been waiting for my whole life. *And* it felt like an astonishing miracle. If this was all I ever got, it would be the best thing that had ever happened to me, and if this was all I ever got, I'd never stop wanting more of it.

And then he pulled his head a full foot back, and also took a step back, though his hands were still cupping my jaw on either side and his expression was still tender. "I have something to show you," he said.

It was because I was a comedy writer, and not because I was sexually fearless, that I was tempted to say, "Your penis?" Instead, I said, "Is it better than this?"

He laughed. "It's in the kitchen."

"Is it sourdough bread?"

"No, although I'll make dinner if you're hungry, like some salmon and a salad, or else Margit left some premade stuff for us."

Who cares about dinner? I thought.

I said, "Is it an NDA for me to sign?"

He laughed. "Also no." He placed a hand on the small of my back to steer me toward the bedroom door. "It's kind of a present, but it isn't key chains."

Did he think I was a bad kisser? Was the kissing not supposed to have happened? Was the kissing supposed to have happened, but when it wasn't some guy off a dating site, was it paced differently and the subsequent stuff didn't occur as quickly? Was it weird that I didn't know how this all worked even though I was thirty-eight years old, or did nobody know? Counting Martin Biersch, my ex-husband, two earlier guys in college, and the assortment of online serial hookups, I'd had sex with a total of nine men. If someone had told me of this figure when I was in high school, I'd have thought it sounded like an embarrassment of riches, but surely it was nothing compared to Noah's number. Even a pop star who eschewed the term *playboy* had to be, by normal standards, a playboy.

Back in the kitchen, on the wood-topped island, I noticed a shiny black folder. He pulled a single sheet of paper from it, with printed words I couldn't read, and said, "It's something I made as a surprise. Not a song. More of an activity."

"This is very intriguing."

"You'll know what it is pretty quickly. Okay." He cleared his throat. "I need you to give me a noun."

I wasn't sure I'd heard him correctly. "A *noun*? Like a person, place, or thing?"

"Yeah."

"Any particular kind of noun?"

He shook his head.

"Let's see," I said. "How about *door*?"

He used a ballpoint pen to write then said, "Verb ending in -*ing*?"

"This is like Mad Libs. *Fidgeting*."

He looked sheepish. "It *is* Mad Libs. But personalized for you." He began reading. "I just drove my door from Kansas City, Missouri, to Los Angeles, California. As I drove, I was fidgeting about whether I'd—" He looked up from the page. "This is incredibly corny, huh?"

"Well, we've barely started. Don't give away the punch line."

"We don't have to do this."

"I'm happy to. Do you need an adjective?"

His brow furrowed. "I thought this was clever before you got here, but now it seems very contrived."

"It's fun," I insisted.

"I want you to think coming here was a good idea," he said, and there was a catch in my chest, less from swooning than from being startled. "I want you to think I'm not boring, even though I don't work at *TNO*."

I could tell that he wasn't being sarcastic, or even flirty. He was being completely unguarded and sincere, and I tried to be equally sincere as I said, "I don't want to alarm you, but no one has ever made anything like this for me. It's so, like, premeditatedly sweet. And *I* want *you* to think my visit was a good idea. In your room just then—" I trailed off and looked at him uncertainly.

"No, that was awesome," he said. "That was great. To be honest, I was afraid of going too fast and I just—I want to let you get settled here and get comfortable. I don't want you to feel pressured."

"I'm actually pretty comfortable."

"Don't get me wrong, that's definitely what I want. But I worry that I've spooked you in the past."

I could feel my forehead wrinkle. "When?"

"At the bar after the after-party."

"Oh—I was really confused that night. I almost thought—well, I wondered if you were about to kiss me, but I couldn't believe you'd want to."

"I was planning on asking you out. Of course I *wanted* to kiss you, but I wouldn't have done it there."

It was slightly easier to summon my courage this time. I said, "Do you want to kiss me now?"

We were standing with a corner of the island between us, and he stepped around it, leaned his face into mine, and kissed my lips. "Does that answer your question?"

I smiled as I said, "Have I mentioned that I'm very comfortable right now? And not at all spooked?"

And then we were making out in the kitchen, and this time he was a tiny bit more familiar, the taste of his mouth and skin and the feel of his body, and I was a tiny bit more relaxed, and again it was overwhelming and exhilarating. And again, after a minute or two, he stepped back, this time with his hands holding my upper arms. He nodded down once with his chin and said, "See? I just—I don't want to jump the gun or, like, freak you out."

I understood, as I hadn't before, that he meant because he had an erection; even before he'd said anything, I'd been able to feel it. And I'd been delighted. Looking at him, I thought that he was so handsome, but also so endearing. "You know what?" I said. "Let's go back to your room and jump the gun."

We did not end up eating the salmon. We didn't end up eating at all until after midnight when we went out to the kitchen with him wearing nothing and me wearing only my black T-shirt, when we both ate a handful of cashews, split a banana, and chugged water from the same huge glass that he then carried back to the bedroom.

First we'd had fast, ravenous, pulling-off-each-other's clothes, first-time-with-each-other sex that was also there's-a-pandemic-happening-and-we-might-be-in-the-twilight-of-humankind sex. I didn't expect to climax and certainly not while we were in the missionary position—for Christ's sake, it was still light out at that point and I was sober—which may have been why I did. In fact, I did before he did, and as I moaned, with his right shoulder by my mouth and his mouth by my left ear, he said in a low, quiet voice, "Oh, Sally," and then he pulled out and ejaculated all over my stomach and I thought about how Jessa, the older daughter of my mother's best friend, had told me when I was thirteen that when you didn't like a guy, the disgusting things about sex were disgusting, and when you did like a guy, the disgusting things about sex were sexy. I tugged Noah onto me, and he said, "Am I too heavy?" and I said, "You're perfect," and we both lay still for a long time, my arms wrapped around him, his full weight on me, his face pressed against my neck, his left hand fiddling with my hair. My mind wasn't racing; I wasn't nervous; there was nothing other than this that I wanted.

After some number of minutes—eight? Or twenty-five?—he rolled off me, onto his side, and pulled me so I was on my side, too, so we were facing each other and he looked at me from about three inches away with such intensity and affection that I had to avert my gaze; I couldn't help it. But then I looked back at him and said, "You're definitely worth driving twenty-six hours for. And definitely not boring, even though you don't work at *TNO*."

He laughed. "And you haven't even tasted my pan-seared salmon yet."

"By the way I have an IUD. In case next time you want to—" I paused and raised my eyebrows, aware again of the strangeness of how the most precise and succinct way of saying something could feel splendidly obscene. I continued, "In case next time you want to come inside me."

"I'd love to come inside you next time." He grinned. "I hope I didn't make too much of a mess before."

"It was a good kind of mess," I said. "And I also have, uh, a clean bill of health. Sexually."

"Good to know and same for me."

He leaned in and kissed my mouth and the sex we had that time was slower and calmer before it reverted to clawing and devouring each other.

After the second time, before the third time, when it became apparent there was going to be a third time, he was on his back, and I was straddling him, and I didn't care about the pooching of my stomach because I'd decided I was beautiful just as I was. Just kidding! Because it was getting dark and also because presumably sex hormones were coursing through me. He wasn't yet inside me again though I could feel his erection, and I said, "Did you take Viagra?"

"Wow," he said. "Thanks a lot."

"That wasn't an insult. It was a compliment."

"To which one of us?" Without waiting for an answer, he said, "Sorry that I'm really turned on by you. No, I didn't take Viagra."

Sincerely, I said, "I apologize if that was rude."

It was hard to read his expression—he seemed to be analyzing or assessing me almost distantly, though there was also a new haze of closeness between us that no doubt arose from being naked together, our skin smelling like the other's skin, our bodily fluids mixed on his sheets. Even if the knowledge wasn't comprehensive, we abruptly knew each other much better, more thoroughly, than we had a few hours before.

"I think I can forgive you," he said, "under the circumstances." He thrust up once then stopped and said, "Is this okay? Do you need anything?"

"Like what? A vaccine? An overall deal with a studio?"

"I was thinking of lubricant."

As with being gazed at tenderly, as with being given a personalized Mad Libs, I had never before been asked if I needed lubricant. And as when he'd inquired on my arrival if I needed a bathroom, I was touched by both his thoughtfulness and his lack of fear about the biology of the human body.

"I don't right now," I said. "But thank you."

This time he looked at me when he was inside me and I was able to look back for about three seconds, which wasn't nothing; and then I leaned forward, leaned into him, so our torsos were pressed together.

If life were a romantic comedy, I'd have awakened the next morning from a deep, restorative, and gracefully positioned slumber with sunlight streaming in through the windows and Noah standing by the bed holding a mug of coffee for me. Instead, I woke in darkness at 4:13 A.M., my heart hammering, lying on my side with my chin in a pool of my own drool, being spooned by Noah. And even this ostensibly sweet arrangement was compromised by the fact that in a best-case scenario I needed to fart, but I was pretty sure I needed to poop. And he was still naked, and I was still wearing nothing but my T-shirt. In contrast to comparable situations in the past, I felt gratefully not hungover. At the same time, everything that had seemed spontaneous the previous night—not showering upon arriving at his house, not brushing my teeth before going to sleep, him jizzing on my stomach—had caught up with me. I probably was still coated with Albuquerque Hampton Inn residue! Though I didn't exactly feel gross because of Noah, I definitely felt gross adjacent to him, and aware of him behind me not as a smoking-hot person I might be falling in love with but as a rhythmically breathing lump inhabited by a human I didn't *really* know that well.

I could see the time on the cylindrical silver clock on Noah's nightstand, which I lay closer to than he did. What an ugly object, I thought as I tried to determine a strategy for extricating myself. The master bathroom was about twenty feet away and the door was open, and I could go in there, turn on the shower to cover the noise of facing my destiny on the toilet, take a real shower to conceal the fact that I'd just faced my destiny on the toilet, and emerge clean. But where were my clothes and toothbrush and hairbrush? Still in my car? They had to be. And it was very plausible that the house's security alarm was armed, either because Noah had set it the night before or because it was automated. Then I thought, one of the guest rooms. Any of the guest rooms. Any bathroom not right off Noah's bedroom.

All this time, Noah's left arm had been slung over my left side, and, as lightly as possible, I nudged it off. Then I inched forward, to the edge of the mattress, swung my legs down, and quickly stood. Immediately, my new freedom released a surge of adrenaline. The articles of clothing scattered on the rug were indistinguishable in the dark room, and the first thing I picked up was, I was pretty sure, his boxer briefs. The second thing seemed to be his shirt. In the bed, he stirred, and I thought *Fuck* and hurried from the room.

I followed a short hall to the entry hall; crossed it; entered the guest wing; walked to the farthest of the three bedrooms; entered its bathroom; sat on the toilet; peed for a very long time; pooped; immediately felt 60 percent better; remembered I had no underwear on, let alone pants, to pull up; washed and dried my hands; then stood there, unsure what to do next. It occurred to me that, as at the homes of rich people I'd visited in the past, there might be spare toiletries in the cabinet behind the mirror or under the sink. But the mirror was just a mirror, without any cabinet, and under the sink all

I found were a toilet brush, a plunger, and an unopened package of six rolls of toilet paper. In lieu of a toothbrush, I used my index finger and water, and as I did, I noticed the puffy tangle behind my head of triple-orgasm hair. I washed and dried my hands a second time and attempted to run my fingers through the tangles with little success, and as I did I fully apprehended the absurdity of the situation. My phone was in Noah's room, in the pocket of my discarded jeans. My laptop was in the car. I was wearing nothing from the waist down. If I were a different person, presumably this was when I'd have returned to Noah's room, climbed in his bed, snuggled against him, and gone back to sleep. Instead I walked pantsless into the kitchen, pulling my T-shirt over my nether regions, hoping there really was no closed-circuit TV, helped myself to a tangerine in a bowl of citrus on the island, then—as quietly as possible—opened seven cabinets before finding the one with side-by-side compost and trash bins. I saw on the microwave clock that it was 4:31. I walked back to the guest room adjacent to the bathroom I'd besmirched, climbed under the covers, and began crafting the sentences I'd use to express to Noah that I really appreciated his hospitality but that staying in a hotel seemed to make more sense after all. Would I say that I felt overwhelmed, or was that obvious? Would I specify that while I knew there were people who could handle an amorphous and open-ended trip in the context of an amorphous and open-ended relationship, I wasn't one of them? *Relationship,* of course, was the wrong word. *Tryst? Fling? Rendezvous?* I frantically revised my hypothetical script for at least an hour before, improbably, falling asleep. When I awakened, sunlight was streaming in through the windows, and Noah was standing by the bed holding a mug of coffee for me. But before I realized it was him, I only knew that I was in a strange room with a strange man, and I yelped.

"Sally, it's me," he said. "I'm sorry. I didn't mean to scare you."

"What time is it?"

"Nine forty-five." He passed me the mug then sat on the edge of the mattress. He was wearing a gray T-shirt, blue shorts, ankle socks, and sneakers. The perfect golden hair on his perfect arms and legs was visible, and his face was kind and handsome. "I guessed at how much oat milk you put in, so if it's wrong, we can start over."

"I hope it's okay I came in here. I just thought—" The words that a few hours before had seemed necessary—*amorphous* and *open-ended, relationship, tryst*—were eluding me. Instead, I felt very happy to see Noah, while also wondering if my eyes were visibly crusty or my lips were visibly scummy.

"Yeah, of course." His voice was friendly and utterly unfazed. "It's always weird sleeping in a new place for the first time. And I apologize that we didn't get you more settled last night, but I guess we were distracted." He smiled affably. "Your bags are all in the hall. I brought them in from the car. And your clothes are there." He nodded to the left, and I saw that on the white armchair, in a tidy pile, were my folded jeans and folded bra. "I think your phone is in the pocket," he said.

Where, I wondered, was my underwear?

Noah patted my calf beneath the coverlet. "My trainer is about to arrive. Remember Bobby, the one I *don't* have three-hour work-outs with? I'll shower after that, then I thought we could hike or go have a picnic lunch at the beach if that sounds fun to you? Or we could hang out and swim." He smiled and I felt a fizzy sort of scrambling, like the tide gathering itself to go back out: how attracted to him I was, how much I liked him, and how confusing it was to find myself at his house. "We can play it by ear today, but I'm really happy that you're here."

Would a person who wasn't anxious and uncomfortable sit up and kiss him? But I hadn't brushed my teeth since the gas station bathroom! Instead, I said, "Me, too."

Noah's hand remained on my calf, and he squeezed it. "Just text me if you need anything in the next hour. I'll be in the yard by the studio." Then he leaned in and kissed me on the mouth, and the kiss was so quick that it probably didn't matter if I had scummy lips or not.

———

Good news I successfully pooped, I texted Viv. *Also we had sex last night X 3 and it was great*

Bad news is I have no idea what I'm doing here

It's like 13 hours until bedtime

Seriously how do you get through a day with another person?

In the folded jeans on the chair, I'd found my phone in one front pocket and my underwear in the other, which was cringe-inducing but not as bad as if the underwear was still at large. Viv didn't respond immediately, so I opened the door that Noah had closed when he'd left, peered out, saw no one, and pulled in my suitcase, backpack, purse, and the cardboard box with its two remaining protein bars, both of which I ate. I located and used my toothbrush then showered. After I emerged from the bathroom, a text from Viv was waiting: *Day sex*

Then: *OK can we back up a second and savor SEX THREE TIMES WITH NOAH BREWSTER*

AND THAT IT WAS GREAT

THAT'S THE ONLY GOOD THING THAT'S HAPPENED IN 2020

You can't talk now can you?

I called her right away. "He's outside with his trainer."

In a singsong, Viv said, "Sally Milz got laid last night, doo dah, doo dah."

"I'm kind of freaking out," I said.

"Why?"

The answer was both so all-encompassing and so self-evident that it was oddly hard to articulate. After a few seconds, I said, "What if we run out of things to say? What if I fart in front of him?"

"If this is a real relationship, then those things will for sure happen. And then if you get pregnant, you'll fart in front of him so much that both of you will only notice the rare moments when you're *not* farting in front of him."

"How many breakfasts and lunches have you eaten today?"

"I ordered kung pao shrimp for lunch, then I got horrible heartburn and now I'm drinking ginger tea, and I only have medium heartburn. You haven't decided how long you're staying, right? How long can you tell yourself you'll be there without losing it?"

"From my perspective or his?"

"Since you're not a mind reader, only yours."

"Until, I don't know—Thursday?" It was presently Monday, which sort of made staying until Thursday adhere to the rule of three.

"Great," Viv said. "Tell yourself, but don't tell him, that you'll leave at noon on Thursday. And that after that you'll never see him again. And just enjoy the hell out of yourself until then. Leave it all on the field. Is that the expression? I hate sports metaphors. But for once, don't worry about the future. And for sure don't worry what your butthole looks like when you're doing it doggy style."

"I bet my butthole is less cute than yours. Also, neither of us is drinking at all. I'm abstaining in solidarity."

"Wow, that's kind of beautiful. You can't just lose your inhibitions in the fog of alcohol."

"*Will* I never see him again after Thursday?"

Viv laughed. "Will my baby be born healthy and always stay safe from harm?"

"Fair enough. And I'm sorry about your heartburn."

"Bianca didn't get fired, by the way. They're not firing anyone because of the pandy. But the girl from—what's that improv team with the most annoying name ever?"

"You have to be more specific."

"I can't remember right now, but that's who got hired. So you know how I said day sex? I wasn't kidding. That really is the answer to how you get through the hours with this person you kind of do and kind of don't know."

"I'm excited that you're about to bring a human into the world," I said. "You and Theo are going to be such good parents."

"We realized last night that the age he'll be when our son graduates from high school is the age my dad will be three years from now."

"Theo's young at heart."

"Hmm—young at heartburn—is that anything?"

"Young at fart?" I countered.

"Keep me posted."

"Thank you, Vivvy," I said. "And likewise."

In the bathroom, I heard voices outside, and I discovered that if I raised the shade on the north-facing window, I could see Noah and his trainer. The trainer was visible from the back, and Noah was visible from the front, holding a silver kettlebell near his left shoulder then thrusting it straight up with both hands. I was fairly sure he couldn't see me—no lights were on in the bathroom—and I watched for a few minutes. Sweat had made a messy column down the front of his gray T-shirt and also appeared in large patches when he lifted his arms, and again I felt a wave of attraction. He did some sit-ups, and I wondered if his body felt sore from sex, sore in a good way, like mine did. He went back to lifting the kettlebell, and, more because I didn't want to be creepy than because I'd lost interest, I closed the shade. I then lay on the bed with the latest issue of *The New Yorker* and read the cartoon captions until my phone buzzed.

Hey just finished, he'd texted.

I saw you out the window, I replied. *You looked cute.*

Also sweaty, he replied.

Sweaty in a cute way, I replied. *Want to come visit your own guest room?*

I would love to! he replied.

He showed up within about a minute, this time carrying two water glasses. I took both and set them on the table beside the armchair then hugged and kissed him. He kissed me back before saying, "Are you sure you don't care if I'm sweaty?"

"I'm very sure," I said.

Afterward, when he'd collapsed on me and I was running my fingertips over his back, I said, "So have you, uh, dated much during the pandemic?"

"Well," he said, "the last person I had sex with is you. And the person before that was also you and the person before that was *also* you."

"Who was the person before that?"

He lifted his head. "This is kind of a complicated answer. The last serious relationship I had was with a woman named Louisiana. We broke up almost four years ago."

"I know who she is," I said. "And I know you dated her." This was the jewelry designer / pest control heiress.

"We've never officially gotten back together, but—well, for lack of a better way to say it, we've hooked up a few times over the years. Including this past April. And I don't want to sound disrespectful to her, but I remembered pretty quickly why we'd broken up. That's always how it's been with her."

"Can you be more specific and thorough about her unappealing qualities?"

He laughed. "I can picture her wearing a *Good Vibes Only* T-shirt," he said. "How about that? Or, this is a lot more serious, but she's very preoccupied with food and her weight and counting calories. She's extremely thin. And I feel for her, but I have enough issues of my own on that front that I find it challenging to be around."

"Was she staying here?"

"Sometimes. She lives in Malibu."

I wondered but didn't ask if her Malibu house had been funded by cockroaches or necklaces.

"Ending things again with her is what made me resolve to email you," Noah said. "It still took a while to work up the nerve. But I'd felt lonely after being sick, with everything shut down. And then being around Louisiana felt equally lonely. It wasn't her fault, but there was just something missing."

With my thumb and pointer finger, I flicked his left bicep. "I almost resent how good you are at saying the perfect thing."

"Really, perfect? Phew." He leaned down and kissed my forehead. "Who's the last person you were involved with?"

"Before Covid, there was a guy I never quite dated but, you know, met up with. Like friends with benefits, except we weren't friends."

"I bet he was smitten with you."

"He definitely wasn't. And I definitely wasn't smitten with him. It was a holding pattern for both of us. The last time I saw him was in 2019, in September or October. Then we weren't in touch for a few months, and I texted him, and he texted back that he had a girlfriend but wished me the best of luck." Noah's head was still raised, and I rolled my eyes. "And that's the story of how I was dumped by my mediocre fuck buddy."

"That sends chills down my spine."

"Which part?"

"Being called a mediocre fuck buddy, for one thing. Poor guy."

"You're not a mediocre fuck buddy. You're a stellar fuck buddy."

I was slightly surprised that Noah didn't laugh or even seem pleased.

"Anyway," I said, "the dynamic between Gene and me was completely different from our dynamic. He and I never really talked about anything. And not because we had such an animal attraction that we tore off each other's clothes the minute we were together. Our conversations were just pointless and uninteresting. They were about how it was crazy that Christmas was almost here, or could you believe that thunderstorm the other day? And also—" I paused. "I lied to him about my job. And I'd done that before, lied to other guys. I said I was still a medical newsletter writer because I didn't want to talk to them about *TNO* or be asked for tickets. After the text where Gene told me he had a girlfriend, he sent another text saying, *By the way it's cool you're a writer for TNO.* I asked how he knew, and he said he'd seen a fleece jacket with the *TNO* logo at my apartment and assumed I'd bought it at the gift shop in the 66 Building, but later he'd also seen a mug that Henrietta had made for my birthday one year that had a picture of me, her, and Viv on it. So then he googled me." I was quiet, and Noah looked at me.

"How'd you feel about that?"

"Remorseful. Not because he deserved better, although of course he did, but because who was I really pulling one over on? What was I achieving by sleeping with someone I didn't want to tell the most basic information about my life?"

"Before seeing Louisiana," Noah said, "I hadn't had sex for almost a year. In 2019, I went on a bunch of first dates, and a couple second dates, but I felt like I knew beforehand how they'd play out and it just wasn't worth the energy. If you're our age and single, dating kind of has to be an act of reckless optimism, right? The triumph of hope over experience?"

"Did you really not have sex for almost a year?"

"Yes."

"I'm not judging you, I'm just surprised."

"Because I'm a guy?"

"Partly."

"Do you buy into the idea of all men as constantly horny? I thought the younger *TNO* staffers were teaching you that gender stereotypes are nonsense."

"I don't know if you know this, but you're also a celebrity. A good-looking celebrity. Don't women throw their bras at you onstage?"

"I don't think that happens in real life."

"Never? Not even once or twice?"

He smiled sheepishly. "Maybe once or twice." Then he burrowed into me. "I *am* constantly horny for you, in case that's not clear."

Margit and Glenn came back in the afternoon, and even though I knew they weren't Noah's parents, I felt a little like they were, and I wanted their approval. They appeared to be in their sixties—Margit was petite and dark-haired, and Glenn was tall—and I further realized that I'd half expected them to have on uniforms like the servants in a British period drama. Instead, they were wearing shorts and T-shirts, and when Noah introduced me in the kitchen, they greeted me in a friendly but brief way, and then Noah told Margit that we hadn't eaten the salmon the night before so it would probably be good to have it for dinner. Equally casually, Noah said to me, "Do you want Glenn to vacuum your car?"

"Oh," I said. "No, that's okay."

"If you change your mind, just give him the keys."

Then we went out to the pool and splashed around and treaded water for a while and stood in the shallow end pressed against each other, making out—did Margit, whom I had the vague impression was still in the kitchen, care? Had she seen a version of this many times?—and Noah said, "I think it's very important for you to be kissed a lot while you're in a swimming pool because I hear that Martin Biersch was negligent on that front."

"I appreciate that," I said.

Then we lay on the inflatables, and I almost fell asleep, with the sunny blue Topanga sky above us and the green hills around us and a sort of natural ambient buzzing in the air. I wasn't, of course, totally un-self-conscious about how I looked in a bathing suit, but I was only about 17 percent as self-conscious as I'd have anticipated. First because of all the sex we'd had and second because, as per Viv's pep talk, I was staying for just three more days, until Thursday at noon, so really, wouldn't it have been a waste of time to fret about my thighs or belly?

After that, he showed me his studio: the live room, which held another grand piano and a drum set in addition to a dozen guitars of various shapes and sizes stored on stands; the control room, with a vast mixing console like the one in the control room at *TNO;* and the isolation booth, with its foam-covered walls and standing mic. Back in the live room, he picked up an acoustic guitar and tuned it and then, while looking at me, began playing a song I soon recognized as "Revolution" by the Beatles. He kept playing as we talked about something else, and I felt a tidal wave in my stomach, this reminder of the thing he could do exceptionally well and easily and the strange preciousness of his doing it when no one was around except me.

He stopped playing and said, "It's weird we've never discussed this, but do you play any instruments?"

I shook my head. "I wish."

He began to play another song and said, "You know this one?"

It took me a moment, then I said, " 'Sultans of Swing'?"

He nodded, closed his eyes, and sang. I thought about the embarrassment I had experienced watching him rehearse his songs at *TNO*, and it seemed in retrospect to have been a kind of foreknowledge but also a kind of misunderstanding. I didn't feel embarrassed in his studio; I felt admiration. And my embarrassment from before now seemed like a protectiveness.

"Last one," he said, and he segued into "Ain't No Sunshine"—the title was revealed in the first line—and his eyes were closed again and he was belting it out unabashedly, and I wondered then if there was always a loneliness to loving a very talented person because their talent was only of them, not of both of you, and then I thought, *Jesus Christ, do I love Noah? I only got here yesterday!* And then I thought, was there anyone who would ever feel lonely because of my talent? Was I as talented as Noah? I was competent, but nobody would want to stand still and just watch me. If you were a writer, you could be impressive in a cerebral sort of way, but if you were a musician, you got to be viscerally magical.

As casually as he'd reached for the guitar, he put it back, and grabbed my hand.

We returned to the main house and ate the dinner Margit had made, though we didn't see Margit until we were halfway through eating, when she came to check if we needed anything and then came back to clear the plates. (Was it reprehensible that a couple in their sixties worked for Noah in this way? Was it fine? Was it my responsibility to decide?)

Then, in Noah's bedroom, we watched a futuristic movie about astronauts, but halfway through we began messing around and the movie was still playing on the wall-mounted screen as he peeled off my jeans and underwear and kissed the insides of my thighs, so my consciousness was split between the surreal ecstasy of his mouth on me while my eyes were closed and the characters saying things like "But the commander has no idea that the electromagnetic currents from the storm damaged the satellite!"

I woke the next morning, and moved from Noah's bed to the one in the guest room (with a long and, I hoped, surreptitious stop in the bathroom between) not at 4:15 but at 5:27, which seemed like progress. The next morning I woke and moved at 5:55. On the fourth morning, I woke at 6:10, went to the guest bathroom, then returned to his bed, and when I did, he sleepily scooted toward me and wrapped me in his arms.

This was the day I had planned to depart, a plan I'd never mentioned to Noah, a plan that seemed, from the vantage point of his bed and his arms, to be ridiculous.

A rhythm asserted itself: outrageously delicious yet healthy meals prepared by Margit and eaten outside; Noah's trainer every other morning, which was when I attended to the Sisyphean task of body hair removal, except with a razor blade and tweezers instead of a boulder; responding to emails or, in Noah's case, to phone calls after lunch; driving to various trails in the late afternoon to hike and sometimes swimming on our return; watching movies before bed; and random but regular intervals of sex that was sometimes fun and lighthearted, almost joking, and sometimes passionate and serious, like we were the futuristic astronauts who'd made it back from our mission successfully and could finally take off our space suits and go at it with our earthly flesh.

It was somewhere in this stretch that I remembered the Mad Libs and convinced him to let us finish it, and my favorite line from our collaboration was *"Forsooth!" I said, "California is truly the most axiomatic and piquant bellybutton I've ever square danced!"* It was also during this stretch that I was reading by the pool one afternoon while Noah was inside on the phone with his manager discussing a livestream show that would be filmed in September at a concert hall with no audience. The conversation went on for a long time, and at some point, I became aware of a mild but persistent longing. And then I thought, *I miss him.*

It was on the ninth day of my visit, while we were lying naked in his bed at 11:40 A.M., that he patted the hamster on my right bicep and said, "That's still the greatest tattoo of all time." I was flat on my back and he was on his side, facing me.

"It really encapsulates my badass lifestyle, doesn't it?" I touched the inside of his left forearm, the music notes on a staff. I now knew, as I had not when the glimpses of and proximity to his skin had tormented me at *TNO*, that he'd gotten the "Blackbird" notes after his first album came out, the crow after his bandmate Christopher had died, and the Celtic knot after his first year of sobriety. I said, "Do you think you're done or not done with body art?"

"Probably done. What about you?"

"Also probably done, unless I form an unexpected attachment to a guinea pig or a raccoon."

He laughed, and I said, "I have a question for you. You know over email when I asked if you were trying to seduce me during your song rehearsal at *TNO*? When you said no, I kind of interpreted it as you saying, no, you weren't interested in me."

He shook his head rapidly. "I knew I was walking the knife's edge with that one. In the emails, I mean. And I blew it, didn't I? It was the word *seduce* that confused me—I think of that as being sleazy, like what a scoundrel does to an innocent young woman in a nineteenth-century novel. I didn't understand what you were asking. If you had just said, 'Do you like me?' I could have said, 'I sure do.'"

I laughed. "What if I had said, 'Do you like me in a wholesome, non-scoundrel-ish way?'"

"No." He was shaking his head again. "It was never wholesome. But I didn't know if it was safe then to convey that."

"Couldn't you tell that 'Do you like me?' was basically what I was asking when I had that email freakout? And you were like, 'I don't know what we're doing, but it's fun, huh?'" I poked a finger against his chest. "I needed more affirmation than that."

"After you dressed me down with the stuff about how I'm not a toxic narcissist but only barely, I did know I'd fucked up, but I wasn't sure how."

"But then I apologized."

"Did you?" Noah was regarding me dubiously.

"I expressed remorse!" I might, even then, have been reluctant to let it slip that I had practically memorized our emails, except that his recall of them seemed similarly detailed. And he was correct that I hadn't actually written the words *I'm sorry.*

"I'm very happy to give you affirmation," he said. "I want to give you affirmation. But if I don't give you enough, you should ask for it."

"Isn't asking for affirmation—I don't know—needy?"

He looked perplexed. "Isn't the point of something like this that the other person tries to meet your needs, and you try to meet theirs?"

I was quiet for a few seconds before saying, "Is this what they teach in therapy? Because it's blowing my mind."

He laughed. "I have an idea. Instead of going back to New York in September, what if you quit *TNO* and stay here? Isn't L.A. better if you want to pivot to screenwriting?"

I raised one arm to gesture around the room. "This is very fun. But it's not real."

"In what way is it not real?"

"Having sex all the time while barely interacting with any other human beings."

"It *should* be real." He raised his head and propped it on his left hand, his elbow just below the pillow. Our faces were a few inches apart.

I looked at a wood beam in the ceiling. "I have to tell you something. I felt so overwhelmed about staying with you that I told myself after I got here I'd only stay three days. I've been acting all breezy, like I'm not intimidated by this whole situation, but the truth is that I'm a super-anxious person. That's how it's not real."

Kindly, he said, "Do you think I didn't realize you're anxious?"

"Wait, really?"

"It seems like you've found ways to manage it that work for you. And, I mean, coming from a recovery background, three days is impressive. Most of us just take it one day at a time." I didn't say anything, and he added, "Isn't the goal to live with our demons, not to expect them to go away?"

"Also," I said then stopped.

"Also," he repeated.

"Sometimes when I speak, I feel like I'm writing dialogue for the character of myself. I'm impersonating a normal human when really I'm a confused freak."

He laughed. "We're all confused freaks. It's just that most of us aren't professional writers." We made eye contact, and he said, "It seems like you're describing what everyone does in all sorts of situations. Fake it 'til you make it. How do you think I felt the first time I performed at a big awards show? While a virgin, might I remind you." He leaned forward and kissed me on the lips. "In fact, we're even, because I've been pretending I'm not intimidated by being around someone much smarter than I am."

"That's very gentlemanly of you," I said. "But come on."

"You're so terrifyingly, awesomely perceptive. That thing about writing dialogue for the character of yourself, that's so clever. I wish I had thought of it years ago, so in interviews I could have pretended I was playing the part of a musician promoting an album."

Wasn't this more than I'd ever imagined I could wish for, that a kind, thoughtful, smoking-hot man would think I was terrifyingly, awesomely perceptive? That he understood how neurotic I was, and didn't seem to mind? That he saw neediness not as annoying but as normal? Hadn't it all seemed so unlikely that I'd genuinely made peace with never finding someone like Noah except perhaps in the pages of a screenplay I wrote?

He reached out and smoothed back my hair, which was something he did a lot. He said, "None of that means that what's happening between us isn't real."

———

We'd gone for a hike in Temescal Canyon, walking a loop of just under four miles, and it was late afternoon as we returned to the trailhead. We both wore baseball caps, and Noah wore a backpack that contained our water bottles and the wrappers from the same brand of protein bars he'd sent to me in Kansas City. We'd eaten the bars while sitting on a boulder near an outcropping apparently known as Skull Rock, from which we could see Santa Monica Bay. Gesturing at the view, I'd said, "It's so painful being reminded that the smugness of people who live in California is justified."

As we approached the trailhead, we were discussing Noah's wish to get a dog, and he said, "Do you think a golden retriever would mean my WASPy parents successfully brainwashed me after all?"

"What about a beagle?" I said. "To renounce your WASPiness and also because they're objectively the best dogs."

He took my hand. "Beagles are the best small dog. I'll grant you that."

"But they're not small dogs. I mean, I'm sure no beagle thinks that. Small dogs are Pomeranians or Chihuahuas."

"Doesn't it depend on the beagle?" We'd reached the parking lot, and we were walking toward Noah's car, which was a silver Lexus hybrid SUV.

"Sugar weighs twenty-five pounds," I said. "Twenty-five pounds of beautiful, lustrous, formidable canine that could never fit in someone's purse."

"I'm not disagreeing that Sugar—" Noah began, but he was interrupted by a male voice saying with some urgency, "Hey, Noah!"

Immediately, Noah dropped my hand and said very quietly, "Keep walking."

The parking lot was half-full, and about ten people in configurations of twos and threes were milling around. After scanning the line of cars to figure out who'd spoken, I spotted a man kneeling by a Volvo sedan. "Noah, who's your friend?" the man said. "What's your friend's name?" The man looked to be in his twenties, holding a big black camera with its lens extended, and in the ensuing quiet, I could hear the shutter click repeatedly.

"Come on, man," Noah said. "Not now."

"You cut off your hair, right?" the man said. "Did you shave your head? When did you do that?"

Noah was walking so quickly that I'd fallen a foot or two behind him. He'd removed the keys from his shorts pocket, and there was a beep just before he climbed in the driver's side door of the Lexus and started the engine. As I entered the passenger side, the paparazzo said to me, "Hey, what's your name? Are you and Noah dating? How long have you known Noah?"

Noah's jaw was clenched as he reversed out of the parking space and drove toward the exit. I glanced back toward the paparazzo, and Noah said in a low voice, "Don't look at him." He'd turned onto the road when, still in a tight voice, he said, "You'd think those guys would lay off with everything happening now."

I said nothing, and when he turned his head toward me, we made eye contact for the first time in several minutes.

"Are you okay?" he asked.

We both were quiet as we passed a high school that was low and palm-tree-bedecked like a high school in a movie, and finally I said, "Are you afraid he'll sell a picture of you holding my hand?" I could hear that my voice was weird, too, though not how Noah's was— mine was sharp and distant. There was a warmly teasing way we'd gotten in the habit of speaking to each other, and this was its opposite.

"I hope he doesn't for your sake," Noah said.

"Oh, really? For my sake?"

Noah looked over again as he said, "Are you accusing me of something? Because that's what it sounds like."

"If I were a hot twenty-five-year-old actress, would you have dropped my hand like that?"

He squinted. "Are you serious? Did you *want* the guy to take our picture?"

"There was something very—" I paused. "Instinctive. About how you pulled away from me."

"I thought you'd hate it. Yes, you. Not me. You. Because you're a private person and I know you've walked red carpets a few times, but I don't think you're used to being ambushed in normal life like I am."

In front of us, the ocean appeared again, turquoise beneath a cornflower sky, and the beauty of the view was an unpleasant contrast to the disagreeable energy inside the car. At least sixty seconds had passed when, taking pains to keep my tone matter-of-fact rather than resentful, I said, "There's nothing you promised me. I'm complicit in how undefined whatever we're doing is. I admit that. And I believe you genuinely like me, or at least you genuinely like me enough to be your secret pandemic hookup. But I don't think I have a low enough opinion of myself to be your secret pandemic hookup."

"Wow," he said. "I don't even know where to start. The fact that you could think any of that is so off base that it makes me wonder if we've been having completely different experiences the whole time you've been here. I thought we were having a great time."

"Secret pandemic hookups and having a great time aren't mutually exclusive."

While looking straight ahead, he pulled the car over to a parking lane abutting a dusty upward slope dotted with sage scrub. He moved the gear shift into park before facing me, his expression bewildered and displeased. "Do you remember when I told you I was attracted to you from the moment you started talking at the pitch meeting in Nigel's office?"

"Yes."

"Part of the reason was that you seemed so confident, like one of the most confident women I'd ever met. One of the most confident *people*. You had very clear ideas for your sketches, and it was obvious that you knew you could will them into being. And you talked in this way where it seemed like you were planning to be polite and professional with me, but you assumed I wasn't very bright, and you were prepared to overcome my lack of intelligence. I've worked with tons of creative people, tons of talented people, but there was something so refreshing about you, something so cool, where you just really knew who you were and how to get shit done. I had this overwhelming feeling of *I want to know her. I want to be around her.* Then in your office, you were incredibly kind and supportive. You've probably told me seven times, starting that night, what an asshole you are, but you almost never are. Or when you are, it seems like some kind of bluster. It doesn't seem like who you really are."

I was fascinated, silenced, and unsure where this was going. On the other side of the windshield, a big white bird I couldn't identify swooped down and then up again.

Noah exhaled deeply. "You and I hung out in person that week at *TNO* and it was fun and great. Even after things went off the rails at the bar, I felt like there was a conversation we hadn't finished, and for the next two years, I wondered how the rest of it would have gone. From the minute you responded to my first email, it was like that conversation picked up exactly where it had stopped. Emailing with you was fun and great, and then we talked on the phone, and it was fun and great, and you came here, and, yeah, it's not effortless, there are little bumps where we need to figure out how to be around each other. But that's just life, and having you here has been even better than fun and great. When we're hanging out by the pool and when we're watching a movie and above all when we're making love, and I already know you'll mock me for saying *making love,* but that's what it is—all of that is amazing. I've waited my whole life to feel connected to someone in the ways I feel connected to you. I don't even know if this registered with you, but when we were emailing, after I got worried I'd offended you by telling you to send me a pdf about your divorce, I told you that I didn't want you to ever stop emailing me. But I wrote a different sentence first that I was too scared to send. And it was that I wanted you to be part of my life forever. I want you and my sister to get to know each other, and I want to introduce you to all my favorite people that I work with. When everything isn't shut down, there are so many experiences I want to share with you, like taking you to this really cool restaurant in Tokyo or to my favorite park in Sydney. I think of *marrying* you. And to feel this way and then hear you say crap about how I'm embarrassed to hold your hand in front of some fucking paparazzo—it's like The Danny Horst Rule wasn't just a funny sketch idea. It's your philosophy of life. That version of you in Nigel's office that I fell in love with, you *are* that person and you do have that confidence. But at the same time, you might be the most insecure adult I've ever met."

Really, I had been completely silenced. I had never been on the receiving end of this kind of—well, I didn't even know what it was. An admonition? A declaration? An encomium? None of it was clearly wrong; much of it was heart-stoppingly flattering; a small but significant portion was humiliating.

"I'm not sure what to say," I said.

"I love you, Sally," he said. "For you to suggest that I'm ashamed of you—you're not just insulting yourself. You're insulting me."

He loved me? He loved me! Or had he loved me five minutes earlier but changed his mind since then because of what I'd said since we'd left the parking lot? "For what it's worth," I said, "I think it's easier to dismiss entrenched dating patterns when you can date anyone you want."

He said nothing.

"Setting aside The Danny Horst Rule as a generalization," I continued, "I guess the thing I don't understand is that you can do better than me. You can find someone prettier."

He was looking at me with a not-warm expression. "Is that a question I'm supposed to answer?"

"Please."

"Will you at least acknowledge how fucked-up it is that first you accuse me of not thinking you're attractive enough to date, and after I tell you that's not true, you ask why I'm not dating someone better-looking?"

"You just admitted that you liked me at first because you could tell I didn't think you were smart. What's that Groucho Marx line about not wanting to belong to any club that would have you as a member?"

He turned his head so he was gazing out the windshield again. "There's a picture of the cast and crew of *TNO* taken every year on the main stage, right? I'm sure I've seen it online or in a magazine. And if I was looking at that, would I pick you out from everyone else and say, 'That's the most gorgeous woman I've ever seen'? If I'm being honest, no. But human beings aren't static images. We're dynamic and kinetic, and it's like I said before—right away, I wanted to talk to you, and every time I've talked to you since I've always wanted to keep talking to you."

That I didn't feel completely uninsulted by his admission that I wasn't the most gorgeous woman he'd ever seen meant—what? That I'd nursed some private hope that he thought I was? Either because he had unusual taste or because I'd been holding on to the belief that, as with many a romantic comedy heroine, I was far more beautiful than I realized? At the same time, I didn't feel the impulse to cling to the insult as I might have when I was younger; I appreciated his candor. I said, "Do you know what *sapiosexual* means?"

"No."

"It means being attracted to someone's brain."

"I am attracted to your brain," he said. "But I'm also attracted to the rest of you." We both were quiet for a few seconds, then he said, "When you told me that thing about swearing off dating at *TNO* because Elliot rejected you, a part of me was like, *Thank God for that*. Even though your decision seems over the top, if you hadn't made it, you'd probably be married to another writer. But now I wonder if it's a cautionary tale about how you want to stew in your aloneness. Because, sure, I'm discreet when I'm dating someone new in order to avoid media drama, but I'm not the one who's into secret hookups as a way of life."

"Why would I want to stew in my aloneness?"

"Because you're scared."

"What am I scared of?"

"Getting hurt. Knowing another person really well and another person knowing you really well. Feelings you can't make fun of. Interactions that go on for long enough that they maybe turn a little awkward or a little tedious instead of ending after ten minutes with a zinger."

"If you're referring to *TNO* sketches, they're more like five minutes. Ten minutes is an eternity on TV."

He looked at me then said, "Okay, Sally," and turned on the ignition.

"I love you, too," I blurted out.

"Do you?" His brow was furrowed.

"The truth is that I can't believe you exist. I've never known anyone with the combination of qualities you have. You're so deeply nice and so humble and so insightful in this very non-show-offy way. And even though your fame does fuck with my head, I really respect your creativity and talent and work ethic. Sometimes I feel silly expressing this to you because I'm the fifty-million-and-first person to say it, but I do think your songs are beautiful. And spending time with you, it *is* fun and great. Everything you said, I feel that, too, that I loved being around you at *TNO* and I loved emailing with you and I loved talking to you on the phone and I love—" I paused but then I made myself say it. "I love when we make love. It's definitely different from anything I've ever experienced. And I can't believe that we met and I get to be the person who's eating dinner with you and hiking with you and being naked with you. For that matter, that I'm the person who just looks up and there you are in the same room with me, and, yes, you are smoking hot. And how unique and incredible you are does make me kind of karmically or existentially terrified. Because how could anyone deserve you, let alone me? But I'm also really grateful because I always wanted to feel disbelief at my own luck. At my romantic luck, I mean, not my luck related to Nigel giving me a career break."

By this point, Noah was smiling, looking at me with that great affection—with love—and as he leaned forward and kissed me, I was struck by how forgiving he was, how he wasn't going to make me grovel. "Let's go home," he said. "Okay? Since we're in agreement about how good we are at being naked together—let's go do that."

"You make me want to be a better man," I said. "That's what I'm trying to say."

Back at his house, in his bed, we looked into each other's eyes the most that we ever had, we touched each other the most tenderly, and a few times I wasn't sure if I could maintain the eye contact, but I did. At one point, he stopped moving while he was still inside me and smiled, his face above and so close to mine. Quietly, I said, "This is the happiest I've ever been."

Then we kissed for a long time, moving together.

After, while I rested my head on his chest, he said, "You know that thing I said about if I saw a picture of the cast and crew of *TNO*? I feel like it came out wrong, because you *are* really pretty." He squeezed my waist. "I love every part of you."

"When I didn't think you were smart at the pitch meeting, it was only for ten minutes," I said. "Ever since then, I've thought you are."

He laughed. "There's a compliment I've wanted to give you, but I'm not sure I've figured out how to say it in a way that doesn't make me sound self-centered."

"Everyone is self-centered," I said. "Go for it."

"Do you remember when we were on the phone and you asked if I'm the type of Airbnb host who leaves my family photos out and my food in the refrigerator, and I said that I would make my house very clean so that you'd give me five stars?"

"Yes."

"I realize my response wasn't, like, *TNO*-quality. But I was proud of myself because, honestly, I'm not usually that quick-witted. You bring out that side of me. You know the advice about how you should always play tennis with people better than you? When I'm talking to you, I'm a funnier and smarter version of myself because you're funny and smart."

"Ironically," I said, "I've played tennis about twice, and I'm awful at it."

But Noah's voice was serious as he said, "For a long time, I've known that the best parts of my life were the public parts. I can't complain, because those parts have been really great, like touring in another country or being part of a ceremony at the White House. But in my romantic relationships, away from audiences and cameras—I don't want to insult the women I've dated, because it takes two to have mundane conversations, but they *were* mundane. It was like what you said about you and that guy Gene. Either we were talking about predictable topics or talking about potentially interesting topics in a predictable way. Sometimes I'd tell myself, Well, sure, it's hard for normal life to measure up after you hang out with the Obamas. But other times, I felt like, behind the scenes, there was this emptiness. At night, when I was going to bed, I was more relaxed when I was by myself, whether I wasn't dating anyone or was dating someone but they weren't there that night. I wanted to find a real partner, but I couldn't picture who the partner would be." He paused. My ear was over his heart, and I could hear its steady beat. "When I'm with you," he continued, "the best, most interesting part of my life is behind the scenes. I felt this emailing you, and I even felt it in your *TNO* office when you were helping with my sketch. Like, no one in the world knows what we're up to except us and it's awesome. It's not for social media, it's not for a documentary about the making of an album, it's not an anecdote to tell on a talk show. It's just because we think it's fun and we like each other and we like being together."

Listening to him, it had occurred to me to say, "I'm honored that you find me more interesting than the Obamas," but what came out of my mouth instead was "That's the nicest thing anyone has ever said to me in my entire life." I raised my head to look at him. "And I don't think it's self-centered."

"Oh, good." He grinned.

"Just so you know," I said, "you weren't wrong about me being private and hating to have my picture taken, or at least by a random dude jumping out of the bushes."

"I did know," he said. "Because you threatened to stay at a hotel when I mentioned there might be paparazzi at that shopping center when you were arriving. If I'm not mistaken, you also once told me you were a goblin who'd never appeared onstage at *TNO*."

"Oh, right." I brought my hand up to my face in embarrass-ment. "I mean, there wasn't a second when I actually wanted to stay at a hotel. I always wanted to stay with you. I just got anx-ious."

"I like that you're private. You realize that there are women who dated me in order to get their picture in magazines, don't you?"

This was an aspect of the situation I hadn't considered. "I bet that was more of a fringe benefit than the main reason," I said. "I'm sure you being charming and adorable was the main reason."

Dryly, he said, "You might be surprised."

"I may have a flaw or two, but I solemnly swear that I'll never use you to try to advance my modeling career. Or to get my cannabis-infused-jams-and-jellies small business off the ground."

He laughed. "That reminds me there are two jokes I've thought about making when we're"—he patted my bare hip—"like this. Should I try them out on you?"

"You definitely should."

"The first one, the joke part isn't the sentiment. It's the callback."

I was smiling as I said, "Not to discourage you, but preemptively explaining a joke rarely enhances it."

"Okay," he said. "Baby, you don't know how beautiful you are. You're so perfect, I never thought I'd find this, am I in heaven?" When I laughed, he said, "Do you know what that's a reference to?"

"Yes." I leaned in and kissed him. "And I do think it's funny."

"But you also get that it's really how I feel? That's why I think of it whenever we're in bed."

"Thank you for your delusionally generous view of me. What's the other joke?"

"This one is a little crude."

"Even better."

"I'm so happy that I can't wipe the smile off my penis."

This time, I really, really laughed, and he said, "Seriously, the sound of you laughing—there's nothing else like it."

To my surprise, the first person to contact me about the photos wasn't Henrietta; it was Danny. *Yo Chuckles,* read his text, which arrived that night just after 10 P.M. Pacific time. He'd included a link to an online tabloid with the headline "Noah Brewster Spotted on Hike with Mystery Woman." Noah and I were watching a movie in the sitting area off the kitchen but had paused it while he got up to pee.

Danny's next text was *Aren't u a dark horse*

Weird huh? I replied. *How are you doing?*

From Danny: *Trying to hide how much I dig the pandemic.* This was followed by a photo of a placid, empty pool in the foreground, then some well-manicured hedges, then part of a vast white brick house that I assumed to be Nigel's Hamptons mansion, an assumption confirmed when Danny added, *Nigel likes to keep it at a sweet 81 degrees*

The pool? I replied. *Or all of the Hamptons?*

From Danny: *Are u and NB cuffed?*

I replied with the shrugging brown-haired white woman emoji then added, *Pretty sure Noah keeps his closer to a sweet 75 degrees*

Danny: *To each his/her own sugar daddy*

I didn't love this, nor was I convinced that the implication was unfair.

Btw he and Annabel never really dated back in 2018, I wrote.

Danny: *Old news Chuckles*

Danny: *Good to see u enjoying yourself for once*

The next text was indeed from Henrietta, after a screenshot taken of a different online gossip site: *My fav hetero headline ever!* This one was "Does Noah Brewster Have a New Girlfriend?"

I skimmed both articles. I could see that already there were many more, all regurgitating the same minimal information—*Noah, debuting a newly shorn look, and the unidentified woman took a hike in the celeb-popular Temescal Canyon Park. . . . Brewster, who was last linked with jewelry designer Louisiana Williams . . . Noah Brewster, almost unrecognizable without his signature long hair, and his brunette date were all smiles following the afternoon stroll.* . . . The photos, of which there seemed to be just three, were of us before we'd realized the paparazzo was there, when we were holding hands and both looking slightly downward at the path in front of us, except in one Noah was facing me and speaking. Though I'd been wearing what I thought of as my cutest and sleekest leggings, my thighs looked lumpier than they did in my mind's eye. On the gossip site, some of the photos helpfully included superimposed bright green arrows pointing at the absence of Noah's hair under his baseball cap.

I could hear Noah returning, and I had the impulse to toss my phone behind a cushion, but I hadn't done so by the time he appeared. "Is everything okay?" he asked.

I hesitated then said, "I think the photos are online. I mean they *are* online."

He looked displeased. "Can I make a suggestion? Ignore it completely, and let's let my publicist deal with anything that needs to be dealt with tomorrow."

I hesitated—I didn't want to upset him, but it felt odd for him not to know—then said, "Are those the first photos since you shaved your head?"

He grimaced. "Is that what they're making this about?"

"Partly. Is that also some of the reason you didn't want your picture taken?" Had my essential mistake been the assumption that his displeasure in the parking lot was at all connected to me?

But he shook his head. "When I had Covid, I wondered if I was going to die. Or, I know I told you this, but if I was going to permanently lose my voice. And compared to either of those, if they're going to mock me for a haircut"—he shrugged—"so be it."

"They're treating it more as breaking news than mocking it. But yeah." He was still standing, and I held open my arms. "Fuck 'em," I said. He sat and leaned into me, letting me enfold him from the side, and I hugged him tightly.

But my ability to keep things in perspective was short-lived. I'd placed my phone on the table in front of the couch, then after the movie ended, I glanced at it and recoiled; I had twelve new texts, which was a lot for me, especially at this hour. While Noah was brushing his teeth, I set my phone on the floor in the hall outside his bedroom and closed the door. We cuddled without having sex before he fell asleep (*I guess the passion is gone forever,* I thought), then I lay awake for a solid two hours, fell asleep briefly, awakened, and scurried to the guest room to read every article and every comment. Among the comments, blatant insults such as *Nhoa Brewster would never date a women who looks like that shes obviously his assitant* and *His music sucks he looks so old with no hair now no wonder he cant get hotties* were interspersed with backhanded compliments along the lines of *In our superficial times I respect Noah even more for not caring what his GF looks like!* I also read every text and email I'd received overnight from about fifty people, including my college roommate, Denise; a childhood babysitter; and a co-worker from the credit card magazine. Also from my agent, manager, and the director of publicity for *TNO;* apparently, at some point, I'd been identified by name and occupation, and the online articles had been updated to reflect this information.

There was one email unrelated to the photos, and it was from Jerry; the subject was *Food For Thought. Dear Sally,* he'd written, *Do you know there is something called "pupcakes"? They are cupcakes for dogs! Most of the ingredients are suitable for people, but they put a bone on top for "decoration." Sugar and I miss you! Love, Jerry*

If I had responded to any of the messages, this was the one I'd have chosen. But I was too agitated from bingeing on gossip about myself, exhausted and immobilized. I responded to nothing and left my phone in the guest room when I returned to Noah.

Two days passed, days during which both of us communicated a preposterous number of times with our respective agents and managers, and they all spoke to each other. The tone of these conversations could have made an observer conclude that we were discussing a topic of major significance—a respiratory pandemic, say, or systemic racism—but, even as my stomach churned, I found it hard to be dismissive. The consensus was that Noah's publicist would say nothing for the time being and wait until we were photographed again to make a statement, and the statement, which would be released to a weekly magazine known for its obsequious treatment of celebrities and attributed to a source who knew both of us would be: *Noah and Sally developed a friendship when he hosted* The Night Owls *in 2018. They're now enjoying spending time together and seeing where it goes.*

For us, the conversations to hash out this anodyne non-declaration mostly took place in the sitting area off the kitchen, sometimes on Zoom on Noah's laptop and other times on Noah's phone, set on the coffee table on speaker. Before the conclusive one ended, Noah said to the seven other people who'd dialed in, "I know the reason not to shout from the rooftops that I'm madly in love with Sally is that that would be baiting the paparazzi. But to be clear, I'm madly in love with Sally."

There was an uncharacteristic silence from the agents and managers, then, finally, in a way that belied the sentiment, a female voice that I thought belonged to Noah's agent said, "That's wonderful news, Noah."

After the call ended, I said, "At least now I understand why you dropped my hand in the parking lot." I'd meant the comment ruefully, but I could hear that it sounded bitter.

He took my hand then, lifted it to his mouth, and kissed the back. "This part blows over," he said.

It was after lunch the next day—Margit had prepared a spinach frittata and fresh berries—that Noah said, "I have something to show you." He led me to his study, opened the door, looked at me, and said with a boyish sort of pride, "What do you think?"

As when he'd shown me the room on the day of my arrival, the long and rough-hewn desk was empty except for a dark blue ceramic lamp, and the room was uncluttered. Then I realized that the built-in shelves behind the desk, which had previously been about a third full, were entirely empty. He waved me over to the desk and opened the one large, shallow drawer. It, too, was empty.

"It's yours," he said. "This room is your office so you can stay forever and write your screenplays."

I hadn't pulled my laptop out of my backpack since getting to his house.

Slowly, I said, "But I have a job."

"That you've been telling me for the last two years you want to quit."

"But I signed a contract saying I'd go back."

"Isn't that what agents are for?"

"But I'm not flaky. I'm responsible."

We looked at each other, and he said, "I didn't mean to upset you. I meant to make you feel welcome."

"If I stayed here forever, what does that even mean? Would I pay you rent?"

"Of course not."

"So I'd suddenly become a person generating no income while living in some man's mansion?"

"I'll be shocked if the studios don't fight each other to buy any screenplay you write." His voice was cooler as he said, "And I don't think of myself as some man, but I guess you do."

"If I were to quit *TNO* and stay here, it would cost you nothing. If we break up in two months, or in eight months, you can just proceed like this never happened. But I'd have given up my job and my apartment and my life in the city where I have friends."

"Then hold on to your apartment."

"I'd have given up my *identity*. Instead of being a *TNO* writer, I'll be like, Example Seven in an article about nineteen celebs who are totally dating normies. I've heard from more people about those parking lot pictures than about any sketch I've ever written."

"I thought you'd like having a place to write, but now I see that I was moving too fast and being presumptuous. Sally, I'm sorry that

I didn't think through how this would look from your perspective."
But in his voice, along with contrition, there was impatience.

"It's not that you've done anything wrong," I said, "but I don't
know how to do this."

"This what?"

"I don't know how to be in a relationship. I think I should go.
Like stay somewhere else for a few days and just try to get some
perspective. I don't want to give up my career because of how good
it feels when you go down on me." Immediately, I could see that I
had distracted us both with the specificity of this example, that there
was an off-ramp for the conversation we were having as well as the
course of action I had suggested. And maybe I was being rash but I
also was being sincere—I didn't want to leave TNO because of
Noah. I wanted to leave TNO because it was time to leave TNO. As
if this resolved anything, I added, "I need to think this stuff through."

Once, years before, I'd stayed on for a few days after the Emmys
ceremony, moving from the downtown hotel where the network put
us up to an oceanfront room at a boutique hotel in Santa Monica.
This was early on in the time when I could have afforded such a
thing, and I'd done little during my stay—I'd read, and walked on
the beach, and eaten takeout on the balcony—and, pretty much
continuously, I'd experienced disbelief at my good fortune. I didn't
live in Missouri or North Carolina anymore! I didn't work for a
medical newsletter! I wasn't married to a man who thought I wasn't
funny! I was a TNO writer who had been nominated for an Emmy
and could stay at a hotel that cost four hundred dollars a night!

Returning to the same boutique hotel, I tried to remind myself
that these facts were still true—by now, I'd won Emmys and could
afford to stay at a hotel that currently cost five hundred and thirty
dollars a night—but I felt bereft. Though the beach was open, the
pier, which I could see from my balcony, was eerily empty, and the
streets nearby were quiet. A powerful sense of misgiving had begun

to grip me in Noah's guest room, as I set my clothes in my suitcase then loaded my aunt Donna's car, which I hadn't driven since pulling onto his property. He had walked out to the driveway with me, and as he kissed my cheek with an unfamiliar formality, I wondered if I'd lost him already. My regret hadn't been total as I wound south around the roads of Topanga. But my regret was already strong, and grew stronger as the minutes and hours passed. Why had I voluntarily left? What was I proving, and to whom? Was this when my interlude with Noah would begin to recede as a pandemic fever dream?

I'd checked into the hotel at 3:30, then lay on the bed for a while, planning to read and instead crying myself to sleep for an afternoon nap. When I awakened, I wasn't sure what time it was, or at first, where I was, and then I realized: 7:18 P.M., and a hotel. I thought of ordering dinner, but instead I texted Viv and Henrietta: *Had bad conversation with NB, now in hotel, maybe things are over*

From Viv: *Oh no what happened*

From Henrietta: *Are you okay*

From me: *Weird part is I think he wants a serious relationship/ wants me to stay here*

From Viv: *Of course he does you're a catch*

From Henrietta: *Is that what fight was about*

From me: *Kind of*

From me: *Would it be crazy if I don't come back to TNO*

From Henrietta: *Then who will write my sketches about the 35 year old who hasn't figured out how to use a tampon*

From Henrietta: *JK it's your one wild and precious*

From Viv: *Do you WANT to stay out there*

From me: *I don't know*

From Viv: *Pretend it's Monday and you're about to leave your apt and come to 66 and sit in Nigel's office for the pitch meeting*

From Viv: *Are you psyched to be back or are you over it all*

From Henrietta: *As you inhale the aroma of Danny's burps*

From Henrietta: *Or maybe not bc we'll all be wearing masks?*

For almost a minute, I held the phone, biting my lip. Then I wrote, *It makes me so sad to think of not seeing you guys in the middle of the night*

From Henrietta: *FWIW I'm willing to haunt your dreams*

In the morning, I went out for coffee and an egg sandwich that I ate standing outside the café, then I walked on the beach before it got crowded, as the surf roared beside me, not washing away my thoughts. Back in the room, I considered texting Noah but instead googled his name. The so-called top stories were about our hike, and I looked at the photos again, and again felt dismayed at the fit of my leggings, though the dismay was almost immediately eclipsed by a nostalgia for this moment four days before, when we'd been casually holding hands, casually chatting.

I took my laptop onto the balcony, sat, and created a new document that I named *Pros/Cons*. Then I observed the blinking cursor, listing neither pros nor cons of quitting *TNO* and moving to L.A. I needed some classical music to help me. I went into the room to find my earbuds, and when I returned to the balcony, my phone was buzzing with an incoming text, but it wasn't from Noah; it was from Viv.

How you feeling today?

Okay, I texted back. *Thanks for checking. How you feeling?*

She replied with a photo in which she stood in profile in front of a mirror, her belly truly enormous beneath a gray tank top.

Amazing!!!! I replied. *You look great*

When my phone buzzed again, I assumed it was her, but this time it *was* a message from Noah: *Hey*

My heart clutched.

Hey, I wrote back. *How are you?*

The three dots pulsated for what felt like fifteen minutes but was probably ten seconds. Then finally: *The house is really quiet without you*

This was so . . . nice? Mature? Non-game-playing?

As I began typing, another text from him appeared: *I'm sorry that I made you feel like I don't respect your job*

From him: *I do respect your job*

From me: *I'm sorry that I failed to express the slightest appreciation about you clearing out your study*

From me: *That was very kind of you*

From me: *Even if I turned it into something weird and symbolic*

I typed, *I miss you,* but before I could send it, he texted: *About to workout w/ Bobby*

From him: *Have a good day*

I waited a few seconds then deleted *I miss you*

But by the afternoon, I was looking up how much it would cost to transport my aunt Donna's car back to Kansas City if I flew directly from L.A. to New York. Although I didn't usually need to be back at *TNO* until the last week in September, there were rumors that we'd have additional days of training for the new Covid protocols and that attendance might be staggered because of limits on how many people could be in a room at a time. Plus, I'd been away for four months; maybe it made sense to go back early, to reacclimate to the city in a pandemic. By evening, however, I'd decided that eleven years of pitch meetings—along with eleven years of Tuesday all-nighters and Wednesday read-throughs and Thursday rewrites and Friday rehearsals and, yes, even Saturday shows—was enough. I didn't need a twelfth year. And there were more reasons I didn't want a twelfth year than reasons I did.

I kept moving in and out of certainty and uncertainty, composure and despair. As the sun set over the ocean, a loneliness seized me that didn't pass. By this point, it was nine in L.A. and midnight on the East Coast, and while there was a time I wouldn't have hesitated to call Viv or Henrietta at midnight, that time had been prior to them or their wife being extremely pregnant. *I really should have made more than two friends back when making friends was still possible,* I thought, and then I thought, *Danny.*

I texted *Can you talk now?* and a few seconds later, he was face-timing me, wearing a tie-dyed T-shirt, reclined on a floral sofa. He said, "What's shakin', Chuckles?"

"Can you imagine Noah being my boyfriend? Not just as a pandemic hookup, as a real long-term thing."

"Hank and Roy have always said you're a eunuch, and I'm like, 'Nah, man, she's got a beating heart.'"

"Thanks?"

"Are you in a cave right now?"

"I'm in a hotel room, and only the bathroom light is on."

"That doesn't sound at all depressing." Just as I decided that reaching out to him had been a mistake, his expression turned serious. "You okay, Chuckles?"

"Not really. I didn't have contact with Noah from the time he hosted until about a month ago, then he emailed me, then we had this emailing frenzy, then I drove out here to L.A. and we had a great time, then I ruined it. I think I want to quit *TNO* and stay here with him, but why should I get to be Noah's girlfriend? What makes me deserving? And anyway, isn't being in a relationship with a famous person kind of terrible?"

"Okay, back up. To be crystal clear, you and Noah have been banging?"

"Correct."

"You're asking separate questions, so let's go in order. Why should you get to be Noah's girlfriend? You're in overlapping industries, you met, and obviously you hit it off if he was still thinking of you two years later. And the banging was decent?"

"Yes."

"And you're easy to talk to, so that covers the conversation part. It's not necessarily more complicated than that. Next up, what makes you deserving? You're funny, you're cool, and you pretend to be tough but you're a softie."

"I'm sorry to beg for compliments, but aren't I the least cool person you know?"

"I don't mean I'd take advice from you on what sneakers to buy.

I mean cool like having your shit together. For the isn't-being-in-a-relationship-with-a-famous-person-terrible question—yeah, probably. Or it has some sucky parts, but all relationships have sucky parts. Here's my question for you. Do you like him a lot or a little?"

"More than anyone I've ever met."

"Then what's the problem?"

"Lots of people don't get what they want in life. Why should I?"

"Didn't we already cover this?"

"I think I'm better at using rage and disappointment to fuel my creativity. Happiness makes me uneasy."

When he laughed, I said, "I wish I was kidding."

"I know you're not. Here's another way of looking at it. You're, like, forty, yeah?"

"Thirty-eight."

"But you've experienced your share of hookups and relationships that didn't work out. Elliot or whoever?"

"Who told you I had a thing for Elliot? Elliot?"

"I never reveal my sources. My point is that even if Noah is the love of your life, your batting average is still pretty bad. So is mine, and so is most people's. Of all the couples that ever existed, most aren't together now. You're not together with your ex-husband. I'm not together with Annabel. I believe you that you're bad at dating, but you can be bad at dating and still fall in love once a lifetime."

"That logic is enticing yet very, very tenuous."

He grinned. "I'm good at falling in love, and it makes my batting average a lot worse than yours."

"How are things with you and Lucy?"

"Are we finished with you and Noah?"

"The fact that he's way more attractive than I am—you really think that doesn't matter?"

"Oh, man, I'm excited you asked me this. There are three topics I'm an authority on. You know what they are?"

I shook my head.

"The movies of Bethany Brick. The menu at the Big Wings on Forty-eighth Street. And I don't know if you've heard of this, but there's something called the Danny Horst Rule. And the amazing thing is, *I'm* Danny Horst."

"Touché."

"Chuckles, you and Noah are the ones who decide if it matters. It doesn't seem like it matters to him so that just leaves you."

"When you put it like that, it almost makes me sound like a self-sabotaging asshat."

"I'm not going to say the rule doesn't exist, but it's like Santa Claus. It's only real if you believe in it."

"Well, if you're Jewish and I'm agnostic . . . thank you for this, Danny."

"Anytime, Chuckles. And things are good with me and Lucy."

"Give my regards to Nigel."

When my phone rang the next morning at seven, I again, of course, thought it was Noah, until I saw on the screen that the call was from my aunt Donna.

"Oh, Sally, Jerry isn't doing well," she said after I'd answered. "I think he has it."

"You think he has—" I paused, but I already knew. "Covid?"

"On Sunday we went over there with Barbara, and we were sitting on the deck, but it started raining so we went inside. We tried to stay six feet apart, then Barbara tested positive and I'm sure it's because her grandsons are staying with her, and Nicholas works at Starbucks."

"When you say Jerry isn't doing well—do you mean—what do you mean?"

"I talked to him on the phone just now, and he sounds weak and a little, well, a little disoriented. He said something about clearing snow from the driveway. Sweetheart, I want to help, but with my diabetes and Richard's cardiomyopathy, I'm afraid it'll get all of us. I went there this morning and rang the doorbell, hoping he'd come to the window so I could see him for myself, but he didn't. Who's the mother in the family next door?"

"Charlotte?"

"She came out when she saw me on Jerry's stoop and said that at five in the morning Sugar was wandering in their yard with no leash. They also didn't get an answer when they knocked on Jerry's door, and she said she was about to call the police when she saw me pull up in Richard's car."

"Where's Sugar now?"

"I told her Jerry's not well, and she said they'll keep her."

Even more alarming than the idea of Jerry having Covid was the idea of Jerry letting Sugar wander the neighborhood unattended; he *never* did that.

"Okay," I said. "I'll come back. If I get in the car now"—I meant, of course, in Donna's car—"I can be there tomorrow morning, but I'll check flights, too."

I wondered if she'd try to dissuade me. Instead, she said "Sally, he told me not to call you, but I thought you should know."

"Hey," Noah said when he answered his phone, and his voice contained the scratchiness of sleep.

"I think Jerry has Covid," I said. "I just tried to reach him, but he didn't pick up. Sorry for waking you."

"No, it's fine. Are you considering going back there?" The absence of any irritation on his part—the presence of sympathy, the immediate willingness to suspend the unresolved tension between us—felt like a significant data point, one I could have guessed at but not have been sure of.

"I'm definitely going back, but I'm trying to figure out if I should drive or fly."

"How sick is he?"

"I don't know. His sister, my aunt Donna, called, and she has her own health issues so she hasn't seen him, but she said he's disoriented and the neighbors found Sugar in their yard this morning. Jerry's pretty healthy as eighty-one-year-olds go, but—well, he's eighty-one."

"You should fly. Let me make a few calls."

I could have pretended that I didn't understand what he meant, or I could have protested that it was too extravagant, because I already knew I wouldn't be paying for it. Instead, I said, "Thank you, Noah."

It was a Gulfstream, with eight white leather seats in the cabin. In addition to the two pilots, there were two flight attendants, all of them in navy-and-gold uniforms, all of them wearing masks, as Noah and I also were. Noah's presence on the plane was the surprise. He'd called me back forty minutes after I called him and said, "Okay, Leah and I are going to come to you, she'll take us to the airport, you'll give her your car keys, and she'll go later today to your hotel to get your car and drive it back to my house. The flight's out of Van Nuys, not LAX." Leah, whom I hadn't previously met, was his personal assistant.

I had flown on private planes a few times, including when the 2015 Emmy Awards ceremony was the same week that the real Hillary Clinton—and not just the cast member Lynette, who played her—was appearing on *TNO* and I was writing the sketch. Those times on private planes, always at *TNO*'s expense, I'd felt like a cross between an imposter and a tourist, discreetly taking pictures of the interior to send my mother. This time was decidedly less festive.

On the tarmac, after we'd climbed from the car and walked to the boarding stairs, Noah held out an arm to indicate that I should go first. In the front of the cabin, four of the white leather seats were arranged facing each other in pairs, with a table between them on which were water bottles and a dish of mints. I glanced over my shoulder, unsure where I should sit, and Noah said, "Why don't you go there?" and nodded toward the window seat in the pair facing forward. After I had, he slid in next to me, pushed up the white leather armrest between our chairs, and wordlessly set his right arm around my shoulder. I wordlessly turned my face into his chest and closed my eyes. Through my mask, his neck smelled the way he smelled on waking, some combination of being outside in the woods and bread, and I thought how in the last few weeks, the idea of him had sometimes made me nervous but the reality of him always comforted me.

One of the flight attendants offered us coffee, which we both accepted, and blueberry muffins, which he declined and I accepted, pulling down my mask to take bites. Over the sound system, the pilot apologized for our bumpy ascent, then the ride smoothed out, and the flight attendant refilled our mugs. I'd been scrolling on my phone, and Noah had been scrolling on his iPad, and he said, "Do you want to watch a movie?" He told me to choose, and I picked a historical drama that, while not as well written as it seemed to think, was at least somewhat distracting. By the time the credits rolled, we were twenty minutes from landing.

"Unless he's really in horrible shape, he shouldn't go to the hospital," I said. "Right? Because couldn't that be even worse in terms of overcrowding and lack of ventilators?"

"Leah tracked down a doctor who's supposed to meet us at the house at three. I think we let him assess." Noah squeezed my hand. "And she ordered a car to take us from the airport."

I looked at him in confusion. "Like a concierge doctor?"

"Yes," he said. "Like a concierge doctor."

I'd removed the key to Jerry's house before I'd given my car keys to Leah, and I pulled it from my jeans pocket as we walked up the path leading to the front door. The house my mother and I had moved into in 1983 was a modest colonial with maroon shutters. Noah and I kept our masks on as we entered.

I had since the plane took off been gripped by mutually exclusive anxieties. The first was that we'd find Jerry doing chair yoga or eating Raisin Bran, wondering what the fuss was, and it would turn out I'd used Donna's call as an excuse to summon Noah, or to test him. The other anxiety was that we'd find Jerry dead.

I called his name several times, but there was no response. With Noah close behind me, I hurried up the steps, which were covered in a beige carpet from my youth. The door to Jerry's bedroom was open, and when I confirmed the slight rise and fall of his body beneath the sheet, I, too, exhaled. "Jerry, it's Sally," I said. "I came back from L.A."

He was lying on his side, facing the door. His eyes blinked open in his long, thin face. He looked confused, and something in his expression was strangely childlike, an impression exacerbated by the fact that clear mucus was dripping from one nostril.

"It's Sally," I said again. "I'm wearing a mask because of Covid."

"Hi, honey," he said in a subdued voice.

I knelt beside the bed. "How are you feeling? Do you think you should go to the hospital?" I set my palm against his forehead, and it was burning.

"It's my throat." He touched his neck and in his subdued voice said, "It's not good."

"Have you had anything to eat or drink lately?"

Behind me, Noah said, "I'll get him some water."

Jerry closed his eyes, and I recalled not having responded to his email about the pupcakes. It was hard not to think of what I'd been doing while he'd been deteriorating—hiking with Noah, having sex with Noah, declaring to Noah that his cleared-out office was an affront to my independence.

Noah returned with two glasses of water, one with ice and one without, and held them both out to me. As I reached for the one without ice, he said, "I couldn't find any straws, but I can go get some." Because of how close Jerry was to the edge of the bed—unsettlingly close—I couldn't perch beside him on the mattress. Instead, I continued kneeling on the rug and held the glass to his lips. Though some water dribbled down his chin and neck, he drank several sips.

"What about some crackers?" Noah said. "Or applesauce?"

"Maybe crackers," I said. "I don't think he has applesauce."

This time when Noah left the room, I said, "That's the friend I was visiting in L.A., Noah. He came with me to—" I paused. "Check on you."

"Yes," Jerry said, and his eyes shut again.

I had wondered, on entering the room, if I was smelling death, but I'd quickly realized I was smelling feces, and not from the bathroom. Tissues were scattered atop the sheet and on the floor, and there was a low scraping noise that I soon deduced was a humidifier with no water left in it. I set the glass on his nightstand, walked to the outlet, and yanked out the cord.

Noah brought in a small plastic container of vanilla pudding and a teaspoon on a plate with a few Ritz crackers. I said, "If I lift him, will you fluff his pillows so he's more elevated?"

As I reached around Jerry with both arms, he felt shockingly frail. "How about a few bites of food?" I said. "To give yourself a little energy?"

Jerry didn't reply, and I said, "How about some pudding?"

"Pudding," he repeated.

I pulled the tab off the plastic cup, but before I'd peeled back the foil, I said, "Oh, we should wash our hands."

"I did in the kitchen." Noah nodded at the pudding. "Want me to do that?"

I passed it to him and walked into Jerry's bathroom to use the faucet. When I came back, Noah was kneeling where I'd been before, holding the teaspoon to Jerry's lips with the creamy glob on it. As I watched, Jerry parted his lips slightly, and Noah slid the spoon in.

Jerry swallowed then said, "That's enough." Once again, he closed his eyes.

"How much did he have?" I asked.

Noah held up the container, which was still mostly full. "Three or four bites." He stood, motioning with his thumb to the doorway. "Wanna go talk?"

I led him across the hall to my room; neither of us remarked on the white wicker furniture. I instinctively sat sideways in my desk chair, and Noah sat on the bed and lowered his mask to his chin. He said, "I meant to pack the pulse oximeter Margit got when I was sick and I forgot it. I'll go out and see if I can find one."

"He seems horrible, right?"

"He doesn't seem great, but it's hard to separate what's because he's old, what's lying in bed for a few days not really eating or drinking, and what's Covid. And we don't even know that he has Covid."

"This isn't what he's like under normal circumstances. He's not one of those elderly people who runs marathons, but he walks around and makes sense."

"I'm going to go look for a pulse oximeter and straws. Should I call an Uber or take his car?"

"Are you comfortable driving a 2002 Buick?"

Noah smiled slightly, and I said, "That's a serious question."

"Where are the keys?"

"And also, no offense, but if you're going to Target or whatever, do you know *how* to shop at Target? Have you ever done it before?"

"Yes," Noah said. "I know how to shop at Target."

We both went downstairs, and I found the keys where Jerry always left them, on a hook just inside the door that led to the garage; the key chain was a leather oval with a gold metal duck in profile, something Jerry had used for as long as I could remember.

Noah wrapped his arms around me. I hugged him back, and neither of us said anything.

Leah texted Noah to say that the concierge doctor was running late, and he showed up not at three o'clock but at almost seven. Dr. Fischer arrived alone, as I hadn't expected, and wearing so much protective gear that he was barely recognizable as human, which I suspected further disoriented Jerry. I certainly couldn't fault Dr. Fischer for it, but in addition to a white mask over his nose and mouth, he wore a hood with a clear shield in the front and, on his body, pale blue plastic coveralls. On his hands were latex gloves, and, over his shoes, white booties. He administered a Covid test via Jerry's nostrils, the first Covid test I ever saw, and said his office would notify us of the results the following day but that we should operate on the assumption that Jerry did have it. We were to watch for Jerry's skin or lips turning blue, an inability to catch his breath, or complaints of chest pain; if any of these symptoms occurred, we should call an ambulance or take him to the hospital immediately. In the meantime, we should encourage fluids and use the pulse oximeter on him twice a day.

I had thought that the presence of a doctor in the house would feel reassuring, and it hadn't. And that was even before I said, "How worried should I be?" and, a little impatiently, though maybe he was just tired, Dr. Fischer said, "He's in his eighties. It would be highly irresponsible for me to make any promises."

The next few days were a blur, a sort of inverse of the fun blur after my arrival at Noah's house. The way the pulse oximeter worked was that I affixed it to Jerry's pointer finger and confirmed that the number showing the oxygen level in his blood was above 90; if it wasn't, he was supposed to go to the hospital.

At Target, in addition to buying the pulse oximeter, a jumbo pack of tissue boxes, and several jugs of Gatorade, Noah had bought a so-called bedside commode (it was gray with armrests that made it grimly throne-like); a so-called bedside urinal (a sideways-slanting plastic thermos with a glow-in-the-dark cap); and a medical shower chair (a lot like a regular plastic-and-aluminum chair except with a wider seat and suction cups on the bottoms of the legs). At some point on that endlessly long first day back in Kansas City, after Jerry ate a quarter of a scrambled egg I'd made, Noah and I together got him into the shower, and, while Noah wore a mask, running shorts, and nothing else and Jerry wore nothing at all, Noah bathed him and I changed his bedding. As I did, I played the Indigo Girls on my phone at a low volume, so that I could distract myself and have company at the same time that I could hear Noah and Jerry in the shower and help if they needed me.

When Jerry was resettled in fresh sheets, I went outside, crossed the front yard, and rang the Larsen family's doorbell. Then, so as not to be standing overly close when the door opened, I turned and descended the three steps back to the walkway. Both Charlotte and her husband, Keith, came outside, and I thanked them profusely for letting Sugar stay with them for the day. They said it had been the highlight of the pandemic for their daughters. Keith went to get Sugar while Charlotte asked how Jerry was doing, and when Sugar bounded out to me, seeing her mournful eyes and wagging tail—it was two-thirds black and one-third white, at the end—almost made me weep. Instead, I lifted Sugar into my arms and thanked them again.

"Let us know if you need anything," Keith said, and I turned back toward Jerry's house.

"Sally, sorry if this is a weird question," Charlotte said then, and I paused, and Keith said, "Not now, Char," and Charlotte said, "But are you dating Noah Brewster?"

"Oh." I hesitated.

Charlotte was in her midthirties and worked as a buyer for an electronic goods company, and it was the Larsens' older daughter, Stella, who was eleven, who thought she'd caused the pandemic by telling her mother she traveled too much. "I'm not sure," I said.

"It's just that he's my *favorite* favorite singer. For real, since I was a teenager."

"Oh, wow," I said. It seemed safe to assume that revealing Noah was inside Jerry's house, about twenty feet away, would complicate rather than simplify matters.

"I know you meet lots of famous people with your job, but those pictures—was that really you?"

"Charlotte, let her go," Keith said.

"I do know Noah," I said. "Have a good night!"

When we entered Jerry's bedroom, Sugar leapt onto his bed and licked his face, which seemed maybe medically inadvisable. But then, his voice weak, Jerry said, "There's my good girl."

———

That night, when I told Noah that I was going to sleep on the floor in Jerry's room, he said, "With a mask on? Won't you sleep terribly?"

"Presumably," I said, and went to find an ancient sleeping bag in the basement. Noah slept in my bed with the wicker headboard.

On the second afternoon, someone from Dr. Fischer's office called to say that Jerry's Covid test was positive, and offered me the opportunity to speak with Dr. Fischer after he finished seeing patients, but instead I called my pediatrician college roommate, Denise. Although the advice Denise gave echoed Dr. Fischer's recommendations, I had learned my lesson, and instead of asking how worried I should be, I said, "It's completely plausible that he'll recover, right?"

Immediately, she said, "Oh, sure."

The second night, I slept again on the floor of Jerry's room and on the third night, I slept in my old bed with Noah. In contrast to in California, our physical contact was minimal and chaste.

During this time, Jerry continued to have a fever, to report a sore throat, and to mostly sleep and still seem exhausted when he woke, but, with our encouragement, he ate small amounts of bananas and applesauce and chicken broth and toast. He didn't seem to have lost his sense of taste or smell, he didn't vomit, and, once we got the rhythms of the bedside urinal and commode established, he no longer went to the bathroom in the bed. I was usually the one who emptied the bedside urinal, which he used solo after I'd helped him sit up, and Noah was usually the one who helped him onto the commode.

As the days passed, Noah and I increasingly took turns doing things other than taking care of Jerry. I binge-watched a fantasy drama full of dragons and gore, and Noah worked out in the backyard, apparently while facetiming with Bobby, and he went for runs in the neighborhood. On one of his almost-daily outings to Target, he purchased a legal notepad and a guitar that I'd find him playing on the deck, while intermittently pausing to make notes on the pages, as Sugar sunbathed at his feet. "Kansas City is really creatively inspiring, huh?" I said the first time I came upon this scenario, which was on our fifth day at Jerry's house. "Kind of like

Paris in the 1930s." I'd just carried a soup bowl from Jerry's bed-room to the kitchen sink, seen Noah out the window, and slid open the glass and screen doors.

Noah smiled. "Kansas City did produce you."

I stepped onto the deck, and Sugar immediately rolled into belly rub position. Noah was sitting in a folding lawn chair with gray webbing, wearing a baseball cap and sunglasses that he removed. It was eleven in the morning and eighty degrees, which by Midwest summer standards wasn't bad.

"My mom died of stomach cancer so it was, you know, very messy," I said as I crouched to pet Sugar. "I've been through a vari-ation of this. But sometimes I still can't believe how undignified and sad life is."

"I know what you mean," he said, "but I'm sure it makes a huge difference to Jerry that you're here." We both were quiet, and the whisking and tapping of a nearby sprinkler became noticeable. "I wish I could make this easier for you," Noah added.

"You have," I said. "In about a million ways. Have you ever been around a super-sick person before?"

"There was a producer, this beloved guy named Billy Rodriguez, who died in 2010 of glioblastoma. I'd worked with him on all my albums except one. I wasn't directly cleaning up after him, so to speak, but I saw him a bunch of times in the hospital and once in hospice and yeah—it's rough."

"If you want to go back to L.A., I hope you know it's okay. I don't want you to feel trapped here."

"Do you want me to go back to L.A.?"

"No."

Again, we were quiet, and Sugar wagged her tail against the deck and the sprinkler went *tck, tck, tck*. Was it my imagination, or was there a head and a pair of shoulders in the Larsens' second-floor bathroom window, a figure watching us? Which was as likely to be Charlotte as one of her daughters.

"I don't want to go back to L.A.," Noah said. "I do eventually. But not now."

That afternoon, courtesy of Viv and Henrietta, an enormous box arrived from a gourmet grocery store in New York: dried fruit and fancy coffee and cheeses wrapped in gel packs and many kinds of crackers and cookies. I was moved, and almost certain Noah would eat none of it. That night, he made us pan-seared salmon for dinner, and as we were cleaning up in the kitchen, I said, "So I have a question."

Noah raised his eyebrows.

"Do you still want to be my boyfriend—or whatever—now that you've given my stepdad a shower?"

He laughed. "I'd love to be your boyfriend or whatever. I do have a condition, though."

Nervousness surged through me.

"If something upsets you," he said, "it's fine if you need to pause the conversation or go in the other room, but I don't want you to blow everything up, because it's too stressful to live like that."

"Blow everything up meaning what?"

"Meaning check into a hotel. Or throw a bomb about me dating models so we don't talk for two years."

I swallowed. "I think that's fair," I said. "Do you know the movie term *lampshading*?"

"I don't."

"It's when something in the plot or the logic of a film doesn't quite make sense and the screenplay has the characters acknowledge it without resolving it. It's a trick to reassure the audience that you're not trying to trick them."

"Okay." He looked puzzled.

"I want us to stay together," I said. "I want to be your girlfriend. And I know that if I am, your professional identity will overshadow my professional identity and Internet trolls will criticize how I look and say they can't believe you're with me. I can work on not caring about those things or not paying attention to them, but I can't keep them from happening."

"If this helps, I can remind you that Internet trolls are Internet trolls."

"I'm going to lampshade it because I don't know how to resolve it. But you're worth the risk. Even I know that giving up would be a huge mistake."

"Oh, yeah?" He was grinning. "Even you?"

"This might come out wrong, but I haven't been sure until now if you know how to be a normal person. For a celebrity, you're amazing. But I didn't know if you knew how to pick up takeout or live without assistants or stay in a crappy little house with wall-to-wall carpet. And I don't think you've been trying to prove yourself, but if you had, it's clear that you're actually a lot better at being a normal person than I am."

"I'm always trying to prove myself to you." He made a wry face. "But maybe I'm lucky that you underestimate me so it's not that hard."

"I've been meaning to ask—do people recognize you at Target?"

"I don't think so. I'm a middle-aged bald dude wearing a baseball cap and a mask."

"I think it's only a matter of time before the mom next door real-izes you're here, if she hasn't already. Apparently, she's a super-fan." I pointed toward the window facing the side of the Larsens' house.

"Did she say something?" Noah seemed unruffled.

"That she's a superfan." I rolled my eyes. "She's a nice person, and I don't think she'll alert the media or anything like that, but I might have to develop some skills for running interference for you."

"If people ask you for stuff from me, you can always ignore them or else refer them to Leah and let her handle it."

"I don't long to be your secretary, but you're not worried that I'd ignore something important?"

"People tend to be persistent when it's important. And they shouldn't be reaching out through you anyway. Regarding the neighbor—"

"Charlotte."

"Regarding Charlotte, I'm happy to meet her. I can't be all things to all people, but the family who took care of Sugar? I'm glad to."

"That's very nice, and I hope you don't come to regret it." I'd been wiping the kitchen table, and I squeezed the rag over the sink. "Anyway," I said, "for as long as I live, I'll always remember that you went and bought Jerry a bedside commode."

"Don't forget the shower chair."

"And the shower chair. And the portable urinal with the glow-in-the-dark cap."

"The funny thing," he said, "is that when you were staying at that hotel in Santa Monica, I was brainstorming about how to win you back. I was thinking about how in romantic comedies, don't they usually end with one of the people hurrying to be reunited with the other and publicly declaring their love? Like at a party or an airport? I didn't know I just had to buy a urinal at Target."

"The term for that is a grand gesture."

"I was wondering if you'd like it or hate it if I came to your hotel and, well, serenaded you. In front of other people, I mean, like from the sidewalk."

"Good question. I think maybe I'd aspire to hate it but secretly love it."

"Why would it be better to hate it? Because it's cheesy?"

"Well," I said, "I once heard a smart person point out that it's hard to determine where the dividing line is between cheesiness and acceptable emotional extravagance."

He grinned again. "I didn't tell you at the time, but I know exactly where the line is. When it's happening to other people, it's cheesy. When it's happening to you, it's wonderful."

I got into bed a few minutes after he did that night, wearing a T-shirt and underwear, and immediately, before I'd turned out the light, he pulled me toward him, toward his warm, muscled, bread-and-forest-smelling chest—he was wearing only boxer briefs—and it was a joy to be close to him again, so much of our skin touching. When he was on top of me, I set my hands on either side of his head, my palms against the stubble, and said, "I've been meaning to say this since I first got to your house, but you're actually even better looking with your head shaved."

He smiled a little. "Actually?" he said. "Am I?"

"It's true, though. Your hair before—it was okay, but there was something very teenage heartthrob about it. Now you look like an adult man. In the same way that I think meeting in our late thirties made us more interesting to each other, I think you're even more attractive now than you were twenty years ago."

He averted his eyes for a few seconds then looked back at me. "I have a confession," he said. "I sometimes wore hair pieces before. When I was hosting *TNO*, that wasn't all my real hair."

"Well, *TNO* is the world headquarters of wig wearing, so welcome to the club." I felt conscious of not wanting to embarrass him but also not wanting to feign astonishment—not wanting to lie to him, even about something small.

"I wouldn't say I wore a full-on wig. I just had some help." He seemed uncharacteristically abashed. "Do you think that's cringey?"

I shook my head. "I'm very familiar with people in the public eye doing stuff like this. And I don't just mean on camera. But the exact way you are right now, in this moment—you couldn't look any better." I paused. "Given how much has been written and said about how good you look for the last two decades, do you *like* being told that or does it seem boring?"

With his face a few inches from mine, he smiled. "Do I like when the woman I love tells me that I look good? Yes, Sally. I like when you tell me that."

Jerry's progress could be measured by the distance he ventured from his bed: first to use the toilet in his bathroom; two days later, downstairs to the kitchen in his seersucker bathrobe; the day after that, onto the deck. He announced he wanted a hot dog for lunch one day, and while the two of us waited in the kitchen for it to boil, he said, "I hope the male nurse isn't too expensive."

I squinted. "Do you mean Noah?"

"Who's Noah?" Jerry asked.

"My friend. Or, uh, my boyfriend? The guy staying in our house."

Jerry looked equanimous, and not all that interested, as he said, "I thought his name was David."

In the selfie Viv sent Henrietta and me from the hospital, she was wearing a blue mask and a green hospital gown, her eyes were wide open, and she was making a peace sign.

Contractions 3 min apart cervix dilated to 5 cm, she wrote.

Then: *Gloria the doula is my new BFF*

Then: *Epidural heavenly*

OMG!! I texted. *How are you feeling?*

Then Henrietta's reply came through and it was a picture of Lisa, who'd planned a home birth, reclining bare-breasted against the interior wall of an inflatable pool, looking blissed out, holding an actual baby—a tiny, huge-cheeked, closed-eyed, naked little creature.

From Henrietta: *Amazing and also . . . meet Olivia Rose*

From Viv: *WTF?!!!*

Viv: *Meaning congratulations you overachievers*

Viv: *But when did Lisa squeeze that out?!?*

Henrietta: *8 lbs 1 oz, born 7:46 A.M. this morning*

Henrietta: *Mom, Mommy, and Olivia all on cloud nine*

Henrietta: *You'll do great Viv*

Me: *H so happy for you and Lisa!!*

Me: *Vivvy hope you can feel all the love coming toward you*

Me: *I know Theo and Gloria will take such good care of you*

Then Henrietta texted just me: *Don't want to say this to Viv but Lisa's labor so messy it was like a food fight*

Then Viv texted just me: *Don't tell Henrietta I said this but is there ANYTHING fouler than giving birth in a tub*

Viv's first text had arrived a little after 9 A.M. central time. Six hours later, two texts arrived from Theo: first a photo of a baby gazing outward with big brown eyes, wearing a white hat, and wrapped in a striped blanket. And second a message: *Caleb Elijah Elman, 7 pounds, 4 ounces. Caleb & Viv both fantastic!*

I'd invited Charlotte Larsen onto our deck to meet Noah, and she came over after dinner, radiating jubilation and panic, clearly dressed up in a sleeveless flowered blouse, white jeans, and platform mules. When she'd climbed the steps from the yard onto the deck, I said, "Charlotte, this is Noah, and Noah, this is Charlotte," and she said, "Oh my God, I love you so much, Noah." Then she burst into tears.

As she wiped her eyes, she said, "I'm so sorry, but 'Making Love in July'—and also 'Arlington Dawn'—and 'Sober & Thirsty'— sorry, I can't even talk, but our first dance at our wedding was to 'Making Love in July.' My sister and I know all the words to the entire album."

When Noah spoke, it was with a contained, professional kind of friendliness I hadn't seen even during the week he'd hosted, a guarded warmth. "Thank you," he said lightly. "I really appreciate that."

"But what happened to your hair?"

Pleasantly, he said, "It was time for a change."

"Would it be okay if I get a picture?" Charlotte asked. "Sally told me about not posting anything, but just to show my sister. She won't believe it unless I have proof."

As Charlotte passed me her phone, and Charlotte and Noah positioned themselves side by side—"I'd put my arm around you if not for the pandemic," he said, while maintaining a few feet of space between them—I thought once again of another *TNO* writer telling me years before that nonfamous people wanted their interactions with famous people to end as quickly as possible so they could go tell their other nonfamous friends about them. And indeed, Charlotte was within ten minutes walking back toward her own house.

I whispered to Noah, "Fifty bucks she puts that picture on Facebook later tonight."

He whispered back, "What will be will be."

Charlotte disappeared from view, and I said, "Seriously, you're very good at that."

"I've had practice," he replied.

I sat at my wicker desk to write the email to Nigel. Two days before, I had spoken at length to my agent, and my agent had then relayed the particulars of our conversation to the relevant people at *TNO*, which meant that reaching out to Nigel was an act of decorum on my part rather than a disclosure of information. If I'd had more faith in my ability to express myself in speech, I'd have called him, but of course the thing that had propelled me to *TNO* in the first place was my faith in my ability to write.

Dear Nigel, I typed on my laptop,

> I will never be able to adequately thank you for giving me the opportunity to be a writer at TNO. When I think of the best, happiest, and funniest moments of my life, an extremely high proportion of them took place inside the TNO studio or up on the seventeenth floor. I've heard you say more than once that TNO isn't a place for lone wolves or perfectionists, but it was an ideal place for me because it helped me be much less of a lone wolf and much less of a perfectionist. You have created a singular comedic community, and I'll forever be amazed that I was part of it.
>
> All my best,
> Sally

Nigel's reply arrived ten minutes later.

> Sally, apparently "lone wolf" is something of a misnomer. A wolf who strikes out on her own tends to do so only temporarily, when moving on to the next stage, before finding a new pack. As for perfectionism, those of us who have spent time inside the TNO studio know that something so evanescent and silly comes about only through prodigiously hard work. Don't hesitate to be in touch. N

We ended up staying in Kansas City for sixteen days. Jerry's fever had broken after five, and, very slowly, he continued to regain energy. By the time we decided it was okay to leave, he wasn't the same as before, but he was far better than he'd been when Noah and I had shown up. His sister Donna promised me that she'd check on him every day.

For a farewell dinner, we grilled shrimp out on the deck the night before our departure. The Larsens were also on their deck, and Chloe, who was the nine-year-old, asked, "Do you think Sugar knows she's a dog?" Before I could respond, Stella, who was the eleven-year-old, eyed the Greek salad Noah had made and said, "I don't like cucumber because the best part of a cucumber tastes like the worst part of a watermelon."

Noah and I looked at each other, and I said, "I can't disagree."

To surprise Jerry, I'd baked pupcakes for dessert—I'd found a recipe that was indeed edible for both humans and dogs, with flour and peanut butter as the main ingredients—but after we finished dinner, Noah said, "Before you bring out the you-know-whats, there's something I want to do. I'll be right back."

When he reemerged from the house, he was carrying a guitar—not the Target one he'd made do with for a few days but one of his fancier models that Leah had sent from California, along with some clothes, after it had become clear we'd be staying awhile—and I heard Charlotte Larsen gasp. Around his neck, Noah wore a metal contraption that at first glance looked like an intense form of orthodontia but in fact was a harmonica in a holder. He walked to the eastern side of the deck and stood with the railing behind him. Noah glanced at Jerry and me, then at the Larsens, then back at me, and said, "I want to dedicate a song to you, Sally."

Addressing the five other people and one dog, he said, "Sally and I met a couple years ago, but it's only recently that we've reconnected. I feel very grateful. And since the way I express my feelings is through music, I want to sing a little something tonight. Thank you all for humoring me." Looking at me, he said, "So, Sally Milz, this goes out to you."

Next to Jerry, sitting at the table where we'd just eaten, I experienced a sort of internal lurching. Had Noah written a song for me? Was he calling my bluff after I'd said that maybe I'd like such a thing? Could I handle this in front of Jerry and the Larsens? In a different way, could Charlotte Larsen handle this?

Then Noah glanced down and began strumming. I knew right away, just from the first few chords, even before he looked at me and sang, "I heard that you were drunk and mean / Down at the Dairy Queen . . ."

I didn't need to fake-smile; I didn't need to make an effort to express my delight or conceal my distress. It was better than if he'd written a song for me, though perhaps, as I realized he hadn't, I did sort of hope he would in the future? It also was better than if he'd sung some happily-ever-after ballad. There was nothing about Noah Brewster standing on Jerry's deck singing "Dairy Queen" that I didn't love.

He sang, "Ain't it funny how we lose one day / And a lifetime slips away," and in the third verse, after the lines "It was good for a time / I am told," he pressed his lips against the harmonica and closed his eyes as the instrument's magnificently nasal, twangy sound filled the air and Charlotte Larsen whooped and clapped.

The odd part was that, although I had listened to the song hundreds of times, and seen the Indigo Girls perform it, I had always focused on what I thought of as the spectacularly devastating lines about a relationship that hadn't lasted. I'd hardly noticed that the song ended with the lines "Hey, I love you more and more / Oh, I love you more and more"—with those lines in the present tense. Watching Noah as he sang them, as he watched me—his eyes were open again—I wondered if I'd always understood the song a little wrong, or possibly if I'd always understood life a little wrong. Wondering this was not a bad thing; it was a beautiful, unexpected relief.

He bent his head once more to blow on the harmonica while rapidly strumming the guitar strings then slowed down, ending with a last elongated flourish. Lifting his head, he said, "Sally, I do love you more and more. And this is me talking—Noah—not the Indigo Girls, though I bet the Indigo Girls would love you, too, if they knew you."

Because there were only six of us, I can't say the applause was deafening. But it was certainly enthusiastic as I stood, walked toward Noah, and kissed him. I whispered into his ear, "That was a perfect grand gesture."

An hour later, as I was pulling out of the driveway to pick up a few last things from the grocery store for Jerry before we left the next morning, the neighbor on the other side of the house waved at me to stop. When I rolled down the window, she said, "Is Jerry learning to play guitar? Because he sounds wonderful."

EPILOGUE

April 2023

B ecause *TNO* airs live, it comes on at 8:30 P.M. on the West Coast, around the time Noah and I are finishing dinner during a night at home. The first time we watched it together after I left the show, I felt tense and territorial, and I was pretty sure I could guess who'd written which sketches, and I had strong opinions about how they could have been improved. Viv was still on maternity leave for the 2020 season premiere, but Henrietta was back, and I wanted to text both of them right after the ceremonial goodnights and also wanted to leave them alone—to let Viv sleep, or breastfeed, or whatever else she was doing, and to let Henrietta head to the after-party and not feel her phone vibrating. I suppose I was trying to protect myself from feeling ignored. My heart swelled when, as the credits were still rolling, a text arrived from Viv to Henrietta and me: *I miss you bitches*

Simultaneously, Henrietta and I replied, *Same!*

As the weeks and months passed, my feelings of tension, territoriality, and homesickness while watching dissipated. I can't claim to be impartial these days, but the impulse to critique has mostly been replaced by a more relaxed nostalgia. Danny, who now shares an office with his News Desk co-writer, Roy, sometimes texts me threatening to write a sketch called The Sally Milz Rule.

In the summer of 2021, Noah returned to touring in a modified way, and I've gone with him for some shows, including when he performed in Kansas City and also in D.C., where I met his parents. He had described them accurately—palpably affluent, not especially nice—though the good news was that he had also described his sister accurately, and Vicky and I have become close. But usually when Noah travels, I stay put in Topanga.

The first feature for which I wrote the script is now in preproduction and scheduled to be filmed in L.A. in the summer. It isn't, after all my talk, a romantic comedy. Instead, it's a buddy movie starring Viv and Henrietta as the ex-wives of two Silicon Valley billionaires. Though their characters were both heavily involved with the founding of the start-up that made their ex-husbands rich, they've received little money or credit, and they team up to correct the record and seek justice. The working title is Tech Sis, though already I've had several multi-hour discussions with the studio executives about why they think, and why I don't agree, that it should be Tech Sisters, or even more preposterously, Tech Sises. Nigel is one of the producers.

After Noah and I left Kansas City in 2020, I returned two weeks later (on Delta Air Lines, not a private jet) to check on Jerry. That November, I flew again to Kansas City (on a private jet, not Delta Air Lines) and, as planned, Jerry and Sugar flew back with me to Los Angeles for Thanksgiving and stayed until March, setting up camp in the pool house. This was a pattern we repeated in 2021, and in 2022, they came and just stayed. Which is to say that whether you consider beagles to be small or medium-sized, that's the kind of dog that Noah now lives with. Sometimes in the late afternoon, Jerry and I do chair yoga by the pool, though we also regularly do water aerobics. It turns out California agrees with him.

In July 2021, Noah and I got married. On a Friday morning, we went together to get the license, which cost eighty-five dollars, and I provided the date of the dissolution of my previous marriage.

Though there are, I learned, paparazzi that lurk at various L.A. courthouses hoping to catch high-profile people on this very errand, there is also such a thing as a confidential marriage license in California—it's not designed to accommodate celebrities but rather the convenient result of a law from the 1800s meant to allow already-cohabiting couples to marry without public shame. This was the kind of license we obtained, then we drove immediately to a hotel in Montecito, where we'd rented a private villa overlooking the coast. On the villa's lawn, the hotel's general manager officiated at a ceremony with no other witnesses.

I don't know if this is the wedding Noah and I would have had if not for Covid, but of course I don't know if we'd have had any wedding if not for Covid; I don't know if we'd have found each other again. And I realize it's not the wedding most people would want, but I found a deep beauty in its irreducibility. We spent that weekend ordering room service, marveling at our new circumstances, and, well, making love in July. That Monday, we returned to Topanga and called our family and friends to tell them. On Tuesday, Noah's publicist released a statement announcing our marriage and suggesting that anyone who wanted to help us celebrate could do so by making a donation to a nonprofit working to elect Democratic women. "We need to offset my reentry into the ultimate heteropatriarchal institution," I'd said, and he'd laughed and replied, "As newlywed wives often tell their husbands." That, among lots of my former colleagues, both Autumn and Elliot contributed struck me as unnecessarily magnanimous of them.

The Internet had opinions about Noah marrying me, and though I've inferred that some people saw it as a tragedy for him while others considered it a victory for feminism and/or mousy-looking straight women everywhere (two entities that are not, in fact, interchangeable), I've managed to avoid reading the vast majority of the comments.

By the time we got married, Noah and I were both, with effort, in the habit of leaving our phones in a drawer in the kitchen overnight. When I awaken in the morning, I sometimes go to that other far bathroom even now, but I always return. Noah is usually asleep when I do, and his unguarded face is startlingly handsome; the truth is that I still can't believe a hot, smart, kind man loves me back. Often when I climb into bed, he reaches for me, opening his eyes as he does, smiling because he's glad to see me. There are, presumably, texts and tweets and news articles I'm missing, but in these moments none seem all that urgent.

ACKNOWLEDGMENTS

For facts, anecdotes, and analysis, I'm indebted to many sources. These include the books *Live From New York: The Complete, Uncensored History of Saturday Night Live as Told by Its Stars, Writers, and Guests,* edited by James Andrew Miller and Tom Shales; *A Very Punchable Face* by Colin Jost; *Gasping for Airtime: Two Years in the Trenches of Saturday Night Live* by Jay Mohr; *Bossypants* by Tina Fey; *Yes Please* by Amy Poehler; *Girl Walks into a Bar . . . : Comedy Calamities, Dating Disasters, and a Midlife Miracle* by Rachel Dratch; *I Am the New Black* by Tracy Morgan with Anthony Bozza; *Hello, Molly!* by Molly Shannon with Sean Wilsey; and *The Bedwetter: Stories of Courage, Redemption, and Pee* by Sarah Silverman. I also benefited from reading the *New York Times* article "Lives of the After-Party" by Paul Brownfield; the *New York* article "Comedy Isn't Funny" by Chris Smith; and the *New Yorker* article "Leslie Jones: Always Funny, Finally Famous" by Andrew Marantz. I listened to the podcasts *WTF with Marc Maron; Mike Birbiglia's Working It Out; Conan O'Brien Needs a Friend;* and *Fly on the Wall with Dana Carvey and David Spade.*

And I watched the documentary *Saturday Night,* directed by James Franco, as well as *Saturday Night Live*'s YouTube channel and its "Creating Saturday Night Live" videos. Finally, though I hope this is already clear, I was inspired by almost five decades of episodes of *Saturday Night Live* and am grateful to their creators, producers, writers, cast members, hosts, and crew.

Articles on other topics that helped guide my writing include "I'm Not Ready to Perform" by Will Butler and "The Day the Live Concert Returns" by Dave Grohl, both in *The Atlantic;* and "Why America's Black Mothers and Babies Are in a Life-or-Death Crisis" by Linda Villarosa in *The New York Times.*

I'm incredibly lucky to work with people in publishing who are very smart and very kind. Among them are my editor, Jennifer Hershey; my agent, Claudia Ballard; and my publicist, Maria Braeckel. Also at Random House, I am supported by Gina Centrello, Andy Ward, Susan Corcoran, Rachel Rokicki, Windy Dorresteyn, Madison Dettlinger, Jordan Pace, Wendy Wong, Marni Folkman, Paolo Pepe, Cassie Gonzales, Robbin Schiff, Kelly Chian, Theresa Zoro, Leigh Marchant, Benjamin Dreyer, and Elizabeth Eno. At WME, I am supported by Anna DeRoy, Tracy Fisher, Suzanne Gluck, Fiona Baird, Oma Naraine, and Stephanie Shipman. And over at Transworld, I am extremely thankful for Jane Lawson, Larry Finlay, Patsy Irwin, Vicky Palmer, and Richard Ogle.

My first reader for this book was my brother, P. G. Sittenfeld, whose wit and intelligence made writing more fun and whose strength, optimism, and big heart make him my role model. Other early readers were Ellen Battistelli, Tiernan Sittenfeld, Matt Carlson, Essie Chambers, Dessa, Julius Ramsay, Lewis Robinson, Aminatou Sow, Erin White, Bryan Miller, and Rebecca Hollander-Blumoff. I especially appreciated nuanced insights from Essie Chambers and Dessa. Celeste Ballard and Claire Mulaney showed me great generosity and patience. I am so glad to be part of a larger community of writers who include Susanna Daniel, Emily Jeanne Miller, Sheena MJ Cook, Cammie McGovern, Sugi Ganeshananthan, Sally Franson, Lesley Nneka Arimah, Will McGrath, Frank Bures, Jennifer

Weiner, Elin Hilderbrand, Sarah Dessen, and Jodi Picoult. Stephanie Park Zwicker will forever be my Indigo Girls authority; Kari Forde-Thielen is a friend to beagles and Curtises. And my family members, both human and canine, are just such a delight to sit on the couch and watch TV with. Thank you all.

ABOUT THE AUTHOR

CURTIS SITTENFELD is the author of the *Sunday Times* and *New York Times* bestselling *Rodham*. Her other acclaimed and bestselling novels include *American Wife, Prep, The Man of My Dreams, Sisterland, Eligible*, and the acclaimed short-story collections *You Think It, I'll Say It* and *Help Yourself*. Her stories have appeared in the *New Yorker, Esquire, Oprah Magazine* and the *New York Times Magazine*. Sittenfeld was also the guest editor for the 2020 Best American Short Stories anthology. She lives with her family in the American mid-west.

curtissittenfeld.com
Facebook.com/curtissittenfeldbooks
Twitter: @csittenfeld